T. R. Wilson was born and brought up in Peterborough on the edge of the Fens. He attended the University of East Anglia, and his love of East Anglia – its landscape, people and history – has always been central to his life and work. He submitted his first novel, *Master of Morholm*, for publication at the age of twenty-three, at which time he was a student on the University of East Anglia MA Course in Creative Writing, under Malcolm Bradbury and Angela Carter. His MA submission was part of the novel which was later published in 1989 as *Treading on Shadows*. Other novels include *The Ravished Earth*, *The Straw Tower* and *Beauty for Ashes*. His latest novel, *Hester Verney*, is available from Headline. He lives with a word processor in a small flat.

Roses in December

T. R. Wilson

HEADLINE

Copyright © 1992 T. R. Wilson

First published in 1992
by HEADLINE BOOK PUBLISHING PLC

First published in paperback in 1993
by HEADLINE BOOK PUBLISHING PLC

10 9 8 7 6 5 4 3 2 1

ISBN 0 7472 3971 1

Phototypeset by Intype, London

Printed and bound in Great Britain by
HarperCollins Manufacturing, Glasgow

HEADLINE BOOK PUBLISHING PLC
Headline House
79 Great Titchfield Street
London W1P 7FN

For Glenn Patterson

As soon
Seek roses in December – ice in June;
Hope constancy in wind, or corn in chaff.
Byron

Part One

One

I remember the first time I walked through the gates of St Germain House. It was May and I was eighteen. Winter seemed immortal that year, dying slowly, in rain and greyness, above Billingham's long streets. Only two days before, the weather had begun to turn warm at last; and in the front gardens leading up to St Germain House I found that spring had come.

Like everyone in Billingham, I had seen the house from a distance. I had seen its square bulk at an angle from the main road west out of the town, and from the railway I had seen its steep hipped roof rising like a secret behind a curtain of trees. But I had never seen it from the front until that day, and then I nearly turned back.

The gardens were laid out in a formal way that made me think of the public gardens of seaside resorts. Between the topiary hedges the tardy spring had broken out in geometric beds of daffodils and narcissus and trim squares of acid new grass, and the air was sweet with the scent of lilac from the shrubbery alongside the drive. Sunlight poured back from the many windows of the house and, more softly, from its luminous stone. It was very beautiful, after the imprisoning months of dark and cold. But

3

I had an intense feeling of being out of place. For a moment it seemed quite impossible to walk up the drive to that house, so imposingly symmetrical, so florid with pediments and pilasters: and I stopped dead.

It was the car that made me go on. It came through the gateway in a sudden roar that shattered the silence, its tyres spinning out gravel. The hood of the car was down, and as it sped close by me with a blast of the horn I glimpsed four faces, turned my way in a momentary flutter, like flowers in the breeze. The car banked at the end of the drive and disappeared somewhere round the back of the house. It made me remember that I was expected and that it would be rude not to turn up, and I was at that time very conscious of the proprieties; but its effect on me was more complex than that. Something about the exhilarating rush of the car, the flash of its chrome leaving dazzled streaks on my eyes, gave me confidence. And I wondered too who the people in it might be, the four faces, briefly illuminated, and all looking strangely alike.

The job was a temporary one, and my mother and father were against my applying for it. In those days, I am afraid, that alone was sufficient reason to make me want to: curiosity and dissatisfaction did the rest. To lay one's head on the pillow with a little sudden desperate feeling that somewhere, in that irrecoverable day, something has been missed, some opportunity lost, is not peculiar to youth, I now know: but I did not then and I was very restless.

I knew a little about Gerald Crawthorne, before I went to be interviewed by him at St Germain House. He had been a senior colonial administrator, and had made a name for himself as a traveller in North Africa and the Near East before retiring through ill-health. A distinguished man, my father said, though with a slight reservation – he had merely taken St Germain House after the war, he was not local, he was not one of those old rooted gentry whose domination of towns like Billingham lived on in street names and the dedication of foundation stones. For me, the contrast the job seemed to offer with the work I had been doing in the dreary solicitor's office off the High Street was enough. It was enough even to overcome my shyness.

When the maid let me into the hall, I felt as if I had stepped into a cool stone tank. The gloom, after the brightness outside, had the effect of blinding me, and for a moment I could only make out the hulking outline of a great central staircase and the dragonfly wings of the maid's starched apron-strings as she asked me to follow her down the long hall. When my eyes adjusted, I saw stuffed animal heads mounted high on the walls. Their sad empty faces looked down on me as I passed.

I knew nothing of distinguished men, and there seemed little to distinguish the tall elderly man who, in the study, lunged forward to shake my hand. My first impression was of a shabby schoolmaster, even to the leather patches on the elbows of his tweed jacket. When he spoke, however, there was a difference. Many families have some unifying physical characteristic – in one member occurring as a beauty, in another, perhaps, as a blemish, but always proclaiming their relationship: and in the Crawthornes it was that voice. It was a musical voice in the truest sense: one could listen to it as one listens to music.

'Miss Goodacre. So glad you could come,' Mr Crawthorne said, as if it were a party. 'Won't you sit down? Excuse the mess – it's frightful, isn't it? Do tell me about yourself.'

He cleared a chair for me by throwing some magazines, printed in French, on to the floor. He threw them like a fisherman throwing a net off a boat. A cloud of dust went up. The maid had called the room the study, but it was more of a library, and more of a lumber room than either. It confirmed the idea I had had on entering the house, of something very different from the formality of the front gardens, of domesticity pitched, as it were, like a tent among the grandeur. I sat down, conscious of my Sundayfied hat, and told him about my diploma in typing, shorthand and bookkeeping and my secretarial experience in Billingham. An ornate plaster ceiling writhed high above me. I felt as if I were speaking on stage.

Mr Crawthorne jammed a pipe in his mouth, and nodded vigorously, but he did not look at me and I felt he was only half listening. He prowled over to a mahogany desk where an old Olivetti typewriter glinted dully under a bloom of dust. I thought for a moment he was going to ask me to sit at it, perhaps, and actually prove I could type: but after peering suspiciously at it he said, 'I do hope this machine isn't too old. It's been put away in the attic. I did have a permanent secretary once, you see, but that was *long* ago.'

He looked to be in his late fifties, but he spoke as if he were a great age. He worked the pipe around his mouth and went on: 'Blanche volunteered to type for me. She can't, of course: the whole thing was a dreadful mess and she gave it up after a few pages, which is just like her. Now look here.' He yanked open a drawer and pulled out a fat folder of foolscap paper and thumped it on the desk. 'Hand-written, you see.'

I got up to see.

'Some parts of it are five or six years old, that's why the paper's gone so awfully yellow. I put it aside for some time. And then this winter something drew me back to it and I finished it in a rush. My writing's beastly, I'm afraid. And look – look how it changes. I find my writing changes according to what mood I'm in, do you find that?' Without waiting for an answer he went on: 'It covers the whole of my colonial service. I published a little book, a monograph really, about the Arabs, a long time ago – of course T. E. Lawrence rather overshadowed me there. Anyway, the publishers tell me it won't matter if I repeat myself a little. As you can see the pages are rather erratically numbered. I fancy there must be four hundred or more. I did say a temporary post in the advertisement, didn't I? It rather looks to me as if the job would be endless.'

He pawed through the pages, champing on the pipe, in a sort of fierce despondency. I began to say something about the writing being quite legible.

'You think you could manage?' he said, brightening and then frowning again in a moment. 'These emendations are ghastly,' he said, irritably waving a page interlaced with crossings-out. 'I'd have to make fair copies. Unless you could take them down in shorthand at my dictation? Could you do that?'

I said I could.

'There are certain special problems in a work like this that require me to be on hand,' he said. 'The question of proper names, for instance. Some of the

Egyptian names are perfect horrors and I rather think I haven't been consistent in my usage, though of course there is no absolute standard of transliteration . . .'

I began to feel then that Mr Crawthorne was not really speaking to me: that out of habit, rather than rudeness, he addressed his remarks half to himself. For some minutes I had been aware of the faint sound of dance music from somewhere, thinly as if from a gramophone or a wireless: now Mr Crawthorne came out of his musings and heard it too. He went over to the french doors, which opened out on to a terrace, and pulled them shut with a bang.

'The children,' he said.

He looked at me and smiled for the first time. In that moment I think I perceived several things about him: that he was ill; that he had been good-looking when young, but that the illness had made him lined and sallow and left only the eyes, piercingly blue boy's eyes stranded in the harassed wedge of face with its lank fringe of grizzled hair; that he did not like being ill, and so there was something compensating in the ham-fisted energetic way he lunged and bashed at things, applying a disproportionate element of will to small physical tasks.

'The question is, of course, does the world need any more memoirs?' he said, with the sad end of a smile, and then again without waiting for an answer plunged on: 'Now, this desk will be all yours for your hours of work. I'll empty it completely so that you can have everything you need about you. I like to have my own bits and pieces about me when I work, don't you?'

I realised with a start that the interview, such as

it was, must be over; and Mr Crawthorne seemed somehow relieved to have barged so quickly through it. He began to say something about drawing up the terms of my employment – my father had urged me to insist on this, but I had forgotten, as I had forgotten till now about my carefully garnered references – when he abruptly stopped and dragged out the chair from the desk, scraping back the Persian rug as he did so. 'Of course *this* won't do,' he said furiously, 'stupid of me to think so.'

I saw then that the chair was designed for him: he stood at least six feet, and I am not tall. With the same angry self-reproach he said, 'I should think you'd get a pretty hellish backache in about five minutes flat . . . Will you excuse me?'

Carrying the offending chair, up in his arms like a baby, he left me. Remembering what he had said about the children, I went over to the french doors, wondering if I might see them. Beyond the terrace a long lawn flowed down between rosebeds, and amongst the apple trees at the end I could see three adults seated in garden chairs, with a gramophone but no children. It was one of the shibboleths of my upbringing never to 'stare', so I turned back to look at the vault-like room where, it appeared, I was to work for the next couple of months. I knew that St Germain House, impressive as it was against the huddle of Billingham's streets, was no irreplaceable masterpiece, and instinctively I knew that no anti-quary would give this room more than a cursory glance. Still, it was like nowhere I had ever been. The books were not confined to the glass-fronted cases: they had burst out in riot over the gateleg tables, the deep window-sills, the polished floor. Across the chairs, which were an ugly meeting of shabby modern and monstrous Victorian, moulting fur rugs and odd lengths of exotic, dirty fabrics had been thrown with a cheerful defiance: on the panelled walls hung Eastern miniatures, something garish worked in silks, a great barbarous shield of beaten copper. Again I had the sense of the house and the people in it leading quite distinct and separate lives: behind the scent of hyacinths and the pot-pourri that filled the Chinese bowls, there was an old, patient smell of dust and sun-baked floorboards, a just perceptible background like the dim hum of summer bees.

I was looking along the bookshelves when someone passed the open study door and then stopped. As I turned, I thought for a moment that Mr Crawthorne, for some eccentric reason of his own, had changed his clothes for shirt and flannels: the bright blue eyes were the clearest feature in the figure looking in from the dim passage.

The man stepped into the room. 'Hullo,' he said. 'Sorry, did I startle you?'

'No,' I said. I saw now that only the eyes, and the tall loose-knit build, were those of Mr Crawthorne: the man was in his young twenties. He had a sheaf of gramophone records under his arm.

'I say, was that you we passed in the drive?' he said. 'In the car? I'm afraid we nearly ran you over.'

'Oh—' I remembered the car. 'Not at all.'

'Tom always drives like that. We've told him, he'll do somebody an injury one of these days.'

'Really, it's all right,' I said.

He smiled then. The effect softened his eyes, rather distant and blind-looking as blue eyes can sometimes be, like those of classical statues. I wondered how I must look standing about quite alone in the study, and he must have thought of it too for he said, 'Don't tell me my father's kept you waiting all this time?'

'Oh! no,' I said. I explained about the chair, and said I thought Mr Crawthorne had gone to find another.

The young man looked amused, though kindly so, at this. 'So you've got the job then?'

'Well, I think so.' I was pleased about it but a little bemused: I suspected that I had been the first applicant and as such I had simply been given the job.

He nodded. 'Father didn't confirm it formally, I can imagine. Always in a rush to get things over with. I must say I don't envy you. I've looked through those memoirs of his and they seem to be in an awful mess . . . I'm Martin Crawthorne.'

I shook his hand. The very young are not good at introductions and farewells; shy as I was, I believe I did not even say my name.

'We'll have to make sure he looks after you properly, if you're to work here,' the young man said. 'I'm afraid Father doesn't even notice discomfort. It's lucky you'll be here in the warm weather. This room gets perishingly cold in the winter. The whole place does.'

'It's a wonderful house,' I said.

'Well, it's only a fine shell, really. It's a pity, some Victorian colonel practically gutted the interior. There used to be all sorts of fine panelling and carving. Instead he left those ghastly animal trophies in the hall . . . I suppose you saw them?' he added with a wry upward twist of his lips.

I said I had.

'There's even a little antelope there about the size

11

of a cocker spaniel. What sort of a brute would shoot that? Anyway, he got his come-uppance in the end, he overspent and went bankrupt.'

'What did he overspend on?' I said.

'Oh, drink and dissipation, I think.' He pushed back his hair from his forehead. 'Unless he was hounded to his grave by the ghost of a tiny antelope. I hope so. That's rather an eerie idea, isn't it? Make a good ghost story.' With his hands in the pockets of his grey flannels he went over to look at the dusty typewriter. He had very fine clear skin and this, together with his strong smooth neck and his hair which was a dark barley-colour with a faint curl in it, reminded me again of classical sculptures. Some time later I saw a picture of a bust of Alexander the Great and I saw there something of what struck me that first day I met Martin Crawthorne: the brilliantly young, fair, shaped face unrestful in repose.

'Actually, the garden's probably the nicest thing about the house,' he said.

'Mr Crawthorne said the children were there,' I said. 'How many are there?'

His expression was such that I thought I had said something terribly stupid or rude. Then he smiled again with that wonderful softening, expansive effect and said: 'Four in all. But we're all rather big.'

I saw my mistake and began to say something in apology but he laughingly shook it off. 'Not at all,' he said, 'Father and Mother will still refer to us as "the children". It's no wonder it causes confusion. There ought to be a neutral word, really. Something like offspring. Or issue.' He ran a finger along the space bar of the typewriter. 'I wonder if we can persuade Father to buy a new machine – this one's practically out of the ark. Do you know when you're starting?'

I said no, but I could start whenever was convenient.

'I don't know where he'll find another chair. Half the rooms in this place are completely shut up, you know. It's really rather a ridiculous place to live, isn't it?'

I did not know how to answer. I thought it must be a wonderful place to live.

'Well, I'll go out this way.' He opened the french doors, and indicated the records under his arm. 'Came in to fetch Blanche's favourite. "Someone to Watch over Me".'

'Oh! I like that song,' I said.

'Do you?' He paused, his head against the sunlight a bronzy silhouette carved with transparent blue eyes. 'It makes Blanche cry but funnily enough she says she enjoys the tears.' A breeze came into the room, bearing lilac scent: its sweetness caught me for a long, particularly poignant moment while I heard the melody of the song in my head. Martin Crawthorne gestured to the garden. 'Would you like to come and say hello to the other offspring?'

'Oh – well, I think I ought to wait for your father.'

'Yes, of course. You'll be meeting them anyhow. I'll leave you.'

He left me, with a funny, friendly little wave, and only a few seconds later Mr Crawthorne came back.

He had found another chair: he brought it in with much banging and crashing and he was breathing very hard. I think the effort knocked him up – I learnt later that he suffered from a weak chest – but at the same time there was a sort of furtive triumph about him, as of a man tired of being repeatedly told not to overtax himself.

The chair was the right height for me, but not of course for him; and when he sat down at the desk to draft my terms of employment his expression of surprise was comical. He laughed then, in a good-tempered explosion, and I thought, from behind my screen of shyness, how likeable he was.

I was to start a week on Monday: he would have the terms properly drawn up, he said, in a way that made me think he would probably forget. When at last the maid came to show me out he had reverted to his musing mode.

'When I was young typists were sometimes called typewriters. Odd, isn't it? I wonder when precisely the modern usage became fixed . . .' He shook my hand and said how he was looking forward to our tackling those infernal memoirs and then said: 'I meant to ask, have you far to come? How did you get here?'

I had walked. There were buses, and the trams were just trundling out their last days, but it was not far. Mr Crawthorne, however, seemed to think it was. 'Why not cut across the park?' he said. 'You'll find it much quicker,' and he gave me directions.

St Germain House, as befitted its ambiguous status, had a park but not much of it. Once, indeed, the grounds stretched right across the western side of Billingham, but much had been given up to development when the town had thrust out aggressive new streets in the late-Victorian boom, and only a few spinneys remained, with an old riding-path that came out, as if with a start, on to a suburban street of villas. It was this path that I took, at Mr Crawthorne's insistence. One reached it by skirting a bumpy tennis-court at the back of the house, and it was from here that I had a view again of the lawn. Again the people there, from a distance, looked strangely alike: but one was waving me to come over and I realised it was Martin.

To my embarrassment the three men stood up, surrounding me with flannelled tallness. Martin was saying, 'These are the other children, you see. Here you are, Tom – this is the young lady you nearly ran over in the drive.' The others laughed and again I said it was quite all right but the one called Tom flushed red and stammered out, 'Did I really – I say, look, I'm most awfully sorry . . .'

He was a broad muscular young man, very blond, with round brown eyes and a shyly smiling mouth. His hands were huge, the golden hair on his fore-arms running right to the knuckle: when, after all the teasing and apology, I shook hands with him, my own was quite swamped. He continued to stand in an apologetic way, as it were, while Martin intro-duced the others. 'This is Ralph,' Martin said, and I took the cool hand of a dark, slight young man who seemed to step briefly from a sort of background and then return. 'And Blanche, who tried to do your job and should have known better.'

'Oh, Martin, don't.' The young woman lounging in the cane chair reached out a long bangled arm to slap him. Her beauty was fair, pale and translucent: it was complete and undeniable. She made me think of pearls. She stretched out her hand to me, from the chair, in a sort of confidential appeal. 'I'd never touched a typewriter before – I thought anyone could do it,' she said. Her smile, revealing small white teeth, had a curious and charming intimacy: it seemed to tremble like a smile through tears. 'You never saw such a mess. And that huge manuscript! It goes on for ever! Will you be coming every day?'

'Every weekday, starting a week on Monday,' I said.

'Oh! we'll have to look after you, then,' Blanche said.

'Just what I said,' Martin said.

'Father will treat you like an absolute slave,' said Blanche. 'You won't even get a cup of tea unless we remind him. He's not cruel: he just forgets.'

'Have you got to use that ancient typewriter from the attic?' the dark one, Ralph, said, again as it seemed from a little distance.

Martin said, 'I was saying to – I'm sorry, I didn't catch your name—'

'Jenny Goodacre,' I said.

'I was saying to Jenny, we ought to persuade Father to buy a new machine. I'm sure we can do that.'

'Yes, we'll look after you,' Tom said cheerfully, and I felt myself suddenly and warmly enclosed by them; their faces, which had looked so alike from a distance, revealed as so individually and even alarmingly detailed, their voices chiming round me like different bells on the same note. My shyness rose in spite of myself, and as I said goodbye at last, I could not quite meet their friendly interested eyes. Their voices called after me as I took the path through the park – 'Goodbye, Jenny.' 'See you soon!' – and I felt, half pleasurably, that vulnerable nakedness one feels when strangers use one's name. I looked back once, and they all waved, in a jaunty way, exactly as people will wave from a pleasure-boat.

Sheepishly enough, I waved back, and it was only as I entered the spinneys, where drifts of bluebells lay like smoke among the layered shadows of the trees, that a curious elation hit me, the feeling that as a child makes one want to skip. When I emerged from the gate in the enclosing wall, the grey roofs of the town appearing abruptly before me, I felt as if I were seeing them after being away for a long time.

Two

My mother and father thought I was foolish to give up a safe job for a temporary one that would barely last the summer. They looked pained. But characteristically my father talked himself round at last into thinking it a good idea.

'Of course, it'll be very useful experience,' my father said. 'Sort of experience that's not easy to come by. And the reference. Crawthorne, that's a good name to have on your references.'

Names were very important to my father. Important, of course, was his own name picked out in white relief letters above the shop door: but there was something too plain and unadorned about that GOODACRE, compared with the names on the brass plates of offices in the centre of the town.

'Collins, Morley and Petty,' my father would say, tasting the words on his tongue, 'now they're a good firm.' Or, 'Milner and Wall – now they're a very good firm.'

He himself had no experience of these firms, accountants and solicitors and auctioneers, in their tall Georgian and Victorian houses with steps up to the front doors. There was a fund of symbolism in those steps, and in my climbing them.

Billingham in those days was a largely working-

class town of engineering factories and marshalling
yards and straight grey streets of terraced houses.
The professional class were few and they tended to
cling about the old town: the town of the cathedral
and the grammar schools, where their sons mixed
with the sons of prosperous farmers, county men for
whom Billingham was still, as it had been before the
railways, simply the market town that served their
spacious world of wheat and barley and beet fields,
vast under a vaster East Anglian sky. My parents
were anxious for me to join the fringes of this class,
and I of course did not know what I wanted, only
felt that it was something shimmering and elusive,
not to be named, glimpsed from the corner of the
eye.

We lived at the end of a street of Victorian terraces, slate-roofed and identical, each with a tiny
front path two strides long to the front door – which
was never used – and a square of back yard enclosed
by gas-tarred fences. Many of the men worked 'on
the line' – that is, for the Great Northern Railway,
or the Great Eastern or the Midland: others cycled
to work at the factories over the viaduct. The women
stayed at home and boiled up great coppers of washing and beat rugs in the yard and cooked scrag-end
or kippers or liver and onions. It was a straitened
and respectable little world bounded by a Wesleyan
chapel at one end and my father's shop at the other.

My parents were Methodists. My father was a
member of the Total Abstinence League. There
were many pubs in Billingham, and my father, who
in those days still had a horse and cart, kept the
horse in a stable behind one of them, the Queen
Adelaide: but that was as near as he ever got to a
pub and his disapproval of them was the only severe

thing in his character. My own hazy knowledge of pubs was filtered through this disapproval, so that I had a dim idea of them as hot and shadowy places where whiskered men sat in gloom, like greasy walruses, and drank fierce liquors while smoking something called Nut Brown Shag. My father's own pleasures were football and light music. He and my mother had a small pile of gramophone records of songs from the elaborately tuneful operettas that were still popular then and on a Saturday evening they would wipe these carefully and play them one after another, listening intently to John McCormack or Richard Tauber singing full-throated airs from *The Vagabond King* and *Lilac Time*. They were private and gentle people and objected to swearing, chiefly because, like many things in life, they found it painful.

I remember the shop as full to bursting, yet it is remarkable how small the range of goods we sold really was. Behind the counter there were deep drawers where the tobacco was kept and I loved the smell of these. In front, tilted on racks, were large open tins of loose biscuits, petit-beurre and arrow-root and Marie. There were jars of boiled sweets and a few packets of tea and sugar. There were fruit and vegetables for which Goodacre's had a high reputation: sometimes my father would go out in the cart to Snowden's farm and bring back fresh apples and plums or cauliflowers with milk-white heads. The shop window was usually filled with intricate sculptures made of empty cigarette packets flattened like playing cards: a man from the wholesaler's came to make them and as a girl I thought him a wonderful conjuror as I watched him raise these cardboard castles; though they soon became

21

faded, and dead flies, like the corpses of heroic defenders, covered their battlements.

Behind the counter hung a card respectfully requiring that customers should not ask for credit: in practice my father often gave tick to regulars. The immediate neighbourhood was not poor but being 'a bit short' was a condition everyone was familiar with. My parents embraced their respectability all the more tightly because they knew that it was precarious; that a few streets away, where the air was tainted with the sickly smell of the gasworks and the terraced houses crept forward to the pavement, was another world, where the housekeeping money saw the publican before it saw the housewife, where watches and cutlery lived a double life in the pawn-shop, where bare-legged women stood in open doorways, insolently pregnant, in grimy twilights. It was another world but it was really terribly close, no further away than a few shillings or a turn of bad luck.

I think this made them all the more anxious for me to get on. Like parent birds about a fledgling, they hovered benevolently over my studies at the secretarial college, which was lodged in of all places the cathedral gateway, so that the massed clattering of typewriters vied with the piping voices of boy sopranos rehearsing in the Becket Chapel nearby. It was not that my qualifications were to prepare me for any sort of career in the true sense of the word: such things were not really considered important for women, and I do not believe at that time it even crossed my mind. What mattered was the passport to a more secure world, a respectability more unassailable.

What I felt about all this I find it difficult to say.

The self-absorption of youth is so complete that even our later selves can only partly penetrate its seamless shell. My impression of myself is of a sort of sleepwalker. 'You do like it there, don't you?' my mother asked me when I started work at the solicitor's office, and I said yes: but my emotional capital was not invested in such durable stock. It was all in invisible assets, as it were, and it is no wonder my parents could not understand me. I did not understand myself. I fell into deep pockets of dreamy introspection at the sight of a stranger's face on a bus, at a glimpse of a foreign place on the films, at watching the last, infinitely attenuated shadows of the trees in the town park melt away as the sun went down. My mind snagged on these things like a garment caught on a thorn, as I seemed to catch the far-off echo of a promise, a possibility, a whisper to the heart.

I had stopped going to chapel, to the sorrow of my mother and father. Religion was still strong in Billingham in 1929. It was possible to be jaunty about it – even my father referred to the corrugated-iron Mission Hall in Brougham Street as the Tin Tabernacle – but religion, like the railways, was terribly pervasive, in Temperance coffee houses and oratorio concerts and the Salvation Army Band thumping their way from the Citadel to the market place on empty Sunday evenings. 'It's something you've always got to fall back on,' my mother said: but I chose to escape it – and to escape, especially, Billingham's Sabbath of clangorous church bells and cemetery-visiting – by walking or bicycling out of town, as it was still possible to do in those days; to wander the surrounding countryside of farms and coverts and river meadows in a sort of entranced solitariness. I would even stare, affronted, if I found other people at my favourite spots, and would avoid them, as if the shrine were defiled.

It was not in the nature of my mother or my father to remonstrate with me. They themselves were so private that they regarded other people, including their daughter, as mysteries not to be trespassed upon. With my grandmother it was different. She came to us on Sundays for the inevitable tea of tinned salmon and tinned fruit salad. My grandmother was often spoken of as a 'poppet'. She was a tiny fluffy lady with a soft beaming face and something childlike about her brisk little body: her shoes always looked too big for her, like Minnie Mouse on the films. She was also a frightening woman who would have made a sterling member of the Inquisition. Her conservatism of mind was no reflex but an active principle: her sweet fluffy logic led her to the most merciless conclusions. There was much unemployment at that time and my grandmother, scenting a rabbit, soon hunted it down.

'Well, if they're not working, what do they live on?'

'The dole money, Mother,' my father said.

'But why should they get that for not working? That isn't fair, is it?' she said, beaming innocently.

'There isn't any work for them,' my father said.

'But that doesn't mean they should be paid for doing nothing, does it?' my grandmother said. 'It's just not right to pay people money for doing nothing.'

'But they'd starve otherwise,' I said, unwisely.

'Well, then, let them starve, and die,' my grandmother said comfortably, her little legs dangling.

Curiously, she thought of herself as broad-minded. She habitually catechised me about The Young, addressing me as if I were their elected representative, seeking information. 'Why do the young women nowadays cut off their hair?' she asked me. This was the time of bobs and shingles. Her own white hair was piled up like a cottage-loaf, Edwardian-style. 'What makes them do it?'

'It's the fashion,' I said.

'Oh! well, we had fashions when I was young,' she sweetly conceded, 'but not like that. It's not natural. Girls never cut off all their hair before. Not ever.' And though my father often said I mustn't get angry with her I couldn't help it: I even hunted out a book with a picture of the ladies of Queen Anne's time, all with their hair shorter than any shingle. It was no good. It was like attempting to argue with a tyrannical pixie. And so when I stopped going to chapel my grandmother pounced, assaulting me with sharp little questions, trying to trap me.

'If you don't believe in God why don't you go and murder someone?' she said.

I hadn't said I didn't believe in God, but my grandmother's logic vaulted over that. 'Why should I murder someone?' I said.

'Why not? If you don't believe in God then there's nothing wrong with it.'

Then for some time she would seem to have forgotten about it, and I would forget too, until she suddenly flung another of her unanswerable *non sequiturs* at me. 'Who made the roses, then,' she demanded, when I admired a bowl of roses on the table, 'if not God?' And her little body quaked with triumph.

Though to my grandmother I was incorrigibly unconventional, I believe in most ways I conformed, not consciously but in that same abstracted habit of mind which I have likened to sleepwalking. It was because of this that I only slowly became aware of how much I disliked working at Mellows Burrell and Co., the solicitors.

At the college much had been made of the many skills required of The Secretary: but at Mellows Burrell the young girls were really only a typing pool. However, our vanity was none the less for that. The pay was little enough, but we were aware that we had what my father called 'the better sort of jobs' and had not ended up at the corset factory where girls monotonously turned out braid and webbing amongst whining stitching machines. The offices of Mellows Burrell were in a peculiar and typically impractical building, situated in a sunless street like a dry gorge, in the old commercial quarter of Billingham. In lobbies and corridors one fell up and down odd pointless little steps: the filing-bays were jammed into windowless corners, and on winter afternoons the whole place was as dark and damp as a root-cellar. But even this had a sort of lofty authenticity.

The men of the firm were solid Rotarian types who played golf and bridge and inhabited another Billingham, one of red-brick villas and conservatories and timber-framed garages housing newish motor-cars, like a transplanted cutting of the Home Counties. About all our contacts with them, there hung an unspoken question. Though my parents at least would never say it, it was tacitly understood that for girls access to that class would be most fully secured by marrying into it. Over cheap lunches and teas in the Grandee Café, or Mallinson's with its Japanese garden, the other girls and I discussed the men in brittle tones. We aped the sophistication of the films, but we were innocent prudes, appallingly vulnerable: we fancied ourselves in love with the men, and were terrified of them. The men were in fact mostly chill and humourless little tyrants, sexless as monks, and I think it was when I realised this that my discontent with the job began to surface. The advertisement for the temporary post at St Germain House put the spark to a long-smouldering restlessness.

The fascination of St Germain House for me lay in the fact that it corresponded to none of Billingham's aspects. It was as distinct from the suburban villas as it was from the sooty barracks of the railwaymen. Nor indeed was it aristocratic. Ten miles out of the town was a true stately home as big as a palace, filled with treasures, and garlanded with the names of Capability Brown and Robert Adam, where hunts still met for long winter runs across stark clay land, westward into the shires: and compared with that St Germain House was small fry. It merely perched on the edge of town, tolerated like a quaint piece of old furniture. It had been built by one of Oliver Cromwell's close associates, a wealthy lawyer who had been governor of Billingham in the Civil War and had risen high during the Commonwealth: he had, however, been canny enough not to put his name to Charles I's death warrant and had smoothly transferred his loyalties at the Restoration. Thus it had never been a manor house, never the centre of a landed estate: its founder's family soon died out and a succession of owners followed, living out sequestered lives in the large house with its handsome front obliquely hidden by trees, part of the town yet aloof and separate.

I was drawn to this partly because of my own growing feeling of separation. I think our work at Mellows Burrell was not particularly hard but the tension of little jealousies and snobberies made the days exhausting. This was not helped by my shyness. As a blind person apprehends the shape of the world around him with a stick, so it was with the shyness I always carried, tapping, before me. Moreover, I seemed to myself dismayingly young. Some of my contemporaries from school were married; the other girls at the office spoke knowingly of the prices of furniture, of leasing of houses and bringing up of children. They were at home in their future: I was a stranger in my own.

So I left the prim and seething correctness of Mellows Burrell and was not sorry. Claustrophobia oppressed me and on that first visit to St Germain House I had sensed something very different. It was something about the people there: Mr Crawthorne who was kind and ill and the children on the lawn who were not children and who from a distance had all looked strangely alike.

The girls at the office found nothing strange about my leaving – they simply assumed it must be because I was engaged to be married. One by one they cornered me alone, on the pretext of a special friendship, widened their eyes and said, 'Who is it? You know you can tell me!' in a crammed whisper. One even looked down significantly at my belly and hissed: 'You're not . . . ?' They took me out for a farewell tea at the Grandee, where we wolfed cakes and giggled like the schoolgirls we really were; but the truth had disappointed them. 'And you'll be working all on your own,' they said. 'How awful!'

I loved the hours of change in Billingham: those

times of the morning and late afternoon when the
life of the town would brim up into the streets and
then disperse: when people hurried out of one life
into another and for a brief space hovered in
between, exposed and public. I loved the morning
and the smell of watered dust on the pavements,
with the striped awnings of shops coming down and
the factory hooters answering each other across
Billingham's brick-and-slate valleys, and the commercial travellers gripping their hat-brims as they
raced to catch the businessman's train, the eight-
forty, to King's Cross. Over the bridges men pelted
on bicycles, leaving the terraces to aproned wives
and small children turned out to play, as I had once
been, in a back-yard world of cabbage-patches and
pigeon-lofts: until at tea-time the men streamed
back, through the faded light of a day gone dusty
and stale like the last unsold loaves in the bakers'
windows, and the town waited for evening as people
waited unmoving for buses, their eyes fixed on something that was elsewhere and theirs alone.

I loved these times and as I went to and from my
new work that late spring and summer I felt myself
part of them. I moved with Billingham's twice-daily
tides: and yet once I entered the gate to the park of
St Germain House I was strangely removed from
them. It was different there. Train smoke was everywhere in Billingham in those days – it flavoured the
very fish and chips, and washing on the line was
never white for long – but though the main east
railway ran close by the park I believe I never smelt
it there. I remember only the scent of lilac and lime
and grass grown lush and shaggy beneath fragrant
umbrellas of chestnut trees. There was a deep quiet
too in those spinneys, disturbed only by the song of
birds that were mostly invisible except when a wag-

tail would scuttle across the path or a thrush would stand, a brown stillness against the wavering green, holding a snail in its beak.

That backward spring matured into sudden summer and the days were very warm. At St Germain House the big rooms held the sun like a grandfather holding the hand of a child, and the old wood panelling creaked and stirred in the heat. The french doors of the study stood always open and I worked at the desk wafted by breezes flavoured with wistaria and Mexican orange blossom that grew on the terrace outside. Mr Crawthorne donned a pair of old cricket flannels held up with a tie and rolled up his sleeves to reveal arms that his years in the Near East had turned permanently brown. He was very eager about the book.

'I think it will turn out to be jolly interesting to a lot of people,' he said. 'Oh, not because of me. I mean the topography and history. I was just the observer.'

The manuscript, as Martin Crawthorne had said, was an awful mess. Snaking arrows led to interpolated passages scribbled postage-stamp size in the margin or even sideways across the page: a system of asterisks and peremptory instructions – *See* p. 34, when there was no page thirty-four at all – added to the confusion. Sometimes too Mr Crawthorne had dropped into his own private shorthand: *fat and moth* were obviously his father and mother but *E* might in one passage mean Eton and in another Egypt. After a laborious start in which he perched on the edge of the desk and went through every page with me line by line we settled to a system whereby I typed a first draft of each chapter, skimming over the queries, and then retyped to his corrections. His enthusiasm grew as he saw the book emerging in a legible form: and it was interesting work for me after the staccato legalese, the 'insts' and 'ults' and assigns and messuages that had passed through my absent mind and fingers at Mellows Burrell.

That private shorthand was typical of him: there was an element of it in the way he talked. It was not difficult to feel at ease with Mr Crawthorne, for he treated me, as I found he did everyone, as if he had known me well for years. He lived much in his mind and assumed that other people lived there too.

'Rather reminiscent of Alec Stewart, that,' he would say. 'Before his marriage, of course.'

Or: 'Roberta's uncle took up golf when he was eighty, you know.'

I soon learned the trick of murmuring mild interest or acquiescence to these remarks about people I did not and could not possibly know: I came to realise that Mr Crawthorne, with his habits of a man much older, was continually leafing through a mental memoir much more personal than the one I was typing. And in a similar way he would speak familiarly of things far outside my experience. 'That wonderful passage in *Bouvard et Pécuchet*,' he would say, 'you know the one,' or, 'Rather like those remarkable acoustics in the Opera House at Cairo.' I think that in the kindest possible way he was not really aware of other people as separate individuals with different backgrounds at all: they merely swam, occasionally, into his thoughts of books and eastern places and drifted out again.

And so in a curious way we got on well together. The young and shy fear scrutiny most of all – and I think Mr Crawthorne would not have noticed if I had turned up for work dressed in a suit of armour. Despite his abstraction he was uniformly kind and courteous: I found in him the genuine article that is counterfeited in that chill and nasty little phrase 'good manners'. We shared the satisfaction of a job of work that grows and takes shape and has a discernible aim, and the hours passed quickly in the study fragrant with wistaria over a sharp musty odour of sun on old books.

The manuscript was subtitled *Memoirs of a Public Life* and so it was: the parts dealing with his early life before joining the colonial service were brief and summary. From it emerged glimpses of Mr Crawthorne's family, a wealthy late-Victorian clan of doers, vigorous under the Empire's sun at its zenith. His father had been one of those indomitable gentlemen striding with umbrella and topi through Himalayan passes while the sherpas lagged: and Mr Crawthorne, after Eton and Oxford, had wished for nothing better than to be like him. His brother in the army had been decapitated at Omdurman but this, it seemed, had not dimmed his enthusiasm and scholarly love for the lands of the Near East, which quickly took over as the chief subject of the memoirs.

I was typing on a brand new Corona typewriter: the children, it seemed, had been as good as their word. But I saw nothing of them, those first weeks. No gramophone music or young voices broke the quiet, and soon I realised they were not there: and though Mr Crawthorne sometimes mentioned one or other of them in his absent way, I did not ask where they were.

At first I went home at midday for dinner. Even taking the short cut across the park, it was something of a rush, and it typified my rather odd position at St Germain House, where I was an employee working set hours, rather like a domestic servant who did not live in. I think Mr Crawthorne, left to himself, would never have realised this. I disappeared at twelve and reappeared at one and presumably I had, in the interval, taken on nourishment rather like a train taking on coal. It was Mrs Crawthorne who changed that.

There was a photograph of her in the study – as a young society beauty before the war, bosomed and statuesque and dreamy in that rather overripe Edwardian way – but I saw little of the original. She seemed to be out a lot and as she did not come to the study I saw her only by chance, once or twice, in the hall or the passage where she said, 'Good morning. It's Jenny, isn't it?' and afterwards, 'Jenny, hello. Are you well?' She looked rather younger than her husband, in her late forties, elegant and somewhat forbidding as Mr Crawthorne was not.

Then one morning there was a thunderstorm. Since the day before a thick close heat had been building up, fusty and unpleasant, reminding me of the heat given off by rotting straw in the outhouse of Snowden's farm; and by mid-morning the sky was so dark with cloud that we had to have the light on in the study. The electric light did not suit the rooms of St Germain House. It lit up the high ornate ceilings in a bleaching and pitiless way that was very like the harsh flashes of lightning that at last appeared in the choked sky, pulsating between crumps of thunder, directly above the house.

Mr Crawthorne had left me alone in the study some time before noon, and when dinner-time came the maid as usual brought me my hat and coat, and commented on the rain. In between the rattle of my typing I had heard the first fat drops spattering the terrace, and now as I went to the open french doors I saw the rain coming down vertically, in a great pounding hiss of summer storminess. I stood for some minutes, breathing in the wonderful freshness of earth stirred to life again after the deadening strawy heat, and wondering quite incidentally whether I could get home without being soaked to the skin. I did not hear Mrs Crawthorne come in.

'Hello, Jenny,' she said. 'I didn't realise you were still here.'

She came and stood by me at the french doors, looking out at the terrace, where the drumming rain was forming pools on the uneven stone, and the gardens beyond, receding as if behind a veil.

'Good heavens, you'll be drenched,' she said.

I said: 'I was waiting for it to let up a little.'

'It doesn't look as if it will,' Mrs Crawthorne said. 'How far have you to go? How long does it take you to get home?'

'Oh – about fifteen minutes,' I said, though it was more like twenty.

'Well, you simply can't go through that,' she said with decision. 'You must stay here to lunch today.'

I thanked her, but explained that my mother would be expecting me.

'Then we must telephone her,' Mrs Crawthorne said, and I had to explain that we did not have a telephone. My father sometimes spoke vaguely of having one installed, but it was expensive and we could not imagine when we would ever use it.

'That's no go, then,' Mrs Crawthorne said. 'At least you have an umbrella?'

I had no umbrella. I was perversely cavalier about

such things, even going shivering in the snow without a warm coat; but now I felt embarrassed. Mrs Crawthorne seemed to look at me with some perplexity. I was to learn that she had a habit of looking very intently into one's face, even in the most casual contact; but just then I did not know that and somehow I felt a fool about the rain, the telephone and the umbrella. I began to say something about making a dash for it but she stopped me, in a sweet and kind fashion, touching my hand with a sudden smile that immediately made me think of Martin Crawthorne, that first day when he had come into the study with the records under his arm.

'Come with me,' she said. 'I know just the thing.'

In a long closet off the hall like a sort of panelled tunnel she found me a pair of galoshes and a waterproof overcoat.

'They're Blanche's,' she said. 'I'm sure they'll fit. You're a very similar size.' She gave me an umbrella too and then looked at me quite maternally, as one will look at a small child dressed up for the rain. I think I noticed then for the first time how smooth her face was, quite unlined and with a peach-like bloom beneath the lightest dusting of powder. Only between her brows was there a sharp deep cleft that added to the intensity of her gaze. The eyes were as light as Martin's but instead of that blind carved look they were terribly bright and penetrating and I found them difficult to meet.

'Now don't hurry back, if the rain doesn't ease off,' she said. 'We don't want you catching your death. I'll explain to Gerald.'

The rain did ease off, and I was not late back: but it was from then on that Mrs Crawthorne began to take thought for things that would never occur to her husband. From then on, at half-past ten every morning, the maid brought me coffee at the desk. In those days it was not a drink I often had, except occasionally in that bitter liquorice-like version that came in square bottles which we sold in the shop: and this tasted quite different. With the coffee came a doilied plate of biscuits that shattered into delicate fragments when you bit into them. And it was from then on that I began to stay at St Germain House, at Mrs Crawthorne's insistence, for the meal that I called dinner and the Crawthornes called lunch.

The room where we ate was called a morning-room. It was much smaller than the dining-room or the drawing-room which I had glimpsed as a vast and uncomfortable-looking place with chairs gathered in a huddle at one end round a monumental marble fireplace. The morning-room, like the study, had french doors opening on to the terrace and here we sat at a small table in the warm weather. I remember the smell of beeswax in that room and the scent of cut flowers in tall vases standing on china cabinets. There was a marquetry fire-screen too which I found hypnotically hideous and a grand piano which I thought beautiful.

Mrs Crawthorne saw me looking at it and said, 'Do you play, Jenny?'

I was fond of music but I did not play. I asked her, in my diffident way, if she did.

'Not since I was a girl,' she said. 'And then it was compulsory. Girls had to do it. We hated it and no one wanted to listen to us but that was the way of things.' She turned her abrupt smile on me. Whenever she did that I always felt the effect was like having a lamp thrust in one's face. 'No, it's Martin who plays.'

My curiosity about the children had been growing
and at each of these casual little hints and clues
about them it seemed to flare up fierce and intense
as a blown flame. I was as yet too tinglingly conscious of propriety to ask questions about them
point-blank, and so it was only piecemeal, by
indirection, that I learned that Martin had been at
the centre of musical life at Cambridge and afterwards had gone to study for a year with a famous
piano teacher in Paris. It was in the same gradual
way that I learned that he had given it up, at least
as a potential career, and was in London, acting as
aide to a Liberal candidate in the General Election
that took place that May. This experience, Mr
Crawthorne said with approval, was to prepare him
for going into politics himself.

I thought of the young man who had stood framed
by molten sunlight against the glowing garden and
tried to imagine him going, as Mr Crawthorne so
casually put it, into politics. I thought too of the
sentences in Mr Crawthorne's memoirs, telling – in
his rather long-winded oratorical style which
reminded me of those fearful instruments of scholas-
tic torture, the novels of Sir Walter Scott – of his
family's devotion to public service. I looked again
at the piano, on which stood a plaster bust of Mozart
with the blind carved eyes that were rather like
Martin's when the sun was on them, and my curiosity seemed to burn more fiercely and restlessly.

In the same way I gathered that Blanche was with
Martin in London, and both Tom and Ralph were
at Cambridge where Ralph, his father said with
pride, was proving a scholar of brilliant promise. It
was just by chance that they had all been home for
a weekend the day I had been interviewed. I learned

too that Martin was the eldest and Ralph the youngest and that Blanche and Tom, in the middle, were twins: but this information I did not really absorb, for the children seemed to me, as I had seen them in the car and in the garden, almost as a single entity undifferentiated by age.

My hunger for knowledge about them was offset by the barely subdued alarm I felt at sitting down to lunch with Mrs Crawthorne. Impeccably groomed, her waved hair with just a touch of grey, her face with its high cheekbones and tilted nose palely serene under its merest frosting of powder, Mrs Crawthorne was a handsome and charming woman. But I found something intimidating about her. Perhaps it was the terrifying weight she seemed to give to the most casual conversational inquiries, so that I was left groping for an answer, like an unprepared student at a particularly searching examination.

There was a tiger-skin rug in the hall, left by the shooting colonel whom Martin had told me about, and Mrs Crawthorne commenting on it said: 'I always think a skin like that is the merest mockery of the real animal. One must see the muscles moving underneath the skin – *that* is really seeing a tiger.' She turned to me. 'Have you ever seen a tiger, Jenny?'

I had been taken to a zoo as a child, but I could not remember whether I had seen a tiger there or not. Idiotically, with Mrs Crawthorne's lamp-like gaze on me, I racked my brains about this instead of giving a conventional answer. I came out lamely with 'I think so' – for all the world as if I was not entirely sure what a tiger was.

'They're magnificent creatures,' Mrs Crawthorne

said. 'But the animal that impressed me was the cheetah – do you remember the one we saw in Abyssinia, Gerald? Lean, almost like a greyhound.'

There was an extreme crispness and clarity about Mrs Crawthorne's speech and I think it was that that was alarming. She gave to the words *tiger* and *cheetah* a quite ferocious resonance.

'Interesting,' Mr Crawthorne said, 'an animal with a long history of association with man. It's depicted on ancient Egyptian reliefs, as a symbol of courage I believe. The princes of India and Persia tamed it and used it as a hunting animal – there are even records of hunting with cheetah on the plains outside Kiev – of course the range of the species must have been much larger then.'

Mrs Crawthorne paused with the respectful attention she always gave her husband when he made one of these mental dives into his stored learning. I was struck, for the first time, by the thought of Mrs Crawthorne being with her husband at his far-off colonial postings – a memsahib or whatever the equivalent was in Egypt or the Sudan. Her skin looked as if the sun had never touched it. I knew from the memoirs that Mr Crawthorne had come back to England at the end of the war, to work for a short while at the Colonial Office in London before retiring to St Germain House, and it struck me now too that the children must have been born abroad.

'Yes, so they were,' Mrs Crawthorne said when I asked about this. 'We sent them home when the war broke out. Martin remembers Egypt quite clearly. I don't think Ralph really can at all, though he says he does.' I had a fleeting impression of unpleasantness as she said this, like the momentary whine of a fly close to the ear.

'Not a climate to bring children up in, really,' Mr Crawthorne said, throwing down his napkin. He ate little and impatiently, viewing food as an irritating distraction. 'Though oddly enough the French seem to thrive on it.'

'What is your earliest memory, Jenny?' Mrs Crawthorne said.

Again I floundered. I thought of saying the outbreak of war, just to get an answer out, and then I grasped something. 'The windmill,' I said. 'The windmill on Cambridge Road.'

Billingham, as a town of late growth, still retained some rural aspects that had been caught up and held in its ribbons of grey streets: one of these was the tall, six-sailed windmill that towered above the railway cottages on Cambridge Road, the long main road that ran parallel with the railway and cut the town in half. I must have been a very small girl when I saw it for the first time, riding on my father's cart out to Snowden's farm. It was a windy day and the sails were whirling round. I remembered calling out in delight and my father stopping the cart and lifting me up in his arms to look at the windmill with its white sails gaily turning against the sky.

I said something of this but the Crawthornes, to my surprise, did not know the place I meant and I had to describe it. Although I had that feeling of entering another world when I entered the park gates, I still thought of St Germain House as part of Billingham, as familiar a landmark in its way as the cathedral or the railway station. Now I saw that for the Crawthornes it was not so. They did not know about the windmill, or Glassbottle Row where the end wall of the terrace was studded all over with the green bottoms of bottles, or the Temperance Hotel where Nonconformist farmers from the fens met on market days. They were isolated from the town and did not know of these things. And Mr Crawthorne said something that I often thought of later: 'We've never really felt that we belong, somehow.'

Sometimes after lunch, if there was time, Mrs Crawthorne would take me through to the conservatory to show me the flowers there, or to the garden. The first time she did this she asked me, in her alarming catechistic way, 'Do you like flowers?' and 'Do you garden?', and once she had established that I did she began to refer to 'our flowers'.

'Jenny, let's go and have a look at our syringa,' she would say, or: 'I wonder how our fuchsias are coming along.'

The fuchsias were of the standard type, standing erect in terracotta tubs, like vivid parasols, and some were of a delicate contrasting pink and white that always made me think of raspberries and cream. While we admired them or inspected them for whitefly or snails Mrs Crawthorne talked to me of her charity work. She seemed to be what I had heard called 'county', in a way that her husband with his scholarly reclusive habits was not: and her time was much taken up with ladies' committees and fêtes and functions. She had stood beside more tea-urns, she told me humorously, than she cared to think about.

'Gerald tells me I sometimes open fêtes in my sleep,' she said. 'He says I mumble "I'm glad to see you all here today" and things like that. Do you know, I'm not sure he's joking.' We were walking down towards the rose-beds, past tall flowering yucca. 'But of course one has a duty,' she said. 'Doesn't one? Or else life is a poor thing.'

Just then Mrs Crawthorne spotted a snail amongst some leaves of honeysuckle against the old stone wall. She made a dart for it. As often happens it turned out to be much larger than a glimpse of its shell had revealed. It came away with an audible sucking and as Mrs Crawthorne held it between thumb and forefinger it writhed, grey and slimy, and very large indeed.

'Oh!' she exclaimed. We exchanged an appalled sort of glance. 'What shall I do?'

The snail writhed again and I said, unable to think of anything else: 'Oh! throw it away.'

She did so, with a shuddering convulsive flick of the wrist. The snail flew away and hit the stone wall. It lodged there, squashed.

Mrs Crawthorne looked at it and then at me, in a stretched, contrite way. 'What a ghastly thing to do,' she said. 'One never likes killing them at the best of times . . . but what else can one do with them?'

At home if I found a snail I sometimes tossed it over the fence to next door's garden: our neighbours on that side were a youngish and rather slipshod couple who had fancy lace curtains but had let the back garden go to a jungle of juicy weeds. My mother said they were all red hat and no drawers. In their garden the snails could do no harm, I thought, and it would take them an age to make their way back. I said something of this to Mrs Crawthorne as we walked on and she began to laugh.

'Oh! Jenny,' she said, 'you are funny.'

Youth tends to stiffen on being told that, but just

then I did not mind. 'Of course, you can feed snails to pigs if you get enough of them,' I said. 'Pigs love them.'

'Do you keep pigs at home?' she said.

'Oh no! Not at home.'

She knew about my home: her burning curiosity had already elicited from me all its details. Some people in Billingham, however, still kept pigs, at the bottom of long scrubby gardens gritty with train smoke. For many it was only one or two generations since their families had come off the land into the town, and husbandry was still in their blood. Though my own family were townspeople immemorially, I knew about such things as pigs from my long association with Snowden's farm. I told Mrs Crawthorne this, and as we walked down the lawn she asked me, in her intent way, all about the farm. It was as if at such times she were eagerly adding to her mental picture of me, seeking its greater and greater completeness.

So I told her about the farm, ten miles out of the town on heavy clay land, where the Snowdens lived. The Snowdens, father and mother with two sons and a daughter, were friends of my family and I could not remember a time when I had not known them and the farm and the surrounding country of water-meadows and sheep and wheatfields, a country that gravel-pits to the west and brickyards to the east had left untouched. Margaret Snowden, the daughter, was my oldest friend. She was getting married soon and I was to be her bridesmaid. The wedding had been delayed because a few months ago the father, Joe Snowden, a small, crushed and battered man who always had a scorching fragment of cigarette jammed between his lips, had died, leaving

Mrs Snowden and the sons Robert and John to run the farm.

I had not been there or seen them for some time. Somehow it had all seemed quite far away since I had begun working at St Germain House. Now I thought about them again and how different the house would seem without little wheezing Mr Snowden and soon, when she was married, without Margaret.

'Are you fond of the country, Jenny?' Mrs Crawthorne said.

I said I was, very much.

'Oh! so am I,' she said. She lifted her flat serene face to catch the scent of roses, powdery on the shifting summer air. 'One could fancy we're in the country here – though of course we're not really. That's one of the things I liked about the house when we took it. So peaceful.'

I was struck with a sort of baffled admiration when she spoke so casually of 'taking' a place like St Germain House.

'Peaceful,' she repeated, smiling wryly at me. 'Not for long now, of course. Did Gerald not say? The children are coming back.'

'Oh, when?' I said. The little firings of excitement, disturbing and inexplicable, returned to me as she mentioned the children.

'Next week,' Mrs Crawthorne said. 'Tom and Ralph are coming down from Cambridge, and Martin and Blanche are coming back from London for the summer, so they're all planning to come home together.' She put her hands to her temples in mock anguish. 'And descend on us all at once!'

Mr Crawthorne, typically, had not mentioned the

children's coming back. But the very next day, when we were in the study, his winding thoughts brought him to the subject of Martin and the parliamentary candidate whose campaign he had been helping in London.

'Our man got in,' he said. 'Close thing but he got in. Actually it might have been more useful experience for Martin if he *hadn't* got in, in a way. Learn by mistakes, for when his own time comes. Still, it's given him a splendid introduction to practical politics. There's that passage in Stevenson – you know the one – about politics being the only profession for which no preparation is thought necessary.' He gave his snuffling, inward laugh. 'Not true these days, I'm afraid.'

The candidate who had got in was a Liberal, but the government returned by the general election was Labour and Billingham too, for the first time, had gone Labour. My father, who belonged to the Nonconformist Liberal tradition that was still strong in towns like Billingham, only looked mildly anxious about this and said they must be given a chance. My grandmother was more forthright. Ever since *John Bull* had revealed that Ramsay MacDonald had been born illegitimate she had been very fierce against him in her diminutive way.

'It just goes to show what these Socialists think of marriage,' she said on Sunday, perching in the carver chair like a wrathful doll.

'Mr MacDonald is married, Mother,' my father said, with his pained fairness.

'That's what he says,' my grandmother said cryptically; and then, 'I hate to think of that man sleeping in that nice Mr Baldwin's bed!'

'I don't suppose they keep the same bed, you

know, Mother,' my father said. 'Not the same bed.'

'You never know,' she said, 'with Socialists.'

'He can't help being born illegitimate, anyway,' I said.

'It shouldn't be allowed!' my grandmother cried.

I did not ask her what should not be allowed: I was afraid she would say all illegitimate babies should be exposed on the hillside or something like that. I only said, fuming: 'Anyway, it just shows he got on, in spite of his birth.'

My grandmother's steel spectacles glinted at me. It was like the flash of a drawn sword and I waited for the thrust.

'Why don't you go and live in Russia,' she said to me, 'seeing as you like it so much?' And she refused a third helping of fruit salad and read the *News of the World*, her lips moving disapprovingly.

The week the children were due to return to St Germain House was one of pure summer heat unrelieved by breeze. I was glad of the informality of my job there, which meant I could go to work in a light sleeveless dress, though my grandmother was shocked: as if atheism and Bolshevism were not bad enough I was brazen too. My walks through the spinneys of the park took me beneath arcades of lime-tree boughs heavy with sappy leaf. No gardeners seemed to touch the park, unlike the formal front gardens, and it had grown wild and profuse and unchecked. Woodbine and dog-rose grew in tangles, in aromatic and sticky tunnels of greenery, and pollen was like yellow pepper in the air. Always there was a chorus of song from nesting birds, the song deepening and expanding in the dusk or after a sudden shower that, briefly, lifted the heavy veil of heat from the trees.

I arrived at the house one morning, cooled and exhilarated by just such a shower, to find that the children were home. Several pieces of luggage were still stacked in the hall and when Mr Crawthorne came into the study where I had already begun work he made a humorous gesture of tearing out his hair.

'Bedlam again,' he said smiling. 'The brood returned last night – at eleven o'clock, if you please.' He went to knock out his pipe on the fender, with a great hearty hammering. I had seen him break a pipe that way but he never learned to do it more gently. 'Ah, well, we shall be quiet in here, at any rate.'

The chapter of the memoirs we were working on dealt with Mr Crawthorne's travels amongst the Marsh Arabs, or Mad'an, of Mesopotamia. The manuscript was scattered with strange words, with *mudhifs* and *taradas*, that I had to verify with Mr Crawthorne, and the effect of this was to make him excitedly reminiscent. He was fascinated by this unique people in their watery land on the Tigris, and soon his mind was back there with them.

He mused aloud and I murmured absent replies while I typed, and all the time I was aware of noises in the normally quiet house, slamming doors and running feet and sometimes laughing voices. The spacious rooms, the high ceilings, seemed to amplify these sounds so that they hung tantalisingly about me as I worked: and several times I made mistakes in my typing as I thought of the children, Martin and Tom and Blanche and Ralph, and tried to match with my memory of them the disembodied voices floating about the house.

This went on until the morning coffee came. Mr Crawthorne left me then to fetch some more tobacco and I went to the french doors and looked out at the rear garden, where I had first seen the children. They were not there but I could just see figures, dressed in white, moving about on the tennis-court. The apple trees were in full leaf and obscured the view, so I could not tell who was there. I might have been able to see better if I had gone out to the balustrade across the terrace, but I did not do so, partly because of the aggrieved feeling that had been growing in me all morning. The fact that the children were home and I had not seen them afflicted me with a stubborn and piqued resentment that, foolish as it was, I could not suppress. I remembered when I had seen them in the garden and they had said, with cheerful friendly interest, that they would have to look after me. I remembered the way they had waved to me from the lawn and I began to feel, with the same hurt stubbornness, that they had been mocking me in some way: that their kindliness had only been a joke and I would not see them at all. At the same time I told myself that I was merely doing a job of work for their father and there was no reason, after all, why they should be interested in me.

I went on in this rather stupid way for the rest of the morning. I made several more typing mistakes and I even began to feel irritated with Mr Crawthorne as he spun out his reminiscences about the Mad'an and his visit to the tomb of Ezra on the Tigris. As lunch-time approached I made up my mind that I would make an excuse and not stay at St Germain House for lunch today. I felt the children would be there and in my present mood I did not want to face them.

At last Mr Crawthorne took out his watch and

expressed his surprise at the time. 'Well, Jenny,' he said, 'I expect you're ready for some lunch.'

I do not know what excuse I was about to make. It had become an expected thing for me to stay there for lunch, and it would certainly have been rude, whatever I had said, to cry off then. But before I could say anything there was a knock at the study door, and Martin put his head in.

'All right to come in?' he said. 'Literary labours over?'

'We've just finished for lunch,' Mr Crawthorne said. 'You've met our Miss Goodacre, I think?'

'Of course,' Martin said. 'That's why we're here,' and then I saw the other children behind him.

The bluff fresh face of Tom beamed at me. 'Hullo, there!' he called, as if I were half a mile away.

'We've come to take Jenny on a picnic,' Martin said.

'A picnic?' Mr Crawthorne said. 'What about lunch? Is there—'

'It's all settled. We told Mother earlier,' Martin said. 'There's lunch for two in the morning-room.'

I was still seated at the desk. Blanche came into the room and took my arm. 'Come on, Jenny,' she said. 'I swear he works you too hard. You need a break. Oh!' She looked at the pile of typescript on the desk. 'Look at all those beastly Arabic names.'

'You ought to be paid more for that,' Martin said. 'A bonus for every Arabic word. Well, shall we go?' He looked at Mr Crawthorne. 'It is all right, isn't it, Father?'

Mr Crawthorne smiled at me and again made tugging motions at his hair. 'Oh yes, go,' he said. 'Deprive me of my secretary. As long as you bring her back at some point.'

'Come on then,' Martin said. 'The studious atmosphere in here's making Tom ill.'

'It's the books,' Ralph said. 'Bring him out in a rash.'

'I'll have you know I've been studying jolly hard for the last six weeks!' Tom said.

'Studying!' they said. 'Oh yes – we know!'

In this way, laughing and teasing, they went out to the drive at the front of the house, where the car was parked, and I, in a bemused way, went with them.

The car was the one that had passed me in the drive that first day: an open four-seater Riley. The chrome gleamed in the sunlight.

'Tom's driving – you'd better not go in the front,' Martin said. 'It might be too much for you when you're not used to it.'

I climbed into the back seat between Blanche and Ralph. The leather seats were hot and aromatic.

'Where are we going?' I said.

'Oh, anywhere!' Blanche said, waving a slender white arm. 'Somewhere with water – somewhere cool.'

'How about the Nine Bridges?' Tom said, getting in behind the wheel.

'Yes, how about there?' Martin turned round from the passenger-seat to me. 'Do you know the Nine Bridges, Jenny?'

'Yes,' I said. 'Yes, it's . . . it's lovely there.'

Martin looked rather quizzically at me, with the corner of a smile. My state of bewilderment must have shown in my face, for he said, 'Don't look so startled. We're not going to kidnap you, you know.'

'Oh! it's not that,' I said.

'You did know we were back, didn't you?' Blan-

che said, in her small light, clear voice that again,
like her ash-blonde beauty, reminded me of pearls.
'Or did Father forget?'

'No – no, it's not that,' I said. I felt absurdly
relieved, with a breaking of emotions inside me.
After my stupid stubborn mood of this morning,
the effect of this sudden reversal was to lower my
defences, so that I simply said, in a weak sort of
way, 'I thought you'd forgotten all about me.'

'Forgotten, I should jolly well say not!' boomed
Tom, with such tremendous emphasis that the others
laughed and I found myself laughing too.

'Don't be so mealy-mouthed, Tom,' Ralph said,
and Martin said, 'Yes, you will *whisper* so, Tom,'
and amongst this gentle teasing, which he seemed
not to mind a bit, Tom started the car and we swept
down the drive and away.

The Nine Bridges are nine stone arches, a few
miles north of Billingham, carrying a road that goes
back to Roman times across the river and its flood
meadows. I remembered going tiddlering there as a
child. Tiddlers were the tiny young stickleback that
swarmed in the shallow places below the arches and
as a child I loved to dip a jam-jar into the water and
lift it to see the pygmy, perfect fish teeming inside.
The Nine Bridges was a popular picnic spot but that
afternoon when Tom parked the car by the road
and we descended to the meadows we were the only
people there. Butterflies broke into sudden life from
the long grass, fluttering above patches of cow-
parsley and crowfoot and marsh-marigold: and
beneath the elder and the willows that grew by the
river there was a thick murmuring of insects in the
ripe June air.

Tom carried the picnic-hamper, swinging from

one golden-haired hand, as if it were as light as a reticule. He set it down on the bank, close to the arches of the bridge, where the river ran shallow, chattering, over stones. It was a good place, I thought, for tiddlers.

Martin had brought rugs from the car. He spread them out on the grass and toppled over on to his back with a groan and a sigh. 'Tired – why am I so tired? I've done nothing all morning, except unpack I suppose. What time did we go to bed last night?'

'About two,' Ralph said. He stood on the bank looking down into the water. 'After Blanche's recital.'

'Blanche brought a pile of new records from London,' Martin said to me. 'And of course she had to hear them all, then and there. And so we had to stay up and listen too.'

I did not ask why the others had to stay up too. Already it seemed natural to me that they would do such a thing, just as their voices, joking and teasing in the car on the way here, had chimed together and overlapped and blended like the instruments of a quartet, never discordant even when they were all speaking at once.

Tom dived at the hamper. 'I should think you're starving, aren't you, Jenny?' he said.

'Tom means *he's* starving,' Ralph said, turning to look at me and turning away again all in the same movement.

'I'm afraid I am,' Tom said. He began to dig out the contents of the hamper with both hands, exactly as someone in a film or a pantomime digs out treasure from a chest. 'I always am, I'm afraid.'

He began to press the food on me: cold chicken, ham, salad, celery, eggs, watercress, three different

kinds of bread, currant loaf, fruit. I was hungry and
the food was very good. As Tom kept passing me
plates, until my lap was fairly heaped with food, I
was reminded of another thing from my childhood
and at last I said, 'I feel like the Mole in *The Wind
in the Willows* – you know – that part—'

I found them looking expectantly at me, falling
silent. I bit into a sandwich and all the old shyness
seemed to rise lump-like in my throat to meet it. I
half choked and then swallowed and it was as if
something in me made a decision. 'You know,' I
said, 'it's at the beginning when he goes on a picnic
with Rat – and all this food comes out of the hamper
and he holds up his paws and says "O my! O my!" '

The others laughed then, and Ralph slapped Tom
on the shoulder and said: '*The Wind in the Willows*,
Tom – a bit advanced for you. You'll get on to it in
time, you know.'

Tom carried on eating and smiling. His splendid
white teeth crunched away at celery and spring
onions and apples as if the noise of eating were half
the pleasure. Everything he ate he wanted me to try
too – 'Have one of these tomatoes, Jenny,' he said,
and, 'This potato salad's jolly good – try it – and
this ham' – until at last I had to protest that I
couldn't manage any more. Even then he continued
to press me, as if he simply could not understand
someone who did not share his huge and constant
appetite.

Blanche didn't eat much. She lay back as if giving
herself up to the sun like a sacrifice. She had on a
middy-jumper of white crepe de Chine and the sun
seemed to penetrate her skin in just the same pellucid and transparent way as she lay squinting
through her long lashes.

'Oh, look at that blue sky,' she said. 'Is there any sky in London? There might as well not be. One never sees it.' Then she gave a squeal as a large dragonfly circled over her upturned face. She flapped her hands at it and struggled upright.

'Look out, Blanche!' Tom cried with a deep shout of laughter. 'It's an eagle!'

Blanche threw an apple-core at him. 'Well, it was big!'

'I saw in a book somewhere,' Martin said, 'there used to be dragonflies big enough to carry off small animals. Can you imagine? You know, in prehistoric times.'

Tom clapped his hand on the back of Blanche's neck. 'And there's one now!' he said. He ran and Blanche chased him and threw another apple-core. It was one of those casual playful throws that succeed as if they have been aimed. The apple-core hit Tom squarely on the head.

'Waow, it hurt!' he said, rubbing his thick blond hair.

'You can't hurt wood,' Blanche said, pushing him over on the grass.

'Did you hear the hollow sound it made?' Martin said. 'Just like Pinocchio.'

'Don't you think they're rotten to me, Jenny?' Tom said, sprawling on the ground, whilst Blanche tried to push handfuls of grass down his neck.

'Oh! it's because you never mind,' Blanche said, suddenly ruffling his hair with a quick and affectionate movement. I remembered then that Blanche and Tom were twins. Looking at them together I could see their resemblance, not only in the extreme fairness of their colouring, but in a certain soft and appealing quality, in that light hair and the brown unclouded eyes, which was like that of furry domestic animals.

I thought then too of what I had said about the Mole in *The Wind in the Willows*, and it seemed to me that I was very like that; emerging from the dark labours and discontents of that morning into laughter and release and sunlight by the river. I no longer felt shy. I felt, as I had done that first day in the garden, enclosed and embraced by the four of them. My intense curiosity about them was stronger than ever, but without the restless urgency: I could satisfy it at leisure.

Martin had been lying back for some time gazing, with the half-blind look, towards the sheep-pastures above. Now he sat up and fixed his attention on me with a gesture that I had already begun to notice in him, an absent pushing back of the hair that grew heavy and untrimmed over his forehead.

'How are those memoirs coming along?' he said. 'Where are you now?'

'In the Tigris marshes,' I said.

'Oh no! The Marsh Arabs!' Ralph said. 'They're a regular King-Charles's-head with Father.' He turned to me as before, with a certain brusqueness. Ralph's hair and colouring were the darkest of the four: his eyebrows were sharply arched above heavy-lidded eyes, giving him a slightly sardonic expression. His glance at me was narrowly assessing and yet I fancied a certain shyness in it too. 'How much is there left to do?'

'We're about a third of the way in, I think,' I said.

'Is it very boring?' Martin said.

'Oh no!' I said. 'I like it.' And as Ralph seemed to raise further his arched eyebrows I said, 'No, I do. My last job was boring. I hated it. It's awful doing something you hate day in and day out.' And as I said this a violence seemed to enter my words, as if I was realising for the first time just how much I had hated it at Mellows Burrell.

'Ask Martin about that,' Ralph said.

'Poor old Martin!' Blanche said.

'Yes, poor old fellow,' Tom said. He was still working his way through the hamper. 'How did you stand it? All that politics. It would just about drive me round the bend.'

I understood then that they were talking about the work Martin had been doing with the election candidate. Martin only smiled a little and said: 'You make it sound as if I was down the mines or something. There are a lot worse things. It was quite interesting actually.'

There was a silence then, in which the cry of a peewit came clear and startling from the next meadow. I was aware of things being left unsaid and a subject avoided. I felt I should say something so I began to tell them about my grandmother and Ramsay MacDonald and Mr Baldwin's bed.

They laughed about it and I felt glad. I felt I had begun to share in that mutual intuition that bound them and that had made them draw back from something which did not belong with the picnic and the teasing and the summer river. And I felt with the same intuition that Martin hated what he was doing as much as I had hated Mellows Burrell.

Then Blanche remembered that the gramophone was in the boot of the car.

'Go on, Tom,' she said. 'Go and fetch it.'

'I can't move. I'm absolutely stuffed,' Tom said, flat on his back.

'I'll go,' Martin said.

I watched him, up on the road by the bridge, take the gramophone out of the boot of the car. There was a sheaf of records too and he struggled to hold them both. I went up to help him.

'Can I take those?' I said. I had come up behind him and he started.

'Oh! thank you.' He looked blind again and abstracted. 'Sorry. Miles away.'

He handed me the records and closed the boot. I looked at the label of the top record.

'Oh, it's that one again,' I said. ' "Someone to Watch over Me",' and I remembered that first day when Martin had come into the study.

'Mind out,' Martin said, taking my arm and moving me away from the road. A car flashed by, whirling up dust, with a shrill double blast on the horn.

'*The Wind in the Willows* again,' I said. ' "Poop-poop".'

'Mr Toad.' Martin smiled, with the transforming expansive effect I had first noticed in the study. It was a smile I always found myself waiting for with a curious tension and with a wonderful relief when it came. He seemed to emerge, beautifully and touchingly, from some entangling inner maze.

We walked down the path to the river between clumps of scented meadowsweet. 'Now all we need is to see a badger,' Martin said.

'I thought I saw an otter here once, when I was little,' I said. 'I was tiddlering and I thought I saw one slip into the water – but it was probably only a vole or something.'

He looked at me. 'What's tiddlering?'

I explained about tiddlering. It made Martin smile and again I found myself eagerly waiting for the smile and the breaking of tension when it came.

Blanche played 'Someone to Watch over Me' on the gramophone. The thin fluty voice of Gertrude Lawrence floated out above the tattling of the stony river and Blanche's voice followed it, oddly similar, wistful and unemphatic.

Ralph, who was smoking a cigarette and sitting, slight and coiled, on the very edge of the bank, said, 'Really, Blanche, you are sentimental. That bit about it not mattering whether he's handsome. I can just see you falling for some chap with cross eyes and no teeth.'

'I *don't* think!' laughed Tom.

'Oh, but it's such a lovely idea – such a lovely phrase,' Blanche said, still dreamy and lost. 'Someone to watch over you – I think that's a lovely idea.'

'Not always,' Tom said. 'The dean jolly well watches over *me* like a hawk. There's nothing lovely about that.'

'Why?' I said. I was mystified: I believe I was thinking of the dean of the cathedral.

'Tom got into bad odour at Cambridge,' Martin said. 'Too much roaring about on motor-cycles and tinkering with cars. Skipping lectures and chapel.'

'Only a couple of times,' Tom said with indignation.

'So he was warned and had to keep his nose to the grindstone,' Martin said. 'A bad type, our Tom.'

Tom did not in the least look like a bad type as he sat with his arms round his big knees, his brow knotted into the frown of a misunderstood little boy. 'I can't help it,' he said. 'I'm not very patient with studies. I understand cars much better than books. I do try, you know. Anyway,' he waved a hand at Ralph, 'one genius is enough in the family, isn't it?'

Ralph, to my surprise, blushed. Hastily I looked away.

'Well, at least you do something, Tom,' Blanche said. 'You're at university, aren't you? And you can do things with cars and all that. I don't do anything, I'm quite useless. There's Jenny typing away, and Martin with his politics and his music – and I don't do anything.'

'Couldn't you have gone to university too?' I asked. I did not know whether this question was rude: these were things far outside my experience and I was all curiosity.

'I suppose I could,' Blanche said. 'I was supposed to be quite brainy, you know.' She gave a faint uneasy laugh and tugged a lock of her shingled hair across her cheek. It was a sound and a gesture I was to come to know, as something Blanche brought out when she felt vulnerable, something like the flourish of a toy sword or a cardboard shield. It was both self-mocking and defensive. 'But the girls who go to university are so beefy, you see – so hockey-playing and dowdy. And I couldn't bear that. Oh, that sounds awful, doesn't it? You know what I mean,' and there was the laugh, quavering, again.

Blanche was the least beefy girl I had ever seen: I could not imagine her long pale limbs playing hockey or doing anything more strenuous than gracefully swaying to the sentimental dance tunes she loved. I did not like hockey-playing girls myself and I sympathised with her.

I saw then that Martin was tearing up pieces of bread and throwing them across the grass to a couple of sparrows and a starling that had been attracted by the remains of the picnic. He was throwing each piece a little less far, so that the birds had to come closer. Just as Blanche was about to put another record on the gramophone Martin held up his hand and said, 'Hush a minute. I want to see if they'll take it from my hand.'

'Wild birds won't do that,' Tom said.

Martin, squatting on his knees, dropped a piece of bread a foot or so in front of him. The sparrows did not approach, but the starling, after strutting around in a circle for a while, at last darted forward and took the bread and hurriedly waddled back to a safe distance.

Martin placed another piece of bread on his palm and laid his hand flat on the ground. We were quiet, watching him. 'Come on,' he said. He tried to make a chirruping sound.

'Make the starling mating-call, Martin,' Ralph said.

'What is the starling mating-call?' Martin said.

' "Starling, darling",' Blanche said.

Martin joined in the laughter, but his concentration remained fixed on the birds and he did not move. He looked very likeably serious about it all.

'Wild birds won't do it,' Tom repeated. 'Garden birds might possibly. Not out here.'

'Perhaps I look too big and threatening,' Martin said. He began to drop down till he was lying on his stomach, still with his arm outstretched, the bread on his palm. The starling gave a nervous flutter, retreated and then came back, head nodding, eyeing Martin from every possible angle. Oily spectrum colours glistened in and out of sight on its glossy plumage.

'Now it just thinks you're off your head,' said Ralph.

'Perhaps it's because I'm looking at him,' Martin

said. He rolled slowly over on to his back, till he was staring at the sky with his arm outstretched behind him, the bread still on the flat of his palm.

'Martin, you look ridiculous!' Blanche said: but he kept quite still, and the starling, still cocking its head in every direction, began to waddle closer.

I watched with something of the same fascination. Martin's posture did not strike me as ridiculous. The sun was full on his upturned face: I saw his strong, well-modelled throat rising from the open neck of his shirt and the light catching the hairs on his bare forearm.

The starling scurried forward, snatched the bread, and was gone all in a second. It was like a little boy, for a dare, ringing a doorbell and running away.

We shouted with applause. Martin laughed at himself but looked pleased. 'I never felt it,' he said. 'They're so light and quick – I never felt anything.'

'Wild birds never do that. I can't believe it,' Tom kept saying in his sturdy way. 'It must have been a young one – not full-grown.'

It was then that I thought of the time and how I ought to be back at work soon. I said something of this but they would not hear of it.

'Oh! it's not time yet,' Blanche said. 'We'll square it with Father if you're a bit late.'

'Yes, don't you worry about that,' Tom said, springing to his feet. 'I fancy a swim before we go back. Down-river a bit should be just perfect. Who's with me? I put towels and costumes in the car so you've no excuse.'

'Not me,' Blanche said, winding up the gramophone. 'I feel too lazy.'

'All right, I'll come,' Ralph said. 'As long as it's not too cold.'

'Jenny, what about you?' Tom said enthusiastically. 'There's Blanche's costume. Oh, go on, do come.'

I did not know what to say. I could not swim and I did not trust the river: I remembered a brother of one of my schoolfriends drowning in it and I was afraid. But I found I could not say any of this: and together with my anxiety that I should not be late for work, and Tom's friendly, clumsy persistence, its effect was to bring back my old paralysing shyness. I stood helpless and mute while Tom carried on, not understanding, just as he had kept pressing food on me when I could eat no more.

'Go on, Jenny,' he said, 'just a dip. It's so refreshing. Come on—'

Through all this I saw a frown deepening on Ralph's face. He watched Tom and his clever mouth grew pinched and tight and more and more angry. But just as he seemed about to say something Martin took my arm and said, 'No, I want to go tiddlering. Jenny said she'd show me. I don't know how to tiddler. Is that the verb? To tiddler.'

Martin turned me gently away and at that moment Tom seemed all at once to understand. It was as if he had suddenly grasped his own clumsiness and was shocked by it. He seemed to stand back from it, terribly muscular and embarrassed, his lips moving as he groped for words. He began to say something about being sorry but Ralph stopped him, saying, 'Oh, come on, Tom! Let's go in before I change my mind.'

We had no jam-jar but in the hamper there were glass bottles that had contained barley water and these, I said, would do.

'That's the thing about tiddlering,' I said to Martin, 'you don't need a lot of special equipment.'

The water was very shallow beneath the stone arches but the rocks were slippery. After stumbling and sliding about for a minute I went to the bank and took off my shoes and stockings. Martin followed suit, rolling up the legs of his flannels, and we paddled out amongst the rocks with the bottles.

In the shadow of the arches it was wonderfully cool. There was a smell of old stone and weed and sweetly decaying bulrushes. The water flowing over my bare feet and legs felt cool too and I forgot the stiff embarrassment of a minute ago with a sudden rush of childlike happiness as I dipped the bottle in the water.

Martin was holding up his bottle and looking dubiously into it.

'I don't think I've got any tiddlers,' he said. 'It just looks like a lot of silt. Is that right?'

I looked at him standing there, his legs, bare to the knee, planted apart. Against his open white shirt, in the shadow of the bridge, his skin looked very brown and his eyes and teeth very bright. Perhaps because my mind had been running on *The Wind in the Willows* and childish things generally, I was reminded, with great force, of an illustration in a children's book. I did not know whether it was from *The Coral Island* or *The Swiss Family Robinson* or even whether it was one of those mental pictures that children embroider and interweave with their favourite fictions. But somehow as Martin stood there he created an image that was familiar in a dreamlike and poignant way: a traveller or castaway, in old-fashioned breeches perhaps, standing on the untrodden sand of a far-off beach and looking with light wondering eyes into the unknown before him. I stared, transfixed.

Martin shook the bottle. 'No, I can't see anything,' he said. 'Shall I tip it out?'

The vision disappeared: abruptly I felt a fool. He was waiting to be told what to do, and there was really nothing to it. You just dipped the bottle in and tried to catch the tiddlers and looked at them swimming about and then tipped them back: that was tiddlering. The pleasure, I realised, was only in the personal nostalgia. It would mean nothing to Martin and he would think me a fool.

The pain this gave me was so unexpectedly sharp and lacerating that I could not speak. But then Martin dipped the bottle in again, not so deep this time so that the river bed was not disturbed, and as he straightened he gave a cry of pleasure.

'Oh! I see now!' he said. He held the bottle up to the light and this time when the smile came and expanded I felt almost light-headed with relief. 'They're so tiny . . . It's funny you can't really see them when they're in the river.'

'There should be more further in,' I said.

We went further under the arch. The cool was like a slap on the back of the neck. As we pottered about a country bus went over the bridge, sending a tremble through the stones that made the tiddlers dart and teem like blown drifts of smoke under the water: and Martin with quite a genuine look of indignation shook his fist and shouted, 'Hoy! You're scaring the tiddlers!'

At last I noticed Martin's wristwatch as he stooped near to me. He saw me looking at it and straightening said, 'You think you ought to get back?'

I did not want to go back: I did not want to leave the river.

'We can square it with Father, you know,' Martin said.

I knew that: but a certain dogged conscientious-
ness was so integral to my upbringing that I knew I
would be uneasy if I were late back. Martin watched
me and seemed to perceive my feelings.

'We'll go and get the others,' he said.

'I don't want to seem rude,' I said.

'Nonsense,' Martin said. 'It was us who dragged
you out, after all.' We climbed up the bank: my
feet slipped and Martin put out a hand to help me.
'Anyway,' he added, 'if we get you back in time
Father won't mind us stealing you away again.'

The gramophone was on the bank but there was
no sign of Blanche. Shouts and laughter were audible from the river.

'What do we do with the tiddlers?' Martin said.

There was nothing to do with them really, I said;
I always used to tip them back. So we tipped them
back in the river and stood a moment on the bank.
It always made me very slightly sad as a child: the
urge was to keep them though there was nothing to
do with them and they would only die. Now I felt
there was in that something hazily symbolic, of
pleasure and fulfilment and disappointment, but I
could not put it into words that did not seem foolish.

Down-river we found Blanche standing on the
bank, watching Ralph and Tom in the water. Ralph
came to the bank and said he had had enough, but
Tom, out in the middle of the river, was still diving
and blowing and twisting like a porpoise. Seeing
Tom swimming I wondered how I could ever have
thought him clumsy. His body was splendidly muscled and proportioned and he looked more at home
and somehow more himself in that element where
his brilliant physicality was set free. He dived under
and was gone for several seconds and then surfaced

close to the bank, spraying water at Blanche.

'Oh! Tom, you pig – my skirt—'

Tom stood upright in the shallows like a merman, roping back his heavy hair that water had darkened to a colour of burnt almond. He smiled radiantly when he saw me and called, 'Jenny, hullo!' just as if he had not seen me for months.

'Come on, Tom,' Martin said, 'time to get back. One of us has got work to do.'

'Oh – in a minute—' Tom protested.

'Oh, hurry up, Tom,' Ralph said, climbing out of the water. 'It's still pretty cold actually – that long winter – Ow!' He sat down heavily on the grass and lifted his foot. It was bleeding. 'Damn it – I *knew* I trod on something sharp . . .'

The cut was quite deep. Blanche bound Ralph's foot with her handkerchief and when that was not enough I added mine. Ralph crouched on the grass, thin and shivering, and looking somehow in a hawkish way aristocratic.

By now Tom had come out of the water. He stood dripping and helpless. His broad chest heaved.

'I say, is it very bad?' he said.

'It should be all right,' Martin said. 'It wasn't broken glass, was it?'

'I couldn't tell,' Ralph said.

'It was probably just a sharp stone,' Tom said. 'Just a stone – it'll be a clean cut. There are a lot of sharp stones – I noticed that myself—'

'You didn't tread on one though,' Ralph said crossly. 'Damn! I wish I hadn't gone in now.'

'Well, why did you then?' Tom said.

Ralph cast a weary glance up at Tom. 'To keep you company, of course. You would insist—'

Then a curious thing happened. It was the first

time I had heard the Crawthornes come near a quarrel and they seemed suddenly to realise it too and
drew back from it. That same common instinct of
solidarity seemed to bind them all at once. Tom
began in his muddled way to apologise and Ralph
with the last departing traces of crossness told him
it was nothing and then Blanche suggested that Tom
give him a piggy-back to the car.

'Oh! no, honestly,' Ralph said, 'I can walk on it
easily—'

'Go on, Tom,' said Blanche, 'just for fun – like
you used to when we were little.'

'You used to give *me* piggy-backs, and I was the
eldest!' Martin said.

Ralph said he would look a proper fool but he
was laughing now and when they were dressed Tom
scooped him up on his back and carried him up to
the car. His strength was immense, for he did not
even stoop, but he was not rough and he set Ralph
down gently before scooping Blanche up and running with her at full pelt over the bridge and back.

'Oh Tom, I'm all shaken to bits!' she cried. 'What
do they *feed* you on? I think you must have been a
horse in a past life or something . . .'

Then as we were getting into the car Tom suggested I go in front. 'Go on, Jenny,' he said, 'it
blows away the cobwebs wonderfully.'

'Oh! all right,' I said. He was so eager in his
boyish decent way that I wanted to please him. 'You
only live once.'

'Good show!' He revved the engine.

'Hold on to your teeth!' cried Martin from the
back seat.

I had very seldom ridden in motor-cars at that
time and I had certainly never been driven so fast.

The engine thrummed as if it would burst. Cornfields and hayfields, buttery in the sun, appeared momentarily beside the road and were snatched away behind us like conjuror's handkerchiefs. The wind pressed like a hand over my face so that I could hardly get my breath to answer when Tom glanced cheerily at me and said, 'All right, Jenny? Exhilarating, isn't it?' He had no difficulty making himself heard and it struck me then that Tom's habitual booming voice was very like that of someone shouting to be heard over an engine. He looked at home too behind the wheel, just as he had done when swimming, and he said to me: 'Fast enough for you? It can't be fast enough for me. I just love it. I love speed. I can't get enough of it.'

Presently, at the insistence of the others in the back, he slowed down. I glanced back to look at them. Blanche was in the middle, with her arms round Ralph and Martin's shoulders, her milky skin glowing. They were physically at ease with each other in a way that was foreign to my family and indeed to the world I came from, and seeing this I felt a twinge like a flaring up of my old shyness.

'And now you've got to go back to that dreary study!' Blanche said. 'How rotten! Never mind – we'll do it again.'

It was indeed difficult to settle back to work that afternoon. The garden breezes that came laden with scent to my desk had never seemed so seductive, and when I looked at Mr Crawthorne, his too-blue eyes waterily fixed on some enchanting prospect in the landscape of his past, I was reminded of Martin as he had stood under the bridge, and the river and the laughter in the summer afternoon.

But that austere puritan strand running, I suppose, through my long Billingham ancestry made
me apply myself to my work. It even insisted on my
staying at my desk well after my usual time, to
finish the chapter I was typing, as if in some guilty
compensation for the picnic.

I said I would see myself out and Mr Crawthorne
left me to go and change. The house settled into
silence, and then as I finished the last page and
pulled the cover over the typewriter I heard the
piano being played in the morning-room.

In the long hall I hesitated. There was no one
around. At last I went down to the morning-room
and looked in.

Martin was playing. The music was something
quite intimate and wistful but it was not of the tear-
jerking kind that I had heard tinkled out endlessly
from cinema pianos. When it came to an end Martin
was still a few moments and then his hands
wandered about the keyboard, idly doodling soft
chords.

I thought I ought to make my presence known
and I coughed.

He looked round. 'Jenny! Still here?'

'Just going,' I said.

His hands continued to make harmonic shapes on
the keyboard as he looked at me.

'What was it you just played?' I said.

'Schumann. "Papillons".'

'I liked it,' I said.

Something I recognised began to emerge from
Martin's strummings. He gave me a slight, mischievous smile. It was the melody of 'Someone to Watch
over Me'.

'Haven't been able to get this wretched thing out

of my head all day,' he said. His thick fringe of hair was hanging down and as he played he quickly put up one hand to push it back in that abrupt absent gesture I had noticed. 'Sad life, Schumann,' he said. 'Ran out of the house in his slippers one morning and chucked himself in the Rhine.'

'Why?' I said.

'Oh – it was nearer than the Thames, I suppose,' Martin said, and winced. '*Not* a tasteful joke. No, the poor fellow went mad. They fished him out of the Rhine but he ended up in an asylum.'

'They often seem to come to those tragic ends, don't they?' I said. 'Artists.'

'The great ones, anyway,' Martin said. He was playing something different now, something thick and foreboding that I did not know.

'Mrs Crawthorne was saying – ' I hesitated but decided to go on – 'saying you went abroad to study music.'

Martin nodded. 'For a while.'

Again I hesitated.

'Why did you stop?'

For a few horrible moments I thought he would not answer, that I had somehow given him impossible offence and he would not speak to me. But then he shrugged and said in a quite casual voice: 'Well, I was never going to be another Schumann, that's for sure. And if you can't be absolutely first-rate at something then really there's no point in doing it at all. Don't you think?' A frown came and went on his brow.

I said I did not know. I said I thought it must be wonderful to be able to play the piano like that.

'Oh! there's not much to it, really.' He stopped playing and waggled his fingers in the air, smiling at me. 'Bit like typing, really.'

I smiled too.

'I must go,' I said.

He got up. 'Goodbye,' he said. 'Till tomorrow.' And then with sudden energy: 'You know, it is awfully nice having someone who's *not* a Crawthorne about the place. We're so clannish. I think you're good for us, you know, Jenny.'

A few minutes later I was walking through the spinneys towards the park gate into Billingham. The trees were in full leaf, their dense masses of green casting wide nets of shadow that were still charged with the mature heat of the afternoon. But I felt with absolute certitude that the summer had only begun that day.

Three

That summer the weather was very beautiful but I began to feel imprisoned in Billingham just as I did in the town's grey drab winters. I felt a new impatience with the town and the people in it. It was in July, a couple of weeks before the wedding of my friend Margaret Snowden, that an incident, seemingly trivial in itself, brought this impatience sharply to the surface.

It was a Saturday. That was cattle-market day and also the day when people did their shopping and the town was very busy. In the morning I went for a fitting for the dress I was to wear as a bridesmaid at Margaret Snowden's wedding. The shop, Poulter's, was said to be rather exclusive. It was also old-fashioned. Lady assistants in pearls stalked about, straight-backed in stays, on polished creaking floorboards. They came at you out of the gloom and asked you, in a remote suffocated voice, if they might help you in any way? That day was very hot and inside Poulter's, behind drawn blinds, it was baking. As I struggled in and out of the dress I found myself sweating embarrassingly. The dress was too tight in the bust and this caused much dignified clucking and fussing amongst the senior ladies. I was being attended also by a very young scared trainee whom the seniors chivvied and bullied exactly as if she were some scullery skivvy in that Edwardian world of which Poulter's was a relic. I felt sorry for her but my own temper was growing short as the fitting dragged on in the insufferable heat. The whaleboned ladies were perspiring too and the dim shop was filled with an odour which I once heard described as *bouquet de corsage*.

I was in a hurry because I had promised to go and relieve my mother, who was minding a stall at a chapel bazaar down our street. I was half an hour late by the time I got to the chapel hall and more hot and irritable than ever. It did not improve my temper to be told, in my mother's ruefully chiding fashion, that I must have been window-shopping or daydreaming to be so late.

The bazaar was like the countless bazaars I had grown up with and which were held every week in church and chapel halls all over Billingham. Lay preachers circulated, smirking over white chipped cups of tea, whilst neighbours drifted in and pawed articles that they themselves had probably donated and a few desperately poor wives hunted, in a hungry distracted way, amongst piles of deathly old clothes. The stall I was minding sold home-made cakes; the one adjoining it was set out with the sort of knick-knacks made of raffia and macramé that look dusty even when they are brand new. It was being minded by a girl I had been at school with. Her name was Ellen Boocock. We called her Booey. She was a thin sandy freckled girl with a way of licking her lips and looking at you with a terrible expectant eagerness. She had a way, too, arch and repetitive, of saying, 'The mind boggles!' at any occasion of mild surprise. She was a superb and fanatical swimmer. She was in the water so much that her skin was permanently raw and chapped from it and this gave an extra red-rimmed nakedness to her sandy eyes as she stared at you and exclaimed again, 'The mind boggles!'

As we stood behind our stalls Booey talked to me of her swimming and how she had improved on her crawl and how a coach from the county team was coming down to the baths to have a look at her next week. From this she went on to me and what I was doing.

'So you've got another job, I hear?' she said.

I said I had.

'Over at St Germain House – is that right? Who would of thought it! The mind boggles!' Her eyes, lashless and over-candid, burned at me with voracious curiosity. 'What's it like? Do you like it?'

I said it was very nice, and I liked it.

'We never seem to see you at chapel nowadays,' she said.

'No,' I said. 'I stopped going.'

'What about your mum and dad?' Booey said. 'What do they say to that?'

'Nothing, really.'

'What, you mean they don't mind?' Booey said, staring harder. 'I should of thought they'd have something to say. Well! The mind boggles!'

I was very thirsty in the heat. For want of anything else I drank several glasses of a home-made lemon-ade that was sold from another stall. It was warm as tea and little gritty bits of pith swilled about in it, leaving a murky film on the glass.

'I'm so hot,' I said to Booey. 'Aren't you hot?'

'Oh no!' Booey said. 'I like it. I can stand it hotter than this. I can take any amount of heat. What, don't you like the summer?'

'Yes,' I said, 'but not this heat.'

'Oh, I do! I can take this heat.' Booey seemed to find a certain triumph in this. 'I can't get enough heat myself.'

She said something more about the heat but I did not hear what it was because I had just spotted Robert Snowden, Margaret's brother, across the other side of the hall. He was buying something at the bric-à-brac stall. I was surprised to see him here and I could not imagine what he would find to buy amongst the dismal lumber.

At last he made his way over to me. He was carrying in his arms an old wall-barometer, huge and ponderous in dark carved walnut.

'Hullo. Haven't seen you in ages,' he said.

'No,' I said, staring at the barometer.

'Only we usually see you at the farm come summer,' Robert said.

'Well – I've been quite busy with the new job.'

'Ah,' he said. 'Margaret said about that.'

'What brings you here?' I said.

Robert shifted the weight of the barometer in his arms. 'I brought Margaret into town. She's still got a lot of shopping to do – you know, for the wedding. I knew she wouldn't want me trailing after her so I went round to the shop to see your dad. He said you were down here.' He looked at the cakes on my stall. 'Don't seem to be selling very well.'

Booey, who had been following the conversation with interest, put in: 'Perhaps they'd be better if they were hot. You know. They'd sell like hot cakes,' and she laughed. Robert smiled.

'Jenny reckons it's hot enough as it is anyway,' Booey went on. 'She says she can't bear it. I like the heat myself.'

'It's awful,' I said, 'don't you think?'

'I don't really notice it,' Robert said.

He did in fact look quite cool and in my irritated mood I felt resentful and displeased with him because of this. It seemed perverse that he should be so clearly unbothered by the heat. I could not understand either why he had bought the barometer and I said, 'What on earth made you buy that?'

'Oh! Well.' He shrugged. 'You know how it is. I just happened to glance at it and the old girl there started pushing me to buy it.'

'It doesn't look as if it works,' I said.

'No,' he said. 'Can't afford to chuck money about really. But you know how it is. Anyway it's all for charity, isn't it?'

'I suppose so.' I felt just then rather impatient with the things that were done in the name of charity. I knew that the Snowdens, since the death of Robert's father, were having a struggle to manage, and that made the purchase of the barometer seem even more nonsensical. But I could not say anything of this and just then two small boys came to the stall to buy cakes and Robert stepped out of the way.

Then, as I put the boys' money in the tobacco tin behind the stall, Booey said, 'What are you putting it there for?'

'That's where I've put all the money,' I said.

'Oh no!' Booey said. 'That's my tin. You've got that wrong. That's the tin for my stall. Look – that's your tin over there.'

I saw my mistake. 'Oh, sorry,' I said.

Booey flapped around me. 'It's all wrong now,' she said. 'This is the macramé tin – now the cake money's all mixed up with it – you've got it all wrong.'

'Well, what does it matter?' I said. 'It all goes to

the same place. It's all for charity. What difference does it make?'

Booey continued to flap and eventually called over the ladies organising the bazaar to sort it out. Amidst all these fussings I felt the annoyance and frustration of the morning build up with horrible force inside me. It all seemed so monstrously typical of the oppressive pettiness of these affairs that I was overcome with a sort of savage contempt.

'Honestly, Jenny,' Booey said, 'the mind boggles – you are a dreamer, you know. You are a clot.'

'I must be to be doing this,' I said. 'I shan't do it any more. I can't be bothered with it. Thank God it's nearly dinner-time. I've had enough of it.'

Through all this Robert stood waiting, holding the barometer in his arms. For some reason the fact of his watching made it all seem worse and in the same confused way my annoyance became focused on him. It was something to do with his not noticing the heat and seeming to like the awful bazaar even to the extent of wasting his money on the barometer. There seemed to me something fatuous in the way he was carrying it around like a baby: he was tall and bony and broad-shouldered and it looked undignified and yet he seemed unaware of this.

So at last in this irritable confusion I collected my bag and hat ready to go and I suppose I must have presented to him a face of testy incomprehension when he said: 'Thought I'd wait for you if you don't mind. I wanted to speak to you about something.'

I could not think what he might want to speak to me about. We went out into the dusty street, into a searing hot glare.

Robert shifted the barometer in his arms again. Obviously he wanted to put it down, and I wanted to get home; but he slowed his pace until we were hardly moving. He licked his lips several times, staring ahead of him.

I had known Robert since we were children but I had never known him well. Mr and Mrs Snowden were my parents' friends and Margaret was my friend but Robert had always been somehow slightly in the background of the picture. He was the quietest of the Snowdens and as he grew to a young man he became rather solitary in his habits. Often when we visited the farm we did not see him at all, or only saw him briefly when he came in from ploughing or feeding. There would often be something abstracted and abrupt about him as he passed through and murmured hullo, giving me a quick glance from under his strong black brows: and this gave me a curious unease which I felt again now, in spite of my crossness and impatience, as we walked down the sun-dazzled street towards my father's shop.

'It's about the wedding,' he said. 'I wanted to ask you about that.'

'Yes?' Again I could not think what it could be. The heat of the pavement burned through my shoes and I felt weary.

'The thing is, you see, Margaret wants me to give her away,' Robert said. 'You know – at the service.' With difficulty he went on: 'It would have been Dad, you see. That's the usual thing. But now he's gone and we haven't really got any older relations, so she wants me to do it.'

'Don't you want to?' I said.

'Oh! it's not that,' he said, and frowned. 'It's just that it should have been Dad. You know. I keep thinking how it would have been Dad and it just doesn't seem right somehow. You see?'

I did not really see.

'It's one of those things that Dad liked to do. He was good at that sort of thing. I keep thinking it doesn't seem right somehow, now he's gone. Don't you think? I mean you'll be there. You'll be bridesmaid – you'll see what it looks like. I'm only a couple of years older than Margaret. Do you think it will look all right?'

He stopped then, and seemed to lose himself in perplexities where I could not follow. If I had been in a less savage mood I might have understood better. I might perhaps have seen that this inarticulate self-questioning over the simple matter of giving away his sister in place of his dead father was rooted in something more complex: that the death of his father had made Robert as it were the head of the family and the small matter of the wedding was perhaps the thing that had brought this home to him. But just then all I saw was a worry that seemed needless and trivial and I merely said: 'Oh! I can't see as it matters really, if it's what Margaret wants.'

'Oh.' Robert looked hard at me and then away. 'Right,' he said, suddenly curt. It did not occur to me that I too had been curt: partly because my mind was still running exasperatedly over the bazaar and Booey and the dreary pettiness of it all; partly because Robert's manner was often like that. He could be rather short and peremptory and would close up, as he did now. A sort of immobility descended over his face, a strikingly dark, high-cheekboned face, not exactly swarthy but with something of the Slav about it.

We walked in silence to the end of the street where our shop was and where, I now saw, Robert had parked the old Humber that he used as a runabout. He put the barometer in the back seat. At the last minute something made me say, 'Aren't you coming in?'

'I don't think so, thanks all the same,' he said. 'Got to get into town and pick Margaret up.'

'Well! I'll see you at the wedding then,' I said. I felt then, suddenly, that I should have given him some more helpful answer to the question that had been troubling him. But the moment was gone and he said goodbye and got into the car and drove away.

The stupid incident of the bazaar continued to rankle and I suppose it typified my general feeling of dissatisfaction. This in turn grew worse because I had no way of expressing it. I never quarrelled with my parents but I could not confide in them even if I had wanted to: I think they would have found such a thing alarming. They were grave-faced people – my father was a heavy jowly man with a drooping moustache which filtered all his facial expressions, and my mother had a habitual look of adding up a difficult sum in her head – but I think in their worried fashion they were happy people too. They were devoted to each other in an exclusive way: each had had the good fortune to find a mate who shared their peculiar unargumentative privacy and they wanted nothing else. In the bureau in the living-room there were photographs of them when young, gazing with high-collared adoration at each other in front of a studio landscape of funereal pine-woods zooming off in enthusiastic perspective, which I found both hilarious and painful. I did not believe they had ever felt what I was feeling and so I gnawed in silence.

Nor could I really have said what it was that I was

feeling: except perhaps that if I had hitherto been like a sleepwalker, now it was as if I was waking, with all the startling confusion that implies. And it was St Germain House and the people there that were responsible. If I was inattentive to Robert Snowden, it was largely because the Snowdens and the farm and indeed everything that was not connected with the Crawthornes had become shadowy and unreal to me. There was only one reality now.

I do not know how I managed, after the children came back, to keep my mind on my work with Mr Crawthorne. Somehow, however, I did. The work of preparing the memoirs progressed for us as satisfyingly as before. I felt a genuine regard and affection for Mr Crawthorne, and that remained the same through all that subsequently happened. But throughout those summer days as I worked at the desk I was aware of the children, whether it was the sound of their footsteps or voices or the sight of them in the garden or even the very absence of these things. It was as if my emotions were continually flexed in anticipation of them.

'I haven't gone much into theories of heredity,' Mr Crawthorne said to me. 'But I do wonder if my urge to travel has passed on in some debased form to those children.' He snuffled humorously. 'It seems to manifest itself as an inability to stay in one place for two minutes at a time.'

He was referring to the keen restlessness that swept the children in and out of the house and brought them often to the study at lunch-time to bear me off again for picnics. The car whisked us out into a country scorched under a high summer without rain, where hay was turned in fields baked hard between hedges of hawthorn, profoundly green against an enamel sky, and where fields of wheat lay broad and still under breathless layers of heat. Always we went to a different place.

'Oh! not there,' Blanche would say, 'we went there the other week. Somewhere new.'

So Tom would drive us, hurtling, to new places by the river or amongst the woods down the valley. The country roads were very empty then, which given Tom's love of speed was just as well: once he threw the car into a stomach-wrenching turn down a side-track to avoid frightening a farm-horse that was trundling a cart up the road ahead. Sometimes too we went to isolated pubs, out on the flat fenland to the east. Shades of my father's disapproval pursued me and I was surprised and a little disappointed to find that pubs were not dens of vice seething with dark glamour. The fen pubs were strange places that seemed to have been set down in the middle of nowhere: they stood at odd angles, never seeming to face the road, and with no village in sight; and inside leathery men sat in rows against the walls of low, stone-floored rooms, staring over their pipes, as if waiting for something.

I remember one pub that we found by the side of one of the long straight drainage dykes that march across that part of East Anglia. The land was so low that the brink of the dyke came up higher than the slate roof of the pub and I thought how strange it must be to live there and know that a flood would bring the water straight down on top of you. There are many orchards and market-gardens in that country too and at the back of the pub there were plum trees, shading a rambling sort of garden where there were a few wooden seats and tables amidst a

typical fenland mess of broken wheels and rusting
rolls of wire and an ancient pergola drunkenly stag-
gering under a ragged burden of rambler rose.

But what delighted me about this place were the
animals. It was rather like a pets' corner in a zoo.
Besides chickens and rabbits in pens there was a
tethered goat and in a small paddock a donkey that
came to the fence and nuzzled against my hand as
if for sheer pleasure of company. There was a goose
too and Martin wanted to feed it by hand the way
he had with the starling. The goose, however,
needed no persuasion. When the bread was gone it
continued to pursue Martin, honking, in the rather
alarming insistent way tame geese have, until at last
he took refuge behind me.

'Tell it, Jenny,' he said. 'Speak to it. Tell it I
haven't got any more. Speak to it in goose.' He put
his hands on my shoulders, which were shaking with
laughter. 'Honk to the wretched thing!'

'Where's St Francis of Assisi now?' Ralph said in
his ironical way.

We laughed a lot about the goose and as we sat at
one of the wooden tables Martin still kept glancing
behind him. 'Are you sure it's gone?' he said. 'I'm
not sure. I can just imagine it following us home. I
can just imagine waking up in the night and hearing
it honking at my window.'

Above us the plums hung heavy and scented. Tom
had eaten hugely as usual but he said he was still
hungry and several times I saw him looking up at
the plums. At last when the landlady came out to
the garden Tom asked her if the plums were good.

'Oh! very good, usually, from these trees,' the
landlady said. 'Good fruiters, these.' She was a big
woman with coiled bunches of grey hair, shrewd and

unsmiling in the fen way. 'Would you like to try
some?'

'Could I?' Tom said. 'They do look so tempting.'

'As many as you like, dear,' the landlady said.

Tom plucked at the plums in his greedy boyish
way. He had already got several in his mouth before
his expression changed. He spat the plums out. The
bloom on them was deceptive. They were as hard
as stone.

The landlady's big face split in a grin. 'Sorry,
dear,' she said. 'Should have told you.' Tom, caught
out so often, laughed too, but looked so disappointed that the landlady said, 'Come again in a few
weeks, dear, when they're ripe – take all you like
then. You're welcome.'

'You should read your Bible, Tom,' Ralph said.
'Then you'd know better than to eat fruit a woman
offers you.'

Ralph was often ironic in this lightly astringent
way but sometimes he seemed to direct his barbs
especially at Tom. It was not exactly malicious but
it was as if Tom's very imperviousness, his thick
skin, gave Ralph a frustrated urge to prick it. Seeing
Tom and Ralph together – Tom so blond, fresh-
coloured and brawny, Ralph dark and wiry with his
sardonic question-mark eyebrows – I thought of the
ancient idea of the humours and how each person
was made of a different mixture. It seemed to me
there could be no more opposite mixtures than Tom
and Ralph. And yet sometimes, especially when he
had been too cutting, Ralph would seem to be struck
with remorse and out of it would emerge an affectionate protectiveness towards Tom. I watched these
things with fascination.

I did not understand Ralph. Sometimes on these

picnics he hardly spoke to me. At other times, particularly if the others were occupied with something, he talked to me in a quiet confidential way as if we knew each other very well. He spoke of Cambridge and his studies, and it was then that the mocking undertones left his voice. He was fascinated by languages and he soaked them up like a sponge. He knew not just the classical languages and French and German but Czech and Danish and others besides.

'Did you know,' he said to me, 'that God in Serbo-Croat is *Bog*?'

I did not know and I could not help smiling.

'There you are,' he said, seeming pleased. 'That shows how our religious responses are coloured by language – *made* by language. The power of the Word. No wonder the old Catholic Church resisted using the vernacular.'

I could not always follow him when he spoke like this. His mind seemed to flit along its own paths rather like his father's. I said, 'I used to play with a little boy who was partly deaf and he used to mix up the words "dog" and "God". So if we saw a stray dog in the street he'd say, "Mind – mind the God." '

'Beware of the God, eh? Like something out of Joyce. The seriousness of puns.' Ralph smiled his narrow smile and seemed pleased again and I was glad. Sometimes he used his cleverness as a shield to keep you away; but at other times I felt an unspoken understanding with him. I was convinced that there was a key to Ralph and that I might grasp it.

When there were no picnics I still saw the children at lunch. It was served in the dining-room and was no longer the quiet meal punctuated by Mr Crawthorne's scholarly ruminations and Mrs Crawthorne's terrifying conversational salvoes. I had thought the dining-room overlarge and depressing but the vitality of the children filled and transformed it and then overflowed it, for they never stayed at the table for very long. Tom was keen on tennis and had hardly finished eating before he was ready to play.

'Come on, Martin – while the weather's good,' he would say. 'It might rain later. Go on – I'll give you three games' head start.'

The tennis-court behind St Germain House, rather typically, was bumpy and the net sagged. Sometimes the four of them played: more often it was Tom and Martin, who was the only one who could give Tom anything like a game. Even then Tom always won. He played tennis with the same grace and energy with which he swam and he went all out to win.

'Here, that was in, wasn't it?' he cried.

Blanche and I were watching. 'No, no – out – definitely out,' we said.

'Biased judges!' Tom said; but he never minded, and went on peppering Martin with thunderous serves.

'It's funny,' Blanche said, 'Tom's never serious about anything except the things that aren't supposed to be serious. Games. Cars and motor-cycles. Have you seen his motor-cycle? He bought it from a friend at Cambridge. It's terrifying. I went in the side-car and I screamed my head off.'

She slipped her arm through mine as we walked on round the tennis-court. She often did this and at first all the defensive reserve of my upbringing had reacted against it. My shyness and solitariness had seemed to harden but then at last to yield, breaking and dissolving, leaving me relaxed and liberated.

The gesture was one of many small affectionate habits that I found charming in Blanche. 'I'd like to be a serious person – wouldn't you?' she said. 'Really serious about something. Oh, but you are serious anyway, Jenny – I thought so when we first met you. Oh dear, that's rude, isn't it? It isn't meant to be.'

I did not know whether I was a serious person: one effect of what I have called my awakening was that I did not know what sort of person I was. Watching Martin on the tennis-court I said: 'Is Martin a serious person?'

'Oh! I think so,' Blanche said. 'I couldn't exactly say what about.'

Just then Martin came off the tennis-court, having lost again. He flung himself down on the lawn.

'No, no more,' he said to Tom. 'Thrashed again!' He looked up at me, pushing his hair back. 'I did beat Tom at something once, Jenny. I have a clear recollection of an epic game of halma back in 1916 . . .'

'I remember that – I let you win!' Tom called. 'Blanche, how about a game? Just for fun.'

'No thanks,' Blanche said. 'I don't want my tombstone to say "Here lies Blanche Crawthorne, killed by a tennis ball." '

'How about you, Jenny?' Tom said. 'Do you play?'

'I'm afraid I've never played tennis in my life,' I said. At school our sporting recreation had been confined to a single stony netball-court like the exercise yard of a Victorian prison: I think there was supposed to be something character-building about bruised and bleeding knees.

'Have a go,' Tom said. 'Just to get the feel. Blanche has tennis shoes.'

I did want to have a go. But I soon found that Tom was not the best person to teach a beginner. He merely played his normal game: he could no more tap the ball over the net than an elephant can tiptoe. After fifteen minutes, during which I flailed my racket and hardly touched the ball once, we called a halt and Tom said with awkward kindness, 'I think you're getting the feel a bit,' and looked disappointed that I was such a weakling.

I did still want to learn very much, and Martin must have perceived this. Late that afternoon when I had finished work and was preparing to leave he appeared at the french doors of the study, still in his whites, and asked if I had to go home just yet.

'I thought we could have a knock-up,' he said. 'If Tom's left any tennis balls in one piece.'

I felt enormously happy then. I went out with Martin into the tender sunshine. 'You just want someone you'll be able to beat,' I said.

'Oh, I'm not counting my chickens,' he said. 'I still can't get over Tom letting me win that game of halma when I was ten. All these years I've been thinking I won it . . .'

I remember how happy I was those late afternoons when Martin taught me how to play tennis. It must have been a boring task at first but he was very patient. We laughed a lot and I remember too the first time I managed to hit something like a recognisable tennis shot. By some fluke the ball bounced off my racket as a volley, wrong-footing Martin completely. Tom and Blanche and Ralph were watching and they gave a great cheer.

Martin solemnly laid down his racket and began to walk off the court. 'That's it,' he said. 'I'm not playing any more.'

I was laughing and then for a second I felt the

laughter catch sickeningly in my throat as it struck me that he might be serious. It was only a momentary feeling and immediately dispelled as Martin smiled and picked up his racket, but just for that moment it had been horribly intense and desolating: the idea of these afternoons being over was unbearable. And across the net there was a sort of pause about Martin that made me think that he had seen it in my face.

Often, as I became a slightly less hopeless amateur, we played on through long bronze dusks roofed over with birdsong, until at last, reluctantly, I had to run home before my tea was spoiled. Hurrying back through the town, crossing the wide, sunstruck emptiness of the market square where pub doors were being unbolted and barbers swept out piebald drifts of hair at their shop doors, I had again the feeling that I had been somewhere far remote from Billingham. The town did not seem real to me any more. My mind, like Mr Crawthorne's, was elsewhere. When on Saturday afternoons I served in the shop I was thinking all the time of the car and the picnics, the bumpy tennis-court and the sound of a piano being played in another room; and I believe I must have looked a perfect simpleton to the old men to whom I gave the wrong brands of tobacco and the women who, making a perfectly reasonable request for a pound of onions, found themselves being blankly handed a tin of golden syrup.

My grandmother scrutinised me. Though I was brown from the sun, she said I was white as a sheet, and went on to ascribe this, with sturdy illogic, to the green-sickness.

'It's being a bridesmaid,' she pronounced. 'That's what's done it. That's brought it on. It makes 'em jealous. They start itching to get married. They can't stop thinking about it.'

I was not jealous of Margaret, and I was not itching to get married. But I was glad when my grandmother dropped the subject.

Although Margaret Snowden was only a year or so older than me, the man she was to marry was over thirty. When I first heard this my reaction was, with youthful intolerance, one of astonishment that my best friend was going to unite herself with an old man. But then I met Bill Long, and had to admit that he did not after all have one foot in the grave. In a grimly real sense, however, he had had much to do with graves, as a young soldier in the war at Passchendaele. He had come through unscathed but had had a breakdown on returning to England: all his friends, it seemed, were dead, and his mother, his only family, died of the Spanish flu just after the Armistice. At last he had become a schoolteacher, at the boys' school in the little pottering market town of Cawley, a few miles down the river from Snowden's farm: and it was there, at a concert given by the boys, that he had met Margaret.

In those days schoolteachers were held in respect rather in the manner of doctors and lawyers, and there was a feeling that Margaret had done pretty well for herself, even though Bill Long's salary was really very little. Margaret was a small and tidy and compact girl with sloe-black eyes of great steadiness and a muted way of speaking. She sang in the cathedral choir and I never forgot the surprise, the first time I went to hear her sing a solo part, of hearing her thrilling deep contralto springing out from that slight body. She was a thoughtfully kind person who always remembered birthdays and sent letters and flowers if you were ill. She and Bill Long, in their quiet undemonstrative way, seemed well suited, and I was very happy for her.

When we went out to Snowden's farm for the wedding the hot dry weather was still unbroken and in grass meadows on the way I saw black patches where fires had broken out. In the fields that led up to the farm the corn was already a pale yellow, and up at the house Robert Snowden, big and stiff and uneasy in his blue serge suit, said they would be cutting early. He scooped a finger under his tight starched collar, his shaven jaw already turning dark again, and spoke nervously of the corn and the dry weather.

'We could do with a spot of rain,' he said to my father. 'Just a spot.'

'Not today, though,' Mrs Snowden said. 'Not for the wedding. It spoils a wedding if it rains.'

Mrs Snowden was a tall and bulky woman with the dark Slav looks that she had passed on to her children. Overworked and capable and anxious, she moved about the big redbrick-floored kitchen, checking once again the food and drink for the guests. 'You're looking well, Jenny,' she said to me. 'We haven't seen much of you this summer.'

Her words were casual and without reproach, but still I suffered a pang. The farm was so much a part of my life and it was strange to feel myself, as I did then, remote and detached from it. It was only when I went up to see Margaret in her wedding-dress that this detachment began to give way. No one, I think, can see their oldest friend dressed to be married without powerful emotions; and I kept down tearfulness, as did Margaret, with a tense, hysterical sort of gaiety.

'I wish I wasn't so short,' Margaret said, looking at herself in the mirror. 'Look at me! Two penn'orth of nothing going up the aisle!'

'I could carry you on my shoulders!' I said.

'I could stand on a stepladder at the altar!'

In this way we giggled ourselves at last downstairs, where Robert, perspiring and muscular, gave his sister a worried searching look as if she were an invalid taking her first convalescing steps. There was something clenched about him as he gave her his arm and I thought again of the day of the bazaar and his troubled inarticulacy over things that I had dismissed then as trivial.

The village church was small but it was not full: Bill Long's side was almost empty. Death had robbed him of family and friends and I remember feeling happy for him that he had found someone of Margaret's warm and loyal nature and then piercingly sad in some way that seemed to relate to myself though I could not have said how. I remember too how a dry gusty wind blew up outside the church after the service. As we stood for the photographs it caught up Margaret's veil and it blew round the long draped skirt of my bridesmaid's dress, fresh and cool on my legs, giving me a sensation of lightness and exhilaration. Scatterings of confetti whirled around the sunken churchyard and it was as if we were enclosed and suspended in a little world very like one of those glass paperweights filled with a miniature snowstorm.

Back at the farmhouse the guests who had not filled the church soon filled the kitchen that was the Snowdens' main living area – I had never known anyone use the parlour, which was a sort of cretonne museum where photographs of past Snowdens stared each other out of countenance across unfaded

floor-rugs that were like luxurious growths of mould.
Mrs Snowden had laid on a lot of food: it was all
home-made and excellent. Many of the guests, it
seemed to me, were local people who in the backbit-
ing village way could not be left out. They were very
interested in the food. They chewed like cows in a
meadow and when Margaret and Bill came round
to speak to them looked affronted, as if that were
not part of the bargain.

'Now you must come and stay with us, Jenny,'
Margaret said to me. The couple were to live in
married quarters attached to the old school in
Cawley. 'There's a lovely spare room – we've been
doing it up specially.'

'Thank you – I'd love to,' I said.

'Mind – I'll hold you to that,' Margaret said.
'We've hardly seen anything of you lately. Where
do you get to all the time?'

'Well, Jenny's got a living to earn, remember,'
Bill said, as if he had seen a shadow of guilt on my
face. He was a fair, gaunt man with quiet watchful
eyes that I felt did not miss much.

The time came for the toasts and the village guests
reluctantly stopped chewing. They stared with the
same glazed affront at Bill's best man, a fellow-
teacher, as if they had never seen a man stand up
and speak before and found it obscurely insulting. I
remember one woman was wearing an ancient fox-
fur, complete with head and paws as was the way
then, and its glassy eyes were very like theirs as they
sucked their teeth and stared through the speeches.
In the heat the fox-fur had begun to stink and I
actually saw Margaret's younger brother, John,
recoil as he passed near it.

Some peculiar unease came over me as the toasts

began and then I realised why: it would fall to Robert to make the response for the bride. Again I was stung by the way I had dismissed his troubles: I began to see how his father's death had thrust him forward into life in all sorts of ways. I tried, rather late, to give him an encouraging smile but he was not looking my way.

He got through it very well. He spoke feelingly of Margaret and Bill and only once lost his thread for a moment when one of the village guests, thinking for some reason that he had finished, gave a terrific single clap like a gunshot before realising his mistake. When Robert sat down at last, smoothing back his heavy crop of black upswept hair, his face flushed with relief, I tried again without success to catch his eye.

It was some time after this, when everyone except my mother and father had had a drink or two and the village guests had loosened up sufficiently to begin swapping gnarled little country jokes, that I noticed Robert was not there any more. Margaret went up to change into her going-away clothes and I went with her to help.

'It's a bit like on Christmas day, isn't it?' she said, stepping out of the wedding-dress and looking at its yards of satin pooled on the floor. 'You know, when all the presents have been opened and the wrapping-paper's lying all over the place.'

I felt my long affection for her keenly as she stood there in her slip, thoughtful but happy in her subdued way. And this affection seemed to fuse, with the happiness of the occasion and the beauty of the late sun striking the old rafters of the attic room and perhaps the sherry I had drunk, into a vague and embracing affection for the farm and everything associated with it.

'I'm sorry I haven't been over much this summer, Margaret,' I said.

Margaret's reflection smiled at me as she fastened her blouse in the mirror. 'We did wonder where you'd got to,' she said. 'I'm dying to hear about it.'

'Oh – well . . .' I found I could not say anything.

'You can tell me all about it when you come to stay,' she said: Margaret was never obtrusive. 'Here, you haven't seen Robert, have you? We'll be going soon.'

'I haven't seen him for about an hour now.'

'He said he was just going out to water the heifers but it can't have taken this long.' Margaret clucked her tongue. 'I'll bet he's sloped off to his workshop. I'll bet that's what he's done. And on our wedding day as well.'

'Shall I fetch him?' I said. 'Where's his workshop?'

'Across the yard – the other side of the barn. He calls it his workshop. He tinkers with things.'

I slipped out. The house was an L-shape, and the outhouses formed the third side of an open court-yard overlooking a small garden of gillyflowers and herbs and beyond that the long sloping field that descended to the road. The land is so flat in this country that I always thought of this as quite a hill. Crossing the yard now I paused to look at the sun sinking, basted in its own rays, and the golden glow thrown on the stubble-field as if a vast furnace door had been opened.

I went round behind the barn, where a derelict horse-brake that had been there as long as I could remember pointed its shafts to the sky, and found the lean-to that was Robert's workshop. Inside there was an astonishing clutter of dismantled farm machinery, of harrows and binders and threshers gutted as if in a slaughterhouse, of petrol engines and wheels and tyres, and of rusting islands of scrap set about with glistening pools of oil. There were holes in the corrugated-iron roof that let in a murky light and in some of these house-martins had built nests, adding their droppings to the mess.

I found Robert bent over the entrails of an engine and, as Margaret had said, tinkering. He was so absorbed that he jumped when I spoke.

'Sorry,' I said. 'Only Margaret and Bill will be going soon.'

'Is it that late?' Robert looked at his grimed hands. He had taken off the jacket of his suit, and by some miracle had kept the trousers clean. 'Damn. I didn't realise.' He found a rag which was only slightly dirtier than his hands and wiped them. 'I came out to water the heifers, you see. And then I popped in here just for a minute . . .'

I thought of saying it was more like an hour but instead I said, 'I thought you made your speech very well.' And when he wiped his hands and did not answer I went on: 'It was just right – just the right note.'

He shrugged. 'Oh – well . . . Thanks,' he said. He did not look at me and I felt the constraint of the day of the bazaar still unlifted.

I said: 'Can you find a use for all these things?'

'Oh! just about, I reckon,' he said, and looked around with an appreciative eye, like a connoisseur at his collection. His glance alighted on me then, very sharp and sudden, and he said, 'I forgot. I wanted to show you something.'

I followed him round to the front of the house.

The front door, half obscured by great stubborn hollyhocks, was seldom used and it squeaked as Robert pushed it open and stepped into the hall.

'There,' he said. 'That's what I wanted to show you.'

It was the barometer he had bought at the bazaar, hanging on the wall. He had transformed it. He had stripped the old stained walnut base, and the brass which had been the colour of liver shone: it was really a very handsome piece. He tapped the glass.

'See,' he said. 'It works. It was just a bit rusted.'

He gave me the sharp look again and somehow I felt a point was being made.

'I'd never have recognised it,' I said and he smiled again.

'Might be able to sell it for a few bob,' he said. 'If things get really tight.'

'Are things tight?' I said.

He hesitated. 'The farm doesn't really pay,' he said, and said no more.

I knew, vaguely, that the post-war promises of a brave new world of small farmers had turned very sour and that the land was in decline. But I did not like to think of Snowden's farm being part of that. In my curious state of detachment I put the thought away from me, just as when we came away from the farm that evening I put away the thought of Mrs Snowden moving big and harassed about the kitchen and Robert solitary and absorbed in his magpie mess of scrap and the transformed barometer hanging on the wall. The single-mindedness of youth is rather terrifying and already in that single-mindedness I had consigned all this to what I thought of as my past life.

The bright dry spell of weather did not so much

break as decompose into days of sultry cloud and mottled evenings troubled with thunder. Spatters of rain fell in violent shudders or, more frequently, hung in the windless air and this humidity affected Mr Crawthorne's health. As I typed at the desk I would hear, clearly above the clattering of the keys, Mr Crawthorne's breathing, terribly cramped and impatient. He persisted in smoking his pipe, however, refusing characteristically to acknowledge his illness. One morning he complained several times of how stifling it was in the study and then as he stood at the french doors and lit his pipe I heard him explode into racking coughs.

The coughs went on and on and left him doubled up and purple in the face. I was alarmed and was going to run for some water but he stopped me and gestured me to slap his back.

'Harder,' he gasped, and I thumped again between his hunched and bony shoulders: and at last the coughs subsided and he sank into a chair.

'Thank you so much,' he said, his courtly tone unaltered even as he struggled for breath. 'Awfully sorry . . . Remarkable how efficacious that is, you know – a good thumping . . .' He managed to smile; and I saw how furiously he hated being ill. 'Perhaps I won't light this just now,' he said, putting down his pipe. 'I'm sure Catherine would think it very foolish of me.'

I understood then from his look that he would prefer it if I did not mention his attack to Mrs Crawthorne. I did not: I knew he dreaded to be fussed and I did not dislike the idea of something for once eluding Mrs Crawthorne's relentless curiosity. Later a fierce shower of rain cooled the air and made him feel better; but it left me wondering whether the tennis-court was playable. I felt stuffy myself and longed for a game.

I finished work but Martin did not appear. I could hear him playing the piano. I stood at the open morning-room door, watching and listening; and had a sudden apprehension of myself as a nuisance, dragging him away from his music for no good reason. He turned and saw me just as I was on the point of going away.

'Sorry,' I said. 'Didn't mean to disturb you.'

'You didn't,' he said. 'I've had enough now. Ready for a game? Hope the court isn't too damp.'

'What were you playing?' It had been something quite modern, very spare and angular and haunting.

'Nothing really. Just tinkering.' He closed the piano lid, rather abruptly, and shuffled together some sheets of music. I saw the row of sharpened pencils.

'Oh! something you wrote!' I said. I picked up the sheets of music, in a sort of marvelling pain. Though I loved music I was technically illiterate and the very idea of composition was a wonder to me. 'I didn't realise it was yours – I didn't know I was interrupting that.'

'You didn't interrupt,' Martin said. He was frowning. 'It's nothing. It's not finished. I can't really say I wrote it anyway – it's such a flagrant imitation of Debussy. It isn't anything.' He snatched the sheets of music from my hands and stuffed them, quite savagely, into the canterbury by the piano.

He seemed annoyed and I had got it into my head that I was responsible. As we went outside I said, blunderingly, something more about having disturbed him.

On the lawn he turned and jammed his hands on

his hips. 'Look,' he said, frowning still. 'You haven't. You haven't, Jenny. It isn't you. Honestly.' All at once the smile broke out, transforming and compelling, and I realised how anxiously I had been waiting for it. 'Now come and thrash me at tennis.'

And so we played. There was still a nap of dampness on the uneven court and the ball jinked and bounced in unexpected ways; and at last, inevitably, it sprang wildly off my racket and disappeared over Martin's head into the trees behind the court.

We had got into the habit of leaving lost balls and this was the last one left, so we trudged into the trees to look for it. In those dark green tunnels, overgrown with weeds and moss and festooned with blights and cuckoo-spit, the earlier rain had not dried. It dripped and pattered everywhere and I felt its wetness on my bare arms and clinging moistly to my legs through my thin summer dress, giving me an exhilarated feeling very like the gusts of wind outside the church on the day of Margaret's wedding.

'I'm getting drenched!' Martin said, turning to me: and I stood there and laughed and said, 'So am I. It's wonderful – it feels so cool.' And a lightness seemed to come over Martin then too.

'We'll probably find no end of lost tennis balls in here,' he said, plunging further into the spinney, through waist-high weeds. 'From years ago. Generations of them – nests of them. Old whiskery grandfather tennis balls – and breeding pairs – '

'And little baby ones like marbles – '

We laughed at this fantasy, and our laughter was loud under the tent of leaves where there was no sound but the dainty patter of a past rain. Then to my everlasting astonishment I saw the tennis ball above me, wedged into the crook of a branch, just as if the tree had put out an arm to catch it: and we laughed again.

'Like an enchanted forest,' Martin said, clambering up to get the ball. 'I warn you, Jenny, if these trees start moving I shan't wait for you. I'll be off . . .'

'Martin,' I said, 'Look here.'

'Not another one?'

'No.' The thing I was staring at was taller than me and at first I had taken it for the dead trunk of a tree or shrub, twined all about with bindweed and ivy and surrounded with towering thistles. I trampled the weeds down to get near it and began to tug at the sinewy wreaths of ivy.

'I can't believe it,' Martin said. 'I never knew this was here.'

It was a statue on a pedestal, almost buried under the climbing plants and moss. When we had cleared some of the ivy it was revealed as a male figure, about four feet high, in classical dress with a bow and quiver on his back. The hair was knotted above the forehead and bound with a laurel wreath. Moss and damp had turned the statue almost entirely green but that seemed to me only to enhance the romantic strangeness of the graceful figure. Lost among the leaves, he seemed to stare back into the springlike groves of a mystic past that had borne him when the world was young.

'Who is it?' I said. 'Is it Cupid?'

'I don't think so,' Martin said. 'I think it might be Apollo.' He knelt down and began to tear away the brambles round the pedestal. As he did so I looked at his shoulders, broad and young, and thought of Mr Crawthorne earlier, hunched over in the agonies of coughing. This, with the image of the beautiful statue lost but uncorrupted through time, fused in my mind to a moment of panicked pain as I realised that Martin's shoulders too would one day be narrow and bent like his father's.

Something of this, I suppose, made me lay my hand on his shoulder as I knelt down beside him. The casual affectionate physicality of the Crawthornes made this natural; but I had difficulty in taking my hand away.

'Aha,' Martin said. His finger traced the moss-grown letters incised into the stone pedestal. 'Apollo.'

We stood, and looked at the god half revealed amidst the lush greenery, like some growing living thing himself.

'They show him with a lyre sometimes,' Martin said. 'He's the god of music, and light, and the protector of fields and flocks as well, I think. Those Greek gods always seem rather overworked to me.' He reached out and touched the statue's upraised arm. 'That's the first time my classical education's been any use to me since I left school.'

'What's he made of?'

Martin tapped. 'Bronze, I think. Just a decorative reproduction. Victorian, maybe – could be earlier. Must have been overgrown for years. Father doesn't know it's here, that's for sure – this spinney's never been touched since we came.'

'No one knows it's here but us,' I said. Something about this excited me. 'We're the only ones to see him . . . Shall you tell your father?'

Martin looked at me. 'No,' he said smiling. 'We found him . . . and he doesn't look as if he wants to be disturbed, does he?'

I was glad. 'He's our secret,' I said.

'I say, wouldn't it be strange if we came back to look for him some time and he'd gone?' Martin said. 'An empty pedestal – and the ivy all torn away— '

'Why do you always think of these spooky things?' I said: laughing, but not without a shudder.

'Warped mind.' Martin plucked a leaf of ivy. 'Sorry I was a brute earlier, Jenny – about the music.'

I did not know what to say.

'Did me good to come out,' he said. 'Plugging away in there, indoors – you get crotchety.'

'I'm the same when I've been at the desk a long time.'

'Are you? I wonder if it's being sedentary – the sitting position, you know, low down, there's a sort of lowering of the spirits . . .'

'Tut, Martin, don't get profound,' I said.

His smile answered mine. 'Damn, I missed a joke there, didn't I?' he said. 'Crotchety – I could have made a joke about crotchets—'

'You could have made it with a quaver in your voice,' I said.

Martin looked at me, keenly, with amusement. 'You cheer me up, Jenny,' he said. 'You're a good influence on me.'

'Oh dear! – you make me sound like Pollyanna,' I said. I had to turn away: my face was burning in a way that I thought I had overcome long ago.

We left our statue, and went back to the tennis-court, where the other children had just arrived. Moments of great change in our interior lives may pass unnoticed; and if that afternoon a leaven was added to feelings that had lain in me raw and amorphous, I was as yet unaware of it and could not have known that the fermentation had begun. Within a few minutes I was caught up by the four children, their peculiar mutual harmony and buoyancy enfolding and enchanting me once again. The god in the trees, the silence under the leaves and the feel of Martin's shoulder through his white shirt – these things might never have been: except when Tom asked how on earth we had found the lost ball in all that jungle, and Martin said with the merest sidelong wink at me: 'The god of lost tennis balls guided us.' And only Ralph in his watchful way seemed to notice that.

We played doubles, and then nonsensical games in which two and then three of us at a time took on Tom; and at last we sat down on the lawn whilst Tom, tirelessly athletic, stayed on the court to practise his serve. I said I ought to be going, though I did not want to go.

'It's Friday, isn't it?' said Blanche, who was often vague about such things. 'We won't be seeing you till Monday . . .' With unaffected interest she said: 'What will you be doing at the weekend, Jenny?'

I told them about what I would be doing: about serving in the shop, about the ritual of Sunday tea and my grandmother cosily pronouncing herself in favour of public hangings. The utter emptiness I felt about it all must have shown, for Blanche said: 'You could come here for Sunday tea – yes, do that, Jenny. We're inviting you.'

'Oh – if you're sure—'

'Of course!' Blanche said. 'Father would have invited you before now, if he ever thought about such things, which he doesn't. You'll be our guest – we're not at all formal, we don't go to church or anything – well, only Ralph does.'

I tried not to show my surprise. It seemed quite of a piece with the Crawthornes, and the fascination they held for me, that they were not churchgoers: what surprised me was that Ralph, so apparently sceptical and self-sufficient, should be the exception.

'You'll be here this weekend, won't you, Martin?' Blanche said.

I understood that Martin often went to London at weekends. For a moment he seemed to me to hesitate.

'Yes, I'll definitely be here,' he said.

'Tom, do you hear?' Blanche called. 'Jenny's going to escape her dreaded grandmother – she's coming here to tea on Sunday.'

'Marvellous!' Tom came pounding off the court like a whistled dog and flung himself down on the grass beside me. His shirt was open to his muscled chest, where blond hairs of an incongruous softness curled, and he smelt faintly of healthy sweat. 'We should have asked you before! I say, when you come we must show you over the house. You never see any of it except that dreary study.'

The children did show me over the house, and it is that – and one room in particular – that remains most significantly in my mind from that Sunday. But first there was tea, with a silver service that rather wanted cleaning and some home-made cakes that were really not very good. At St Germain House there were two gardeners, who tended those formal gardens that made the front so impressive and which, Mr Crawthorne told me, were a relic of the eighteenth century: but inside there were only three staff and I do not think there was even any pretence that this was adequate for the place. And after tea Mrs Crawthorne cornered me first, and insisted on our taking one of our tours of inspection of the conservatory and the garden.

It was warm that day but Mrs Crawthorne, in a suit of cashmere cut in elegant straight lines, was cool as always as she prowled amongst the thickly scented lilies and the tea-roses that hung in wayward smudges of colour from leaning trellises.

'I must say it's quite disorienting to have you here on a Sunday, Jenny,' she said. 'I keep thinking it's a weekday. Now I hope you didn't have to put off any plans to accept the children's invitation?'

I said no, not at all.

'Only I know how insistent they can be – they brook no denial. Brook no denial – that's a legalistic sort of phrase, isn't it? I seem to recall solicitors' letters saying they will *brook no delay*. Of course you would know all about that. Shall you go back to it, do you suppose? That line of work?'

I murmured that I probably would. It was like a cold wind to be reminded of a time when my work at St Germain House would be over. I did not know whether Mrs Crawthorne was conscious of this.

'Well, you seem to have become quite a favourite with the children,' Mrs Crawthorne said. 'They have quite taken you up. I suppose you are rather different from the young people they have generally mixed with – though of course they have chiefly mixed with each other, being so close. It's quite a surprise to me to see an outsider being taken into their circle, as it were, so readily.'

Again a cold wind blew at this talk of outsiders, and then as if reading my mind Mrs Crawthorne touched my arm and added, 'Good for them, too, I think. They are so alike, and they may think everyone is like them, which of course isn't so. Very necessary for Martin to bear in mind, of course, going into politics.'

I said, before I could stop myself: 'Isn't he going to pursue his music, then?'

'Oh no!' Mrs Crawthorne said. 'Oh no, indeed! Politics is the career.' She turned her full naked gaze on me, as if for completer emphasis. 'A political career for Martin. That's a settled thing.'

'He plays very beautifully,' I said. It came out slightly combatively; but Mrs Crawthorne only smiled serenely and said, 'Yes, he does – it will be a splendid relaxation for him.'

I was glad then to see the children waiting for me on the lawn.

'Come on, Mother,' Tom said, 'let go of our guest – we promised we'd show her all round the old mausoleum.'

'*Not* very respectful, Tom dear,' Mrs Crawthorne said, giving me a wry look as if we had just been sharing a joke; and the children bore me off.

I had never been upstairs in the house before. Dust invaded my nostrils and I seemed to sense too something like I had the very first day I had come to St Germain House: the accumulated pressure of past lives, over which the essence of the present occupants lay but lightly. Down the panelled passages our voices and footsteps were loudly echoed, for there was hardly any carpet; and always beyond the next turning it seemed to me that there were further and different echoes, rustling, receding.

A gallery ran the width of the house, and here they showed me some decayed hanging tapestries on which the Apostles, wearing robes that seemed to fall in an unnecessary number of folds, performed their Acts in sinuous attitudes amongst beggars with extravagantly muscled backs.

'They used to frighten me at night when I was a child,' Ralph said. 'I used to run past them with my eyes shut.'

'The Yellow Room!' Blanche said. 'Let's show Jenny that! The worst first.'

It was a large guest room overlooking the front gardens. 'Otherwise known as the Vomit Room,' Ralph said, 'because it makes you want to.'

'Ooh, Ralph, *please*,' Blanche said.

The room was decorated in bilious shades of saffron and mustard. Crushed velvet hangings and valances, ending in pompons like costive droppings, depended everywhere over elephantine legs of fumed oak. Above the mantelpiece hung a painting of the sort the Victorians apparently found so refreshing, depicting a stag having its guts torn out by hounds watched by gentlemen with anatomical legs.

'Isn't it a fantasy?' Martin said. 'We think it was the hunting colonel's room. Father puts guests here who he doesn't like. They never stay long.'

The room next door was in complete contrast: a frieze of roses, William Morris fabrics, and cool blue and white china. 'This is the real guest room, Jenny,' Martin said. 'This is where we'd put you.'

Then I saw the children's rooms. 'Not mine!' weakly protested Blanche, with her little defensive laugh. 'It's such a mess!' But even the mess, of filmy gowns and blouses thrown around and pieces of jewellery and scent-bottles and combs overflowing the dressing-table, seemed to me expressive of Blanche's peculiarly lazy, unemphatic elegance. Ralph's room was severe, even monastic, except for the books: it might have been designed expressly with the view of giving absolutely nothing away. I saw Ralph watching me as if daring me to give an opinion.

Martin's and Tom's rooms were at the back of the house. Martin's room had a window-seat – something that in my own world of terraced houses and back-yard views of cinder-paths and other back yards seemed the epitome of desirable luxury. It was all fresh white, with crimson Regency-stripe curtains and cushions. I knelt in it to look over the gardens. 'There's a nightingale somewhere down there in the spinneys,' Martin said, leaning over me to open the window. 'I hear him at night – I lie awake listening to him.'

After that Tom's room was like that of a moderately tidy schoolboy, overlaid with strongly masculine elements of pipe-tobacco and hair-oil. With sheepish eagerness he showed me the photographs on the walls, school cricket and football groups with himself as the centre.

'It's so *healthy* in here,' complained Ralph, touching with distaste Tom's Indian clubs and chest-expander. 'These things look like some medieval instruments of torture. I know where we haven't been – the playroom.'

It was in that playroom that I felt most strongly the personalities of the four children, fused into one presence like the blending of the various flower scents in the conservatory. It was a large, white-washed room with a mansard roof and two dormer windows. There were rugs of coloured patchwork and wicker chairs. Tacked to the walls were childish drawings, and scattered about the floor were many old toys.

'Mother suggested packing all this stuff away a

while ago,' Martin said, patting the shiny painted head of a rocking-horse, 'but Blanche got sentimental and wouldn't let her.'

'It wasn't just me!' Blanche said. 'Martin, you were just the same. Anyway, Jenny, look at this – ' she showed me a doll's house – 'isn't this too nice to put away?' She knelt down and opened the front. 'I used to play with it for hours. I always felt this frustrated longing to get in there – you know? – I wanted to actually be in those tiny rooms with the dolls.'

Ralph picked up a toy steam-engine. 'I tied one of the dolls to this railway track once – do you remember?' He laughed. 'Just like in the films. I think I wanted to see what would really happen when the train came along – in the films the girl always gets saved at the last minute.'

'My doll was saved,' Blanche said. 'Tom saved her, didn't you, Tom?'

Tom beamed.

'Just like Rin Tin Tin to the rescue,' Ralph said, with that faintly sardonic tang in his voice.

'Tom always looked after me,' Blanche said.

I picked up a teddy-bear, and found that it was split horizontally across the middle, spilling stuffing.

'He was mine,' Martin said.

'What's his name?'

'Teddy. That's original, isn't it? He got split when Tom and I were sort of mock-fighting. We had a tug-of-war with Teddy and he ripped right across his stomach.' As I held the toy Martin's long brown fingers patted the stuffing back. 'Mother wouldn't sew him together again – she said we had to leave him as he was, as a lesson to us to be more careful.'

Tom turned, smiling, from the window. 'We asked

Blanche if she'd try and sew him up – but she can't
sew to save her life.'

Blanche reclined in a wicker chair. She had a way,
very cat-like, of slipping into curled and relaxed and
comfortable positions wherever she found herself.
'It's true,' she said contentedly, waving her hands
at me. 'I sew not, neither can I cook. Tom thinks
I'm not a proper girl at all. I think I'll have to have
babies – I'll have to spawn a bit to redeem
myself.'

'Blanche, really,' Tom said, colouring, with heavy
embarrassment.

Ralph was taking the wooden animals from a
Noah's Ark. 'I used to love this,' he said. 'You
know, in some religious families this was the only
toy a child would be allowed to touch on a Sunday
– because it's Biblical.'

I remembered then that Ralph went to church and
I said, blurting rather, 'By the way, I – I'm sorry if
you put off church today because of me.'

'Not at all,' Ralph said shortly. I felt then, not for
the first time, that Ralph's sometimes brusque way
came from shyness. Then he looked at me with one
of his rare intimate smiles. 'I don't suppose it will
put my immortal soul in peril, you know.'

'And this is where you used to play,' I said, gazing
round. 'I'm trying to picture you all.'

'Ralph looked exactly the same,' Blanche said.
'Tom had hairy knees from a very early age and
they were always covered in bruises. I was fat – ' I
goggled at this, for I could no more imagine a fat
Blanche than a fat gazelle, but she nodded with
conviction – 'and Martin had a mop of curls.'

'You didn't,' I said.

'Afraid so.' Martin grimaced. 'I looked just like

112

that little beast in the Pears Soap advertisement.'

I laughed. I remember that I felt, in the oddest way, a little dizzy: I was so stirred by the sheer brilliant fact of the Crawthornes, here at the top of the house in this airy room that was charged with their presence, and by my being with them.

'I say, look at that!' cried Tom, pointing out of the window.

We went to look. It was an aeroplane, still not a common sight in those days. It was circling slowly, quite low and close, glittering in the blue.

'Wonderful!' Tom said. He looked as if he had seen a vision. 'Imagine – just imagine being up there. Lucky beggar.' He shook his fist. 'You lucky beggar!'

'No good for me,' Blanche said. 'I can't bear heights.'

Tom glanced round, and said, fumblingly earnest: 'But just think – to fly – to fly a plane – just think . . .'

'*You* fly in a car, Tom,' Martin said. 'You just about take off in it, anyway.'

Tom was not listening. 'I wonder where it's from. We never see planes over here.'

'The Agricultural Showground, I should think,' I said. 'It's the show next week – they're probably having a flying display there.'

'We'll have to go then – I must see that,' Tom said. Suddenly he pulled in his head from the dormer window. 'I can't see properly here. I'm going up on the roof.'

We followed him to an iron spiral staircase that went up to a small area of leads on the very summit of the roof. Tom pounded up the iron steps.

'Anybody coming?' he called down.

'Nobody's been up there for years, Tom,' Martin said. 'The leads were never very safe.'

But Tom was already up on the roof. Looking up the stairwell, I could see him, in dramatic fore-shortening, gazing rapturously up at the sky. 'Lucky beggar!' he cried again. 'Oh! to fly like that – imagine.'

There was a loud creaking of leads as he moved out of sight. All at once Ralph ran up the steps. His face was pinched.

'Tom!' he barked. 'For God's sake mind what you're doing,' and I found myself climbing after him.

On the roof I saw, with shock, just how old and run-down St Germain House was. The decaying leads were covered with shaggy moss that grew between pools of stagnant water. The stonework of the chimneys was crumbling away and there was the carcase of a dead bird like a black stain. Across the other side of the roof Tom stood with his head thrown back, gazing at the aeroplane. I have never seen anyone look so uplifted. The wind buffeted him, making chaos of his blond thatch of hair, but he was aware of nothing. He seemed unaware even of how close he was to the edge of the roof.

Ralph stormed at him. His voice took on a high fluty note as he called: 'Tom, come away from the edge, will you! It isn't safe! Dear *God* . . .' and his anxiety infected me too.

'Tom,' I said, 'come down, please – it's too dangerous': and just then he seemed to wake up, and gave a startled glance down at the drop below him.

'It isn't even railed,' Ralph said as Tom followed us down the stairs at last. 'You just weren't looking . . .'

Tom still looked slightly dazed. 'I get like that,' he said. 'Forget everything – just forget where I am. Same with the motor-bike – the speed. You know. I'll forget my head one of these days.'

'Well, *that* won't matter much,' Ralph said; and Tom said, 'True – true enough,' awkwardly patting Ralph's arm.

Instinctively I laughed as they did: nervous soothing laughter. Again the quarrel had been averted; again the Crawthornes had closed ranks. But now I did not feel excluded by this. That Sunday, the bedrooms and the roof and the aeroplane and above all the playroom, were like a chain of small strong stitches binding me to them. If in my involvement with them there had remained a core of my shy reserve, it was gone now. When at last I thanked them for having me and said goodbye, Mrs Crawthorne shook my hand, and I remembered what she had said about my being an outsider. The word still stung but I did not believe it was true.

I have mentioned Martin's sometimes going to London. The week following that Sunday tea, he was away there for two days. Mr Crawthorne called my attention to this, commenting that I would miss my tennis lesson: he appeared not to notice that it was pouring with rain. He spoke then of the political contacts he had made for Martin in London.

'It isn't right, of course, that he should have to begin his career by these means – I mean through social contacts made by his father. The old school tie and so on. But that's the way of it, I'm afraid. And it would be simply perverse of me *not* to make the introductions.'

When I say that I thought constantly about Martin during those two days, I do not mean I had any clear picture of what he was doing in London, in that other life of which he seldom spoke. The world of which Mr Crawthorne spoke, of parliamentary secretaries and retired diplomats and constituency selection procedures, sounded to me so dry and dull that I simply could not picture Martin in it or connect him with it at all. I believe that, paradoxically, as our fascination with a person increases, our capacity mentally to visualise that person decreases. I could summon up, for example, a photographic image of Booey with her eager gristly eyes; but Martin became a shifting series of impressions of which the strongest was of him standing by me in the stream beneath the Nine Bridges, his shirt open at the throat and his eyes translucent in the cool stone shade. And I looked forward with a sort of uneasy hunger to his return to St Germain House, so that I could see him again and match these impressions and perhaps make sense of them. But it happened that I saw him before I expected to, and not at the house.

I have often thought of the sheer chance that brought this about, and what a trivial thing it was. One of our neighbours, an old widowed lady named Mrs Craven, had her sister coming to stay with her from London. Mrs Craven was a kindly timid body with such a bad case of halitosis that one could only speak to her in awkward profile like a figure on an Egyptian frieze. She wanted to meet her sister at the station but was nervous of going alone after dusk and so I went with her.

Several times as we stood on the London platform Mrs Craven spoke fondly of her sister, saying how they were like two peas in a pod and had never had a cross word. The rain had lifted an hour ago, and now an orange sun, washed and clear, hung just above the horizon, casting a late glow over the heaps of blue-black coal in the yards across the tracks. The London train was on time and I had no difficulty in recognising a slightly younger version of Mrs Craven, berating a porter, in amongst the steam and the hurrying businessmen.

'You brought enough luggage with you, didn't you?' Mrs Craven said. 'Where am I going to put all that?'

'Oh! don't start,' her sister said. 'You've got pots of room.' And they embarked happily on a good hammer-and-tongs argument, leaving me to disappear quietly into the background.

This touching reunion amused me and I suppose I was still smiling to myself when I saw Martin, getting off the train. He carried a small suitcase. For a moment he did not see me and then his eyebrows went up in surprise. I thought his eyes looked smoky and tired.

'Hullo, Jenny,' he said. 'Were you meeting someone?'

I explained about Mrs Craven and her sister, who were now quarrelling with the porter. Martin smiled and then as the engine sent out a great animal hiss of steam and smuts he seemed to wince at it in a taut, harried fashion.

'Has it been raining here?' he said. 'It was pouring in London.'

'All day,' I said. 'No good for tennis.'

His brow seemed to clear for a moment as I said this and then he frowned again and looked at his watch.

'Jenny, do you have to be home just yet?' he said. 'It doesn't matter if you do – you know – but . . .'

117

'No,' I said. 'I don't have to go yet.'

'I could fancy a drink,' he said. 'Could you? It was stuffy on the train. Ever been in the Great Northern? It's cool in there.'

The Great Northern Hotel, a big Victorian brick building with something suggestive of railway carriages about its long ranks of identical sash windows, stood directly opposite the railway station. I had never been in there, as I had never been in any licensed premises before I met the Crawthornes. The voice of my upbringing piped up in alarm: in Billingham in those days, unbelievable as it seems, it was daring to go for a public drink with a man to whom one was not married.

But I had ceased to listen to that voice, and in the hotel lounge a weighty respectability reigned. All the upholstery was overstuffed, and even the fish mounted in glass cases seemed to be bursting in a pop-eyed way. Pier-glasses reflected brass and aspidistras and palms, dingy against fleur-de-lys wallpaper. A little sunken shuffling waiter brought our drinks on a tray. The only thing I knew how to drink was sherry: Martin had whisky. He drank it quickly, his fingers gripping the glass, seeming tense and overstrung. A couple of times he asked me whether he was keeping me. 'Sorry – you probably want to get home,' he said, and at last I said, 'Martin – don't make a stranger of me.'

'Sorry,' he said again.

He was wearing a grey herringbone suit. I was used to seeing him dressed more informally and I suppose he must have noticed me looking at the suit for he said, 'Be glad to get into a pair of old flannels. I did miss our game of tennis.'

'So did I,' I said.

An express train thundered through the station across the road from the hotel. I felt the vibration through the floor and the potted ferns in the lounge quivered. Martin smoked a cigarette and this, with the suit and the drawn, preoccupied look on his face, made him seem to me a much older person.

'Ever see much of London?' he asked me suddenly.

I said I had only been there a handful of times in my life.

Martin nodded. 'To tell the truth I don't really like it that much,' he said. 'Not for any length of time anyway. Not the best lookout for a political career, is it?'

'No,' I said, and I thought I began to understand, then, what lay at the root of his troubled and entangled mood.

'By the way,' he said with a sort of determined lightness, 'while I was there I went to see a music publisher. I sent them one or two of my things.'

'Oh! that piece you were playing – that piece I heard?'

'No. Not that one. Just little things.' Martin rang the bell for the waiter. 'Anyway, they said they couldn't see their way to publishing them, but they would be interested in seeing more of my stuff.'

'That's wonderful,' I said, and as he looked dubious I went on: 'It's encouraging. Isn't it? Surely.'

'It's – yes, I suppose.'

'After all, you're still very young.'

'Mozart composed his first opera when he was twelve.'

'Well,' I said, 'it probably wasn't a very good one.'

It was just a facetious remark, nervously thrown

119

in, but Martin smiled and then laughed. The waiter came and Martin ordered another whisky and then said, 'There – you've cheered me up again. Or perhaps I shouldn't say that. You didn't seem to like it last time.'

'Oh! it isn't that.' I did in fact feel glad that I had done this; and inside me there were beatings of cramped excitement at being alone and confidential with Martin in this way. The lounge was empty except for a commercial traveller sitting in the far corner; and when I found myself, for various reasons, unable to keep looking at Martin, I glanced over at the commercial traveller. He was a fat-necked man, going with great thoroughness through a notebook, and at every page he put out a pink tongue and licked the end of a stub of pencil as if it were a tasty delicacy before writing something in the book. Each time I looked I could see a black streak growing on his pink tongue.

'What do your mother and father think of you working at St Germain House, Jenny?' Martin said, again with abruptness. And as I hesitated he said, 'I'm sorry, do you mind me asking?'

'No,' I said.

'I mean, do they have their own ideas for you – make plans for you? Or just accept you as you are?'

I tried to explain my parents' gentle mixture of solicitude and unobtrusiveness. Martin listened with concentrated attention.

'So they just want you to be yourself?'

'I suppose so.'

'That's the main thing, isn't it,' Martin said, with an absent push at his fringe of hair. 'To be yourself . . . but it's not that easy, is it?'

Across the road a slow goods train groaned and clanked. The commercial traveller turned a page and daintily tasted his pencil.

'They sound awfully nice – your parents,' Martin said. 'I'd like to meet them. Are they Billingham people?'

'Oh yes!' I said. 'We're Billingham people since the year dot.' That perhaps had something to do with my new impatience with the town. Billingham was in my bones: though I felt such a completely altered person, I could not get that out. Martin asked me more about my parents, leaning earnestly over the table: he seemed to tease out the tortuous complexities that were troubling him by asking about me.

'I imagine you're like them in some ways,' he said. 'Are you? There's something – something calm about you, something calm and clear.'

I had never been, perhaps, less calm and clear in my life. Probably ingrained shyness had given me that look as a defence. I said: 'I'm not like that really. You can't imagine how nervous I was coming to work at your house.'

'Were you? I suppose we are a bit of a circus. But you seem to think – not like us. We don't think. That's the trouble.' I knew when he said 'we' he meant the children: it was something they all said. 'It's made me start to think seriously about things – meeting you.'

I cannot say what confusion of feelings were working in me at that moment: I only know that the waves of strange excitement continued to beat at me while I sat there, as Martin said, apparently calm. I did not ask him what things I had made him think about. I felt that I understood without words.

'It's very sweet of you to sit here and listen to all this,' Martin said.

'Now you're making a stranger of me again.'

'Well – you know. Waffling on. It's London – going there seems to put me in this funny mood and—'

Quite without forethought and hardly knowing what I was doing, I reached out and put my fingers on his lips. 'Hush,' I said, 'and stop apologising.' And even then I believe I kept that appearance of calmness, though my hand began shaking as I drew it back and I had to clench it into a fist under the table.

Just then the waiter opened a door at the end of the lounge. The door opened on to the walled garden of the hotel. The lawn had been cut some time that day and the freshness of it came stealing into the lounge, wonderfully sharpened by rain. Martin lifted his face to it.

'That's delicious,' he said. 'You know – I don't want this summer to end. I wish it could just go on – just like this.'

'So do I,' I said. My fingers still seemed to burn where they had touched Martin's lips.

We left the hotel by the door that the waiter had opened, and stood for a minute looking out over the newly cut lawn. All about was the deep thrilling song of birds in a bright rain-pure evening.

'Just think,' Martin said, 'our statue must have stood out in all that rain.' He looked at me and I saw that the furrowed tension was gone from his face. 'Shall we go and see him tomorrow?'

'If he's there,' I said, and saw Martin's smile break out, sudden and disarming, as if he had emerged at last from the tight coils of introspection.

'Oh! he'll be there,' he said.

'Have you finished that piano piece?' I said. 'The one I heard?'

'No,' he said. 'I'm afraid I put it aside.'

'Finish it, Martin,' I said. The impulse to touch him came again but I resisted it. 'Go on. Do finish it.'

He seemed to hesitate and then said with decision: 'All right. I will.'

We parted outside the hotel where Martin took a taxi to St Germain House. He asked if he could drop me off but I said it was only a few minutes' walk.

But instead of going straight home I walked by myself through the municipal park, over on the north side of the town centre. I did not feel ready to face other people yet. Spurts of moisture were shaken from the high leaves of the limes, spattering on the path around me, and I felt the waves of suppressed excitement recede and then beat at me again as I thought of Martin. I believed I understood the dissatisfaction that gnawed at him but it was not merely that which excited me. Not only had I prompted him to examine what he wanted in life but I suspected that I was actually a factor in that equation.

Amongst the trees the daylight was seeping away in molten gold patterns and a park-keeper was beginning his round of locking the gates. I lingered. A sort of delirium pounded in my head. I felt I would never stop thinking about Martin and about where I stood in relation to the dreary politics and London and the frustrations that oppressed him. There is a certain stage of youth and love when emotions can whip us with an almost physical lash and I was feeling that for the first time. I did not know what to do. I only knew that like Martin I did not want our summer to end and I dared to think that it would not.

Four

I hovered between reality and dream. Two days after that meeting with Martin at the station I went as I did every year to Billingham Agricultural Show. It was a ritual and everyone in Billingham went. Men who all year worked in foundries and at lathes tramped about the showground on the edge of the town staring at prize cattle and thoroughbred horses and displays of oilcake and fodder, in a sort of uncomprehending homage to a past Billingham that they had never known. But for the rural community it was still an important occasion and working farmers from all over East Anglia came to the show along with the county types in tweeds who got drunk and rhapsodised about Hounds. Usually too the show was attended by one of those minor offshoots of royalty whose titles sound like something out of a Shakespeare play, but I do not remember which scion of Kent or Gloucester was there that day. Far more significant for me was the presence there of both Robert Snowden and the Crawthornes – though the true importance of this I did not realise until much later.

I did not recognise Robert at first. I had been leaning for some time on a barrier watching saddle-horses being taken from the collecting-ring into the parade-ring when one of the stewards waved at me and then came jogging over.

'Did you know it was me?' Robert said. 'Did you know I was doing this?'

'I had no idea,' I said.

'Dad used to do it sometimes. I got roped in.'

He looked very unfamiliar dressed in the steward's outfit of hacking jacket and breeches, which the lean muscles of his body seemed to fill to bursting. For a moment as he stood there I was somehow reminded as I had been with Martin of a picture, a book illustration, but I could not place it and the impression was swiftly gone. Robert leaned on the barrier and pointed to the last horse leaving the ring.

'See that one?' he said. 'That one's been gingered. No doubt about it. You can always tell.'

'What's gingered?' I said.

Robert looked round at me in surprise and then broke into a laugh. He started to say something and then laughed again. I did not much like the feeling that it was me that he was laughing at and I said, 'Well? What is it? What's the joke?'

He stopped laughing at last. 'I don't know quite how to put it,' he said. 'It's to make the horse's tail stand out from the body instead of just hanging down. The dealer keeps some powdered ginger in his pocket and dips his finger in it and – well, pokes it up the horse's behind. The stinging makes the tail stand out.'

'That's a bit cruel, isn't it?' I said. 'Anyway, isn't that cheating?'

'Oh well, most of them do it,' Robert said. 'They're all a lot of shysters really. See that horse there – the roan? That's entered as a cob, which has to be under fifteen hands high. They've got a vet's certificate to say it is but anyone can tell it's more than that. They slip the vet a few bob, you see. They're like that. If a horse is lame in one hoof they'll lame the opposite one so it doesn't show.'

I have spoken of being caught between dream and reality. Just then, as Robert spoke casually of these things, the reality seemed very harsh. He must have seen something of this in my face for he said, 'They're show horses. We wouldn't treat working animals like that. Hang on a minute.'

He went to speak to one of the other stewards and then came trotting back to the barrier.

'They won't need me for another half an hour,' he said. 'Come over to the car-park – I've got something to show you.'

'Not another barometer?' I said.

He smiled a little grimly. 'Nothing like that,' he said.

Many people waved or said hello to Robert as we walked over to the enclosure where the cars were parked. He was at home amongst these people, seedsmen and market-gardeners and farmers of an old-fashioned type with bowlers and side-whiskers. He shared their abrupt taciturnity and yet too there was something that set him apart from them. There was something a little too rangy and restless about the strong body barely contained in the steward's outfit: above all there was the solitariness, which he seemed to carry about with him in the thickest crowd.

I could not see Robert's Humber anywhere. Then Robert stopped in front of an elderly high-chassised Morris-Cowley, burnished and handsome, like a well-groomed dowager.

'There,' Robert said. 'What do you reckon?'

'Is it yours?' I said.

He nodded. 'Sold the old Humber. How much do you reckon I paid for this one?'

I shook my head.

'Nothing.' Robert patted the gleaming grille and then wiped at the fingermarks with his sleeve. He looked pleased and triumphant. 'It had been lying behind Charlie Vere's barn for years. Derelict. He let me have it. He wanted to get shut of it. I've been working on it since the spring, every minute I had spare. All that scrap in the workshop – you remember. Mum said I'd never make anything of it.' A flush of pleasure crept up his dark face, making it look as if it were lit from below. All the difficult inarticulacy of his manner seemed to unwind and release itself as he spoke of the car and touched its shining paintwork with his fingers. 'What do you reckon?' he said again.

'It's beautiful,' I said. In a way I had not been far off when I mentioned the barometer, for here was the same devoted transformation of plainness and dereliction, strangely and surprisingly, into beauty. 'I didn't know you knew about cars.'

'Oh, it's one of those things, I suppose,' he said. 'You know, you have a sort of feeling—' And in his pleasure about the car and my reaction to it he seemed to make a sort of leap into candour. 'I'm not cut out for farming really,' he said. 'I never liked to let on to Dad about it, but – this is more where I feel at home. Cars and machines. I mean – ' he gestured towards the parade ring – 'all that horse-flesh. It's had its day now. This is the future.'

Again, as when he had spoken of the financial troubles of the farm, I felt a vague nostalgic pity:

but at the time it made no greater impact on my mind than that.

'Like I say, I never let on to Dad. You know how it is – how they have plans for you but you know deep down you want something different.' Robert opened the car door to show me the interior. 'She goes like a dream,' he said; and just as he began to ask whether I would like a ride I heard my name being called and turned to see Blanche and Tom Crawthorne.

'I wondered if we would see you here!' Tom almost shouted his delight. 'Hullo! Blanche spotted you from a long way away – she's so sharp-eyed.'

'It's your hair,' Blanche said, taking my hand in her boneless, affectionate way. She was dressed as so often in the white silk that matched her pure blonde beauty. 'There's that hint of copper in it and I'd recognise it anywhere. I always look at people's hair and mouths – never their eyes – it's rather rude isn't it?'

Robert still stood holding the car door. As I introduced him to Tom and Blanche I glowed – stupidly enough as it now seems – with the sheer pride of knowing the Crawthornes and the feeling that their brilliance was reflected on me. I felt intolerably superior in being so casually intimate with them and this was magnified as I watched Robert shaking Blanche's hand. A sort of startled immobility froze his face almost as if he were physically blinded by the bright white and gold glamour of Blanche; and when she said, in her small neat voice that was always just audible, that she had heard a lot about the farm and was so glad to meet him, he seemed scarcely able to reply.

Tom gazed with great interest at the car. 'This old

girl's in awfully good nick,' he said to Robert. 'Is she yours?'

Robert, still with the half-blinded look, said yes.

I said: 'Robert renovated it – it was just a wreck.'

'Not it – she,' Tom said. 'You don't call cars it.' He walked round the car. 'You've made the most wonderful job of her. I've never seen one look this good. Could I have a peep under the bonnet?'

Robert seemed to come gropingly out of his daze. 'Oh! please do,' he said.

'You've caught an enthusiast, Mr Snowden,' Blanche said. 'He'll want to take it all apart again,' and again Robert did not reply.

Tom thrust his big blond head under the bonnet. 'I say, could I just listen to her?' he said. 'Would you mind?'

'Of course,' Robert said. He started the engine. Tom's expression was rapt as if he were listening to music. He began to talk with Robert of gaskets and crankshafts and at last Blanche took my arm and said, 'Oh come on, Jenny – let's go and get some tea. There's no understanding men once they get talking about engines.'

So we left Robert with Tom going over the reno-vated car and again as I walked to the refreshment marquee with Blanche I was swelled with pride. There was a sort of confident ease about the way Blanche walked, leaning back slightly at the hips, and this in turn gave me confidence too.

'I hope Tom won't bore your friend,' Blanche said as we queued for tea. 'He was just the same earlier with the aeroplane – the one on display. He got talking to the pilot and persuaded him to show him the cockpit. He went over and over it. He's got a friend in the RAF and I think he'd like to throw up

Cambridge and join up himself – except it would disappoint Father.'

'Is your father here?' I said.

'And Mother. She's presenting some prize or other later. She's being very county and leaning over rails to inspect pigs with a sort of thoughtful expression. I mean her expression, not the pigs'. Ralph's gone to stay with a friend this weekend. Mother often says to invite him to our place but he never does. Oh, cakes! – don't let me have any, Jenny. I mustn't. Stop me . . . Too late.'

'I suppose Martin's gone to London,' I said lightly.

'No, he's at home. He intended coming with us this afternoon but he got a stinker of a migraine. He was working at his music all morning and didn't let up for a minute – I bet that's what brought it on. Staring at all those dots and squiggles. No wonder Handel went blind. Or is it Haydn? I always get them mixed up.'

'Is he all on his own?'

'Well, Tom offered to stay behind, but Martin said no. There's not much you can do with a migraine except sit it out. Jenny, you have one of these eclairs too, then I won't feel so guilty.'

Through tea I had difficulty in concentrating on what Blanche was saying. I kept thinking of Martin left alone at the house with a migraine. It made me unhappy to think of him like that whilst everyone was enjoying themselves at the show and I felt someone should be with him. At last Blanche said she ought to go and find Tom. When she said, 'Are you coming?' I said I had to go and meet my mother and father.

I watched Blanche move off into the crowd, wil-

lowy and elegant, with a wave of her white hand.
Instead of going to meet my mother and father I set
off to walk to St Germain House. I could not stop
thinking of Martin being alone there and sick and I
felt I had to go and see him.

The route took me down Cambridge Road, the
long road that ran the gamut of Billingham's social
range, from the railway cottages that people called
the Barracks right out to square-bayed villas on the
edge of open country. It was by the Barracks that a
car pulled up beside me and I heard Robert Snowden calling my name.

'Jenny!' he said, opening the passenger door.
'Want a lift home? Hop in.'

It was an awkward moment. My home was in
the opposite direction from St Germain House; and
somehow I could not say that that was where I was
going. 'Oh – it's all right, thanks,' I said, 'I can
walk.'

'It's no trouble,' Robert said cheerfully. 'It's not
out of my way. I wanted you to have a ride in the
car anyway—'

I have said that there is something frightening
about the single-mindedness of youth and so it was
then. I was set on going to St Germain House and
nothing would stop me.

'No, really,' I said. 'I'd rather walk. Thanks all
the same.'

I believe I was not fully aware then of the rudeness of this or of the hurt that appeared in Robert's
eyes, stiffening quickly into hostility. I can only say
that, in my obsessive conviction that I must go and
see Martin, a sort of blindness came over me not
unlike the blindness that had seemed to paralyse
Robert as he shook Blanche's hand. And in this

unseeing state I was only dimly aware of Robert's face suddenly averted as he fumbled at the gears of the car and then drew away, the exhaust giving out a great hoarse cough. The passenger door was still open as the car began to move and Robert's arm came groping out and flung it shut and the bang cut off, with finality, the words of apology that I was still feebly piecing together.

After that something made me hurry. I was almost running by the time I got to St Germain House. I was hot and flushed and the maid looked at me in surprise.

'There's only Mr Martin here, miss – in the morning-room,' she said, and I said it was all right and I would announce myself.

Martin was seated at the writing-bureau, leaning his head on his hand. There were sheets of paper in front of him. The curtains at the french doors were drawn and this gave the light in the room a liquid and subterranean look in the late afternoon.

'Hullo, Martin,' I said. 'I came to see if you were all right. I met Blanche at the show and she said you had a migraine.'

I spoke in a rush. I was still breathless from my haste and as Martin did not speak for a moment a feeling of monstrous foolishness and futility swept over me. The urge that had brought me here had been so single-minded that I had not even thought of what I was going to do or say. Martin must surely think me quite mad.

'Jenny,' he said, 'you came all this way because of me?'

'Well,' I said, 'I was worried about you – a migraine can be pretty horrible after all—'

With something of his father's courtliness Martin

stood and placed a chair for me. 'You're all out of breath,' he said. 'It's very kind of you but really you shouldn't have done it.'

'Are you better?' I said.

'Oh yes, it's gone off now,' he said. He passed a hand over his forehead. He looked pale. 'I only get one once in a blue moon. It goes off quite suddenly.'

'Blanche said you'd been working hard and that brought it on.'

'Did she?' He smiled, with the characteristic little twist at the corner of his mouth, but this time it was without humour. 'Well, I wouldn't really call it working.'

He went and opened the curtains and stood there with his hands dug in his pockets. I saw the manuscript music on the piano and said, 'Is that it? Is it the piece I heard?'

He glanced round, with an irritable sort of twitch. 'Yes,' he said. 'It's finished now.'

'Shall you send it to the publishers?'

'Oh, I suppose so.'

'You might sound more enthusiastic,' I said.

The wry look returned. 'Well – it isn't really getting anywhere. There's something pathetic about – just picking at things. Don't you think? I think the ugliest word in the English language is *dilettante*.'

'It's Italian, isn't it?' I said.

Again a flippant throwaway remark seemed to cheer him. He laughed and came away from the window and said, 'You must be thirsty. Have some tea – or some lemonade—'

'No, I'm all right,' I said. 'Martin, can't you – can't you get your life the way you want it?'

His face contracted again. 'That assumes that one knows what one wants,' he said.

'Don't you?'

He stood quite close to me, looking at me with attention. 'Do you, Jenny?' he said.

I said: 'Yes.'

All at once he smiled and its effect on me, a tingling, fascinated uneasiness, was stronger than ever. He picked up the music from the piano and took it to the desk.

'I'm going to dedicate this piece to you,' he said. 'Do you mind?'

For a moment I was unable to answer. My throat seemed to close.

'Of course not,' I said finally.

Martin wrote on the top sheet. ' "Nocturne in E flat",' he read out. ' "For Jenny". Is that all right?'

Again I could not answer. It seemed so wonderfully more than all right that my throat seemed to close tighter and I was left in a burning schoolgirl muteness. Martin seemed to notice this. He coughed and put the music down and went to breathe the air at the open french doors.

'Well! it's a pity I missed the show,' he said. 'I wanted to go. I hate being stuck indoors and missing a day of the summer . . . That's really what I want to do, Jenny.' He turned to me in appeal. 'Enjoy things – go out and enjoy life. It's wrong of me I suppose. But it's like we said about the summer – not wanting it to end – do you know what I mean?'

'And that's what you can't do when you have to be in London,' I said. Again I believed that I understood him.

'I don't know . . . All that seems like another world somehow.'

'And not the real one,' I said, for it was very close to my own feeling of being split between dream and reality.

He did not answer that. Then as he spoke he

made a sudden transition, in a manner I had noticed in him before, from listless inwardness to energy. 'Do you dance, Jenny?' he said.

'Yes, sometimes – at least, I haven't lately.' I had gone regularly with Margaret Snowden to dances at the Co-op Hall, but then she had become engaged and the gritty chalked floorboards and watery ices that had amused us together began to depress me, and I had got out of the habit.

'We've got a book of tickets for a dance at Market Downing next week,' Martin said. 'Mother got hold of them – she's always being given such things. Why don't you come? It's at the Falcon Hotel – it ought to be a good one. Next Saturday. Say you're free.'

'Oh! yes, I am—'

'You needn't worry about getting home and everything – well, perhaps you should, seeing as Tom will be driving, but you know what I mean. We'll look after you.'

When he said that I remembered the first time I had come to the house, with the children on the lawn saying they would look after me, and I was shot through with a delighted feeling as if all that summer were coming to one concentrated pitch of happiness.

Martin too looked excited. 'What do you say?' he said.

'It would be lovely,' I said, and added with some belated formality born of my upbringing, 'Thank you very much for asking me.'

'Jenny,' he said with a coaxing reproachful smile, 'now you're making a stranger of me.'

I laughed with nervous, breaking relief. 'It's so long since I danced,' I said.

'I'm a bit rusty myself,' Martin said. 'I shall have to brush up – let's do it now.'

'What?'

'I'll get the gramophone. We can put in a bit of practice.'

He fetched the gramophone and placed it on the table and as he wound it he said, 'Blanche is the great one for dancing. It's strange how she's so lazy and yet she can dance till everyone else is dead on their feet. She absolutely floats,' and it struck me then for the first time that a dancer was exactly what Blanche's languidly graceful figure suggested.

'Foxtrot first,' Martin said. He turned to me and then a sort of light mischief moved in his eyes. 'Let's go on the terrace,' he said. 'There's no one around to see. Shall we?'

'I've never danced on a terrace,' I said.

He took my hand and we went out.

'Everyone should dance on a terrace once in their lives,' he said. 'Of course it ought to be evening really – it ought to be evening and starlight like on the films.'

But I did not mind that there was no evening starlight. The late afternoon sun was warm and blown lightly with odours of wistaria. I could hardly believe that an hour ago I had been tramping about the showground amongst cattle and hay-balers and now I was dancing on the terrace with Martin. My life seemed to have moved on to strange new currents which I did not want to fight.

We danced out there quite alone and, exalted and transfigured as I was, I did not even give a thought to my steps. Then all at once I thought about them and as is often the way it made me go wrong.

'That was my fault,' Martin said, with such gentlemanly correctness that I laughed and then he laughed too.

'This is fine, isn't it?' he said. 'In the open air. I

wish I could go dressed like this to the dance on Saturday.' He was wearing an open shirt and pullover.

'I've never seen you in a dress suit,' I said.

'I've never seen you in an evening gown,' he said, and I had a remote moment of panic, like a shout from very far off, as I thought of the single evening dress hanging in my closet: I had not worn it for a long time and I knew I had filled out this year.

'I've only got one,' I said.

His face was gently mischievous again as he said, 'In that case, Jenny, I advise you to wear that one.'

I remember the tunes that we danced to: 'You're the Cream in My Coffee' and 'I Can't Give You Anything But Love' and 'I Want to be Happy'. We practised the waltz to 'A Kiss in the Dark' and then Martin put on 'Softly as in a Morning Sunrise'.

'Oh no! This is a tango,' I said. I disliked the tango and always felt clumsy doing it. 'I can't do that.'

'Try it,' Martin said.

We tried, with much laughter. 'No,' I said, 'I shan't dance this on Saturday.'

'Not even with me?' Martin said.

I could not answer that. I said: 'I'm glad your headache's gone.'

'It feels wonderful when it goes off,' Martin said. I had never been so close to his face before and I noticed a faint cleft between his brows. He smiled at me. 'I still can't get over you coming to see how I was.'

'I was worried about you,' I said.

'Oh! don't do that,' he said. 'You shouldn't worry about me.'

Soon the needle on the gramophone began to go

blunt. Martin was going to look for another but I said I must be going: my parents would be expecting me. We left the terrace, which was striped with long bars of shadow from the balustrade as the sun declined, and Martin walked with me as far as the path into the spinneys.

'I'll see you at the dance on Saturday then,' he said.

'Well, I'll be here during the week anyway,' I said.

'I know,' he said. All the fun seemed to go out of him. 'But I think I shall be in London this week.'

'Oh.' My own disappointment quickly receded at the prospect of the dance. 'Well – till Saturday then.'

'How about getting there?' Martin said. 'It would be easiest if we picked you up, wouldn't it?'

I looked at him, I suppose, rather blankly: so completely separate had my two worlds become that the idea of the Crawthornes' car coming down our street seemed physically impossible, as if he had suggested travelling through time. But after a moment I said – and I am glad I did – that that would be best.

'You'll have to let Tom know where it is,' Martin said; and, rather as his father had once said, he added, 'We don't really know Billingham – we're quite strangers there.'

We said goodbye and then Martin said with a renewed firing of gaiety: 'I think we dance rather well together, don't you?'

'All except the tango,' I said.

'All except the tango.' He smiled. 'Nothing's ever perfect.'

Our shop was still open when I got back. Behind the counter my father was painting with brush and ink a cardboard notice for some Victoria plums he had just got in. He took great trouble with these signs and always surrounded them with quotation marks as if the baldness of the announcement troubled him, so that PLEASE MIND THE STEP became a disembodied voice offering the modest suggestion "PLEASE MIND THE STEP".

'Well, how was the show?' he asked me.

'Oh, it was lovely!' I said. Somehow the show seemed a long time ago.

'You're looking very pleased about something,' he said. But characteristically he did not press me and I simply said, 'It's the summer. Such a lovely summer – it seems like it will never end.'

Market Downing, where I went to the dance with the Crawthorne children, was a little limestone town astride the river north of Billingham. It lay on the edge of old shire hunting country and this was reflected in the lobby and the saloon bar of the Falcon Hotel, where a few old gentlemen pegged at whisky amongst stuffed pheasants and shooting prints. The hotel ballroom however was full of people when we arrived that Saturday night and the room was decorated with flowers and coloured streamers that hung in an expanding web from the great central chandelier. Outside, the quiet of the twisting High Street was disturbed by cars and by the clip of dance shoes as people went laughing up the steps of the hotel, between strings of coloured Chinese lanterns.

I had had some agonies over my dress. It was a straight, sleeveless, taffeta affair with a deep V at the back, and my mother and I had knelt about on the floor for hours altering it so that, as was the fashion then, it should scarcely show my figure at all. But when I shed my coat Tom said with hearty admiration: 'I say, Jenny, you do look corking,' and I felt reassured.

Curiously enough it seemed natural that Tom should compliment me rather than Martin and it seemed natural too that I should have the first dance with Tom. I was a little nervous and I always found something comforting about Tom who, big and colt-ish and constrained in his dress suit, impelled me about the floor as if I were something on wheels.

'I forgot to ask you, Jenny,' Tom said. 'That friend of yours – the one we met at the show—'

'Robert Snowden,' I said, and in a moment of pure pain I remembered the slamming of a car door and a pair of black eyes hardening into hostility.

'That's him. Farmer, isn't he? Has he ever thought about going into cars – you know, as a business? He seems jolly clever with them.'

'Well – I don't know. I suppose the Snowdens have always been farmers and you know how it is.' I did not want to think of that and I said: 'What about you, Tom? What are you going to do?'

'Me? Oh, I've got Cambridge to get through yet. No use planning now. What do you think I should do? What am I fit for, do you think?'

'Oh! I should think you could do anything you wanted,' I said, for I liked him very much and wanted to make some tribute to his shy, genial warm-heartedness.

He laughed, showing his white teeth. 'That's sweet of you,' he said, 'and not true at all. I'll tell you what I'm going to do – I'm going to dance with you all night.'

'That would make people talk,' I said.

'I don't care,' he said. 'You know, I've enjoyed the summer so much since you came to the house. We said we'd look after you – and we have, haven't we?'

'I've loved it,' I said, and I smiled as I thought with warmth of the drives, the picnics and tennis and all the embracing vitality of the Crawthornes.

'I hope you haven't nearly finished those memoirs of Father's,' Tom said. 'You haven't, have you?'

'No,' I said. In fact the end of the manuscript was in sight – we were working on the breaking up of the Turkish Empire at the close of the war – but tonight that prospect did not trouble me.

With Blanche I sat out a dance. I saw several men edging near her and then, as if their nerve had failed at the last moment, moving away.

'Oh, dear – is it me?' I said. 'Do I put them off?'

Blanche laughed. Her laugh was a small silvery shimmer.

'They're afraid of me – I don't know why,' she said. 'Do I look frightening? Like an ogre or a bear or something?'

'No,' I said, laughing too as she turned her wide-eyed, disingenuous face to me and opened her lips in a mock snarl. And yet in a way I did know why the men were afraid to ask Blanche to dance. They were intimidated by her beauty and its impression of cool self-sufficiency: they would only be a clumsy encumbrance to it, just as I often felt hoydenish beside her.

'Or is it the cigarette?' Blanche said, putting down the cigarette in its tortoiseshell holder. 'No one ever lights them for me anyway. That man on the films – what's his name – John Gilbert. *He* would light it for me. Wouldn't you like to be swept off your

feet by someone like John Gilbert? You know –
dramatically.' She did a quick economical mime of
lying helpless in someone's arms. She was constantly, amusingly making illustrative gestures in this
way and sometimes I felt she was hardly aware of
doing it. It was almost as if she were acting her own
character. 'Nothing ever happens dramatically, does
it?' she said. 'I'd love to be pitched headlong into a
drama – I'm sure I'd rise to it.'

I have not spoken yet of Martin. I have said how
I believe that the more fascinated one becomes with
someone the less one can picture them: and in a
similar way coming to the dance that night I had
been so bristlingly aware of Martin that I was barely
able to look at him. I do not think it is possible to
pinpoint exactly when one falls in love with a person.
My inner turbulence of the past few months had
been further confused by the terrible complexities
of youth and I could not say when my feeling for
Martin had emerged from it: I only knew that that
night at the Falcon it was so piercingly clear that I
did not even try to deny it.

And yet in spite of, or perhaps because of, the
tension of young excitement inside me, I found
myself behaving with a curious surface serenity. I
was moving on a high, rarefied plane where I did
not and could not know what would happen next.
And so when I danced with Martin I think I gave
no sign of what I was feeling: how the place where
his hand rested on the hollow of my back seemed
to burn and how I seemed to feel the very pulse of
the blood in his fingertips against mine. I accepted
these things and could not fight them.

'I wanted to have the first with you,' Martin said.
'Tom got in before me – I wasn't expecting that.'

'Why?'

'Oh well, he's rather shy with girls usually.'

'Perhaps it's because he knows me,' I said. 'I'm shy with people I don't know. I've been to dances and sat down all night because I wouldn't come out of my shell. I'd have to wait for the Ladies' Excuse Me and then I was too shy even for that.'

'Poor Jenny!' Martin said. Above the white starched expanse of his dress-front his face, a few inches from mine, was all living colour. It concentrated on me with something of that lamp-like quality that disconcerted me in Mrs Crawthorne, but in Martin the effect was very different. It was as if that gaze could not see anyone or indeed anything in the world but you and the cleft formed between his brows in the effort of excluding everything else. 'You don't seem shy with me . . . but then you know me, don't you?'

'I don't know,' I said. 'I want to.' And still I felt myself suspended in the same curious calm.

'How much do you want to know?' he said, and his eyes were very still on my face.

'Oh, everything,' I said, and somehow I twisted the words to make them flippant.

Martin did not smile. He said: 'I always thought your eyes were brown. They look different. This light must be deceptive.'

'They're supposed to be hazel,' I said. 'But I never know quite what that means, do you? It's not really a colour – hazel – it's so vague.'

'Your eyes are a definite colour,' he said. 'It's something – there's a word for it and I can't think what it is.'

'It must be the light,' I said. I could see his tongue moving behind his lips as he spoke. 'The light must be deceptive.'

I did not see the others when we went to sit down: I am not sure that I could see anything at all. But I remember that we sat on a chaise-longue with fat cushions of the sort that continually yield up little sharp feathers through the upholstery and that my fingers absently plucked these out as I waited for Martin to return with drinks. I remember too a vase of maidenhair ferns behind us and how they tickled Martin's neck as he sat down. He did not see them and he slapped at his neck.

'What's the matter?' I said.

'Something bit me, I think,' he said, and I laughed and pointed to the ferns.

'Was it that?' I said. 'Did that bite you?'

Martin laughed, frowning. 'I'm not sure about that,' he said. 'I don't know – it felt like a bite,' and he turned the back of his neck to me. 'Are you sure?'

'Of course,' I said, 'see,' and I ran my fingers up his neck, touching the short shaved hairs at the nape, 'nothing there.'

I swallowed suddenly at my drink.

Martin said, 'How's the champagne?'

In my haste I had not noticed what I was drinking. I said: 'It's lovely – I never had champagne before.' It was cold and refreshing and did not seem notice-ably alcoholic. 'You're spoiling me.'

'Why not? It's like we said last week. We should just enjoy things – take them while we can. Shouldn't we?'

Just then Blanche appeared. 'Oh! champagne,' she said. 'Martin, be a dutiful brother and fetch me a glass.'

When Martin returned I was dancing with Ralph. What surprised me was not so much that Tom was shy of girls he did not know as that Ralph was not.

Ralph, who seemed so reserved and distant and a little austere, looked dapper in evening dress. He had looked mature and again aristocratic as he danced with a tall flame-haired girl who threw back her head and laughed up at the ceiling at something he said. But when he danced with me and I mentioned her he looked puzzled for a moment and then said, 'Oh, her,' as if he had forgotten her. He glanced back to where the girl was laughing again with that extravagant throwing back of her head. 'The one with the hinged face,' he said.

'You do say some things,' I said. 'I dread to think what you say about me when I'm not around.'

'No you don't,' he said. 'You're very curious to know what I say. Women would rather hear anything about themselves than be ignored. But I shan't tell you anyway.'

'All right,' I said. 'I know I should never take you seriously anyway, Ralph.'

'Shouldn't you?' He looked hard at me, his head cocked, like a dark angular bird. 'Have you ever had champagne before, Jenny?'

'No,' I said.

'I thought as much.'

'You seem to have been watching me very closely,' I said.

'You need someone to watch over you,' he said, and immediately I thought of Blanche's favourite song: but Ralph pronounced the words in a tart and ambiguous way. 'Who better than me?'

In all of this there was such a peculiar mixture of intimacy and sarcasm that I was perplexed and again at a loss as to what Ralph really thought of me. I would almost have said that he despised me had he not made a point of dancing with me again, snatching me up just as Martin was about to ask me.

'I shouldn't have any more of that champagne if I were you,' he said.

'Why not?' I said. 'We're here to enjoy ourselves, aren't we? – enjoy things while we can?'

Ralph's eyes were flinty. 'Because you're not used to it.'

'I've only had two glasses,' I said, and with lightness: 'Anyway, Ralph, what's it to you?'

'I told you,' he said, 'I'm watching over you. That's what friends are for, isn't it? I hope I'm your friend.'

'Yes, Ralph,' I said, 'you are . . .'

'You don't sound very sure.'

'Well – sometimes you're *not* very friendly.'

He laughed. 'It's all a question of comparison – you should see how unfriendly I am with most people.' His face was suddenly serious again and he said, 'My dear girl, don't you know I speak more freely to you than anyone?'

'Not even the other children?' I said.

'Oh well – that's different. We can say anything because we'll always back each other up. That's our trouble. We depend so much on each other. We've always got each other to fall back on.'

'That must be nice,' I said.

'Not necessarily.' Ralph's smile was a little grim. 'That's why it's been good for us meeting you.'

'It's been good for me too,' I said.

'I hope so,' he said. 'As long as you don't let us swallow you up.'

I was not sure what he meant by that: it was on my lips to say that I was very happy to be swallowed up by the Crawthornes. But I did not say anything because I had been struck by a surmise about Ralph.

All at once I wondered whether his feelings towards me were more than that of a friend and whether that was the key to him that I had long felt I might grasp. And yet after we danced he soon left me and I saw him dancing with another strange girl, the same expression of aloof disinterest on his face.

For some reason, however, I heeded his warning about the champagne and did not drink any more before supper. I noticed that Tom too did not drink: I supposed it was because of his driving the car but he merely said cheerfully that he did not need anything. 'I feel just as happy without,' he said.

'He does, too,' Martin said. 'It's disgusting. I wonder if it's something in his make-up. I wonder if we could sort of tap him and extract it. Essence of Tom. We could market it as a stimulant—'

'Have to give a warning about the side-effects though,' Ralph said. 'This product can cause serious shrinking of the brain.'

Blanche drank plentifully of the champagne. Its effect was to make her more soft and affectionate and more than ever like some sleek luxurious cat known for its good nature. She began matchmaking for Tom, trying to get him interested in a girl in fringed and beaded georgette whose bronzed, lissom limbs spoke of golf and tennis pursued with the dedication of a votaress: but in typical Crawthorne fashion she realised when his laughter about this became genuinely uncomfortable and stopped, putting her arm through his and asking him to take her into supper.

There was a good-humoured crush at the supper tables and I saw many white penguin dress-fronts plashed, like babies' bibs, with jogged food. But it was one of those occasions when the atmosphere is

right and nobody minds. Sandwiched in between
the Crawthornes, while in the ballroom the band
continued to play and a few dancers still drifted with
dreamy swishing noises where streamers had fallen
to the floor, I felt my happiness as keenly as if it
were a tangible shape to be held in the hands. We
toasted each other in champagne and then Blanche
said, 'Oh, it feels like a special occasion – it feels
like we should be saying Happy New Year or something. Isn't there an occasion?'

'It's the Jewish New Year in a few weeks,' Ralph
said.

'What about midsummer?' Martin said. 'No, that
was ages ago, of course. It just feels like
midsummer.'

'Just the summer then,' I said. 'Happy summer –
how does that sound?'

I remember that after supper I found myself dancing with Martin again and once more it was as if I
was being carried on currents beyond my own volition. Then the band broke into a stealthy rhythm
that seemed to wake me. I looked up into Martin's
face and saw amusement lurking there.

'Oh no!' I said. 'It's the tango.'

'We'll manage,' he said. 'We can do it.'

'No – really – I can't,' I said, uncomfortable: I
was afraid of being a spoilsport. 'I'm sorry—'

'Would you rather sit out?' Martin said.

'Please.'

We left the floor, where the girl with, as Ralph
had said, the hinged face was stalking very pro-
fessionally in the arms of a large haughty man who
looked like a sort of brilliantined horse. We could
not find any seats, so we followed some other people
out into the hotel gardens.

The gardens too were strung with Chinese lanterns, and about the lawns there was that glow, acid and unreal, of grass under artificial light. The sky was crowded with blown stars and in the still warm air there was the full night-scent of honeysuckle. As Martin had said there was a feeling of midsummer, poised and rich, and as we walked down the gardens the phrase, 'A Midsummer Night's Dream' began to beat, drowsily repetitive, in my head.

At the bottom of the gardens was the river. Beside the towpath was a small boathouse and a bespectacled man was standing there looking out at the river. He turned to us and smiled and said, 'The porter opened it up for us. It's delicious on the river – I've just had a turn,' and he pointed to where a rowing-boat was slowly making its way back to the bank. There was a young couple in the boat and the girl called out, 'It's lovely – still as glass!'

They climbed out, laughing and excited, on to the dry towpath.

'You two have a go,' the bespectacled man said to us. 'I'll keep an eye out for you. There are cushions – you won't spoil your clothes.'

'Shall we?' Martin said.

I have mentioned how nervous I was of the river. I knew it was shallow here and I could hear its gentle lappings, tiny and innocuous, below the towpath, but still the old fear pierced me. At the same time I did not want Martin to see this.

'Is it light enough?' I said. 'I mean—'

Just then Martin put his hand on my arm. It did not urge me: the touch was merely full of reassurance.

'Let's try it,' he said. 'Just a little way. You'll be all right with me. Rowing is about the only thing three years at Cambridge taught me.'

And so I got into the boat and again I felt not fully responsible for what I was doing. As we moved out on to the river, the movements of unease inside me, barely perceptible as the lapping of the dark water round the prow of the boat, still failed to disturb my curious serenity.

There was a great quietness on the river: the lights of the hotel were clearly visible but it seemed somehow far distant, and the only noise to be heard was the sudden liquid flap of a fish. On the opposite bank the branches of willows hung in long, drooping curtains. The warm starriness of the night seemed to hold a secret, enchanted and separate, while the rest of the world turned its face.

'All right?' Martin said, and his voice too seemed different, like a breeze sending a shiver down my back. He rowed slowly and expertly, his graceful figure as incisive in its black and white as a woodcut drawing.

'Sorry about the tango, Martin,' I said. 'I lost my nerve.'

Martin shook his head slightly.

'I'd rather be out here,' he said.

A shape moved above us: I thought it was a cloud passing across the stars and then I saw, turned full my way for a moment, the pale, heart-shaped mask of a barn owl before it mounted away on unhurried wings. As Martin turned his face up to look I saw the whites of his eyes and this seemed to give him an expression of wonder. It was as if we were passing, between the ghostly willows, into a place where all was strangeness.

'It's midnight,' Martin said, glancing at his watch. 'Even if it's not midsummer.'

'It ought to be midsummer,' I said.

Then we slid past an old, giant, hoary willow, leaning right out into the river, and all at once a house was there. It actually stood at the top of a short steep garden, but at first sight it seemed to rise directly from the water like some brilliant Venetian palace. It was a tall townhouse, from the days of Market Downing's Georgian prosperity, and many of the windows were lit: and it was this that helped to give the impression of something extravagant and half fantastical, blazing up straight out of the river. Martin rested on the oars and we looked up at the house, the boat drifting on water that was no longer dark but swept with changing shards of light.

'What a place to live,' I said. 'Don't you envy them?' and then as I said it I remembered St Germain House.

But Martin said, 'I don't envy anyone just at the moment.'

'Neither do I,' I said. Suddenly Martin's eyes held mine as surely as if he had reached out and grasped my arm.

I said, 'Martin—'

'Now I know what colour your eyes are,' he said. 'It's funny when you can't think of a word—'

But I did not learn what colour my eyes were because just then he leaned forward and kissed me on the lips. The slight motion set the water rippling round the bow of the boat and I remember hearing this, with that distant tremor of unease, as Martin kissed me and then as I put my hands up to touch his face and kissed him too.

I did not know whether anyone could see us there: now I suspect not, but at the time I did not care and indeed I did not care about anything, even though,

all the time my lips touched Martin's, I was aware
of that faint ripple of unease coinciding with the
movement of the boat. After a while Martin took
my hands in his, turning them and kissing the inside
of my fingers. The feeling I had was almost like
sickness.

'Martin—'

'Hush.' He put his lips on mine again for a
moment, silencing me. 'We don't need to say anything, do we?'

The light from the townhouse danced on the surface of the water. It scribbled shadows on Martin's
face and then rubbed them out. His hands stroked
gently up and down my bare arms.

'You're warm,' he said.

'Because of you,' I said. 'Because of you, Martin
– because of you.' A terrible shudder seemed to go
through me. I simply did not know that the emotion
of love could be so oppressive, so lacerating.

'You are lovely,' Martin said.

'No, no,' I said, confusedly: for what I really
wanted to say was that all the beauty was his, to
give back to him all the mystery and the almost cruel
joy of the moment.

'I've always thought so,' he said.

'That's all that matters,' I gripped his hands. It
was as if I had never touched a human hand before.
'There's no one else – no one else but you, Martin.'

Water licked at the sides of the boat.

'Jenny,' he said. 'Jenny.'

At such a pitch of feeling for someone, it has the
impact of a blow to hear your name simply spoken
by them. As Martin kissed me again my unease too
seemed to die, gone along with everything else in
the world: and so when a moment later the lights

suddenly began to go out in the townhouse I felt no surprise at the plunge into darkness, when my own sensations too seemed to swoop to some violent extinguishing.

One by one someone in the house was turning off the lights in the rooms. Out on the river the effect was more as if the darkness were carving slices out of the light, until at last there was none left. In the sudden transition I could not see anything and the brushing of Martin's lips across my face might have been the touch of a warm phantom.

'Are you glad you came to the dance, Jenny?' Martin said.

I pressed my burning face against his. I could hear my own breath soughing in the hollow of his neck below the jaw.

I said: 'I can hardly see you.'

'I can hardly see you either,' he said.

We might have laughed then. Perhaps it would have been better: perhaps then there would have been some slackening, some easing of the agonised young tensions of love that seemed to lie like a physical bond across my chest. But just then, with the magnified intensity of youth, there seemed to me no question of such a relief and I could only say, 'I wish we didn't have to go back.'

'So do I,' Martin said. 'I wish we could stay like this for ever.'

At last he released me and took up the oars again. As the boat slid smoothly back in the direction of the hotel I thought of the phrase that had been beating in my head earlier and found myself saying it out loud: 'A Midsummer Night's Dream.'

After a moment Martin said, 'Yes. That's just how it is.'

But already the phrase to me was inadequate. The night on the river and its revelations were real, frighteningly real; and as we drew up to the towpath below the boat-house, where the garden lights threw their rainbow pennants on the water, I wondered whether I could manage the return to cheerful normality. The bespectacled man stepped forward to help me out of the boat, asking me how I liked it, and then I saw a slight figure standing with hands in pockets behind him.

It was Ralph. 'I was wondering where you two had got to,' he said, and his voice was very dry and crisp, cutting through the mild, starry air.

'Ralph, it's lovely on the river,' I said. 'Are you going to have a go?'

'Me, no,' Ralph said. 'I came here to dance. It's my turn. Come on.'

And so, rather reluctantly, I went to dance with Ralph. The tune the band played was 'Someone to Watch over Me': I saw Blanche drag Tom out on to the floor.

Remembering what Ralph had said earlier, I said: 'This tune's rather appropriate.'

Ralph lifted his eyebrows, a sort of transposed shrug. 'Not entirely,' he said.

'No?' I said. Uplifted as I was, I felt equal to fencing with him. 'Why not?'

'Because I can't watch over you all the time,' Ralph said. His heavy-lidded eyes were bleak. 'That's the trouble. I wish I could.'

'Well,' I said, 'thank you.' If my surmise about Ralph was true – and I was still far from sure about that – then I was sorry for him, though I felt he was not a person who would take kindly to being felt sorry for. But what had happened on the river had set the seal on feelings that had begun, for all I knew, that very first day I had seen Martin in the study, and though I would have wished it otherwise, it had also shifted my ground in relation to the other children. All love has the nature of a shared secret, and though I believe I behaved, for the remainder of the dance at the Falcon, with perfect normality, I was conscious of withholding something from the others. And yet this did not at all diminish them for me. Together the Crawthornes made up the bright flame that had drawn me, and now I had reached its white, searing heart.

And so when I danced once more with Martin there was a sort of mute, rapt suspense about me, and Martin too did not speak much. In another of those paradoxes of love our intimacy had seemed to render him a stranger and my eyes dwelt endlessly on his face, his eyes and nose and lips and chin, and they became mysterious just as a word repeated over and over ultimately becomes strange beyond meaning. And then at last we were in the car heading back towards Billingham, the country around softly laid in quiet folds of night. Blanche was singing under her breath, her voice as tiny and unemphatic as if it came from a cat's-whisker wireless:

> I'm a little lamb who's lost in the wood
> I know I could, could always be good
> To one who'll watch over me . . .

In the town there was no movement but the quivering of stars above the ranks of chimneys. Our street was dark and silent and asleep as I got out of the car and said good night. Then Blanche, still floating on affectionate waves of champagne, kissed me goodnight and so too did Tom and then Ralph. Martin was standing holding the door for me and Tom said, 'Go on, Martin – or I'll take yours.'

'No you won't,' Martin said, and bent and kissed me, a warm flicker that was like an echo of what had happened on the river, an echo that reverberated as I went into the house and up the stairs and persisted, unfading, into my dreams.

I did not find it easy, back at work at St Germain House the following week, to be alone with Martin. Perhaps it seems surprising that I was not overtly disappointed about this. But the richness of that revelation at the Falcon sustained me and there was a sort of pleasure too in postponement, like a gift hidden in a cupboard. I held my secret knowledge, and at lunch could scarcely bear to look at Martin's hands across the table. I remembered them touching me.

Nor, the first day, did we play tennis: for when I had finished work that afternoon Mrs Crawthorne came to the study.

'Jenny, could I take a little of your time?' she said. 'There was something I wished particularly to speak to you about.'

We took our old walk through the conservatory and round the flowerbeds, and my heart hammered. My first thought was that it was something about myself and Martin and all my stupid tongue-tied fear of Mrs Crawthorne seemed to come back.

But then Mrs Crawthorne, lifting her flat, cat-like face to the mellow sunshine, spoke of a fête to be held in the grounds of St Germain House in a fortnight's time.

'It's to raise money for the new wing of the sanatorium at Cawley,' she said. 'We've held such things before. But I wondered about making this a little different and I wanted to ask your advice.'

'Yes?' I said. The idea of the sophisticated Mrs Crawthorne asking my advice was bizarre to me.

'There will be the usual stalls and a raffle and so on,' she said. 'But I thought it would be nice if we could spread our net a little wider – get more of a mix. My idea is to extend the occasion into a garden-party in the evening. Nothing stuffy – I have quite enough of stuffy occasions. A marquee or two, and a little band on the terrace, and perhaps there could be dancing. But quite informal. I'd like people from the town to feel they could come and mingle and relax. Do you think that is a practical idea? Tell me what you think.'

I said I thought it was a practical idea and a nice one.

'I am glad to hear you say that,' she said. 'I am most relieved to hear you say that. We are rather separated from Billingham, as you know. It would establish a sort of bridge with the town. But above all it mustn't be stuffy. I don't want anyone to be put off. Do you think people will come? How can I make sure?'

Remembering Billingham's endless bazaars, I said that the best way to get people to come was to emphasise that the whole affair was for charity. 'I sometimes think Billingham people can't enjoy any pleasure unless there's some self-sacrifice attached to it,' I said.

'Jenny, really,' she said, amused, 'I never suspected you were so cynical.'

At that time I was probably less cynical about everything than at any time in my life before or since: after the Falcon you could have told me that it was possible to ride on moonbeams and I would have happily acquiesced. But I rather liked the idea of myself, as Mrs Crawthorne seemed to imply, as urbane and shrewd.

'Of course we can rely on you to come,' Mrs Crawthorne said. 'What about your parents? Would they enjoy it? And those nice friends of yours from the farm – what about them?'

I said I was sure they would be glad to come. Mrs Crawthorne plucked off a withered rose-head and stood looking out across the lawn, smiling as she often did at nothing in particular; she was a person entirely without gestural habits, no finger-tappings or hair-smoothings, and it was as if the abstract smile did duty for them all. 'It should be lovely,' she said, 'early September – so often the pleasantest weather in early September.' And then she turned the smile on me and said: 'In a way too it will be a nice farewell for you, Jenny – as your time with us is nearly over. And of course the children will be going their various ways again. We shall all miss you and it's a pity these things have to end – but the party will be a nice way of marking it, won't it?'

'Yes,' I said. And I thought, with the rather pitying complacence of youth, how little the older generation knew.

Another reason why I did not see Martin alone was Ralph. He had seldom played tennis before, but the next day and the next and the next he was always at the tennis-court when I finished work. I could not have put into words what characterised his behaviour: anyone else might have noticed nothing unusual. But I, with that peculiar feeling of unspoken intimacy with Ralph, felt his watchfulness of me. It was a feminine sort of watchfulness and reminded me a little of when my father was ill and yet would not stop work: my mother would never utter a word of reproach and neither would she obtrusively follow him with her eyes, yet all the time her watchfulness attended him like a spotlight. And so when I heard the sound of the piano as I was finishing work and hurried to the morning-room, saying 'Martin!' as I opened the door, I should perhaps not have been surprised to find that it was Ralph.

He was sitting at the piano and picking out some simple tune. 'It's not Martin,' he said without looking round. 'It's me, Jenny.'

He struck a last sour discord and stood up like a jack-in-the-box. 'He's out, I think,' he said. 'Will I do?'

'Oh! It's just that I heard the piano and I assumed—'

'I can play a little bit,' Ralph said. He snapped a cigarette into his mouth as if he were going to eat it. 'Nothing like Martin of course. I used to fly into terrific rages when I was a child because I couldn't keep up with him. Until I realised my limitations. It's important to recognise your limitations, isn't it?'

He blew out scornful smoke.

'Not just limitations,' I said.

'No? What else?'

'Oh . . .' I could not think of the word. 'Possibilities. Potential.'

Ralph flung himself deep into a chair and regarded me over one jittery swinging leg. 'Has Mother been quizzing you about her garden-party?'

'She asked me what I thought about it.'

'It'll be horrendous,' Ralph said fiercely. 'She

wants to play Lady Bountiful. I swear she thinks Billingham's the estate and the townspeople are the tenants. Christmas in the orphanage. She lives in a world of her own – far more than Father does.'

I was fascinated. I had heard the grating of an abrasiveness between Ralph and his mother before but this hostility was the more surprising in that it was offered so frankly to me.

'I'll tell Martin you wanted to see him, shall I?'

'Oh! no – it's all right.'

'He's off to London again tomorrow,' Ralph said. 'I shall be away again myself. I wonder if I can skip off for the garden-party too.'

I remembered what Blanche had said at the show. 'Are you going to see your friend from university?' I said: it seemed impossible to be over-inquisitive when he was in this candid mood.

'That's the one,' Ralph said. His crossed leg waved almost as if in a parody of casualness. 'Lives over in Suffolk. Simon. Simon Payne. I'd like you to meet him, Jenny.'

'Couldn't you have him to stay here?' I said.

'In the Yellow Room, perhaps?' Ralph said, smiling for the first time. 'I don't know . . . I rather doubt whether he and Mother would get on . . .' He studied the glowing tip of his cigarette, looking clever, taut and saturnine. 'I'm afraid I don't know where Martin's gone, Jenny.'

'It's all right,' I said lightly. 'I must go. Goodbye.'

I made a conscious effort to speak lightly: for somewhere between us, as if neither he nor I had wholly originated it, hovered the idea that Martin was avoiding me. But even if there were any truth in the idea, it was more complex than Ralph knew. No one understood Martin as I did.

And then I met him. I was taking the path through the spinneys to go home, and just before the gate I met Martin coming the other way.

We stopped and I looked up at him, and in spite of all my reasoning the only thing I could say was, 'Martin, you've been avoiding me.'

'Don't say that.' He looked down at my hands and then took them in his. 'I haven't meant to.'

His touch both calmed and excited me. Everything was all right.

'Let's go and see our statue,' I said. 'Shall we?'

Under the trees there was no birdsong now but the small piping of a yellowhammer. The beautiful god still stared from his bower of twining leaves back to a lost and haunted time. I sat down at his feet, in long grass dusty with seed, and after a moment Martin sat down beside me.

'There are always people around, aren't there?' I said.

Martin nodded.

'I didn't know what you thought,' he said. 'I couldn't tell . . . After Saturday – I didn't know whether you hated me.'

'I don't hate you,' I said. 'I love you. There's a difference.'

I think I added this flippant tailpiece out of some notion of softening the terrible ache inside me. The pain of love can be a very real thing and I felt it then.

'You shouldn't, you know,' Martin said. 'Really you shouldn't.'

'Shouldn't I?' I said. 'I can't help it, Martin.'

'Oh dear . . . It would be better . . . It would be more sensible—'

A moment later he was kissing me. Above us the

late afternoon sunlight came through the leaves in
random broken stabbings that were very like the
stabbings of Martin's lips on my face and then of
mine on his.

'No,' I said, 'I don't hate you,' and I ran my hands
through his hair. For so long I had wanted to touch
it and absurd as it seems I did so with a sort of
reverence. 'Can you tell?'

He smiled, an incomplete smile. His hand lay
lightly on my bare arm.

'It isn't easy, is it?' he said.

'Nothing worthwhile ever is,' I said. 'Like your
music.'

'But that's just it,' he said. 'Life isn't all music, is
it? Life isn't all summer nights on the river. I wish
it was.'

'My life is. It is now – with you.'

Martin leaned on one elbow. There were grass-
seeds in his hair.

'Jenny – I'm going to London again tomorrow,'
he said.

'I know,' I said. 'Ralph told me.'

'The real world, you see,' he said. 'All that – I
forget about it when I'm with you. But it is real. It's
all so complicated and it bears down so . . . There's
no ignoring it.'

I placed my hand on his neck, my fingers inside
the collar of his shirt. 'They expect a lot of you,
don't they?' I said. 'I know. I do know your father
– and your mother. I understand.'

'Do you?' He moved his neck against my hand,
like a young stroked animal. 'Jenny – that night –
on the river. Can't we just think of it as a little –
a little harmless midsummer madness? Everyone's
allowed a little midsummer madness, you know.'

I was very conscious of my own breathing.

'Is that how you want to think of it?' I said.

The muscles in Martin's jaw worked a moment.

'I'm only saying that it might be better,' he said.

'It wouldn't be better for me.'

Martin knelt up and held my shoulders. 'I do care for you, Jenny,' he said. 'You're very special to me. You must know that. It's just that – it's not easy—'

'I know,' I said. 'I've told you – I understand. I understand, Martin.'

'I wish things were different,' he said. 'I wish *I* were different. It would be better for you.'

I looked at his eyes, their blueness refined almost to transparency in the sunlight.

'I don't,' I said. 'I wouldn't wish things any different.'

He kissed me again, lightly; and then smiled. Almost without knowing it I had been waiting for the smile, freeing him from doubtful complexities and freeing me too.

'Anyway,' I said, 'it wasn't really midsummer.'

'No. I wish it was. I wish we could go back and have the summer all over again.'

'You're full of wishes, aren't you?' I said. I brushed my lips against his face. 'How long will you be in London?'

'A week,' he said. 'Perhaps ten days.'

'Oh well,' I said. 'I shall still be here when you get back. I'll still be here. Don't look so serious, Martin.'

'Sorry.' The corner of his mouth lifted wryly in the way I loved. 'We shouldn't be serious on a day like this, should we?'

'No.'

With that sudden flex of energy I had noticed before he twisted and held me close. 'And it's not as if the summer's over,' he said.

'Of course not.' Above us the god gazed and the moving leaves twinkled. I lay back in the seed-strewn grass and felt quite simply that I wanted Martin to hold me for ever.

'It's the here and now that matters, isn't it?' he said, and kissed me, deeply, before I could answer.

I remember how, that week while Martin was away, a coolness began to creep into the evenings. The days were still cloudless and brilliant but at dusk there was the faintest smoky tang in the air as the sun died in heroic bronze. I remember too opening my bedroom window in the evenings to look out over Billingham's back alleys and hearing a little girl down the street calling to her friend next door, over the fence, to come out and play: 'Dai-see! Dai-see-ee!' on a falling note. Billingham in those days seemed to be full of these music-hall names, Daisys and Tillys and Lotties: and it seemed to me there was some elusive nostalgia in the sound, lifted on late summer air above the enclosing jetties of pigeon-lofts and gas-tarred fences.

And so it was appropriate that that week I began typing the last chapter of Mr Crawthorne's memoirs. It was a rambling précis of the post-war years and had given him more trouble, he told me, than the rest of the book put together. The children and St Germain House made a fleeting appearance but much of the chapter was taken up with ruminations on the Balfour Declaration and the Arab–Jewish question and the future of the Near Eastern lands which he loved so passionately. The fact that he dealt so summarily and even impatiently with his life since retiring from the colonial service seemed to me significant. The loss of a public life was more to him than simply the loss of an occupation.

'When this is finished, of course, we must check through the whole thing – stand back from the picture as it were,' Mr Crawthorne said. 'And there's the question of a preface – I shall have to think about that. The book of course will be dedicated to Catherine. But I want also to make a special acknowledgement – ' he bowed to me, humorous but genuine too – 'of the invaluable work of the typist – the midwife at the birth.'

I was touched and pleased and though he was often forgetful Mr Crawthorne did not forget. I have a copy of the published book still, with the acknowledgement to Miss Jenny Goodacre in the front. I have only to open the page to bring back unbidden the atmosphere of that week, when workmen were erecting a marquee on the lawn behind St Germain House, when Mrs Crawthorne, tirelessly busy with the fête, was always rattling at the handle of the old-fashioned telephone that hung in the hall beneath the moulting animal heads, and I was wrapped in restless memories of lying in sun-dappled grass, at the foot of a lost statue.

Before parting from Martin I asked him if he would write to me. 'Would you?' I said. 'Write me a letter from London – I'd like that.'

'All right,' he said. 'I will.'

The letter did not come until the following Saturday. I took it out with me to town and read it sitting on a seat in the gardens behind the cathedral. It was only a brief note. *I've started to write but now it comes to it I don't think it's such a good idea. There*

*were many things I should have said to you, Jenny,
last time. Your face makes me forget. I would be
better to talk to you when I come back. I must say
those things then. You are very sweet. Love, Martin.*

I looked at the *Love, Martin*, I suppose, hundreds
of times and thought of the things that he had not
said.

When at last I came to myself and put the letter
away I found an elderly couple standing on the path
near me and gazing up at the long south side of the
cathedral beyond the trees. As I stood up I heard
them say something about finding the way in and I
asked if I could help them. The gate into the precinct
from the south side is hidden and difficult for visitors
to find.

I was right about the couple: they were visitors
exploring East Anglia and had come to see the
cathedral. They talked in strong and friendly West
Midland accents, calling each other Father and
Mother and mentioning the churches they had been
to, as they followed me on stout, noiseless walking
shoes through the hidden gate and round the little
dark stone path, never touched by sun, to the front
of the building.

'We've heard a lot about the west front, haven't
we, Mother?' the man said. 'It's supposed to be
rather wonderful,' and as he spoke we emerged into
the open space of the grassy close, with the west
front of the cathedral silhouetted against the sky. I
was pleased with the dramatic effect of this and
as the couple stood gazing up and murmuring in
admiration I felt too rather proud of the cathedral
and the glory of our East Anglian churches in general. It was this that made me decide, after the
couple had shaken my hand and thanked me, to

go inside and look round the cathedral for a few minutes.

In the south transept I stopped to look at a monument to an eighteenth-century Billingham benefactor: I was always struck by the incongruity of the words on the tomb, denouncing vanity, and the figure on top, smugly reclining on a skull, decked out in curled wig and quantities of carved lace. Then I became aware of a person I recognised seated in a pew to the left, his head leaning on his hands. I have always felt an acute embarrassment, as of glimpsed nudity, at the sight of devotions, and I began to move away, but Ralph lifted his head and saw me.

'I'm sorry,' I said as he got up: my Nonconformist upbringing prevented me from whispering. 'I didn't mean to disturb you.'

'What are you doing here?' Ralph said in his short way. 'I thought you were chapel.'

'Well – I'm not anything really,' I said, and I explained about the elderly couple.

'When did you get back from Suffolk?' I said.

'Hm? Oh, last night.'

He took my arm and walked with me down the nave, stopping to look up at the painted ceiling, its pattern gorgeously and endlessly repeating itself.

'It makes me giddy,' I said.

'I suppose it's meant to.' Ralph gazed upwards. 'I'm a regular haunter of churches, you know, Jenny. I always wanted to take orders – not that that's necessarily anything to do with it. I was determined to be a priest from an early age . . . You look surprised.'

'You're not like any priests I know,' I said.

That seemed to amuse him. His eyelids crinkled

at the edges and he took my arm again. 'Let's go to the cloister.'

'What changed your mind?' I said as we walked out of the side door into the quiet green square of the cloister, penned with high golden walls.

'It wasn't really a question of changing my mind. It's like I said the other day about realising your limitations. You have to give your whole self to the priesthood and I couldn't do that. Not and be honest with myself.'

'It would have been a waste of your talents, anyway, wouldn't it?' I said.

'There speaks a person with no religion,' Ralph said: but he smiled.

We sat down on a wooden bench. The ancient stone basin of the cloister brimmed with sunlight. I thought again of the letter in my bag and I said: 'Is Martin back from London yet?'

'No.' Ralph narrowed his eyes at a blackbird that came pecking within a few feet of us. 'He'll be back before the dreaded garden-party no doubt.'

'It surely won't be as awful as you say, Ralph,' I said. In fact I was looking forward to it: as I had watched the lawn being cut and the marquee erected, and thought of the band playing on the terrace, it had seemed to me that it might well re-create something of that enchantment of the night on the river at Market Downing, spinning together a wonderful setting again for a love that was surely inhibited by the pressures and complexities of everyday life. In my imagination I was already dancing on the lawn with Martin, and so Ralph's next words struck me with the force of a slap.

'Jenny,' he said. 'I'm not blind. Just how deep in are you with Martin?'

I glanced at him and could not speak: my face burnt.

He sighed. 'I see,' he said.

'Well,' I said, choosing a rapid brightness, 'there's no need to look like that, Ralph. It's no great secret really I suppose. You'd know sooner or later, of course. Soon—'

'Jenny,' Ralph said harshly, 'you don't know the first thing about Martin.'

I was held by a glacial and unnatural calm. 'That's what you think, is it?' I said. 'As a matter of fact there's a great deal I know about him. I understand a lot about Martin that no one else seems to have taken the trouble to—'

'Oh, Jenny, I've lived with Martin for twenty years and I can assure you everyone has taken a lot of trouble about him.'

I seemed to hear an inflection of malice in Ralph's voice: I thought of the abrasiveness between him and his mother and how when I had first met him he seemed always to be slightly in the background. I said: 'Well, is that wrong? Isn't he worth it? I think so.'

'Oh, I know Martin's got charm—'

'Yes, he has,' I said. 'Is that a bad thing to have, then?'

'No.' Ralph seemed to consider some words and then reject them. 'But he can't help using it. He doesn't even realise when he is using it.'

'You shouldn't talk about him behind his back like this,' I said – feebly: for I was stuck. My automatic reaction was simply to say that Ralph was jealous; but at a deeper level something told me it was not that. The key to Ralph was something quite different.

Ralph fished for his cigarette case with nervous, elegant hands. 'I could see this happening,' he said. 'I could see it coming – I could tell what was going on in your head—'

'I didn't know they taught mind-reading at Cambridge,' I said. At moments of emotional tension we are often not ourselves, and I did not know where this stupid flippancy came from. Ralph looked at me coolly, unpleasantly.

'You don't have to be a mind-reader to see a woman making a fool of herself,' he said, with such sharpness that the blackbird was startled and flew away.

I was hurt: hurt by this scathing dismissal of what was to me wonderful and precious, hurt too by a momentary fear that it might be true. In such moments of hurt there is not only a desire to hit back but an instinctive knowledge of the vulnerable spot where the pain will be greatest. Deliberately I said, 'And how would you know about such things, Ralph? How would you know anything about women?'

Ralph went red: and in that moment of unconscious cruelty I grasped what it was that had so long eluded me about Ralph.

'Perhaps I don't,' Ralph said after a long moment, and added something the full significance of which I did not appreciate till later. 'But I do know about love.'

I sat still: confused, sorry, and unable to speak.

'Well.' Ralph lit his cigarette at last, plucking tobacco shreds from his lips. 'I dare say you despise me, but I'll say it anyway: I just don't want you to get hurt, Jenny.' He looked at me with eyes that were utterly defenceless. 'Just because I don't – can't

– feel for you in that way – it doesn't mean I don't care for you in other ways. And I don't want to see you get hurt.'

'I don't despise you, Ralph,' I said. 'And I'm not going to get hurt. I'm a grown woman, you know – I'm not a child.'

Ralph seemed to wince. 'Martin has a whole life you know nothing of,' he said. 'There's a whole part of his life that you don't—'

'I know he hates it,' I said impetuously. 'I know that much about it.'

Ralph fell silent. I reached out and touched his hand: he looked startled. 'Ralph,' I said, 'why should we quarrel over this? There's no need. Martin doesn't know much about my life either. All sorts of different people can fall in love . . .' I saw the relevance of this to him as I said it: I stumbled. 'I'm sorry about what I said – about—'

'It's all right.' He squeezed my hand briefly, and with something of his old tart irony said: 'How can I have any secrets from a woman's intuition?'

As he said that I thought suddenly of Mrs Crawthorne and I felt something fierce and protective for him.

'Drop it, Jenny,' he said, gently. 'Let it go.'

'I know what I'm doing, Ralph,' I said. 'Really.'

He looked at me for a long time. I did not flinch from his gaze: there were, in a real sense, no secrets between us now.

'Well, if you say so,' he said at last. 'I suppose I shouldn't go interfering anyway – should I?'

'You haven't been interfering,' I said.

'That means I have. Never mind. You've been very sweet about it. I must go.'

I did not think I had been very sweet about anything. Ralph stood up and poked at the velvety turf with the toe of his immaculately polished shoe. 'You know, don't you,' he said, 'that if ever you want to talk – if ever you need someone to talk to – I'm here. Whatever it is. If you want to.'

'Thank you, Ralph,' I said.

'Father confessor,' he said, wry. 'Perhaps I've found the vocation after all . . . But you see now why it would never have done.'

He stalked away, head bent, with a backward wave of his hand.

Five

Two days before the fête and garden party at St Germain House, Martin was back, bringing with him as guests three people from London.

I was in the study, working alone, when I met them. Mr Crawthorne opened the door and I heard him say, 'Now this is my study. We won't linger because it's a fearful mess but I'd like you to meet Miss Goodacre who's been typing the book and doing an absolutely sterling job . . .'

I shook hands with an upright elderly man who looked remarkably like pictures I had seen of Elgar and then with an even more handsomely aquiline young man and then with a young woman of such striking looks that the whole family seemed like a successful experiment in the breeding out of imperfections. The elderly man's name was not Elgar but Marsden. He was the Member of Parliament under whose wing Martin was beginning his political career and there was indeed something habitually vote-seeking in the way he benevolently bent his flared nostrils over me and asked me how I liked my work. As they left the study I saw Martin waiting in the doorway. I held his eyes for a moment and he smiled slightly. The smile seemed to say, 'You see how it is.'

The mere sight of him was enough to make me feel happy. I turned back to my work, hearing their receding footsteps as Mr Crawthorne showed his guests over the house, and thought of going home this evening and telling my parents I had met a Member of Parliament. I knew they would laugh and remember the time when I was small and the mayor of Billingham had come to visit the school: this had impressed me almost as much as a visit from royalty and great had been my disillusion when I told my father and he merely said, 'Oh! old Ernest Foster. Used to keep the ironmonger's down Jubilee Street.'

This light mood persisted through lunch, where to my relief I was placed between Tom and Blanche and could observe the guests from a distance. Blanche whispered to me that she found the young male Marsden, whose name was Ronald, too attractive to be true: 'He must have some perfectly repulsive habit in compensation,' she said. But there was no fault to be seen in the young woman, Ursula. I was fascinated, and afraid that I stared. Her hair was cut in a very short bob and when she was not speaking she looked like a beautiful pensive boy. When her wide lips opened in a smile the shape of her face, impossibly, seemed to become even lovelier. If I did not envy her as much as I might have, it was because I was in love, and that is one of the few times when envy is in abeyance.

Their presence was, of course, a further obstacle to seeing Martin alone. I felt both that I could and could not wait. That afternoon they played tennis and when I finished work I went to the french doors to see. The two young Marsdens were playing with Tom and Blanche, and Martin was off court watching. Silently I begged him to see me there in the window and to realise I was alone.

He saw me. I turned and fiddled about with the cover of the typewriter and at last he appeared at the french doors, silhouetted against the light just as he had been that very first day.

'Martin,' I said, 'it's seemed ages . . . I got your letter.'

'Did you?' He came into the room slowly. 'I'm sorry it wasn't very long.'

'It was a bit disappointing,' I said.

'I couldn't really say what I wanted to say in a letter,' he said. 'It didn't seem right somehow.'

'Martin—'

'Look, Jenny, we can't talk properly now.' He glanced back at the tennis-court. 'It's difficult—'

'It's all right,' I said. I felt sorry for him having to play host to the Marsdens: already he looked cramped, his face set and elsewhere. 'As long as I can see you again – I'm happy.'

He almost spoke, then I heard Blanche's voice, across the garden: 'Martin – where's Martin?' He glanced back again and I seemed to see him pulled, like a pin between two magnets. But I was confident about which force was the greater: I was confident of the power of the coming party on the lawn, the re-spinning of an enchantment of dancing and summer starlight that had brought us together.

'Tomorrow,' Martin said, 'I must see you tomorrow.' And as he left his eyes seemed, again as on that very first day, to be blindly drained of colour.

Tomorrow did come and was a day of caterers' calls and of workmen on the lawn, talking to each other in the crooning guttural of native Billingham, as musical in its way as operatic recitative: 'Not the-ere – yu don' wanna pud it the-ere, di'yu? You wanna pud it uvver 'e-ere, thass wheer yu wan' it – thass wheer yu wan' it, uvver 'e-ere.' The Crawthornes were busy with their guests and for much of the day I worked alone, and I was alone when just before five that afternoon I finished typing the last page of Mr Crawthorne's memoirs.

I laid the last page on the pile. There was some retyping to do of earlier sections about which Mr Crawthorne had changed his mind, and there was still the preface, but still it was a satisfying and significant moment. I was combing through the chapter for errors when Mr Crawthorne came in.

'I'm so sorry to neglect you in this way,' he said, 'I'm sure you understand how it is – I do hope you haven't had any problems—'

'None at all,' I said, 'it's finished.'

'Oh! marvellous,' Mr Crawthorne said, and there was an expression of touching and childlike pleasure about his face as he picked up the heavy typescript. 'I really never thought we'd get this into shape, you know. It seemed such a "loose and baggy monster" – Henry James's phrase, you know – though some might say his own works tended to monstrosity. Well, this really calls for a celebration of some kind – but of course there's already one planned for tomorrow. You will be coming, of course? And your parents? I'm so looking forward to meeting them. Yes, I imagine Martin will choose tomorrow to announce his engagement. Ursula Marsden, you know. That's my impression anyway. Been in the wind some time – though young people seem to do these things far more at their ease these days: it was rather like negotiating a complex treaty when I was young . . .'

At some point, after talking on for some time about things when he was young, Mr Crawthorne left the study again. I suppose I must have murmured conventional replies out of habit. Habit may cushion emotional blows more effectively than we know; certainly it acted as a crucial brake on my hurtling mind, as I sat on at the desk, pencilling typing errors, stacking the pages neatly, and at last pulling the cover over the typewriter. It was only as I stood up to do this that I realised my legs were not there.

I stood for several minutes gripping the edge of the desk. I remember wondering if I could get out of the house without anyone seeing me. Numbly I gnawed over this problem as if it were the only thing that mattered.

At last I put my hands to my face: I gasped and the sound startled me. I had never believed people gasped out loud in real life and it sounded like an animal in pain.

And then suddenly it was all right. Suddenly I was shaken with a relief that had something of the laughably trivial about it. It was very like the relief that follows the panic of thinking you have lost your purse – and then you realise you are holding it in the other hand. I felt the stopped blood move and flow in my veins again.

The key was Mr Crawthorne, of course. Mr Crawthorne who was sweet and ill and so abstracted that much of the time he was not mentally living in the present at all. He understood the historical forces in the development of the Ottoman Empire but towards the everyday and personal he displayed a sort of refined obtuseness – an obtuseness that was quite capable, even, of getting something connected with his own son spectacularly wrong.

That was the answer and I seized it. I even found myself shaking my head in a pitying sort of tenderness for Mr Crawthorne, as over the innocence of a child. It was such a wild mistake and Martin would laugh when he heard of it. I was quite in control of myself when, a few moments later, the maid brought me my hat and coat.

When she had gone I hurried to the morning-room, confident that Martin would be there, at the piano. The room was empty. Then I thought of the lost statue in the spinney. Martin had said he would meet me today and there could be no likelier place. Our statue.

On the lawn two marquees were already in place and some coloured pennants had been strung from the apple trees at the end. I remember how the wind was getting up, flapping the pennants, and I hoped it would not spoil the party tomorrow. In amongst the trees the wind raved and shivered and the god, lapped by twitching leaves, seemed on the point of stirring into life too. I stood there waiting for some time. When Martin did not appear my disappointment was manageable because I was still buoyed up by my relief at Mr Crawthorne's mistake. I took the path to the gate. After all, it was difficult for Martin with the Marsdens there.

Ursula Marsden. It was a wild mistake and I did not want to think of it any more.

I came out of the gate into the suburban street and a car was there. I did not recognise the car, a sleek tourer with the hood up, but I recognised the voice calling me from it.

'Martin!' I climbed in, reaching over to kiss him. He held my shoulders a moment. 'Is this yours?'

'It's Tom's,' he said. 'He just got it – traded in the old one. You're not in a hurry?'

'You know I'm not,' I said.

Martin started the car, fumbling at the unfamiliar gears. He drove a little way out into the country, to where the river curves in an ox-bow round patches of reedy lake, amongst stumpy sallows. I remember the hard glitter of water struck by low sun as Martin parked the car at the side of the country road and the way, in the ensuing silence, he continued to fiddle in a distracted way at the gears.

'I'm sorry,' he said, 'it hasn't been easy to talk to you – people around and so forth.' He stared through the windscreen at the road. 'I meant to do it as soon as I could – well, I meant to do it in a letter but it seemed not right somehow that way – I really am so sorry—'

Oh God – it is true. It is true. I am still uncertain whether I said those words. Certainly they appeared in my mind as clearly and exactly as if I had said them out loud.

Martin continued to stare at the empty road ahead. 'I realise now that we should have been more sensible – well, I should have been more sensible. Somehow it all seemed quite harmless. The summer was so lovely and somehow—'

I gave a cry and tried to get out of the car. In the confusion of distress and unfamiliarity with the car I could not find the door handle. Cruel glints of sunlight on water moved across the windscreen and I scrabbled amongst thick upholstery for a handle that did not seem to be there and at last, with a terrible sort of exhaustion, I gave it up and listened as Martin spoke of his engagement to Ursula Marsden.

181

'. . . It had been brewing for some time and it was a thing that seemed quite separate somehow. I know that doesn't excuse it but I just want you to understand . . . I do care for you, Jenny, very much – that's why I don't want you to be hurt. That's why I wanted you to think of what happened between us as something not serious – part of the summer – sort of a lovely foolishness. And then forget all about it.'

It was like submitting, helplessly, to some brutal and nerve-tearing operation. My voice came out flat and empty as I said: 'I can't forget about it. It means so much more – I thought you meant so much more . . .'

Martin looked at me edgily and then away at the road again. His hands clasped and unclasped on the steering wheel. 'I'm sorry,' he said again. 'I'm afraid you misunderstood me. That's my fault. I should have made it clearer . . .'

I sat there, not moving. Pain left me dry and seared, too drained for bitterness. The only clear thought in my head was what Ralph had said about me making a fool of myself.

'Your father said something about you and—' Stupidly I could not say her name. 'He said something but I thought he must have got it wrong.'

'We haven't really announced it yet,' Martin said, and I heard in that *we* a great ugly metallic clang, killing hope. 'When I was here – that all seemed far away and remote somehow. I know I should have been more sensible and made you understand. It will be so much better if you forget all about it, Jenny—'

'How can I when I love you?' I said, and the question was not so much asked of him as myself, wretched and unanswerable.

'You mustn't,' he said. 'Really – it would be so much better if you didn't—'

'Better, you keep saying things will be better,' I said, and now the bitterness came in a scalding flood, 'how can it be better? How can this be better? – this is worse – worse than anything . . .'

'Perhaps I should have told you before,' he said, 'but time went on and I didn't . . . and then it seemed if I did tell you it would be like saying you don't mean anything to me, and you do—'

'It was just a lark,' I said. 'That's what you're saying. Just a lark—'

'No,' he said, 'that's not what I'm saying.' His hands left the steering-wheel and I thought for a moment he was going to touch me and how that would be the crowning agony. But he did not touch me. He fiddled with the ignition key and almost involuntarily started the car. The engine throbbed and idled and Martin said, 'What I'm saying is you shouldn't waste a moment's regret over it. I'd rather you absolutely hate me than that. I thought you might hate me after that night at Market Downing – I can't pretend I wanted you to but I knew it would have been better if you had.'

Again I remembered Ralph's words, curt and astringent, about a woman making a fool of herself. My love for Martin, into which all myself had been poured, stood revealed as a fatuous and humiliating illusion. And the worst thing of all was that I could not let it go. Even as I stared at the truth, even as I sat frozen beside the man whose hands did not touch me and who was engaged to be married, my love for him like some parasitic creature gnawed and battened closer.

'You seemed – you always seemed so open with me,' I said. 'The way you talked to me – I thought I understood you and the things you wanted in life. I thought we were so close—'

'We were – we are . . . But things aren't as simple as that.'

'Of course. I remember your telling me,' I said with bitterness.

All the time I did not cry. I remember wanting to but resisting because there would seem to be acquiescence in it. I did not cry and nor did I look at him except at his hands, nervous and never still.

'I should have known we shouldn't have been light-hearted about such things, that it's dangerous to do that – but I didn't until it was too late,' he said. 'Saying one meant no harm is never any sort of excuse, I know.'

'I loved you and you let me,' I said. 'Still, you warned me, didn't you? You warned me,' and I looked at him for the first time. His face was lost and thoughtful and even now as I looked at it something in me readied itself for the swift transforming smile, breaking up the shadows, that always moved me with an absurd tenderness. Then I realised that that was not going to happen any more and with a wrenching sensation I turned and found the door handle at last and got out of the car.

'Jenny,' he said, getting out too, 'wait. Don't go like that – not like that. Let me drive you home—'

I walked on, towards the town, not looking back. I heard him calling me for some moments. Then there was the sound of the car door and at last the car driving away, in the other direction.

I walked along the grass verge, head bent into the wind, half dazzled by the glitter of sun-stained water between the tossing willows. Beneath my feet a few yellow leaves curled and crackled and slowly, dully, I realised that the summer was almost over.

The saddest thing about love is that it has no pride. Self-destructively, it entertains no ideas of dignified retreat. It would have been difficult but not impossible for me to find an excuse the next day for not going to the garden-party at St Germain House and it would have saved me pain. But I could not keep away.

Many people I knew were going: there was the double attraction of a charity beano and of getting a close look at a place that had always been – as it once had for me – a curious anachronistic secret on the edge of the town. That the occasion had held for me a romantic promise which could now never be fulfilled should have been a further warning to me not to go. But love engenders fatalism too. I would go, and see Martin with his fiancée. I did not believe that I could feel any worse.

That evening all the house was lit up and this made me think for a piercing moment of the house that Martin and I had seen on the river at Market Downing. But the effect here was not so much of a Venetian palace as of something very English and civilised and Augustan: it seemed as if there should have been ladies in hoops and gentlemen in frizzed wigs moving about the lawns. But as Mrs Crawthorne had promised the whole affair was very informal. There was a drinks tent but also, appropriately for Billingham's large Nonconformist element, tea and coffee stalls, and a raffle and bran-tubs took the edge off any lingering stuffiness, and a couple of clergymen circulated, threatening to break out into speeches. But there was a small band on the terrace too, and it was the sound of the music threading sweetly in and out of the babble of voices that under-mined my carefully maintained calm. I saw one or two people dancing and I knew I should not have come.

'Well, all the time we were praying that it wouldn't rain,' Mr Crawthorne said, when I had introduced him to my mother and father, 'and we never gave a thought to the wind.' The breeze that I had noticed getting up yesterday had strengthened to a gusty easterly that whipped at the marquees, whistling the first muted tremolo notes of autumn. People held on to hats and scarves and Mr Craw-thorne, in an impossibly crumpled linen suit, looked like a great shabby white bird feebly flapping. 'Very distinguished,' my father said afterwards: I think he felt that anyone who dared wear such a suit must be distinguished.

Soon I met up with Robert Snowden and Marga-ret and Bill Long and I found them full of an excitement I could not share.

'Isn't the house a glorious place?' Margaret said. 'I've never really seen it properly – you can't see anything much from the road. Fancy coming here to work every day – you are lucky.'

'Not for long, now,' I said.

Robert too was interested. 'What's it like inside?' he asked me.

'Oh well, half of it's closed up. It's a bit of a shambles really,' I said. I remembered how puffed with pride I had been last time about the Crawthor-nes and I realised that the very casualness of this reply might sound vain too. 'I don't see much of it except the room where I work,' I said.

'Jenny, you still haven't been to visit us,' Margaret said. 'You must come – we're already bored with each other, aren't we, Bill?'

'It's awful,' Bill said. 'We fight every night just to break the monotony.'

'Come and see us – a week – as long as you like.'

'As soon as the job's finished, I'd love to,' I said. I had neglected them: nothing good, it seemed, had come out of my love for Martin. At the same time I knew that Margaret and Bill were far from bored with each other: they were in love and happy and, cheerfully, wanted everyone to know it. What should have been pleasant knowledge oppressed me and I turned rather desperately to Robert and said: 'How's your mother, Robert? And John – and the farm? Have you been renovating any more old cars?'

Robert, looking rather taken aback by this conversational fusillade, said the family were well. 'As a matter of fact I've been studying up on it – car mechanics. At the Technical School. Turns out I've been doing nearly everything wrong – even though it worked.'

'Tom was asking about you,' I said. 'He said you could make a good living out of it.'

'Tom?' he said. 'Oh! yes,' and I could see him thinking of the day of the Agricultural Show, when I had refused his lift. A moment of antagonism seemed to flare up between us and die away, leaving Robert withdrawn and hardened again, without words.

'He looks tired, don't you think?' Margaret said to me later when Robert was out of earshot. 'He's working the farm nearly single-handed – John's not much help – and then he has these evening classes.'

That Robert should be struggling seemed to me

at that time to be no more than part of the general darkness of things. I had just had my first sight of Martin. He was on the terrace, with Ursula Marsden. She had her arm through his. She was wearing a lavender art-silk dress with yokes at hip and shoulder and a jaunty hat with a feather: it gave the impression of a sort of chic Maid Marian, more beautiful and brilliant than in any of the story-books. She was the real life Martin had been living: the real life from which I had been a pleasant moment's diversion, a brief flame of caprice lightly blown out again. I looked at her and tried to hate and blame her, but there is never any conviction in such things. Hers had been the prior claim and probably Martin was to blame for not telling me. Probably I was to blame for hurling myself so passionately into an involvement with a man of whom, as Ralph had said, I knew very little. Probably his parents were to blame for both expecting so much of him and, again as Ralph had said, spoiling him so that his charm became a kind of intoxicant he could not help indulging. I had been brought up in tenets of earnestness and sincerity, where even irony was a suspect frivolity, and you always said only what you meant: perhaps that too was to blame. It did not matter. All these hypotheses were the merest sophistry beside the simple, unbearable fact that not only was Martin lost to me but that I had never really possessed him.

Ursula laughed at something, leaning against Martin, teasing. I turned and walked blindly down the lawn, through a blur of faces, towards the trees at the end where coloured lights wavered in the wind.

'Jenny.'

It was Ralph, sitting on a garden chair amongst the trees.

'You see, I came after all,' he said, snapping himself upright. 'I want to see how Mother copes when the wind blows a marquee over the roof. How are you?' He held my hand for a moment, very gently, and then said: 'This is the friend I've told you about. Simon Payne.'

I had not seen the other man at first, lounging in a cane chair in the shadows. He did not get up but loosely stretched out a hand rather as Blanche did, with a sort of self-mocking admission of laziness.

'How do you do, Jenny,' he said. 'So you're the amanuensis for the great memoirs? Tell me, are there any shocking revelations about people in high places?'

'They're not that sort of memoirs, Simon,' Ralph said, giving me his chair.

'Oh, I *see*. The sort that nobody reads.'

He was a small, fair and handsome man, wiry like Ralph, but in place of Ralph's narrow reserve he had a flouncing way of turning his face about as if to be photographed. Airily he waved a cigarette in a long holder, curling his legs like a dancer at rest, but about these mannerisms – the import of which was obvious even to my innocence – there was something mocking too. I felt that he was playing at it and wanted to see my reaction.

'I took your advice,' Ralph said to me, 'and asked Simon down for the weekend,' and his eyes met mine with the directness of a challenge.

'Yes, my dear, I've been angling for an invitation for *ages*,' the young man said. 'I was simply longing to see this old barn that one of Cromwell's cronies built. This was rather his stamping ground around

189

these parts, wasn't it? Perhaps that's why we're still
so puritanical. Ralph, be a saint and go and fetch
me another drink, my tongue's hanging out. I am a
guest after all.'

Ralph went. Simon seemed to leave the burden
of speaking to me and at last I got out: 'Ralph tells
me you're from Suffolk?'

He gave me an exaggerated attention. 'Yes, my
dear. At least that's where my parental nest is.
Ralph and I met at Cambridge, of course – and the
rest of the time I try to spread myself amongst my
friends because you know rural Suffolk is *not* the
place for me, to be completely honest with you.'

'How do you like St Germain House?' I said.

'Oh, I adore it,' he said. 'There's a sort of pictur-
esque decrepitude, isn't there – the way none of the
curtains quite fit the windows – you might almost
think it's done for effect. Oh, but it's Ralph's family
that completes the picture – at Cambridge he was
always so *close* about them, you know – and I can't
think why because they are quite charming. And
such a handsome brood too: it doesn't seem fair,
does it? Martin with that melting look – and Tom
such a splendid blond beast – and I don't think I'm
quite qualified to speak of Blanche but I'm told she's
universally admired. Unfair, as I say. There must
be some catch, mustn't there?'

Just then a gust of wind swung the lights in the
trees, illuminating the young man's eyes, and they
looked both hard and shallow.

'Of course it's our hostess who holds it all
together, isn't it?' He made a burlesque of lowering
his voice. 'Rather an alarming woman altogether: a
touch of the Mother Superior, a hint of the lady
of the manor – and a little dash of those Roman

Emperors' wives who used to pop something in the soup when they wanted to get rid of an unwelcome guest. I'm sure that's where Ralph gets his cleverness from – and I've noticed, you know, that clever people never really get on with each other.' He cocked his head at me, like a monkey, mischievous and intent. 'Doesn't she strike you that way? Oh, but of course, my dear, you can't say anything against them, can you?'

'Can't I?' I said, wondering how much Ralph had told him.

'I mean because you're employed by them. Temporarily anyhow. And by the way, how much do they pay you?'

I told him.

'Not overwhelmingly generous, is it?' Simon said. 'One wonders whether they've really got the money to keep this place up. Oh, obviously there's money, but there really isn't any more coming in, is there? But then I'm sure you must know much more about it than I do.'

Ralph came back with drinks, and soon afterwards I left them. I did not know what to make of Ralph's friend, except insofar as his acid insinuations served to reinforce my new apprehension of myself as appallingly and foolishly naïve. Nor did I understand what impulse had moved Ralph to bring him here. I felt sore and deadened and incurious: I longed for the evening to end yet could not make myself leave. There seemed no choice between being here, where I could see Martin walking about with Ursula on his arm, and being elsewhere and seeing the same thing with hellish clarity in my mind's eye.

The main thing was to avoid meeting them face to face. I executed all sorts of manoeuvres about

the garden to this end. At another time it might
have been comic. But it is integral to the agony of
such a situation that nothing is funny. The sense of
loss is embracing: the world is depleted of more than
just love. My feelings had been confined to a narrow
compass and I moved about the garden with something of the cramped desperation of a hunted
animal. And there was something too of fatal
inevitability at last in my turning from talking to my
parents and finding Martin and Ursula behind me.

I introduced them to my parents. Perhaps the
worst thing was that the huge significance of this was
not there. There was nothing to show, except a slight
nervous over-emphasis in the way Martin spoke.
There was nothing to show. The most important
thing in my life might never have happened.

Some time after this – I do not know how long –
Mrs Crawthorne made the draw for the raffle and
then gave a speech from the terrace, thanking everyone for coming and for their support in raising
money for the new sanatorium wing. And then Mr
Crawthorne stood up too and spoke of this as the
perfect occasion for making an announcement and
I saw Martin and Ursula standing behind him.

I began walking towards the trees just as the band
on the terrace began playing the tune of 'For he's a
jolly good fellow'. I had I suppose some idea of
hiding till it was over but just then Ralph appeared.
He took my arm and very firmly steered me into a
marquee and gave me a drink. He waited, quite
patiently, until I was able to speak.

'Did you know?' I said.

'No. I knew he was seeing her in London but I
wasn't sure how advanced it was. That's why I didn't
know how much to say to you – at the cathedral. I

didn't want to hurt you unnecessarily.'

The wind rattled and flapped at the canvas of the marquee. A wish went through me that a gale would come and flatten the whole lot.

'What's she like?' I said.

'Oh, she . . .' Ralph stopped and gave me a straight unsentimental look. 'You don't really want to know, do you?'

'No.'

'Father tells me the typing's finished.'

'Yes. Just a few odds and ends to do.'

'Good. I'm glad – and you know what I mean. It's for the best.'

I said nothing: there seemed no question of best or worst any more.

'Well, I'd better go and see what Simon's up to,' Ralph said. 'Will you be all right?'

I nodded. 'Is he staying long?'

'I don't know.' Again Ralph's look was very direct. 'That depends . . . There's Tom. Tom! – here's Jenny – she's been asking for you.'

I do not know why Ralph said that but it was as if he had discerned a feeling that I myself was hardly aware of: that of all people it was Tom, with his comforting boyish decency, that I would be most cheered to see at that moment.

'Jenny! There you are.' Tom came half running, large and fresh and agile. 'I tried to see you – but I got caught up with some dreary people from Cambridge. What do you think of Martin being engaged? Quite a turn-up, isn't it? Blanche is being all wise after the event and saying she knew something was on the cards but I don't believe she did really. Have you met her – Ursula?'

'Yes.'

'She frightens me a bit, to tell you the truth – she's so damned poised.' Tom looked a little startled at his own candour and then, seeming emboldened by it, added: 'And have you met Ralph's friend? Bit of a rum character if you ask me – I don't think Mother's too thrilled with him. Still, you see all sorts of odd birds at Cambridge. I dare say he's terribly intellectual and all that. I'm just not very good at meeting new people somehow.'

'Neither am I,' I said. An impulse of sad affection moved me to touch Tom's arm. 'Well, we know each other anyway, don't we, Tom?'

'I should say so.' Tom smiled radiantly. 'The band's playing again – would you like to dance?'

He was so eager and happy to see me and I did not want to refuse. But when we went on to the terrace and danced, with the evening darkness thickening in the sky and the smell of bruised grass rising from the crowded lawn, I thought of when I had danced here with Martin, alone in the summer afternoon.

'Do you mind – shall we sit down, Tom?' I said. 'It's a bit of a crush, isn't it?'

Tom did not mind. He was all easiness. We sat at one of the garden tables that had been set round the balustrade and I pretended to eat a strawberry ice that stuck in my throat like a pink slimy oyster.

'All this good news,' Tom said. 'I just keep thinking about the bad news – your job's nearly over, Jenny. I shall hate that. I shall hate it when you're not around. It's been such good fun this summer – I can't remember when I enjoyed a summer so much.'

'Neither can I, Tom.'

'And I've got to go back to beastly Cambridge

next month. It feels as if I've only just come down.'
Gloom did not sit well on Tom's face: it gave him
a look of perplexed strain.

'Do you have to go back?' I said. 'Isn't there
something else you want to do?'

'Oh! race,' Tom said. 'That would be ideal – you
know, like at Brooklands. But I know it's not a
career. What I keep thinking of is the RAF. I'd love
to fly. I feel it's something I'm made to do. Or does
that sound stupid?'

'No.'

'But the thing is, I know Father was disappointed
in me last term – and I feel I ought to make more
of a go of it, you know. I hate being a disappointment to him.'

'I don't think you could be a disappointment to
anyone,' I said. Again I felt comforted by Tom's
stalwart presence, his shy brown eyes that were
untreacherous and without desire. 'I should think
anybody ought to be proud of you.'

Tom brightened visibly, his scalp lifting as he
smiled. 'It's good of you to say that. It's funny, you
know – I can say these things to you – things I don't
even say to the others. You seem to understand and
I—' His fair cheeks coloured. 'I'm not very good
with girls sometimes. At Cambridge, you know, the
girls are sort of intimidating and terribly smart – and
you're not a bit like that. Oh! I don't mean it that
way,' he said blushing harder, 'I didn't mean it to
sound like that—'

'It's all right,' I said, trying to smile. 'I know what
you mean, Tom.'

'Anyway – what I wanted to say was, just because
the job's finished doesn't mean we can't see you any
more – does it? I'd hate that.'

'No,' I said. 'Of course not.'

'I forgot – I've got a new car – did you know?'

'Martin—' I stopped myself in time. 'Martin told me.'

'She's a beauty. Had her up to seventy the other day on a quiet road and she absolutely glided along. You must have a ride in her some time – or how about now? Get away from this crush and blow the old cobwebs away.'

I heard a rippling laugh from the terrace and wondered if it was Ursula. All at once I wanted very much for Tom to drive me away from all this. I wanted to be taken away from the lights and the sweetness of bruised grass and the empty broken promise of music in the September evening. 'Yes,' I said, 'I'd like that.'

As we walked round the terrace Blanche appeared and when she heard where we were going wanted to come too. 'I need a break from this,' she said to me. 'I can't remember *names*. I keep calling people Mr Hmm.' Then Tom spotted Robert Snowden. 'I say,' he said, 'isn't that your friend – Mr Snowden, the car wizard? I'll ask him to come, shall I?'

With hearty friendliness Tom shook Robert's hand and asked him to join us. 'Come and see her – see what you think. The engine purrs at forty but as you go up to fifty I think there's a bit of a knock . . .'

Robert, with one stiff surprised glance round at Tom and then at Blanche and then at me, thanked him and said he would like to. As we walked round to the old coach-house that served as a garage Blanche, who already had an arm through mine, slipped her other arm through Robert's and said, 'Oh! this is better, isn't it? Sneaking away – escaping. Like skipping off school – are there any grown-up pleasures to compare with that thrill of missing lessons, I wonder? Did you play truant from school, Mr Snowden?'

Robert seemed to pull himself with an effort out of the same dazzled and blinded paralysis that Blanche had produced in him before. 'I always did when the harvest was early,' he said. 'Me and thirty others. The teacher never even bothered opening the school then.'

Robert got in the front, so as to listen to the engine, and I sat in the back with Blanche, who sank like a kitten into the deep upholstery; and in a moment we had roared away from the bright scene in the gardens and were turning out of the front gates. We cruised out into the evening country that despite the afterglow of sunset seemed very dark after the lights of the party. I heard Tom saying, 'Now here – this is when she seems to drag a bit,' as he accelerated, and then Blanche curled closer to me and said, 'Now we can gossip at last – so tell me – did you meet Ursula Marsden? What did you think?'

I murmured something about her seeming very nice.

'When Martin telephoned and said he was inviting the Marsdens down for the week I *knew*,' Blanche said. 'I'd met her in London before, of course. I suppose when they're married and Martin finally goes into politics it will just go to show how nepotistic the establishment is, or something. Not that it's a marriage of convenience – I don't mean that. They've definitely got all those irritating habits that people get when it's the real thing – you say something to them and they just stare dreamily through you.'

'Is there a date for the wedding?' I said. I was

surprised at my voice. It seemed to come from far off.

'I don't think it will be for a while yet. Anyway whenever it is, you'll be there, Jenny – you can be sure of that. Just because the job's finished doesn't mean we won't see you. You're our friend – I was going to say you're an honorary Crawthorne but I wouldn't wish that on anybody.'

In the front I heard Tom saying to Robert: 'You're right – they are the future. And especially in Billingham, with the main road and the town still growing . . .' and saw Robert's strong profile turned in the frowningly attentive look that could seem like a dark suspiciousness.

'I'll tell you one thing – it's made me jealous,' Blanche said. 'When am I going to have a love affair? Where's my John Gilbert? I can't go on having a romance with a shadow on a screen. Though most men are just as two-dimensional. I tell you what, though, Jenny – ' she whispered in my ear – 'I think your friend has something of the look of John Gilbert, don't you?'

'Robert? Oh, certainly not,' I said. I thought John Gilbert pretty wet: and I did not know why it gave me such indignation to hear Robert Snowden compared with him.

Suddenly Blanche leaned forward and cried, 'Oh! stop here, Tom – just for a minute. Look – look at the moon.'

Tom pulled over to the side of the road and Blanche pointed to where the three-quarter moon, its face swept with rapidly moving cloud, was reflected brilliantly in a stretch of water. 'Isn't it lovely?' she said. 'It reminds me of a painting, I can't think which one. Where is that water?'

'Oulton Staunch,' Robert said.

I stared without speaking at the scene. Pure stark shapes of willows were caught by the alien glitter and I knew that this was the same stretch of road, perhaps the same spot, where Martin had parked the car and told me of his engagement and I had struggled to find the door-handle and escape that quiet destruction of all my hope. I thought of Martin and I longed for him; and the deep ache that had been festering in me all that evening seemed to burst in a suppuration of anguish.

'Oh! drive on, Tom,' I said, 'show us what the car can do,' and I saw Robert turn and look at me more closely than I cared to be looked at just then.

'Here we go, then,' Tom said. The engine gave a great sensual growl as he took off. The headlights raked the hedgerows and then the empty road ahead with their chill light. I felt the acceleration of the car press me back into the padded seat. The sensation of speed gave me a bitter inhuman thrill. A featureless blur of dark country whipped past the windows and I said, 'Faster, Tom – go faster.' In a sort of savage bleakness I wanted only to be whisked, dizzily and numbingly, away from the party and Billingham and St Germain House and into an accelerating emptiness that might, at least, be bearable.

'She goes a bit, doesn't she?' Tom said. I saw the tension of his broad shoulders and the way his hands rested negligently, with an exultant confidence, on the steering-wheel, so that he was virtually driving by his fingertips. 'All right in the back there?' he said, and he laughed as he put his food down harder and Blanche gave a sort of exhilarated wail.

'There's a sharp bend up here – better slow down,' Robert said, and in the dashboard light I saw the whites of his eyes as he kept looking at the speed indicator.

'It's all right,' Tom said, 'she takes corners like a dream,' and the next moment we slewed sickeningly round the curve. In an effort to keep my balance I lurched up in my seat, pressed against Blanche, and that was how I saw the rabbit sitting in the middle of the road, mesmerised by the glare of the headlights.

Robert shouted a warning but Tom was going too fast to stop in time. Above the screech of brakes I heard the thump, horribly loud, underneath the car.

'Oh, Lord – I hit it, didn't I?' Tom stilled the engine and looked imploringly round at us. 'I couldn't stop – it just sat there . . .'

We got out of the car. I was stiff and sick and trembling. The road was empty and I thought for a second that perhaps we had missed it after all and then Robert pointed grimly to the grass verge where, somehow, the rabbit had ended up. I had heard that rabbits screamed but I had never heard the sound till now.

'Oh! the poor thing – the poor thing,' said Blanche. She stood quite still in the road, her hands covering her face.

'God – what do we do?' Tom too stood quite helpless, glancing round with honest, stricken eyes. 'What do we do?'

'You can't just leave it,' Robert said. Frowning, he walked over to the grass verge. With the merciful deftness of the countryman he put an end to the screaming.

Tom was white. He had the embarrassed and impeded look that muscular men have when they are at a loss as he plucked at his lip and looked over at the grass verge and then away again. 'Shouldn't we

– well, bury it or something?' he said.

Robert wiped his hands on his handkerchief and there was an edge of hard impatience in his voice as he said, 'If you happen to have a shovel about you. Otherwise I think we might as well go.'

I saw the whites of Robert's eyes flash again as I stood frozen in the road and for a moment I did not understand where the light came from. Then he said: 'Car coming – mind out. Don't want any more casualties,' and he came over and took my elbow and Blanche's and urged us over to the side of the road.

He was very capable. Suddenly, in purest misery, I hated him for it. I hated Robert's arrogant practicality and I hated the gentle helplessness of the Crawthornes. I hated the pointless cruelty of the world; most of all I hated my own stupidity that had brought me to this, skewered on the sharp point of a love that was no good to me. The other car drove past, and curious faces peered out at us. I hated it all, and did not know what to do.

No one spoke much on the drive back to St Germain House, and when we arrived I said: 'My mother and father will be wondering where I am – I'd better go and find them,' and said my goodbyes. All I wanted was to find my parents and be gone.

There were still many people in the garden and the band still played, liltingly, beneath the coloured lights. I found my mother and father quite ready to go home – they took their social life, like most things, in the mildest doses – but my father asked me whether I oughtn't first to find our host or hostess and thank them for a lovely evening.

Impatiently I pushed my way through the dancers on the terrace. Mr Crawthorne's flapping linen was nowhere to be seen. Then I saw Simon Payne. He was sitting on top of the balustrade, legs elegantly crossed at the knee, with a wine bottle in one hand and a glass in the other. He took a huge drink and waved the tips of his fingers at me.

'Jenny – my dear girl!' he called at the top of his voice, his mouth stretching with tipsy elasticity. 'Come and sit up here with me. Such a view. One can see the bald patches on the gentlemen's heads. And down the ladies' cleavages too, if one cared to.'

I went over to him and explained my errand.

'Can't help you there, my dear,' Simon said. He raised his eyebrows and pointed his chin at a woman who was staring at him from the other side of the terrace. 'Seen enough, madam?' he crowed, turning his head about. 'Every bit as handsome in profile – though this is my best side – see? Satisfied?' As I was about to go he tapped me on the shoulder with his glass. 'Mrs C was here a while ago – took Ralph off for a *chat* of some kind. Such an *affectionate* family.'

I walked round the back of the terrace, and then I saw Mrs Crawthorne standing at the open french doors to the morning-room. She wore her usual absently smiling look; and only when I was within a few feet of her did I realise that Ralph was with her, standing in the shadows with his hands dug in his pockets.

'Then he will just have to go to an hotel,' Mrs Crawthorne was saying, and her voice, coldly clenched, was so different from her bland expression that it was like watching ventriloquism. 'Not here. Never. That's the end of it.'

Just then she turned her head and saw me. 'Jenny!

There you are,' she said, and seemed with a motion of her hand to put Ralph away. 'I hope you've been having a nice time.'

She turned the searchlight of her attention on me, all charm: but Ralph would not be put away.

'No, Mother, that's not the end of it,' he said, addressing her as if I was not there. 'You can't just ignore things you don't like, you know, and hope they'll go away. Not for ever.'

Still smiling at me, Mrs Crawthorne spoke as it were sideways: 'Ralph, dear, I really don't want to discuss it just now.'

'We must be going now, Mrs Crawthorne,' I said quickly, shaking her hand, 'thank you for a lovely evening.'

'Mother, you tell me you won't have "someone like that" in the house – have I got that right?' Ralph persisted, still ignoring my presence completely. He spoke loudly, but he was not I think drunk: he looked grim and dogged. 'So what about me? You won't have me in the house either, then?'

Mrs Crawthorne still retained my hand, and I felt her fingers tighten painfully about mine as Ralph spoke.

'What you think of Simon must be what you think of me too. Mother,' Ralph said, 'let's be logical about it.'

Mrs Crawthorne's grip had actually made my fingers numb and the flow of returning blood pained me as at last she let go of my hand. 'Goodbye, Jenny,' she said, her smile supernaturally bright, 'do thank your parents for coming, won't you,' and as I hurried away I realised that each of the three of us had been pretending one of the others was not there: the scene seemed in its unreal way the crowning monstrosity of the evening. At the time I did not fully appreciate the implications of what Ralph was saying to his mother, out there in the incongruous conviviality of the lamplit terrace: but I was aware of an unhappiness, different in kind but quite as distinct as my own.

Six

On my last day at St Germain House there was sherry and a special lunch at which Mr and Mrs Crawthorne and Blanche and Tom and Ralph toasted me and wished me success in the future. Only Martin was not there. The day before, he had come to the study when I was working alone, to say goodbye.

The Marsdens had returned to London earlier in the week; but still I had hardly seen Martin and I knew he was arranging it that way. Now he came into the study and sat on the arm of a chair, his elbows on his knees.

'I'm going to London this afternoon,' he said. 'I shan't be here to say goodbye tomorrow, so I thought I'd do it now.'

Just before he had come in I had been nursing a memory of unbearable sweetness, of when I had slipped and fallen on the tennis-court, laughing because it did not hurt at all, and Martin had put out his hands and lifted me up towards him: and now I could not bear to look at him.

'I don't suppose I shall see you again,' I said.

'No . . . perhaps not. I wish it didn't have to be that way but perhaps it's better in the long run. I shall miss you—'

205

'Oh, Martin, don't.'

I averted my burning face. I remember thinking that if I could only not look at him, I might get through it.

He got up and came to the desk, leaning one hand on it.

'I'm sorry, Jenny. All I meant was – I didn't want to say goodbye without saying I'll think of you often. I know you don't want that and I don't blame you. I just didn't want to go as if we were strangers.'

I seized his wrist where his hand leant on the desk. Still I did not look at his face. The warmth of his skin gave me a stunned and beaten feeling. He slipped his hand into mine and for a moment I held it as people will catch and hold a paper streamer from a departing ship. At last the warm fingers slipped from mine and still I could not lift my head until I heard the door close and Martin was not there any more.

That day I did not leave by the path through the spinneys, where the lost god was. I left by the front door and walked down the gravel drive between the topiaries, where I had hesitated and almost turned back that very first day. I saw the geometrical parterres were covered with the starlings that came into Billingham from the open fen to the east in vast flocks, returning again at dusk in whirring clouds that blackened the sky. At my approach the starlings rose in a mass, with a great shrieking and a beating of wings that was like the throbbing of a tremendous engine as they wheeled and banked into the wind. For a moment it was as strange and alarming as walking into a cave full of bats. I stopped and placed my hands over my ears as the clouds of starlings veered and yawed about me, threshing the air, and in a moment I found myself crying like an idiot and quite unable to stop.

Then the engine of wings was gone and I became aware of a more familiar throbbing sound. Tom's car drew up beside me and Tom's cheerful face appeared like the sun at the window.

'I'm going into town, Jenny – let me give you a lift. Hop in.'

I remember scrubbing my face in the brisk way that we always think will somehow disguise the fact that we are in tears. Tom sprang out of the car.

'Why, whatever's the matter?'

'Nothing – it's the cold wind . . .'

Tom looked robustly sceptical.

'Oh – it's just I'm sorry to be leaving,' I said desperately. 'Tomorrow being my last day and everything.'

'Come on,' Tom said. 'Get in – I'll take you home.'

I got in. The new car already had Tom's own very clean tweedy masculine smell about it; and once again I found in his presence something soothing, something that had about it the comforting solidity of the car's upholstery, insulating me from pain. Tom got in beside me and his large golden-haired hand came out and patted mine.

'Don't be sad,' he said, and then as if it had just struck him: 'I say, you're not worrying about finding another job, are you? Father'll give you first-class references, you know. You needn't worry about that.'

'No,' I said. I had not given a thought to what I would do next. Luckily, I was not in the position of the breadwinners who lingered in anxious numbers about Billingham's Labour Exchange, whose num-

bers were soon to become so much greater and
whose anxiety would become despair.

'I should think not too. Smart girl like you.'

We drove between the baroque gateposts. Leaves
were turning on the trees. Tom clasped his unlit
pipe between his lips. He never looked easy with
that pipe – its effect, paradoxically, was to make
him look more boyish than ever, and I think it was
a habit he had picked up at Cambridge as a sort of
duty – and soon he took it out again and said, 'Look,
Jenny – it's like I tried to say the other night. It
doesn't have to be the end, does it?' He glanced at
me and with terrible hurried shyness went on: 'I'd
like so much to go on seeing you – I do get on
awfully well with you, you know, at least what I
mean is . . .' he lost himself and began again. 'I've
got another month till I have to go up to dreary
Cambridge. I would love it if you'd come out with
me sometimes. For fun – like we did this summer.'

I did not say anything. I thought of the summer:
and once more the pain of it seemed to be muffled
and distanced by Tom, cocooning me with his
uncomplicated decency.

'Of course if you'd rather not—'

'No, no,' I said. 'Of course I'd love to.'

'Would you? That's wonderful.' His whole fair
face flushed with pleasure and it was pleasant for
me too, locked into sterile sorrow as I was, to know
that I had made him happy. 'I've got the car – we
can go all over the place and do just what we want.'

'Tom, you are kind,' I said.

'Nonsense!' He patted my hand again. 'Feeling
any better now?'

'Yes.' I smiled at him: if there was anything worth
smiling at that day it was Tom, with his kindly faith
in making things better.

Tom parked the car outside our shop and came in with me, to buy pipe tobacco. Smiling with his superb teeth, he talked with hearty respectfulness to my father, who with his mournful moustache made such a contrast to Tom that the pair of them together looked like the two masks on a stage curtain.

I felt, with that same effect of blurred and soothing distances, proud of Tom. I went back out with him to the car. I saw several women from our street, gossiping in a group around the pillar-box as if it were a brazier, and I noticed the way their eyes slid round and speculated on who the young man with me might be even as their mouths kept talking.

With his hand on the car door Tom turned and said: 'Jenny – what about this weekend – what about going to that pub with the animals that you liked? We never did go back. What do you say?'

Out of the corner of my eye I saw the women staring, wondering. I remembered Martin saying goodbye and the way I had broken down. All at once I wanted, with the murky confusion of love, to get a sort of revenge on Martin. All I had shown him was my hurt and bewilderment and now it struck me that I could show him something else. Instead of mourning I would prove that I could get along very well without him.

'Thank you, Tom – I'd love that,' I said.

'I'll call for you, shall I?'

Tom's voice rang: he was delighted. He roared off with a toot on the horn, and the women stared again. So I was making Tom happy too. That was good.

But it was not of Tom that I was thinking when I sat at my bedroom window and listened to the little girl calling her friend across the fence in the dusk:

'Dai-see! Dai-see!' And when I lay in bed and gazed into shadows it was not the image of Tom that kept me from sleep but the memory of a moving canopy of leaves, and the treacherousness of a midsummer night that was not midsummer at all.

September, as Mrs Crawthorne said, often gives the loveliest weather of all, rather like a special present kept back till the end, and so it was that summer. Billingham, lying exposed where the river valley gives way to low fens, is cradled by no hills: in a sense it has skies instead. The kind of pellucid and gemlike light that people associate with the sea wrapped the valley that early autumn. It shone through tender mornings of vanishing mists and slow afternoons marked by the passage of absurd and wonderful cumulus clouds that were like Olympian cauliflowers. The air had a drowsy elderly warmth and in the apricot glow of sunset, in our wide flat land, you could almost feel the long turning of the earth, inclining unhurriedly to the winter that must come.

I remember how happy Tom was and how this happiness affected me in rather the same way as the September weather. It was gently pleasing and without excitement. For a long time, it seemed, he asked for nothing better than to drive out to the country with me and eat mountainous picnic lunches and tramp across field-paths, vaulting fences and lifting me over stiles the way one lifts a kitten out of a chair. He was never tired and he had a way of singing very quietly under his breath, in utter relaxation of mind, that was reminiscent of the easy cruising of the powerful motor-cars that he loved. There was nothing of the show-off in the athleticism which made him climb into trees or run full pelt up river banks: it simply was, quite unsentimentally, the expression of his soul.

At the little marooned pub on the fen we fed the animals in the yard. I stroked the nuzzling head of the donkey and remembered, against my will, the way the goose had chased Martin. I was trying to work up a technique of as it were blanking out these insistent memories, by fastening my attention quickly on Tom whenever they came: and so I often found myself, as I did now, desperately calling 'Tom!' without knowing what I was going to say.

'Yes?' Tom was at my side, prompt as a dog.

'I – I was just thinking – this is where you tried those plums. Do you remember? – and they weren't ripe.'

'So I did! I wonder if there are any left?'

The plums had all been picked, and the landlady had none to sell, but she directed us to a house a little way down the dyke-side: a typical fenland curiosity of clapboard and brick and chicken-wire where punnets of plums were sold from a trestle outside as well as apples and flowers and field mush-rooms that were like round, sooty cushions. All the way back to the town Tom steadily ate the plums he had bought until, shame-faced, he found they were all gone.

'I am an awful pig,' he said. 'I'm so sorry – you hardly had any.'

'It's all right,' I said. He looked so contrite and I felt so fond of him that I ruffled his hair. 'You enjoyed them.'

I have spoken of myself as a sleepwalker and of the impact of the Crawthornes as waking me. That September with Tom it was as if I was in a doze that

was like neither of those things. I had a curious
sense that I was not there at all, that I was a third
person, watching at a distance, so profoundly unin-
volved were my feelings.

This detachment was what was comforting. Once
or twice Tom took a fishing-rod down to the river
and I sat on the bank watching him. I noticed how
his body had the same suppleness and snap as the
fishing-rod as he drew in the line and examined the
bait and then cast again. He was happy and that
in itself contented me: I could hold those crawling
clinging memories at arm's length. Then he would
turn and look at me with his pure delighted smile
and come running up the bank. 'No luck,' he would
say. 'Ready for another walk?' And even as I was
disarmed by the sheer animal vitality that Tom radi-
ated I was smitten with a suspicion that at last it
would get on my nerves.

So my contact with the Crawthornes, for the time,
narrowed to the single focus of Tom. I did not know
where Ralph stood with Mrs Crawthorne after what
had flared up on the night of the garden-party, but
something had made him disappear into his deepest
reserve, and he withdrew into punishing studies for
his return to Cambridge. At first Blanche sometimes
came out with us, but then she stopped: and Martin
– Martin of course was the person I was proving I
could do very well without.

Sometimes, inevitably, Tom would mention him.

'Martin was saying yesterday—' he would begin,
and the very mention of the name would send a sort
of flex through me and I would cut him off, jumping
up:

'Come on, Tom – let's play ducks-and-drakes.'

It was a desperate and tiring expedient but it

seemed to work. My feelings for Martin could not be overcome or destroyed and so I had to simply block them out: it was a question of sheer survival. That Tom's large generous presence should be the thing to block them out seemed to be of a piece with his general kindness and dependability. I was grateful to him and increasingly fond of him.

Then I began to see something that should, perhaps, have been obvious. Blanche did not come out with us any more because Tom did not ask her. He wanted me to himself and it was typical of him that he expressed this, at last, through talk of machines and speed and his wistful dream of flying.

We were at Raseby Hanglands, a relic of ancient heath and wood on what is by Billingham's standards high ground: there were many dry local jokes, impenetrable to the outsider, about the dizziness of Raseby Hill. We had found a spot near a tiny brook that was like a green thread amongst the furze and Tom lay on his back and looked up at a sky that had the blueness and also the fragility of egg-shell. He spoke of his longing to be up there.

'Air travel is changing everything,' he said. 'Even the Atlantic's becoming just another sea. And nobody seems to take any notice. Don't they see the possibilities? In Italy they're building up a huge air force of modern planes. What about our RAF?'

'Tom, you don't want to fight in a war, do you?' I said.

He turned his face and grinned. 'No. I can't pretend I'm a bit warlike personally. I can't even stand the sight of blood.'

'Can't you?'

He sat up, shaking his head. 'I go all faint . . . There, now my secret's out. Somehow – I can always

213

tell you these things, Jenny – things I wouldn't dare
with other girls. Perhaps it's because I know you'll
understand.'

'Lots of people don't like blood,' I said. 'I should
think plenty of other girls would understand that.'

'Oh! other girls – I don't want other girls!' Tom
said, and flung himself down again, his brown eyes
dwelling on my face.

It was then that I became fully aware of the way
those eyes, so shy and yet undisguised, dwelt often
on me. The look was kind and protective but there
was also a sort of anxious expectancy about it. I felt
then that I must begin to think seriously about what
was happening and this feeling was reinforced when
Tom spoke again.

'Jenny – when I'm back at Cambridge, would you
mind terribly if I wrote to you?'

'Of course not,' I said. 'Why on earth should I
mind?'

'Oh well, I'm not a very good letter-writer, for a
start. Awful scrawls.' His smile turned into a frown.
'Besides, I want to be sure that – well, that you like
me, you know.'

'I like you very much, Tom.'

His relief, and his awkward struggles to say something more, were touching to see.

'Well – you know I like you too, Jenny.' He sat
up and took my hand. 'In fact it's rather stronger
than like. It's – well . . .' and he struggled again,
entangled with shy perplexities. He stroked my hand
and began to say something about how much he
cared for me and I think it was with some idea of
helping him out of these tortuous coils, rather as
one is tempted to supply the word that eludes a
stutterer, that I kissed him. It was something done

to relieve the awkwardness of a person of whom I was fond and wanted to help. And when I had kissed him I allowed him, the taut drum-skin of his shyness broken at last, to kiss me. I sat back in the circle of his big-boned arms and while a pulse in my mind still insisted that I must think seriously about what was happening I did not do anything about it. The kisses, boyish and gentle, seemed so natural an extension of Tom's kindness, a further element – like the clean tweedy smell of his plush car – of the enveloping comfort of his presence: and it did not seem that there could be any harm in accepting them.

'Jenny,' Tom said. He put one great hand against my face, and beamed with sun-like happiness. 'I don't know what to say.'

'It doesn't matter,' I said. His happiness proceeded from me, and I was glad of that.

'I wish—' he said, and stopped.

'What?'

'Nothing. I don't wish anything just now.'

Somehow I felt I knew what he wished. He wished he were more sure of me; and even as the pulse of warning still beat distantly, I thought: Why not? Why shouldn't he be more sure of me?

'I've always been very sweet on you, you know,' he said. 'But I didn't think – well, I didn't think I'd ever kiss you.'

'Didn't you, Tom?' I said. I kissed his cheek lightly: it was such a simple thing, without effort; and I wanted him to be happy.

'I was dreading your job being finished. Not seeing you any more,' he said. 'Still – it's all right now, isn't it?'

'Yes,' I said, 'it's all right now.'

We walked back across the heath to the car hand-in-hand, and the only shadow on Tom's spirits, it seemed, was a faint disappointment that there were no gates or stiles to whisk me over. Still I found myself curiously quiescent and without response. Confusedly, I had sought revenge on Martin by turning to Tom. I had not thought that Tom might be in love with me: but now I knew, there seemed only one logical step. Martin was lost to me, and though I did not love Tom I was very fond of him and I had it in my power, it seemed, to make him happy. Thus, in that strange state that was neither waking nor sleeping, I held Tom's hand and my mind settled itself again, like a lost and tired animal, into a sort of doze.

Tom came to Sunday tea. My grandmother, learning that he was a Crawthorne, was determined to be impressed. Like most people of her kind, she had a peculiarly masochistic snobbery. While she would have had a workless man flogged for taking a piece of coal from a railway-line, she always crooned sympathetically over the spectacular crimes of the rich in the *News of the World:* they were our betters, and could not be judged by the same standards. I believe if Tom had come barging in like a wicked squire and belaboured her with a riding-crop she would have been delighted.

Tom arrived slightly late. 'Awfully sorry,' he said. 'Just as I was setting out Martin arrived back from London, with Ursula. I don't know how long she's staying, but she brings enough luggage with her for an army. I think she's got even more frocks and hats than Blanche.'

'You're making me jealous,' I said lightly.

'Oh! well, I'm not keen on those terribly smart

sort of women myself. I never notice what people are wearing.'

Tom looked very large in our sitting-room behind the shop. The room, always dark and made darker by a plethora of net curtaining, was cramped with its framed photographs and a chain-hung mirror of the sort that always looks fly-blown and a china-cabinet like a glass cage all dominated by a great brute of a sideboard. Tom did not know what to do with his knees and nor I think did he know what to make of my grandmother, who sat in the carver chair in a hunched attitude as if she were fighting an urge to curtsey. All through tea, like someone exhibiting the scars of a wound, she took a lugubrious pleasure in telling him how hard her life had been and how few comforts she had ever had and how, by implication, it was all the likes of her deserved.

'I've never asked for nothing,' she said. 'Not me – never ask for nothing – ' which did not prevent her from asking for another slice of the cake of which she had polished off three-quarters already.

I had told my mother of Tom's vast appetite, and the small table was so crowded with sandwiches and currant loaf and pork-pie and watercress and celery and tomatoes that you could not move without putting your elbow in something. But Tom did not eat as hugely as usual: it was as if he were remembering times when we had laughed about his greed, and was holding himself in check. And I had begun to notice Tom holding himself back in other things. His happiness was delightful to see but as a by-blow of it he seemed to become self-conscious and some of the naturalness went out of him. I was aware when I was with him of his constant anxiety to do the right thing and it was, occasionally, a little wearing.

At the same time part of me realised why this was. Tom was still not sure of me. After tea we went for a walk and I thought about that. I thought too – as in truth I had been doing all through tea – of what Tom had said about Martin coming back with Ursula. I thought of her in one of those smart frocks, leaning against Martin, teasing, as I had seen them at the garden-party, and of his enigmatic face as he looked down at her, half serious and half amused. I thought too of his music and wondered whether he talked of it to her and whether she listened to him play. And it was I suppose because of these thoughts that I answered as I did when Tom spoke of the future.

We walked, at first, towards the park: but when I happened to mention that the school I had gone to was nearby Tom wanted to see it. So we turned that way, walking in the smoky late afternoon through Billingham's Sunday-muffled streets, with here and there the yap of a dog and the drawing back of bolts at chapel doors, preparing for evening service.

'It's funny,' Tom said, looking up at the gaunt school where various lumpy spinsters had taught us to hate learning, 'it's so difficult to imagine people as younger than when you met them,' and he squeezed my arm.

We went onto the Harmon recreation ground where I had played as a child. Harmon was one of Billingham's small captains of industry, an iron-master who had donated the land, and I always felt there was something grimly industrial and iron-bound about the recreation-ground, with its swings hanging from great clanking chains and the concrete settings that were apparently thought so much less likely to break children's heads than grass. Tom was interested in all this. To me Billingham was a drearily known quantity but it was different for him and he kept trying, as he said, to picture me as a girl about these old haunts.

'I'll have to find you an old photograph,' I said. 'Me in woollen stockings and an awful sort of pageboy bob.'

Tom licked his lips in the way that preceded his saying something important. 'What would be really nice,' he said, 'would be a picture of you now – to take back to Cambridge. Only a week to go till I have to go back – I hate the thought even more now. You know – with not being able to see you.' He examined his shoes, stuffing his hands in his pockets with affecting awkwardness. 'I just know that it'll all seem as if it never happened when I get back there.'

'Will it?' I said.

He nodded.

'I mean,' he said, 'it's not even as if we're engaged or anything.'

We had been walking a long time. I felt tired – abysmally tired. I said: 'Would you like us to get engaged?'

'Oh! would you? Jenny – would you?' And again his happiness was like the sun coming out.

'Let's sit down,' I said, 'I feel so tired.'

We sat down on a park bench, Tom hovering protectively over me because I was tired. 'Yes, Tom,' I said. 'Yes, let's get engaged.'

And so it happened. Tom took my hands in his and said they were cold and rubbed them and again I felt myself soothed by him. I became engaged because of the pain of thinking of Martin, of thinking of him and loving and hating him, and because of a confused feeling arising out of all this that Tom could be the one to save me from that pain.

And yet, from this cottony confusion of resentment and consolation, something clear emerged that made me say: 'Let's not tell anyone just yet, shall we, Tom? Not yet. It's between us – our secret.'

'Of course, of course, whatever you like.' He was transfixed and somehow quietened: he stammered as he rubbed my hands between his and said something about how he supposed he was a little young to be engaged but he didn't care a jot. 'I never expected –' he said several times, 'you know – I never expected—' and at last, characteristically, he had to find physical relief for his feelings by jumping up and pushing me on a swing.

So when we returned we said nothing to my parents. And after Tom had gone, having shaken hands with my father and mother and thanked them for having him with all the frankness and charm that the Crawthornes could not help exuding any more than they could help breathing, my grandmother shook her head at me and said: 'Too good for *you*, my girl.' And I knew that yes, in a quite different sense from what my grandmother intended, he was.

Self-deception can be quite complete but I do not believe it can ever last long. Like building a house of cards, it is a process of constant renewal; and each renewal brings nearer the collapse. Sooner or later something would have woken me out of what I have called a doze and into an awareness of what I was doing: it was quite by chance that it was a meeting with Ursula Marsden that was the trigger.

I saw her in Billingham town centre on a Friday morning. She was standing on the corner of The Causeway, looking around her, not knowing which way to go. Somehow it was the very explicitness of that uncertainty that told me what self-possession and confidence she commanded. I knew that if I lost my way in a strange town I would try not to show it. She was wearing a long waisted coat with the huge fur collar and cuffs of that time and it gave her a snug plush look, rather suggestive of the lined insides of jewellery boxes. She saw me, and raised a hand.

'Jenny – it is Jenny, isn't it? How are you? I wonder if you can help me – I'm looking for the bank – I seem to have gone completely the wrong way.'

'Which bank did you want?' I said.

'I really don't know – Martin just said to meet him at the bank in half an hour.'

Martin – how that name seemed to haunt me.

'The banks are down this way,' I said. I walked with her down to the corner around which stood Billingham's banks, mock-Gothic, mock-Georgian, and real Georgian, like three old gentlemen who disagreed.

'You know you've left quite a gap at the house,' Ursula said. 'Mr Crawthorne doesn't know what to do with himself now the book's finished. It is such a pity about his health, isn't it? My father says a man of his experience has so much to offer.'

I thought affectionately of Mr Crawthorne. It had been sad saying goodbye to him and to our labours in the lumber-filled study: all the rest did not alter that.

'He's been showing me all over the house,' Ursula

said. 'It's a mad sort of place. That playroom with
all the toys still in it – did you ever see it? Rather
creepy, I thought. There are one or two quite nice
shops here, aren't there? It's such an old chestnut
about not being able to find anything in provincial
shops. Some of the worst service I ever had was in
Oxford Street.'

She had a way, which I could only admire, of
making all the conversation whilst giving the
impression that you were taking part in it. I resisted
her friendliness, obscurely feeling that if I were true
to myself I should be affronted by it. But there was
no conviction in this, simply because I still could not
fully connect her with Martin. Like him she was a
striking and beautiful person and like him too she
had a way of concentrating on you that was uneasily
flattering, but in my mind I could not associate them
any more clearly than that.

'Are you staying long?' I said.

'I'd like to,' she said. 'It's a bit dreary for me at
home once Parliament opens. I've no mother and
Father's so busy. Now where is Martin? It's supposed to be women who are always late.'

As she spoke I saw Martin emerge from the bank
across the street. He took off his hat and smoothed
back his hair and as he stood on the steps of the
bank I was reminded of the first time I had seen
him in the study and how his eyes had seemed blind
and carved. Then I saw why this was. He was looking in my direction but not at me. It was Ursula that
he saw and it was at Ursula that he smiled and
waved as he came running down the steps. He did
not see me at all. And in that moment my mind
accepted what it had resisted and they were not
separate any more. I had a sensation of things falling

with horrible finality into place and I said 'Goodbye'
to Ursula and hurried away, not looking back.

I walked with blank impulse down the street. I
remember ending up at the river, where the old
customs' house stood by the wharf. I walked along
the embankment, with the old decaying grain warehouses on the other side stumbling into the water.
I was not going anywhere: only slowly did I realise
that what I was doing was putting off going home.
And I did not want to go home because Tom might
call and I did not want to face him. I was awake
now: sharply and painfully awake. That Martin's
smile was for Ursula and not me was a simple and
obvious fact but it was enough to undermine the
cloudy structures that I had built and inhabited as a
refuge. In that refuge I revenged myself on Martin
by means of Tom: whilst still daring to hope, dimly,
that what bound Martin to me was deeper and more
real than what bound him to Ursula and he might
come to realise that. Now I knew it was just not
true. All this past month I had hidden in a terrible
lie.

I do not know if anyone has ever claimed that
love makes you a better person: if so, it is nonsense.
The worst part of the lie which I had forged from
the bitterness of love was that I had involved Tom
in it. And I did not know how to get either of us
out.

The following day was Tom's last in Billingham
before going up to Cambridge for the new term. He
was busy all day with packing; but in the evening
we were to go to a dance together.

The Talbot Hotel was an old coaching-inn of the
sort local historians always claim is the original of

something in *Pickwick Papers*. It was supposed to be
Billingham's superior hotel and had all the draughty
discomfort that implies. That night Tom and I
laughed once or twice at the hideous ottomans and
at the ancient fossilised chambermaids who could be
seen occasionally creeping about behind green baize
doors; but in general Tom was not a person who
noticed such things or found much humour in them.
In fact it was quite a crowded and noisy affair and
we did not talk much. I was preoccupied with
thoughts that one moment turned me oppressively
hot and the next moment clammy with cold perspiration, and sometimes as we danced Tom would
speak and I would look up in bewilderment, not
having heard a word.

'Sorry,' I said, with an attempt at spontaneity, 'I
was dreaming again.'

'You're a dreamer tonight,' Tom said. He looked
down into my face. 'Are you all right?' And again
when we sat out a dance, on one of the ottomans
covered with something like greasy tapestry, he
would sit on the edge of the seat, unrelaxed, saying
'All right?' and watching me in the solicitous and
protective way that was sweet and just a little
wearing.

But I could tell from the way he continually licked
his lips as if to say something important that there
was something on his mind too. At last he came
back from a visit to the men's room, telling me he
had taken a look outside and it was a most wonderful
starlit night, and then he stopped and said, 'I've got
a confession to make.'

'What is it?'

Tom's hand swallowed up mine. 'Well – I know
you said we should keep it secret – about us. I'm

afraid I let something slip to Ralph. I didn't mean to. It was just in passing and – well, I hardly needed to say anything really. Ralph's such a sharp old bird, he seems to be able to see right into one's head – do you know what I mean?'

'Yes, I know.' I thought of Ralph and the way, as Tom said, he could see into one's head. I imagined him looking into my head at that moment. I did not like the thought.

'Anyway,' Tom said, 'old Ralph won't say anything. I mean – that's if you still don't want to make it public. Do you?'

'No, Tom – not yet. Do you mind? Not yet.'

He looked searchingly at me, his eyes reluctant to leave my face. 'All right,' he said. I do not know whether that look held the first cloud of a dawning suspicion, or whether it was simply the continuing watchfulness that Tom bent on me that night, as if he feared I might somehow escape. I wondered if he could tell what was in my mind, horribly clear now: that I would never marry him. After the disaster of Martin, I had run to Tom with the blind selfish pique of a child. To go on with it, without love on my part and motivated only by a hurt vengefulness that itself had become hollow, would be to do Tom a terrible wrong. I knew that now and I had to tell him. It was an ugly choice between giving him pain and giving him greater pain later.

We left the dance not long after supper. Outside it was, as he had said, a night of wonderful autumn clarity, the sky covered with a net of thrilling cold stars interrupted by a shapely space that was the tower of the cathedral. Tom left the car where he had parked it in the market square and we walked back to my home, through a quiet and magnified suspense of empty streets under starlight, sharp with a taste of the year's first frost.

Tom spoke of motoring down to Cambridge tomorrow. 'I can't do without the car,' he said, 'even though it's a bit of an encumbrance at Cambridge. And there are always people wanting to borrow it, which is a nuisance. Some of them are even more reckless drivers than me, if you can believe that.'

'You're not looking forward to going, are you?'

He sighed. 'No. But I'll be home every weekend I can. And at least I've got some nice thoughts to take with me.'

He squeezed my arm and I tried to answer his smile. It was intolerable to think of him taking those thoughts of me back to Cambridge with him, like something precious, when I knew they were a sham. It would be a betrayal of all his decency if I did not tell him the truth.

'Well,' I said lamely, 'you don't know what I'm really like, Tom.'

'I know enough,' he said, kissing my hair.

As we approached my street the stillness was broken, barely, by the soft sound of shunting engines in the marshalling yards, away beyond the railway bridge. The street was almost all in darkness and the clipping sound of our dance shoes was amplified in the tense frostiness of October air.

'You will write, won't you?' Tom said.

'Oh yes!' I said. 'I'll write.' Momentarily a mean little hope went through me that I might tell him that way. Then I remembered Martin and the way he had tried to break the news to me by letter and failed – and I despaired. It was all such a hopeless mess.

Tom came with me down the narrow alley leading

to the back of the shop. At the back door he took my hands in his. Distantly I heard the slow clank of train couplings in the marshalling yards and, as faint as a breath, a hiss of dying steam.

'Well,' Tom said. 'I'd better say goodnight . . . Jenny, I'm sorry – you know, about letting it slip to Ralph.'

'Oh! it's all right,' I said.

'Are you sure? It's just – you know, I've had this feeling you were worried about something.'

I could not speak.

'The trouble is, you see, I keep wanting to tell people. It keeps bubbling up inside me. Jenny – couldn't we tell Martin at least? He's so damned happy with Ursula – and I keep wanting to show him that I—'

'No!' I cried, and my voice went up and I could not stop it, 'not Martin – no, not Martin, Tom, not Martin—' and neither could I stop the tears springing to my eyes. I turned away, hiding my face, trying to wrest my voice into some sort of normality. 'Don't – don't tell anyone, Tom. Not yet. Leave it, please.'

The tears did not, I think, fall; and I managed in a moment to present my face to him again. I could see him quite clearly in the scullery light left on by my parents. His face had gone terribly still, like someone paralysed by a complete loss of memory. He did not even blink. I knew what he was seeing. He was seeing the truth: the truth I had been still too cowardly, at last, to tell him. He took a deep breath and glanced away. He knew.

'All right, Jenny,' he said. He gave a curious little smile and I could not tell what the smile meant: I could not tell whether it was irony or despair or understanding or simple acceptance. He leaned down and kissed me lightly. 'All right, my dear. Goodnight.'

He turned and walked back down the alley, and I heard the clip of his shoes receding, it seemed, for an immensely long time in the crisp air, as if he were going far away.

An endless night troubled with groping reproaches and regrets gave way at last to a morning in which, to my own surprise, I began to feel a little better. I studied my face in the dressing-table mirror. The air was strenuous with the ringing of church bells. I had been a coward: there was no denying that. To have told Tom straight out that I was never going to marry him would have been preferable to that awful moment of realisation that had paralysed him: there was no denying that either. But he knew and it was better now than later. To have gone on with it, with what I now knew to be my motives, would have been a mockery. Tom deserved so much more: indeed he had had a lucky escape and I hoped that quite soon he would come to understand that and realise he was well out of it.

There was something of guilty relief in all this but something of tenderness too. After Sunday dinner, when Billingham lay under a stupefied satiety of Yorkshire pudding and prayer, I bicycled out to the country and I thought after all about writing a letter to Tom. I wanted to write something warm and grateful: something that would explain fully but also convey my true unchanged affection for him. For a couple of hours I wandered about the open country south of the town, where river meadows gave way to swathes of farmland gouged here and there by deep claypits, and composed the letter in my head.

I was still mulling over the vague phrases when I came back, at four o'clock, to help my mother prepare tea.

My grandmother was already installed in the sitting-room, delivering herself of the opinion that the Prince of Wales was an angel in human form. I glanced up from the sink and through the scullery window saw Ralph Crawthorne walking down the passage. I remember how unutterably strange it seemed to see Ralph coming to my home: I remember thinking too, as I ran out of the back door to meet him, that it was typical of him to realise that no one in our district ever used the front door. Only doctors and policemen came knocking there.

'Ralph, what a surprise – Would you like to come in? We're just making tea—'

'No, thank you, Jenny.'

I noticed Ralph's tie was fat and crooked rather like that of a schoolboy. It was unusual in Ralph, who was always immaculate. He stood looking at me in a flat empty way for a few moments and then turned to look down the ash-path at the garden.

'Is this your garden?' he said.

'Yes,' I said, 'not much to see,' but he put a hand on my elbow and walked me down the ash-path and it was in our square of garden, amongst the gritty decaying leaves and the bare rose-bushes, that I noticed that Ralph's normally pale face was like stiff cold wax. He stood with his hands in his pockets, looking from me to the rose-bushes and back again, and told me at last that Tom was dead.

'It was an accident,' he said. 'He set out for Cambridge this morning in the car . . . It was just outside Huntingdon. Apparently it was a bad corner and he went off the road . . . he was driving awfully fast, they say – you know the way he used to drive – and there was really no chance – at that speed there was just no chance . . .'

I did not say anything. I remember staring at Ralph's tie and dully wishing to straighten it.

'There was nothing anyone could do,' Ralph was saying. 'It must have been – just instantaneous. At that speed . . . Martin's gone with Mother down to Huntingdon to identify him. Father wasn't up to it . . . It's just one of those terrible accidents.'

Still I could say nothing. I thought of Tom's face in the passageway last night and the curious little smile.

'The thing is,' Ralph said, 'I was meant to be driving to Cambridge with him – but I got behind with my packing and said I'd go up by train tomorrow instead. I can't stop thinking – I keep thinking that if I'd been with him I'd probably have nagged at him to slow down, and – you know . . .'

I stirred. 'No,' I said, 'you mustn't think like that, Ralph.'

'I suppose not.' He sounded relieved. 'It's just – just one of those terrible accidents . . .'

I stood looking, like Ralph, at the black spikes of the rose-bushes. He was insistent that it was an accident: it was as if – just as Tom had said – he could see inside my head and was determined to scotch any other idea that he saw there. Probably it was an accident: I would never know. I could grasp nothing at that moment but the image of Tom's face last night, pitilessly defined by the scullery light, stricken with realisation.

'Anyway,' Ralph said, 'I thought you should know – straight away . . .'

'Thank you, Ralph,' I said. 'It was good of you to come.'

Some minutes later Ralph was gone and I was still standing in the garden amongst the damp leaves. I had an obscure tugging sense of something left undone, something I was supposed to be getting on with. The golden October air was turning swiftly cold but I stood there for some time, chilled and numb, trying to think what that missing thing was. It was only as I went into the house at last that I remembered that I had a letter to write: and it dawned on me with the same frozen slowness that it was one of those letters that are doomed never to be written.

I vividly remember the leaves at the funeral. They had just begun to fall, and a few drifted into the open grave. There seemed something ghastly and mocking in that.

I remember too a strangeness about Tom's being buried in Billingham's municipal cemetery. I had thought vaguely of the Crawthornes having some sort of family plot; but of course, it was one of the special things about them that they did not really come from anywhere. And as I stood in that breezy cemetery, a sense of terrible appropriateness began to cut through the stunned insulation that had wrapped my feelings till then. The Crawthornes did not belong to Billingham: it was me who had brought them into contact with it; and it was me who had brought Tom here. It was me who had brought him to this most dreadful, irrevocable involvement with the town he hardly knew.

And it was as if then I saw Tom for the first time – Tom himself, Tom alone, not one of the Crawthornes. I thought of his kindness, his clumsiness, his love of speed, his impulsive affection. In death his own vital identity seemed to stand forward from the background into which my confused feelings had blended it. Standing by that leafy grave I was hardly aware of the rest of the family nearby: the world seemed to contain nothing but myself and Tom's insistent presence.

I needed no other reproach. The tears that began to fall from my eyes then were for Tom, not for my own guilt – though there could never be enough for either.

Seven

Billingham's flat plain is not often troubled with heavy snow and that winter following Tom's death was mostly dry. But the town is cruelly exposed to the east wind that comes straight across the fens and funnels up the valley. 'That wind comes all the way from Siberia with nothing in the way to stop it,' my father told me when I was a child; and it is that harsh and biting wind that I remember from that winter. Days of dark steel skies were interrupted only by momentary patches of sun that was all glare and no warmth and always there was the wind, a level blast scouring the long grey streets, chilling you to the bone within seconds. 'It blows right through you and buttons up at the back,' my mother said.

I do not think at that time we understood the full significance of the great financial crash that had happened in America: the strongest ripples radiating out from that earthquake had yet to reach us. What we saw was still more men out of work. They wandered about the town at odd hours of the day, adrift and lost in the alien timetable of the housewife and small child. In our shop, women stood for long ages at the counter, eyebrows painfully drawn together as they added up in their heads and tried to match what they could afford with what they needed. My father said it reminded him of winters before the war, the sort that were never supposed to happen again: and even my grandmother, eating a plate of crumpets before the fire, was less severe than usual and merely said these people should put something by for a rainy day and they only had themselves to blame.

It was a grinding and testing time and in the state of my mind too there was something of the harsh rigour of the winter. The grinding that afflicted me was guilt. Whether Tom's death was, as seemed probable, merely an accident or whether it was something more I would never know: and in a sense it did not matter. I felt that I had as good as killed him. And so I withdrew into a hard world of expiation. Lonely, I sought no company. My passionate involvement with the Crawthornes had ended in the death of one of them and so, with the perverse inventiveness of the young mind in pain, I created for myself a sterile separation. I did not go out much: even on the rare bright days I denied myself the consolation of bicycle rides or walks out into the country. Most of the time I helped in my father's shop. I took on myself long, grim tasks, removing everything from the shelves and wiping and scrubbing and sandpapering down; I climbed stepladders, flourishing a mop into far corners where there was a positive archaeology of spiders' webs. With money everywhere so tight my father was feeling the pinch too and so I volunteered to keep the shop open for longer hours. In hopes of catching a few extra customers amongst men cycling to and from shift-work on the railway and in the factories I got up to open the shop in the icy foredawn; and at night I sat on behind the counter listening for the footsteps of the odd passer-by who might pause and then open the jingling door, with a sort of cold burst that sometimes had about it the savage rawness of fog thickened with the smoke of coal fires. I wore a pair of cut-off mittens and there must have been something grotesquely Dickensian about me, sitting there in the dark winter night and sorting through the biscuits to put the broken ones in tuppenny bags, waiting for customers that sometimes never came.

My father and mother were glad of this but also worried, or more worried than usual. They were worried about my being so grimly unsociable that I would make an escape if one of the neighbours called at the house; it worried them too that in the loveless, self-punishing vacuum I inhabited I shunned amusements and diversions and declined when friends invited me to go with them to dances. Part of this they obviously attributed to grief over Tom's death, but equally obviously part of it was not that and I believe what troubled them most was that I made no plans for the future. I have spoken of their anxiety for me to get on and it was with perplexity that they saw me now, armed with a glowing reference from Mr Crawthorne of St Germain House, doing just the opposite.

And so when I went at last, some time before Christmas, to stay with Margaret and Bill Long it was more at the promptings of my parents than of my own volition. They thought it would take me out of myself; and it was typical of my cramped and knotted mood that I could not explain to them that to be taken out of myself was not what I wanted. The terrible complexities and confusions of youth are often distortions of simplicity and the simple fact was that I embraced solitude because it was the only thing that was tolerable. And only a constant treadmill-like occupation, the less stimulating the better, kept me from reflecting on the Crawthornes and the events of the summer and endlessly tracing the way they had swept on to disaster.

How much of this Margaret and Bill sensed or guessed I do not know. I know they were very kind to me; and the little town of Cawley, to a mind less transfixed with self-laceration than mine, would have acted as a balm in itself. The town lay on the upland, west of the fen, and was all built of limestone. It was beautiful throughout, as only small towns with a single provenance – in this case the school – can be: even the meanest of its cottages would not have looked out of place in a Cambridge college. But then Cambridge colleges were among the things I could not bear to think about.

Margaret and Bill's married quarters, with bow windows and a low passage on which Bill invariably cracked his head, were small and Bill's salary was little more than he would have got as a clerk in a Billingham factory: but they were enjoying life. It was the sort of life, domestic yet continually and busily involved with others, that exactly suited Margaret. She was helping to coach the school choir and one evening I went to hear them in the chapel rehearsing a concert of carols for the end of term. The boys clearly regarded women as an exotic species and were as impressed as I always was when Margaret, stopping them to correct their pitch, sprang out a rich contralto note that seemed altogether too large for her small, tidy body.

Unobtrusively Margaret did her best to lift my spirits and if she did not succeed it was because I was defensively resistant to any incursions of feeling. But when she suggested that we go over to the farm one day and see her family, feeling broke through at last, in a wave of nostalgia.

'I'd like that,' I said. 'It seems so long since I was there.'

'I go over quite often,' Margaret said. 'It's only five minutes on the bus.'

We were sitting over a late breakfast and as Margaret spoke of the farm she began picking up crumbs from the cloth with tense, finicky movements. Once or twice before when she had mentioned her family there had been something diffident about her and now I said: 'They're all well, aren't they?'

'Oh! yes. There's nothing wrong. It's just that sometimes – it's like a battle up there. Can I – do you mind if I tell you?'

It brought home to me just how blank and empty I must have appeared, for Margaret to need to ask me that. 'Of course not,' I said.

'Things haven't been easy for a while – you know that. We know several farmers who've gone bust this year. Then there was Dad going and Robert having to take over. I don't reckon his heart's in it but he's always done his best. The trouble is he's so tired all the time, and it doesn't seem as if John really pulls his weight, and – well, Mother tries to keep the peace but it's not a nice atmosphere.'

I thought of John, Margaret and Robert's younger brother. He was a big boy of seventeen with a bashful pink complexion and a ready smile that was sometimes, I felt, too ready.

'Is Robert still doing evening classes?' I said.

'Yes – and he's been doing jobs on cars and vans for some of his friends. I've seen him fall asleep at the kitchen table. Still, there are people a lot worse off . . . We'll go over tomorrow then, shall we? I know they'd like to see you – it would be just like old times.'

That it could never be quite like old times was, I thought, chiefly due to the change in myself. But still I went back to Snowden's farm with something of the hungry wistfulness of a seeker after lost innocence. It seemed unchanged: the old brake in the yard with its shafts lifted to the sky, the boot-scrapers of wrought-iron before the door, the long brick-floored kitchen smelling of laundry and cooking mixed and the mantelshelf stacked with years of letters that had gone crisp and brown as parchment. Mrs Snowden, big and husky-voiced and sympathetic, gave us tea and baked stuffed apples warm from the range and I felt that here, at least, was something solid and stable and untouched by complication. Perhaps I did not want to accept that this too might be deceptive.

Mrs Snowden, in her friendly way, was very interested to know what I had been doing with myself lately; and often Margaret had to rescue me when, numbly, I could not answer her mother's questions. I had done nothing and felt nothing and wanted nothing. Her kindly curiosity was like pressure on a raw bruise and I was glad when we were interrupted at last by Robert, coming in from late ploughing.

'Oh, hullo,' he said, standing just inside the back doorway, in shirt sleeves and an old waistcoat, with a fresh outside smell about him.

'Hello,' I said. 'Long time no see.' For a moment, it seemed, the curious stiffness, the mutual mistrust sharpened by our recent meetings, was not there, and I smiled. 'How are you?' I said.

'I'm very well.'

'You look well,' I said, and then Mrs Snowden gave a cry and said, 'Oh, Robert, your boots!'

'Can't help it,' he said, glancing down at his mud-caked boots, 'I can't get them off – not with one hand,' and then I saw that he was holding his left hand wrapped in a handkerchief, stained with blood.

'Whatever have you done?' Mrs Snowden said.

'Cut it on a blade. It's all right.' Robert tramped through to the wash-house and Mrs Snowden followed him, saying, 'You'll want a bandage.' I heard the sound of running water and then Mrs Snowden's voice again: 'Ach! look, there's blood all on your shirt as well . . .'

'Oh, it's all right – it's only an old one. I'm not planning on meeting the King in it, you know—'

Margaret smiled at me and then her smile faded as the door opened again and Robert's voice called, sharp now: 'Is that John?'

John came in, very pink and cheerful, throwing off his coat and rubbing his hands together.

'Hello, you two. Visiting day, eh? Any more tea in that pot?' He lifted the lid of the tea-pot.

Robert came out of the wash-house. He had taken off his shirt and he stood there in his singlet with the deep tan on his forearms contrasting with the white, muscle-taut skin of his upper arms and shoulders. He was still holding his cut left hand in his right and I saw a drop of blood drip from it on to the brick floor. His eyes under their deep shelf of brows were like black stones as he stared at his brother.

'Where the hell have you been?' he said.

'Billingham,' John said. He poured a cup of tea. 'I said, didn't I?'

'No, you never said.'

'I thought I did. I thought I said I was going into Billingham to get my hair cut.'

'You never said.'

'All right, I never said.' Bland and unconcerned, John sat down at the table. The tea was cold but he drank it thirstily, swilling it around in the cup.

'You were supposed to be helping me this morning,' Robert said. 'I needed you this morning. You know Jack's off sick. What the bloody hell do you think you're doing?'

There was a naked disturbing edge to Robert's voice that was very like the aggressive bareness of his skin as he stood there in his singlet, his hand red with blood. He stared and stared at John.

'All right, I forgot,' John said. 'Don't get in a sweat about it.' He turned to me with his light boy's smile. 'What have you been up to, then, Jenny? Still working for that old chap with the book?'

'Don't you turn away from me like that,' Robert said. 'I'm talking to you – don't you ignore me like that.'

'All right, all right! What's the matter with you? Who rattled your cage this morning?'

There was something bright and mocking about John that seemed to infuriate Robert further. 'You,' he said, 'that's who,' and as he made a sweeping gesture with his left hand I saw a crimson spot of blood fly through the air and spatter on the door behind him. 'You urge me to death! Haven't we got enough trouble without you sloping off when you're wanted? You never lift a finger – you just eat and never lift a finger.'

'I've got to get my hair cut, haven't I?' John said. He took another slurp of the cold, milk-skinned tea. 'You look as if you could do with a haircut yourself.

You look as if you want smartening up.'

'Don't start,' Robert said. 'Just don't start, that's all.'

'Stop it, the pair of you,' Mrs Snowden said. 'We've got company – we don't want any shouting matches. Jenny, could you fancy another apple? Or a piece of cake – I made a walnut loaf yesterday—'

'That's right,' Robert said. 'Eat everything – eat the lot. There'll be nothing left soon so you might as well.' I had never seen him like this, his temper so near the surface, a fierce flush darkening his face further and seeming to smoulder, like fresh bruises, at the high cheekbones beneath his eyes. Suddenly I knew what Margaret meant about the atmosphere in the house. It was a very bad atmosphere and I wanted to get away.

'What do you think, Jenny?' John said, leaning confidentially across the table. 'Don't you think he looks as if he wants a haircut?'

Robert made another sweeping angry gesture, scattering blood, and said he was a cheeky little bugger and he'd do something he'd be sorry for in a minute.

'There,' John said to me, 'I bet you never heard language like that at St Germain House, did you?'

This remark seemed to be the last straw for Robert. A squirm went through his naked shoulders and he grabbed John's arm, making him spill the stewed tea all over the table.

'I dare say she didn't,' Robert said, 'and she knows where she can go if she doesn't like it. Now you go and get changed, boy.'

'Robert!' Margaret said.

'Well? I never asked her here, did I?'

John, protesting that he had got blood on his

jacket, shook his brother's hand off and went to the stairs door. I got up. 'I think it's time for us to go anyway, isn't it, Margaret?' I said.

'Sorry we can't treat you like your posh friends do,' Robert said. He spoke at me without looking at me, savagely, his voice full of controlled bitterness. 'This is what we're like and I'm sure it's all a bit of a come-down for you but there it is.'

He went back into the wash-house; and soon afterwards Margaret and I got the bus back to Cawley. For Margaret's sake I tried not to show how the visit had affected me. I had thought of the farmhouse and the warm brick kitchen, sentimentally I suppose, as a bastion of unglamorous decency; and the scene with Robert and John, Robert's bare shoulders sinewy with anger and the blood dripping on to the floor and the shouting amidst the spillings of cold tea, afflicted me with a sense of sordid ugliness. There was a refiring of guilty unease too: for there was truth in what Robert had said about me. I had thought, in my intimacy with the Crawthornes, that I had grown out of the Snowdens' world and into one that was lofty and subtle and brilliant. I had been vain with the pride of this and now when he saw me in his kitchen the pride was all he saw. There was even perhaps a miserable defiance in the squalid scene; but I did not fully understand this until much later and for now my chief feeling was of all the fixed reference points of my life slipping away from me. I felt the vague beating of a crisis about me that must come to some resolution, and when I left Margaret and Bill's and returned to Billingham two things happened, at last, to bring it about.

The first was in February, when the new year

seemed already haggard and old with the unending pinch of winter. One afternoon in town I ran into an old schoolfellow of mine named Gwyneth Mills. She treated me to tea at the Grandee: she had just heard that she had landed a job she had applied for in London. Over tea she asked me what I was doing and said there was more work to be had in London and how she was rather nervous of living there on her own. Then my mention of St Germain House came back to her and she showed me an item in the local paper she had with her.

It was an announcement of the marriage of Martin Crawthorne and Ursula Marsden. The wedding had taken place in London.

'Yes, I knew about it,' I said, handing the paper back to Gwyneth.

I knew about it: there wasn't any more to say. There was much to feel, of course. My night and dawn vigils behind the counter of the shop seemed longer than ever. My overriding impression was of finality: of everything being, terribly and pointlessly, over. It was as if someone had told me that all my life had been a dream, without substance.

The second thing came, in some ways, as a counter to the first. In March a letter arrived from Mr Crawthorne: I recognised immediately the looping script from which I had typed for three months. I recognised his voice too, in the courtly tone in which he asked after my health and then, in rambling paraphrases, got round to asking me if I was able to come to the house for a few weeks' more work on the typescript of the memoirs. Some parts, the publishers insisted, needed heavy rewriting:

'Apparently I run the risk of libel in some of my more forthright remarks on various politicians

*involved in the settling of the question of Palestine.
I was prepared to let them stand, but* dis aliter visum.
*Now if you are placed in the slightest difficulty by
this request I trust in your candour to say so. Only
the fact that you worked so splendidly on the book
– and the fact that we would all be so delighted to
see you again – emboldens me to put you to such
trouble, at such short notice . . . '*

And so I went back to St Germain House; and as
I walked down the drive again, between the topiaries
and the parterres all crisp with the unending frost,
I had no feeling of surprise. It was as if I had known
this must happen sooner or later.

I had not seen Mr Crawthorne since Tom's
funeral. Then he had been touchingly dignified, the
public figure once more, braced out of his reclusive
eccentricity into correctness. Now he looked sick
and aged and curiously shrunken. I noticed too that
he felt the cold, where before he had always thrown
open windows and gloried in a good through-
draught. Frequently he grasped the poker and made
a blundering stab at the study fire, clumsily scattering the coals, and complaining that the room was
like an ice-box.

'Are you sure you're warm enough?' he said
several times, and when I had assured him I was he
said: 'You look warm. It is nice, you know, to see
you sitting at that desk again. Quite like old times.'
And hearing this, I felt my affection for Mr Crawthorne fuse painfully with my lingering guilt over
Tom's death.

It was the later chapters that required editing, and
the work was mostly a matter of making cuts and
emendations as were indicated – with the mixture
of cryptic casualness and downright rudeness that

was apparently standard publishers' style – in the editorial notes. Several times as we worked Mr Crawthorne remarked how nice it was to have me back and how it was quite like old times: he did not mention Tom once. Then gradually I realised that these two things were related. My being there typing in the study was exactly like the time before Tom's death – indeed it was rather as if he had not died at all. It was this that made Mr Crawthorne happy and I think it was this, more than anything, which had made him anxious for me to come back for the small job of emending the typescript. Without knowing it he was seeking to re-create that undisturbed, contented period of our joint labours: for, as I learned, there were other troubles to add to the lasting grief of the loss of Tom.

Mr Crawthorne spoke of them indirectly, as was his habit, as if I knew what it was all about. Mentioning something that had happened in January, he said, 'It was about the time those letters came – those awful letters.' He crouched at the fire, his breathing thick and laborious, poking at the ashes. 'I find something like that so appallingly upsetting – I never knew such things really happened,' and then, making his first reference to Tom: 'And in a house of sadness too – that was the awful thing. Such a terrible atmosphere.'

I did not ask him what this meant: it was Blanche who told me. She came running down the stairs to the hall just as I was about to leave at five o'clock.

'Jenny.' Her small, peculiarly affecting smile trembled at me. 'Do you have to go just yet?'

We talked in her luxuriously cluttered room. The wintry afternoon died at the window in a slow sunset of opalescent light, orange-gold, that gave the frothy heaps of dresses and the tumbled jewellery and scent-bottles the look of treasure piled in a fairy-tale cave.

'Did you hear about the wedding?' Blanche said. She sat curled and cat-like on the bed. She smoked a cigarette, without the usual elegant holder: it made her look girlish and inexpert.

I said yes, I had heard about the wedding.

'It was originally planned for Christmas. They put it off because of Tom. They're on their honeymoon now. In Nice.' She hugged herself. 'I'll bet it's warm there. I wish the spring would come – things always seem different when it's light and warm.'

Unlike Mr Crawthorne, she spoke often of Tom. Tom had been her twin and it was, as she said, difficult for her to believe that he was dead. 'I can't believe he's gone,' she said. 'Not while I'm still around. I don't think I ever will believe it really. If I saw him in the street one day I wouldn't be a bit surprised – does that sound silly?'

I said no. I found it difficult to believe too that Tom's abounding vitality could simply vanish from the world without trace.

'It's knocked Father up badly,' Blanche said. 'Mother copes – of course. Father's different. And then there was the business of Ralph.' Her eyes, beautiful and unstirred as a china doll's, sought mine. 'I can tell you, Jenny. I know we can trust you,' she said, and I felt a flaring, like a poignant echo, of all my awed pride at being taken up by the Crawthornes as one of them.

And so I heard about the business of Ralph. It all had such a seedy, Sunday-newspaper fatuity about it that I found it hard to connect with that clever, caustic and self-possessed person I knew. The letters

Mr Crawthorne had mentioned had been a clumsy and vague attempt at blackmail from an anonymous someone who had found out, at Cambridge it seemed, about Ralph's nature. We were still hedged about, in those days, with the shades of Oscar Wilde and Reading Gaol and it was not hard to imagine the shock that had gone through the family – and through Mrs Crawthorne in particular.

'Luckily Father's solicitor said that whoever sent the letters didn't really know what he was doing and there wasn't any real danger. And then the letters stopped coming. But of course the damage was done. And the terrible thing was that Ralph—' Blanche gazed very soberly at me. 'Well, he couldn't deny it.'

I nodded. 'Yes. I knew.'

'Did you . . . ? Sometimes I wondered but I can't say I ever guessed. I suppose it takes an outsider to see these things. It's strange, Jenny – I often felt that you knew more about us than we knew ourselves.'

Pierced by my own misjudgements, I could not answer that. I said: 'Where's Ralph now?'

'At Cambridge. He comes down next week for Easter . . . I'm dreading it.'

'Why?'

'Oh! not because of that. He's still my brother – you can't change towards a person just because of something like that. At least I can't. But when it happened, you see, Mother's first thought was about Martin – about when Martin goes into politics, and how it could damage his career if it got out about Ralph. There were these terrible scenes – Mother raging and raging at Ralph, and Ralph refusing to lie about himself – you know how he is – he'd never do that.'

'Yes,' I said, 'I know.'

'It upset Father – and I just kept thinking of Tom, and how we ought to be just thankful to have Ralph still with us. Alive. I mean, when you lose someone like that – surely it should make you value people even more? Supposing it had been Tom who was that way – wouldn't we give anything to have him back, regardless of what he was like?'

It was strange to hear these things, so sombre and fateful, spoken of in Blanche's light cool voice with its cocktail-party inflections. She sat on the edge of the bed, all fine milky blondeness in the dwindling light, and stubbed out her cigarette.

'Anyhow, Mother doesn't seem to see it that way. She and Ralph are hardly speaking. Father's just terribly bewildered. It's an awful strain . . . You know, Jenny, when you left St Germain House all our luck seemed to go with you – doesn't it seem that way?'

Again I could not answer.

'Well, as soon as spring comes I'm going to stay with friends in Berkshire,' she said. 'They might be going abroad for a while and I'll see if I can go with them – just get away from it all – get clean away. Does that sound bad?'

'No.'

It did not sound bad: I understood. Over the next few days I tried too to understand Mrs Crawthorne. I do not mean to belittle her grief for Tom when I say that she wore it with a certain conscious, head-high nobility. We all have our own species of vanity and none of us can, as it were, unpick it from the weave of our natures: the thread will show up in the light of circumstances happy or tragic. And perhaps too the effect of that grief was uneven: perhaps like some distorted glass it magnified Mrs Crawthorne's already jealous protectiveness of Martin, who was to bear his father's distinguished tradition, and at the same time made of Ralph something monstrous in her eyes, something that made bereavement intolerable. I tried in this way to be fair, and if I failed it was because I could not think about Martin dispassionately and also because Ralph was my friend.

He arrived home from Cambridge one afternoon when a shower of rain had lifted to reveal a thin, pure sunshine like the merest possibility of spring. Mr Crawthorne had been imagining he heard the taxi all day: there was an anxious determination about him to be prompt to welcome Ralph which moved me and made me feel loyal to him. It was about an hour later that Ralph came into the study to see me.

He held both my hands in his, scrutinising my face.

'Here again, Jenny,' he said.

'Here again. Not for long this time.'

He smiled faintly and at last let go my hands. Then as he turned to go he said, 'Will you come to the cinema with me tonight, Jenny?'

'Yes, of course.'

'I'll meet you. Outside the Embassy, about seven.'

Inside the Embassy that night, under the great pall of cigarette smoke that always filled cinemas then, Ralph and I sat through half an hour of a monotonously nasal Hollywood talkie before making our way to the exit. 'Well,' Ralph said with his old wryness, 'it didn't seem quite correct to just ask you to come for a drink with me. We've got to be correct, haven't we? Let's go to the Great Northern.'

So we went to the lounge of the Great Northern Hotel, where I had once met Martin and afterwards had wandered through the park in a nebulous cloud of love and hope. 'What I need,' Ralph said, 'is a very large gin. May I suggest the same for you?'

'All right,' I said. 'Not too large though. I'm of Methodist stock, remember.'

Ralph took his drink in one go as soon as it came and then leant his elbows on the table, looking at me with a face that was no longer taut but quite frank and defenceless. It had the curious nakedness of a person who habitually wears spectacles, when they take them off. 'It's good to see you again,' he said.

'Blanche told me what happened,' I said.

'All rather a mess, isn't it?' he said quite conversationally. 'I'm sorry that it happened when it did – coming on top of Tom and everything. That was terrible. But something had to happen sooner or later – you know that.'

'Not this way.'

'I don't know. Perhaps it took something like this to make Mother face what she knew about me already. So now we've had some good knock-down rows and we know where we stand.'

'She'll come round, surely – somehow . . .'

I did not believe my own words, and Ralph did not trouble to contradict me. He only smiled and said, 'She had to stop herself – in January, it was – she had to bite her tongue. We were arguing it out and she mentioned Tom and she had to stop herself saying – well, you can guess.'

'What?'

'It was on the tip of her tongue to say, "Why Tom – why not you?" Oh, she didn't quite say it,' he went on, noticing my look. 'But, as I say, we know where we stand.' He ordered another large gin. 'I'm fuelling myself up for some confidences. I do seem to land you with these, don't I?'

I had an uneasy suspicion of what he was going to say.

'I shan't be going back to Cambridge,' he said, his bony fingers cupping his glass. 'I've made inquiries about studying on the Continent. I mean leaving completely – permanently. I can support myself by teaching: I'm fluent in five languages – no false modesty. I'm going very soon. You're the first person I've told.'

There was silence between us. The old desiccated waiter unpeeled a fishy eye in our direction and then went back to polishing glasses.

'It isn't right,' I said.

Ralph looked startled. 'What?'

'It isn't right you should have to do this – it isn't fair. I don't pretend to understand it all, but it's just – it's just *wicked* that you've got to become like an exile all because of—'

'Jenny, Jenny.' He gripped my hand. 'No, you don't understand. I haven't *got* to do this. There wasn't any real threat in those letters, and I'm not going because of Mother or because of Martin's political career. I'm not running away from that. I'm going so that I can be myself. Yes, that does include living in a country that recognises that love can take many forms. But it's more than that. I've got to break away from them – the family. The Crawthornes. We're such a unit – even with poor Tom gone. Perhaps more so. You saw that playroom upstairs. Sometimes I think we never left it. I've got to work my passage alone, do you see?'

'Surely Blanche – and Martin – they wouldn't want you to go—'

'But that's just it. Always we've been able to say,

"Well, it doesn't matter, Blanche and Martin and Ralph – and Tom – will be there for me." It doesn't matter what we do because we've always got each other – we're Crawthornes first, and individuals second. It's like a charmed circle and I've got to break it. Make a mess of my life, maybe, but on my own terms.'

It was true that the Crawthornes were like a charmed circle: that was part of their fascination for me. And just as if Ralph, again, had seen into my head he said, 'And this is where you tell me to mind my own business. Because you've got to get out of it, too, Jenny. You know you have. I wish you hadn't come back to do that work for Father – that's going to make it more difficult.'

'Why?'

'Because Martin's coming back from his honeymoon next week. With his wife.'

He seemed to speak with deliberate brutality, watching me closely. It was like a doctor saying, 'Does that hurt?'

Steadily I said, 'That doesn't matter to me. It's all over. I can face that.'

It did hurt. The very mention of Martin set up a nagging and tugging inside me, like a toothache that one knows will not go away. But I did not want to show this to Ralph: I did not want to believe it myself.

'I wonder,' Ralph said. 'Perhaps you think you ought to: but you know, Jenny, there's a thin line between being brave and being plain stupid.'

'Oh! the compliments are flying tonight, Ralph,' I said. I often betrayed myself, I think, by these spasms of flippancy: Ralph looked grim.

'I still think you should get away,' he said. 'We're

not good for people, you know. We're too close and too much alike – even Mother. We swallow people up and they end up being like us. But sooner or later we want the playroom to ourselves again.'

'What about Ursula?' I said. 'See – I can say her name.'

'I don't know about Ursula. Anyway, whatever happens, I shan't be here to see it.'

'I still think it's a shame,' I said. 'I wish you weren't going.'

'There, you see,' he said gently, 'that's just what you mustn't.'

We walked back through the town to my street. The pavements were wet with a clammy, curdled mist: a few mild stars blinked here and there. The frost was over.

I said, 'Shall you be going alone? Can't your friend go with you – Simon?'

Ralph stopped walking. He seemed to hold his breath, and I wondered what I had said. Then he let out the breath, and there was the fragment of a laugh somewhere in it.

'Well,' he said, 'you may as well know it all.' He faced me. 'It was Simon who sent the letters. It didn't take much finding out. There was a quarrel, you see, and that was – well, his revenge, I suppose.'

I was shocked. 'Oh, Ralph – that's terrible.'

'I suppose it is,' he said. He had stopped directly beneath a lamppost, and the light showed me his face: shrewd, sadly amused, rather lovable. 'But then – one doesn't necessarily love the best person. Isn't that right?'

Five days later Martin and Ursula came back to St Germain House as husband and wife.

They were going to make their home there, for the immediate future, though Martin would still be often in London while he was working for Ursula's father. All this Ursula herself told me, coming into the study and with great friendliness pulling up a chair and chatting to me as I worked.

'Father says having two generations in a house doesn't always work,' she said. 'But after all the place is so big you could go a week without seeing each other if you wanted.'

Presently Martin came in. He stood by Ursula's chair, a couple of feet from me. His face was slightly tanned, a sort of warm sand colour, giving a touch of maturity to the brilliant youthfulness of his looks; and when he spoke too his voice seemed deeper and more adult. All this troubled me: and if it is true that there is fear in attraction then I was afraid of Martin at that moment.

'I think you ought to learn typing, Martin,' Ursula said. 'Think how useful it would be. And don't say it's a woman's occupation. The time's coming when there won't be any such thing – isn't that so, Jenny?'

'Except the things we can do better than men,' I said.

'That's right. And there are a lot of those. Aren't there, Martin?'

'Oh! I'm not saying anything – I can see I'm out-numbered here,' Martin said amiably. He was standing with his hands loosely in his pockets and with casual affection Ursula slipped her hand into his, in the pocket, as they talked. I was appallingly conscious of pretending not to notice this. I believe I smiled with an inane brightness all the time they were there; and inwardly begged for them to be gone.

Over lunch that day Martin blinked drowsily and said he was tired from travelling. When I left at five, seeing myself out as usual, I caught a glimpse of white shirt through the open morning-room door. I peeped in to see Martin lying asleep on the sofa. I have spoken before of Martin reminding me of classical sculptures and, as he lay there, his head turned in profile against the dark velvet of the sofa, he seemed again to call up images of the ancient world. Utterly relaxed and abandoned, his face sleep-cleansed of expression, he looked like some foot-soldier of antiquity who had fallen, redeemed and unregretting, in the breach of a hopeless defence. That I thought of these things, whilst knowing that he was a young man tired out from travelling, was ominous for my intention of remaining dispassionate about Martin.

The next day it turned warmer: I saw one or two primroses in the spinneys. At lunch-time Ursula went on to the terrace, her face in the sunlight expanding flower-like and more beautiful, and wanted Martin to play tennis with her.

'Oh! not yet,' he said. 'The court won't be playable – it wants rolling.'

'Idle – that's what it is – fat and idle.' She teased him, patting his flat stomach. She was determined; and at last, in default of tennis, she got him to fetch a shuttlecock and rackets and they played on the lawn. Martin complained of indigestion, and Mr Crawthorne jovially quoted the duel scene of *Hamlet*: 'Give us the foils! Martin, you are fat, and scant of breath!' Ursula was not very good – she had a sort of well-bred absence of reflexes – and she ended up calling Martin a cheat and beating him on the head, with a twanging musical sound, with her racket. Everyone laughed a lot: it was probably the first time they had laughed so much since Tom's death, and I think in this way the arrival of Ursula, fresh and vivacious, was a good thing for them. And if I did not join in the laughter quite whole-heartedly it was because I was haunted by memories of my own that were both elusive and vivid: memories of other laughter and foolery, on the terrace and the bumpy tennis-court, and of the brushing of summer grass-seed against my legs, in the leafy sanctuary of an unseeing god.

I thought that I had got over these things: I thought I was proof against seeing Martin again. I had willed myself to be dispassionate. Now I knew that the will was not enough. I thought of what Ralph had said about working his passage alone. It is hard for the young to accept that there can be salvation in detachment; but I knew that I could not go on like this.

The following Monday, I finished the last of the retyping for Mr Crawthorne. To my surprise he gave me a clumsy fatherly kiss when I said goodbye. Martin shook my hand. In the evening I went to see Gwyneth Mills, who was packing for her move to London, and asked if I might come and stay with her while I looked for a job there too. Two days after that, I saw off Ralph, alone, at the station, as he began his long journey; and the following week I returned to the station again, and left Billingham by the London train.

Part Two

One

My sharing digs with Gwyneth in London was intended as a temporary arrangement. Two years later, I was still there.

I found work as a typist at a solicitor's office off the City Road. I took a bus to and from work, ate my lunch at ABCs, and in the evening cooked with Gwyneth such meals as could be managed on the blackened gas-stove in our digs in Camden Town. These were on the top floor of a Victorian terraced house, with a narrow front and a ramifying back: descending through roofs and annexes and lock-ups and sheds and coal-holes, the house stopped being a house very gradually, and only gave up the effort where a patch of humpy garden at last asserted itself before dropping despairingly into an old railway cutting. On the other floors other single girls lived like us in an atmosphere of frying food and drying stockings, and on the ground floor lived the landlady, a pleasant body who sat constantly in front of a Tudor wireless-set as if it were a warm fire. She told anyone who would listen that she was a medium, and insisted that the house was haunted by the invisible ghost of a Yorkshire terrier which sometimes jumped on her bed at night and nuzzled against her hand with its incorporeal wet nose.

Gwyneth and I got on well. She was a deft pretty girl with the least abrasive personality I have ever known. She had a very high, almost falsetto voice with a habitual tone of gentle, abstracted sympathy. It broke up her words in a musical way. 'Oh, have you-ou?' she would say, if I had a cold or a head-ache. 'What a sha-ame.' Nothing ruffled her amiable calm. I sometimes thought that if I came home one night and announced that I had been struck by light-ning her reaction would still have been the same comfortable, hyphenated commiseration. 'Oh, have you-ou? What a sha-ame. Ne-ver mi-ind.'

Gwyneth was conducting a courtship of infinite slowness with a man who worked in her office. Such things were made more difficult, of course, by the place where we lived: what the landlady called Gentlemen Visitors were discouraged. Still, the tremendous caution and hesitation of Gwyneth and her young man's wooing baffled me, all the more so as they were clearly crazy about each other. He was from Manchester, and when he spent the occasional weekend at home with his family he and Gwyneth wrote to each other. Their letters were as thick as parcels. I knew they could not afford to get married: much of the young man's pay went back to Man-chester, where his father was one of the millions out of work. But I wondered why they did not at least get engaged. 'Oh, I'd have to be *su-ure* of a person,' Gwyneth said, folding up a letter the size of *Old Moore's Almanac*.

But who, after all, was I to criticise? In that cool, smoky spring of 1932, I had been going out with Jocelyn Freeman for six months, and I still did not know how to answer when my mother's letters, fish-ingly, asked about him.

'What a marvellous name – Goodacre,' Jocelyn said when I first met him. 'A name straight from the land.'

Names came up, I think, because of the unfamiliarity of his: in those days Jocelyn was still mainly a man's name but it was an unusual one. It seemed to me rather knightly and medieval and indeed Jocelyn's face, fresh, pale-skinned and shining-eyed, was just the sort that should appear above a chain-mail tunic with a cross on the front. I believe it was this that initially attracted me.

I met him through one of my fellow-typists, who was his cousin; and soon we were going out together for teas and to the cinema and, particularly, to concerts. Jocelyn was Welsh, or at least his parents were, and he had that dreary Welsh conviction that this made him innately musical. One hears of converts being more Catholic than the Pope and there was something of the same obsession about Jocelyn's displaced ethnicity. I remember his eagerness when he met Gwyneth – 'Ah, a Welsh name!' – and his disappointment when she said her parents had just picked the na-ame out of a bo-ook. Though he was about as authentically Celtic as Paul Robeson, he cultivated a sort of bardic mysticism which came out most strongly at concerts, where he went into a trance of communion with the spirits of Beethoven or Haydn or Dvořák or any of the great composers, all of whom, inexplicably, had failed to be born in Wales. He worked as a clerk for a pharmaceutical company.

It was the time of the slump, and we were among the lucky ones. My landlady had cupboards full of bootlaces and garters and pipe-cleaners that she had bought, hating to refuse, from the shiny-suited men who haunted back doors with their cardboard suit-cases. Her husband had been killed in the war and it pained her to see the shabby bemedalled sur-vivors, who had walked into machine-gun fire in order that their children should live on bread and dripping. It was the time too of earnest discussion of the League of Nations and international peace and there was much of that amongst Jocelyn's friends, who met over honey-buns and cocoa, wore sports jackets and felt hats, went on hikes, and agreed with each other a lot.

Jocelyn was very keen to integrate me with his friends.

'You'll love Alec,' he would say, or: 'You must meet Gwen – you'll really like her.' There can scarcely be anything more likely to prejudice you against a person than being told you will love them. I was not sure which bored me most, the endless serious talks about the Disarmament Conference or the endless serious talks about sex: the chief differ-ence, which rather fascinated me, was the way everyone's ears went red during the latter.

Jocelyn talked a lot but he was really rather shy. There was a sort of humility about his diffident kisses that was touching and I wondered if perhaps I might love him. I went to tea at his parents' house in Putney. His father was a youngish, handsome, mad Welshman who talked incessantly in the larger-than-life bombastic vein that such people seem to think is irresistibly poetic and life-enhancing. That I did not succumb to this rough-hewn coalminer charm was only partly due to the fact that I knew he had worked all his life in an insurance office. Mrs Free-man was a whispering blob of a woman who waited on him hand and foot.

'You wouldn't catch me waiting on a man like that,' I said.

'Oh! well – they're a different generation to us, remember,' Jocelyn said; and I saw how much he loved them.

My twenty-first birthday, which I had always expected to be momentous, came and went. The following Friday, I had arranged to go to a concert at Wigmore Hall with Jocelyn. I often think how near I came to not going to that concert. It was pouring with rain; I had one of the colds that seemed universal in the dank backward London spring; the programme was Brahms, not a great favourite of mine. I nearly cried off and did not, at last, only because Jocelyn might be hurt. And I am afraid that only affected me insofar as I wanted to avoid the inevitable post-mortem: we've got to talk haven't we and so on. So I went, on a black night of sizzling rain, expecting nothing and chiefly looking forward to getting back home and burrowing under a pile of blankets.

There was a faint smell of damp clothing in the auditorium. It was about half-way through the programme, and I was idly reflecting on Brahms's uncanny ability to make a symphony orchestra sound like the pouring of wet cement, when something caught my eye away to my right. I say something, because although it was a person's head its effect on me was nothing so precise as recognition. It was rather as if a voice had called out through the steamy labouring of the music. I was suddenly all attention. And then the head with its shingle of light blonde hair turned, and I saw the face of Blanche Crawthorne for a moment in brilliant profile. In that moment the hall, the orchestra, the audience all seemed so faded and unreal that it is a wonder I did not stand up and call her name.

After the interval someone in that part of the auditorium changed seats and as a result I could not see her any more. I began to wonder if I had been mistaken. I did not hear another note of the concert. When it was over at last and we were making our way to the exits I was in such a state of abstraction that Jocelyn took it as a tribute to the transcendence of the music. 'Wonderful, isn't it?' he said. 'You must hear the Third. You'll love the Third.'

Outside the rain still poured and there was a bat-like flapping of umbrellas and mackintoshes on the pavement and a growling of waiting taxis. Jocelyn and I moved with a wet hurrying crowd down the street to catch our bus.

'The "Alto Rhapsody",' Jocelyn said. 'You'll love that . . .'

I stopped. Between the hurrying shapes I saw Blanche, standing at the kerb, just about to get into a cab. She turned down the deep collar of her coat, revealing again the shining blondeness and the perfect profile.

'Blanche!' I said.

Blanche turned. There was a dazzle of headlights and this gave her the appearance of groping in a blind and curiously lost way as she looked round to see who had spoken. Then she saw me and I let go of Jocelyn's arm and went to her.

'Jenny – what a surprise.'

She seemed to gaze at me with something of the same lost helplessness for some moments.

I said: 'I saw you inside – I wasn't sure if it was you.'

'I didn't see you,' she said. There was a man with

her, waiting to get into the cab, but she did not introduce him. 'Where are you living?' she said.

I told her my address.

'I'll come and see you,' she said, touching my arm; and then got into the cab.

I did not believe that Blanche would come and see me. It was something said out of the old habit of impulsive affection. And indeed I did not know whether I wanted her to come and see me. I had greeted her instinctively, almost involuntarily, and it was not until I got back home that the full impact of seeing her again hit me.

In my attic bedroom I undressed quickly and dived for the bed. The book I was reading was on the night-stand: I picked it up but I could not make sense of it. The book, the chest of drawers, the giant brown wardrobe, everything in the room was just as I had left it. But it all seemed profoundly different. It was as if I was seeing from outside, for the first time, the life I had lived here.

For two years I had lived in an ordered and rational manner, habit-swathed, looking no further ahead than the immediate horizons of work, looking back not at all. The past was something I had deliberately set aside. My contacts with it, like stretched threads, had become more and more attenuated. Margaret and Bill had moved, Bill getting a better job at a school in the West Country, and our letters had declined to brief résumés at Christmas and on birthdays. From my parents came the occasional budget of news, filtered through their scrupulous reticence until scarcely anything was stated at all. It was from them that I had learned, well over a year ago, of Mr Crawthorne's death: it had been in the local paper. He had died of a stroke. My sadness at this was succeeded, quite swiftly, by detachment again. It was all in the past. I went on with my safe and colourless life. That is not entirely hindsight. I think I perceived it at the time as safe and colourless, but that was what I wanted. I made a few friends at work; I began with Gwyneth to brighten up our digs with touches of drapery and glass bought at the market; I began to go out with Jocelyn. If I thought of the Crawthornes at all it was with a flicker of warning, as of some bright, gorgeously scented and poisonous flower. I had no moments of great happiness but neither did I know moments of great unhappiness: and this seemed not only a fair swap but natural. I thought it was part of becoming an adult. And if I was wary of intimacy – to the extent that I knew more than one person described me as 'starchy' – then I ascribed that, too, to growing up.

And so the unexpected sight of Blanche Crawthorne at the concert kept me awake that night. Memories that I had long held at bay returned and as I lay in darkness they began to seem, alarmingly, more vivid than the present. It was a curious sensation rather like that of walking into a very strong wind – that moment when the force of the wind exceeds your forward movement and you find yourself going backwards. I did not like it. It threatened the equilibrium that I had come to value above everything else and had imitated, perhaps, from Gwyneth's placidity. But I consoled myself at last with the thought that it was quite by chance that I had seen Blanche and the chances were equally good that I would not see her again.

I overslept next morning. Coming downstairs to go and buy a pint of milk, I found Blanche in the hall talking to the landlady.

'Good morning, Jenny, how are you?' Blanche

said, just as if we met every Saturday. 'Mrs Baker
was just telling me about the ghost. Have you ever
felt it?'

'No.'

'It doesn't seem to go upstairs,' Mrs Baker said,
'I don't know why.'

'Perhaps there was a gate on the stairs once,'
Blanche said. 'You know, one of those safety-gates
for children. And as far as the dog's concerned, it's
still there. Like when ghosts walk through walls, and
it's because the wall wasn't there when they were
alive.'

'I'll bet that's it,' Mrs Baker said. 'The people
who had this house before me, they had little
children. I'll bet that's why it is.'

I saw at once that the landlady, who normally
subjected visitors to suspicious scrutiny, was completely won over by Blanche. All the Crawthorne
charm was suddenly before me again in the dingy
hall, indefinable and undeniable. I felt resistance
inside, like a squint against the light.

'I've got the car outside,' Blanche said. 'It's
stopped raining. Come and see it.'

The car was exactly as I would have pictured a
car belonging to Blanche: a small open tourer,
white, with coffee-coloured upholstery. 'I've only
just learnt to drive,' Blanche said. 'It's the only
practical thing I've ever managed. It's pretty, isn't
it? I'd give it a name only I hate it when people give
cars names. I know someone who refers to their
car as Bubbles. Can you imagine?' She opened the
passenger door. 'Jump in.'

For a moment I did not move. The memories
of the Crawthornes that had afflicted me last night
paralysed me again.

'Where are we going?' I said.

'Oh! anywhere you like,' Blanche said. She smiled rather shyly at me. 'It's just so lovely to see you again, Jenny. It's been so long. You know, last night I could hardly believe it – I'm afraid I must have stared like an idiot . . . We'll go to my place. There's nobody there and we can have lunch together.'

Still I did not move. Stupidly, I was thinking of my ironing. Always on Saturday mornings I cleaned up and did the ironing and now I thought of this as an insuperable obstacle. All the bewilderment of meeting Blanche again, of the recrudescent memories and the stiffening of my resistance against these things, expressed itself in a stubborn clinging to routine.

'Jenny, I'm sorry,' Blanche said. 'Were you just going somewhere? – I should have thought. Well, let me give you a lift anyway.'

'No,' I said. 'It's not that.'

All at once it seemed impossible to mention the ironing. I had a vivid and unflattering image of myself as the sort of person who would make an excuse like that.

'It's just such a surprise,' I said. 'I hardly know where I am.'

We got into the car. Blanche seemed entirely unchanged. Elegantly lissom, she slipped into the driving-seat as if she were getting into bed. Then I saw her left hand on the steering wheel, and said before I could stop myself: 'Oh! you're married.'

'Yes, didn't you know? I suppose you wouldn't. Nearly a year now. That was Victor you saw last night. I'm Blanche Prentice now.' She started the car. 'I'm not a Crawthorne any more. Light me a cigarette, will you?'

On the drive she told me about her husband, who was a financier and property developer.

'He makes pots of money, don't ask me how. Apparently there's still money to be made even in these times, though he lost a lot in the crash. He's thirty-two but he doesn't look it.'

'Does he look like John Gilbert?'

'No, not a bit.' Blanche laughed. 'Fancy you remembering that.'

There were a lot of things that I remembered: they were coming thick and fast.

'We met and we got married all in three months. That's romantic isn't it? Once he motored all the way down from Scotland to spend a couple of hours with me before he had to motor all the way back. So you see I couldn't refuse him then.'

We drew up outside a large and opulent corner house off the Bayswater Road. I noticed there were no curtains at some of the windows.

'We've only just moved in,' Blanche said. 'Victor had a perfectly nice little place of his own but he insisted on selling up and coming here. I think it's too big.'

The house to me looked wonderfully impressive: more so in a way than St Germain House, which had the familiarity of Billingham about it.

'I don't know,' Blanche said. 'It rather reminds me of one of those unhappy houses in Dickens. Where Mr Dombey lives and everything's covered with dust-sheets. But it's not haunted by any ghostly little dogs, anyway. Jenny, where did you find her? I wanted to ask her if it was house-trained . . .'

In the hall there was a smell of whitewash, and temporary lengths of carpet that led to rooms in various stages of furnishing. The house was full of uncurtained light and cold echoes.

'This is called the breakfast-room. I don't know why one has to have a separate room to eat breakfast in, not that I've ever been able to eat breakfast anyway. I'm a zombie till half-past ten. Victor's out all day today. He's gone to play golf with somebody he wants to butter up. We'll have some tea, shall we? We've got a new housekeeper who's Lithuanian. I never met a Lithuanian person before. I wonder what Lithuania's *like*? I imagine dirndl skirts and wooden steeples but it's probably not a bit like that. Now come and sit here and tell me everything you've been doing.'

I sat with Blanche on a long settee in a window overlooking a drab garden. I had forgotten that too: the way one always sat close to the Crawthornes and never took a chair at a distance. I felt uncomfortable. I told her all I had been doing. It did not take long. Then I remembered something I should have said before.

'I was sorry to hear about your father,' I said.

Blanche nodded. 'I don't think he ever got over Tom, you know. But we had this very brisk doctor who said it's nonsense to talk like that and Father was just ill and grief doesn't make any difference. I don't know whether that's comforting or not. It's funny, I've been imagining you all this time in Billingham. We never heard anything from you and I just assumed . . . How is everything at home?'

I mentioned that my grandmother was now living with my parents, and that my mother suffered from a bad back. It cropped up increasingly in my father's letters, with hints – so careful and costive that they were barely discernible – that they were finding it a struggle to manage the shop alone.

'You haven't asked about the others,' Blanche said.

'Oh, how are they?' I said, with forced spontaneity.

'The last we heard of Ralph he was in Berlin. I don't think he's coming home. Mother never mentions him. Martin and Ursula are still living at St Germain House. Well, it's really Martin's place now, of course. He stood for Parliament last year – it was some London constituency, I can't remember which – anyway he lost. Got thumped out of sight in fact. His father-in-law says it's good experience and so on but it rings a bit hollow because he lost his seat as well. Anyway, Victor says politics is a mug's game – he has these expressions, I don't know where he gets them from – and he says Martin should forget it. They've struck up quite a friendship and Victor's handling the money that came from Father. There wasn't all that much, as it turned out, after the death duties. But Victor's making all these investments for Martin and he says they'll soon be quids in – that's another of his expressions.'

I sat there nodding. I cannot say what I was feeling, and that perhaps indicates that I was not feeling anything. I resisted: I did not want to know.

'Victor hasn't got any family. I suppose that made me feel sorry for him at the beginning. His father was killed in the war and his mother got married again and went to Argentina. The funny thing is he doesn't mind a bit. I should feel quite lost . . . Come and see the rest of the house.'

That was pure Crawthorne: Blanche was restless and could not sit long. We went over the house, Blanche throwing open doors to reveal large-ceil-inged rooms, some finished, some quite empty.

There was something curiously desultory and remote about her as she did this and she seemed to have no ideas of her own about the house. 'Victor wants to turn this into a study,' she said. 'This room's too big – Victor says we could partition it.' I found something depressing about the silence and the chill of the endless rooms that had no inhabitants and no purpose. I found myself remembering the doll's house in the playroom at St Germain House and thinking how much more interested Blanche had seemed in that.

'Jenny, you haven't told me about the man I saw you with last night. I'm nosy, I know, but I'm an old married woman, I'm allowed to be. Is it serious? Tell me about him.'

'Oh . . . he's very nice,' was all I could say. It seemed to satisfy Blanche: perhaps she took it as the tongue-tied utterance of someone deeply in love. For a moment I was angry with Blanche. I was angry because I knew then that it was not serious: that Jocelyn meant nothing. And I was angry, and profoundly bewildered, that it had merely taken one meeting with Blanche Crawthorne (as I still thought of her) to present to me this simple and undeniable fact. Everything on which I had constructed my recent life seemed threatened.

So I ate lunch with Blanche in a state of frigid formality which she appeared not to notice. She talked a great deal and though she mentioned their many friends – casually by name, as if I knew them, just as her father used to – it was as if meeting me had satisfied a desperate hunger for company.

'Do you have to go yet?' she said. 'You could stay for dinner – Victor will be home then – you could meet Victor.'

'No, really,' I said, 'thank you – I've got a lot to do.'

'Oh well, never mind.'

She looked at me, without reproach but searchingly, and I felt that she was thinking with surprise: 'Jenny's changed.' Then I thought, with a renewal of anger and alarm: of course I've changed, what's wrong with that?

My defensiveness increased as Blanche drove me home. If I had changed, it was through a process both natural and necessary. It was the Crawthornes who had made it necessary, and the last thing I wanted was to be reminded of those old times, before I had made the healing amputation from the past.

I got out of the car and began to say goodbye, and Blanche held my hand a moment with the old fondness and said: 'I haven't said half the things I wanted to say. I'm afraid I've rambled on rather – you always did let me do that. Have I stopped you getting on with something? What were you going to do today?'

'Oh! just the ironing,' I said.

'Oh, dear, I am sorry,' Blanche said; and I realised that she had probably never ironed in her life and might well conceive of it as some exacting and momentous task. I think it was this that made me soften suddenly: and this softening that made me, almost against my will, say yes when she asked me to come to a cocktail party the next week.

'Nothing fancy,' she said. 'We're just having a few friends for the evening. Come with your friend – what's his name?'

'Jocelyn.'

'Bring him. Oh, I'll look forward to that!'

Perhaps it seems strange that I was not more pleased and touched by Blanche's warm reception of me. I can only explain by referring to something that I was not fully aware of at the time – the sheer dead nothingness of the two years I had spent since leaving Billingham and the way they had left me cramped and cold and dismayingly turned in on myself. If I was starchy with Blanche it was because she, with her beauty and humour and candour, revealed to me precisely how starchy I was. I flinched from her drawing me out exactly as if it were the physical unravelling of some tortuously complex knot inside myself. And this prevented me too from wondering what the things might be that Blanche had yet to tell me.

I went with Jocelyn to Blanche's cocktail party. Jocelyn was not intimidated by the surroundings. He made much of being open to all sorts of experience. You could name any place in the world and he would be ravished at the thought of going there. I used to set myself a mental test of trying to think of something that he would not find fascinating. I gave it up in the end.

'So where did you meet this woman?' Jocelyn said.

'Oh, I used to work for her father. It was a long time ago. You'll love her,' I added.

It was frightening at Blanche's. It was not like a dance, nor like the parties of Jocelyn's friends where you could sink anonymously into a musty armchair while men held a conversation over you: there was nothing to do but talk. The guests were all youngish. The women had small bird-like heads adorned with earrings and many wore backless dresses: everywhere you looked there seemed to be flaunted vertebrae. Jocelyn met up with a young Scots doctor of the sort who misquotes Burns and was soon swapping bogus Celtic flummery with him: I found myself talking to my host.

As Blanche said, Victor Prentice did not look like John Gilbert, but he did have the look of certain Hollywood leading men: the juvenile college-boy sort, buoyant and athletic, with a grin both innocent and knowing. We talked of how I had met Blanche when working for Mr Crawthorne. 'I never knew him,' Victor said. 'I came on the scene just too late. I feel sad about that. I'm going to read that book of his as soon as I get time.'

He had a habit, probably unconscious, of glancing over your shoulder as he was speaking to you, as if looking for someone else: and when I was speaking he nodded a series of rapid, impatient nods that was rather like the ticking off of a list that he knew by heart.

'That's a wonderful house, isn't it?' he said of St Germain House. 'One could do great things with that house. It's a shame it's so run down.'

'I haven't seen it for two years,' I said.

'No?' His eyes flicked over to some new arrivals. 'Excuse me, won't you? Hope we'll be seeing a lot more of you, Jenny. Blanche was over the moon at running into you again.'

There were more and more new arrivals. The too-large rooms became crowded, and cigarette smoke blanketed everything like a Dickens fog. People called loudly to each other from room to room; no one ever seemed to be near the person they wanted to be near.

A man with an accusing ginger moustache came up to me.

'You must be Cynthia's sister,' he said.

'No,' I said.

He stared. 'Don't you know Cynthia?'

'I don't know anybody here,' I said.

'Oh!' The man went away.

I found Blanche putting a record on the gramophone: 'Dancing in the Dark', which was everywhere that year. 'Not "Someone to Watch over Me"?' I said.

'Oh! no,' Blanche said. 'I don't listen to it any more. I can't bear to somehow,' and I thought she must be thinking of Tom.

'I never showed you the conservatory the other day, did I?' she said. 'It reminds me of the one at home. I must stop saying that – this is home. Let's go and see it now.'

I went with her – accustomed again so quickly to the Crawthornes' impulsive, sudden imperatives. In the green humidity of the conservatory I was reminded, as Blanche had said, of the one at St Germain House. I thought of the way Mrs Crawthorne used to take me there on a tour of inspection, firing at me her little interrogative darts of conversation amongst the ferns and the clanking of the hot-water pipes.

Blanche sat down in a wicker chair. 'Phoo, I think I'm a bit tight,' she said. 'Will your friend be all right on his own?'

I was still thinking of St Germain House and absently I said: 'Jocelyn? Oh! yes, he'll be all right.'

I heard the tone of my voice as if someone else had spoken and immediately I knew that that tone said it all. Blanche looked up at me with a wry smile.

'He's not the one, then,' she said. 'You know.'

'No,' I said. 'No, he isn't.'

There was a sour sort of relief in acknowledging
it. I was a bit tight myself: it was a long time since
I had had a drink. Jocelyn's hikey set did not drink
much: he seemed to disapprove of it, unless it was
taken by charismatic rugby-playing hillmen, and it
made him personally, of all things, sneeze.

'Oh! it's good to get away from that crowd for a
minute,' Blanche said. 'You know, Jenny, I can't
talk to any of these people the way I can to you,
even after all this time.'

I smiled stiffly. Tight I might be, but I was still
tight in another way, tightly defensive and strained:
I saw my reflection in the conservatory glass and
not for the first time I thought that my mouth was
changed, the lips drawing inward to a small grim
bud.

Blanche did not seem to notice. She hesitated,
playing with the fronds of a fern, licking her lips in
a way that reminded me of Tom struggling to say
something important, and at last said: 'Do you ever
wish—'

But she never finished the question, for just then
Victor's cheerful face appeared at the conservatory
door. 'Blanche! Harry's just going, darling – come
and say goodbye.'

Back in the crowd I found Jocelyn still with the
Scots doctor, who was explaining something that
looked, from his copious accompanying gestures,
like the procedure for birthing sheep. Suddenly I
was cornered again by the man with the ginger
moustache, who had forgiven me for not being Cynthia's sister.

'Nice place,' he said, waving his glass around
inclusively. 'Doesn't come cheap. Do you know how
much Victor's worth?'

I said no.

'You'd be surprised,' he said with a smug smile, 'you'd be surprised if I told you – all this is just a drop in the bucket,' from which I gathered that he did not know how much Victor was worth either.

'Do you know how much he started out with?' he went on, after turning away and coming back again all in one movement.

'Tell me.'

'As a matter of fact he started out with nothing. Five thousand – that's all he started out with.'

'Five thousand isn't nothing,' I said.

The ginger man put down his drink the better to wave his hands. 'Built it all up from five thousand – that's what he did. Don't you think that's remarkable?'

'I would if he'd built it up from nothing.'

Suddenly he hunched himself to peer into my face. 'Are you a communist?'

It was like being back with my grandmother.

'Isn't that Cynthia over there?' I said, and escaped while he was turning to look.

In the next room there was a lot of laughter. Victor had got a golf club and a ball and a glass and was showing a girl how to make a putting stroke. 'Loosen up,' he said, standing behind her and holding her wrists as she gripped the handle of the club. 'You're not trying to strangle it!'

'You're making me nervous!' she squealed.

I found Blanche putting another record on the gramophone. It was 'Someone to Watch over Me'. She grimaced at me. 'For old times' sake,' she said.

Victor looked up, still with his arms encircling the girl as he held her wrists. 'Oh! not that one,' he said. 'It's maudlin. Put something cheerful on.'

Blanche did not say anything. She stood with her back to him, close to the gramophone. When the record came to an end she put it on again.

'Jenny, do you enjoy your job?' she said to me abruptly. 'Sorry – I'm sounding like Mother now – when she was opening fêtes and so on. "And what do *you* do?" '

'Does your mother still do that?'

'I think so. Though she's not quite the centre of things like she used to be – not with Ursula there. I think it puts her nose out of joint just the teeniest bit. What was I saying?'

'You asked me if I liked my job. And I was going to say – I don't dislike it.'

Blanche looked at me as if I had said something dreadfully sad. 'Oh, Jenny – what's happened to us? I feel about sixty years old.'

The *us* struck me. I hadn't said I felt old.

Blanche began to mix herself another drink and at that moment Victor came over and gently took the glass and the cocktail shaker from her hands. He poured back about half of the drink, smiling, still with the utmost gentleness. Blanche picked up the cocktail shaker and poured the drink back into her glass. She did not smile. All through this, to my fascination, their eyes did not leave each other's faces. Then Blanche took down the drink at one swallow and turned to me. 'Another one, Jenny?' she said.

I had a sense of being asked to make a choice for which I was not prepared and which I did not understand. Old loyalties moved in me, but they were tangled and ambiguous.

'I'm all right, thanks,' I said, and added with an

ungallant passing of the buck: 'I'm sure Jocelyn would like one.'

'Go and get Jocelyn a drink, Victor,' Blanche said, 'there's a dear.'

Blanche touched my arm in a 'thank you' way. I was not sure I wanted to be thanked for anything: I was not sure I wanted to be on anybody's side. I was getting out of my depth, and my recent life had been a long exercise in never leaving the shallows. Nothing I had seen had given me the impression that Blanche's married life was a contented one; but that, I decided, was her business.

I left the party soon afterwards, with Jocelyn. 'Someone to Watch over Me' was playing again on the gramophone, and just as we descended the steps from the front door I heard the scrape of the needle as it was violently lifted from the record.

Jocelyn was wearing his wide-eyed drinking-it-all-in expression. 'I met some terrifically interesting people,' he said, telling me about them in detail.

The next morning was Saturday: I immersed myself in the routine of sweeping and ironing. I was just squirelling away the ironing-board – in our cramped digs everything had to disappear into caches like in a ship's cabin – when Blanche arrived.

She looked pale and there were puffed bags under her eyes. She brought a large bunch of hothouse flowers.

'Thank you,' I said, 'I feel as if I ought to be ill!'

'Oh! I'm the one who's ill.' She sank into the armchair like a balloon deflating, and gingerly put a hand to the top of her head as if to hold it in place. 'I shouldn't drink, you know. I haven't got the head for it. Or the hollow legs. Mind you, they feel hollow now.'

'I was just going to make some lunch,' I said. 'Would you like some?'

Blanche groaned at the mention of food. Instead she drank cup after cup of strong milky tea, bathing her lips in it in dazed fashion: and after a while she was able to get up on her hollow legs and walk about the room. She stood for some time looking out of the window at the chaotic roof-scape where tom-cats held tremendous bouts through the night, and where one scarred veteran took on all comers even while being bombarded from the rear with the slippers of sleepless neighbours.

'It was pretty bloody last night, wasn't it?' she said.

'Jocelyn enjoyed it.'

'Did I do anything silly?'

'No.'

'That means I did. It doesn't matter anyway.' She raised the sash and leant out. 'I'll risk a taste of fresh air. Ugh . . . Jenny, are you happy here?'

'Well – it's the best I can afford just now,' I said. 'I'm quite lucky – it's a good place for the money really—'

'Oh! no, I don't mean this flat. I mean in London. This life. Are you happy – really happy with it?'

I shrugged. 'I don't know about *happy*,' I said. 'I don't really expect to be happy all the time – you can't expect that, can you—'

'But you know what I mean.'

I knew what she meant. I folded and refolded a slip and then dropped it.

'I don't know,' I said.

'I suppose I'm being interfering,' Blanche said. 'But here, somehow – you don't seem – you don't seem like the person I used to know.'

'Well, I'm not. You can't just stay the same all your life, after all—'

'Can't you?' Blanche said, with surprise; and I saw that for her it was not so.

I folded the slip again. All the tight complexities inside me seemed to twist inward, more confused than ever.

'I just wondered because – Well, I'm fed up with things here just now,' Blanche said. 'I was thinking of going back to Billingham for a while. Victor's got a business trip soon and – I feel I need a break.'

I think even at the time I sensed that something was being left unsaid here: that Blanche was not telling the whole truth. But I did not fully attend to it because of the slow breaking through, at last, of something clear amongst the blurred perplexities that entangled me. I remembered saying goodnight to Jocelyn last night and how we had mechanically arranged our next meeting: I remembered how I had placed it on a sort of mental calendar alongside work and shopping with Gwyneth and how for a moment I had recoiled, appalled, from the prospect. Much of my dissatisfaction proceeded from not knowing what it was I wanted; but there was relief in seeing, at last, what I did not want. Ironically, it had taken Blanche to show me that there was nothing here I wanted: ironically, when it was precisely because of the Crawthornes that I was here.

Blanche watched me closely. 'Why not come with me?' she said. 'This isn't the place for you. We could drive back together.'

'I can't do that,' I said.

'Why not?'

'There's my job. I'd have to give a week's notice.'

'Do that then. And we'll go next weekend. Load

everything in my car and be off.'

I thought of my father's letters, the difficulties with the shop and my mother's bad back. They would never go so far as to ask me to come back, I knew; they would wait for my decision.

'What will I tell Gwyneth?'

'She can easily get somebody else to share. You said yourself it's a good place for the money.'

I folded the slip again and then once again I dropped it. I screwed it up and threw it across the room, laughing for what seemed the first time in an age.

'All right,' I said. 'Let's do it.'

And so I found myself, on a cold April day, motoring back to Billingham with Blanche, with the boot and the back seat crammed with luggage, leaving nothing behind me but two dead years which had made me a stranger to myself.

There had been a last, painful meeting with Jocelyn which he had made easier for me in the end by a stout declaration that we could still be friends. There is nothing to be done for people who say that and I had come away at last without regrets. As we finally broke free of the trailing suburbs of London a pale sun began to shine on damp fields and I felt clear-headed and certain that, no matter how the decision had been forced on me, I had done the right thing.

Blanche was very cheerful. She sang under her breath in just the way that Tom used to: she remarked on every church steeple and every herd of cows as if she had not had an outing for years. Then when we stopped for some tea at an old Great North Road inn near St Neots all this faintly hysterical exhilaration seemed to leave her. She sat silent for a long time crumbling an uneaten biscuit in her fingers until at last I suggested that we ought to be getting along.

'In a minute.' Her lovely eyes, grave as a child's, fixed mine. 'There's something I haven't told you, Jenny. I should have said it before . . . I'm not going back home just for a break. I'm leaving Victor.'

I did not speak. Part of me rose up in recognition and said *I knew it*. But above all I was immediately on my guard, wary of receiving the Crawthorne confidences that had once made me so proud.

'Yes – going back to Mother. Isn't it a farce? Going back to Mother and only married a year. Why did I do it? There must be something wrong with me – with us as a family. Such a fool . . . I know I should have told you. I just couldn't face doing it alone . . . Don't be angry with me.'

'I'm not angry,' I said.

'I wouldn't blame you if you were. Everybody else is going to be.'

'I'm not. I just don't understand.'

'Oh! you would if you knew. It's just been a disaster from start to finish . . . You probably got an idea of it last week. That cocktail party.'

'Well – I don't know—'

'Come on, Jenny, you don't have to pretend to me. You saw him fooling around with that girl. The one with the snub nose. I don't know who brought her. And it's like that all the time—'

'Blanche,' I said, 'I don't think you should be telling me this.'

She looked surprised and hurt. 'But I've got to tell you. You're like a member of the family. That's why I can tell you – ordinary friends are no good – I don't really have friends anyway. You're like one of us.'

I remembered what Ralph had said about not letting the Crawthornes swallow me up. I imagined his sceptical face watching me now.

'Don't they know you're coming – at St Germain House?' I said.

'They know, but they think it's just for a short stay, while Victor's on a business trip. Which he is. But when he gets back I won't be there. And then he can console himself with his little floozies all he likes. Oh, that's what's so awful, you see, Jenny. It's so trivial. They don't mean anything. I could face it if it was something real – something dramatic.' She said this with a certain wistfulness. 'Then it wouldn't all seem so dead and pointless. But it's not. They're just little flirts, and he can't stop himself, and afterwards he's sorry. You do see, don't you? You see why I had to do something. I'd been nerving myself up to admit it for a long time – admit that the whole thing was just a pretty bloody awful mistake. And then when I met you again it gave me the jolt I needed. You do see, don't you?'

'Yes,' I said. 'But Blanche, actually leaving him . . .'

'I've got to. It's no good talking about it – we've done that. I really believe Victor doesn't think he's doing anything wrong. It's the only option.'

'What will you do?'

'I don't know. I can't think yet. It'll be better at home – I can think about it at home. Once I get there . . . Jenny, this is awful of me, but will you come into the house with me? When we get to Billingham? I'm just afraid they'll see it in my face as soon as I walk in there.'

'They've got to know some time,' I said.

'I know – I know. But if you could just help me

285

over that first hurdle. Please. They'll be so glad to see you, too, you know.'

I did not know what to say. Blanche had already drawn me in deeper than I wanted to go. I was curious about St Germain House, of course: I did not even attempt to deny that to myself. But the curiosity was set about with sharp thorns. I had schooled myself in self-preservation over the past two years and it said *do not touch*.

'Please, Jenny,' Blanche said.

'All right. But I don't see how I'll be any use.'

'Oh! of course you will. You're our lucky mascot.'

It was early afternoon when we came to Billingham, passing the brickyard chimneys and river warehouses that mark the south end of the town and then crossing the railway bridge to the road that led out to St Germain House. I could smell the familiar train smoke overlaying the earthy freshness of the surrounding miles of black fields. As we turned up the driveway to St Germain House I had again the dizzying sensation that was like walking into the wind, of being pressed back, against my will, into the past.

'Back at the old mausoleum at last,' Blanche said with forced gaiety. She looked at herself in the driving-mirror before getting out of the car. As we went in she took hold of my arm.

The great cold hall looked different but for a moment I could not work out what had changed. Then I realised that the stuffed animal heads had gone from the walls. I was still looking up in surprise when Mrs Crawthorne and Martin came forward to greet Blanche.

It was inevitable I suppose that Blanche should turn all the attention to me. Rattling away with brittle urbanity she told the story of how we had met up in London and what I had been doing there and how I had decided to come back to Billingham; and soon I found myself in the morning-room and being offered tea and loaded with kindly inquiries. To my astonishment Mrs Crawthorne kissed me. She had gone very thin. Her cheekbones had always been handsomely prominent but now the skin was stretched across them like paper on a kite. That quality about her face which I have called nakedness was painfully magnified: it was like seeing a face projected on an enormous screen.

'. . . It was such a piece of luck us meeting like that,' Blanche said. 'Jenny saw me – I didn't spot her at all and I was always supposed to be the eagle-eyed one – Tom always used to say so.'

'All our family have always had excellent eye-sight,' announced Mrs Crawthorne. 'All except Martin who's a little short-sighted – that's odd, isn't it?'

I did not know that about Martin. I thought of the way his eyes sometimes appeared blind. I glanced at him, inevitably: so far I had managed not to look at him. He had not changed. No, he had not changed.

'And how's Victor?' Mrs Crawthorne said.

'Oh! busy as ever,' Blanche said. 'Yes, very busy.'

'Did you meet Blanche's husband, Jenny?' Mrs Crawthorne said.

'Er – yes, I did,' I said. For a moment there I was lost because I had just noticed another change. The piano was gone.

As if echoing my thoughts Blanche said: 'Where's Ursula?'

'Gone into Billingham to see a dentist,' Martin said. 'She's had awful trouble with a wisdom tooth.

Shall I make a start on your luggage, Blanche? Fred's off today.'

'All right,' Blanche said. 'Mind you don't take Jenny's – all mine's labelled.'

'We've had to cut staff to the bone,' Mrs Crawthorne said to me when Martin had gone. 'Really the house is so impractical; but we can't think of selling it. I know Gerald would be terribly distressed to think of its being sold.'

I said again how sorry I was about Mr Crawthorne.

'Thank you, Jenny dear,' Mrs Crawthorne said with unnerving intensity. 'Do you know we are still receiving letters of condolence even now? From acquaintances scattered around the world, you see, from Gerald's colonial service days – often they've only just heard the news. He was such an enormously admired and distinguished man, you see. He left a great deal to be lived up to. And we can only try.'

I saw Blanche stir uncomfortably, and I thought of Mr Crawthorne's children – Tom dead, Ralph in a sort of exile and never mentioned, and Martin who had failed to get into Parliament. I began to understand Blanche's trepidation at returning home carrying the pieces of a broken marriage.

The door opened again and Martin said, 'Blanche, how long did you say you were staying? There's enough stuff here to kit out an army. Did you leave any behind?'

'Oh! you know what I'm like,' Blanche said. 'Can't bear to wear the same thing twice – always have to . . . you know . . .'

'Blanche, whatever's the matter?' said Mrs Crawthorne who, typically, missed nothing.

I saw all the determined brightness of Blanche's face dissolve. 'I'm sorry,' she said, in tears, 'I can't talk about it just now . . .'

She ran out of the room. Mrs Crawthorne rose, bony and glowing, and with martyred dignity said, 'Excuse me, won't you, Jenny? I do apologise for this.'

She followed Blanche and I was left with Martin.

'Don't say she's left him,' he said.

I nodded.

'Is it serious?'

'I don't know . . .' I did not like this. The wind had blown me too far back: I might never have been away. It was too intimate and I wanted out. 'I don't know anything about it and it's really none of my business,' I said.

'No. Sorry.'

'I ought to be getting home.' I rose. 'Will you thank Blanche for bringing me?'

'You're not walking home,' Martin said.

'It's all right—'

'But there's your luggage.' As he said this there was a hint of the old gentle teasing on his face. I had forgotten the luggage.

He picked up Blanche's keys. 'I'll drive you,' he said.

And so I was driven home by Martin – the last thing I would have wanted. Desperate to find a neutral topic, I asked about the scaffolding I had seen on the roof of St Germain House, and he told me about the repairs they were having done.

'It's really a question of limiting the damage,' he said. 'We've closed up the top floor altogether.'

'Where's the piano?' I said, before I could stop myself.

'We got rid of it. Ursula's been doing a lot of redecoration, and it was rather a battered old thing . . .'

I knew then that there could be no neutral topics between us. My mind roamed from Ursula to the piano, from Martin's failure to get into Parliament to Victor Prentice and the money that was running out; and I found I could speak of none of these things to him. The thorns bristled.

Then as we drew up outside the shop, in my old street, Martin said: 'Can I ask you – does Victor know Blanche has left?'

'No.'

Martin sighed. 'Hell,' he said, 'what a mess.'

I was not, perhaps, quite so firmly back in the past as I thought: otherwise I would have remembered the way the Crawthornes spoke and felt almost as one person, and realised that Martin was not referring only to Blanche when he said that.

TWO

The spring seemed slow in coming and I moved restlessly through a succession of steel-grey days and cold evenings, helping in my father's shop. He had sold his horse and cart by now and often I ran errands on an old sit-up-and-beg bicycle that we kept in the yard behind the wash-house. Sometimes I made deliveries to genteel villas in the tree-lined streets near the park, to old ladies who could no longer afford to buy from the select shops in the town centre but would not admit it. They would make a great thing of coming to the door themselves, as if it happened to be the between-maid's day off, and there was a sour smell of camphor and old clothes and soup from the parqueted halls.

Billingham was a place where few people had been really rich and many had been just above poor, where industry had come in a late rush to impose itself on an East Anglian town of hitherto modest dimensions, and the impact of the slump was perhaps the more profound because people had never thought of it as the sort of place where there would be distress. My father spoke with pained delicacy of neighbours of ours where the man of the household was 'not working at the moment'. People ran up long tick bills, and sometimes at night as he was doing the books and these fairly covered the table-cloth I heard him sigh, while my grandmother with her little shins toasting at the fire advised him to fetch the bobbies in to the lot of them. While the nights were still cold men could often be seen making long bicycle trips out to the country to bring back bundles of such kindling as Billingham's sparsely wooded hinterland afforded; and sometimes after dusk you could smell the wood-smoke, thin and acrid where it was not drawing well. In the gardens and about the cemetery and the park everything was late, and hemmed in by drabness I longed for the sight of new leaves and grass. It was because of this that I agreed to go out for drives in the countryside with Blanche.

That spring I felt cramped and aridly complicated in my mind. I had left the emptiness of my London life but I was still locked in sterile perplexities that made me seem, as Blanche had said, a much older person. A couple of letters from Jocelyn informed me that I was all take and no give and in the short interval between opening them and throwing them in the bin I acknowledged that. Not only did I shun giving but I felt quite simply that I had nothing to give. The one thing I was sure of was that I did not want to be drawn in again by the Crawthornes; but neither did I know what it was that I did want.

And so when Blanche began to turn up at the shop in her car, inviting me to come out, the hackles of my insistent caution rose. I went with her because of the pull of the countryside as spring began to break out at last, and because it was impossible to resist the Crawthornes once they asked you and asked you long enough with that peculiar charm that seemed to lurk, excited and confidential, in their musical voices.

I remembered Mr Crawthorne once joking to me about his urge to travel and how it had come out in his children as an inability to be in one place for five minutes at a time: and that was very true of Blanche that spring. Even when I was not with her she was forever going off on long and apparently pointless jaunts to this place and that.

'I motored over to King's Lynn yesterday,' she would say, or: 'I ended up quite lost this weekend – got up to Lincolnshire, I don't know quite where. Just these miles of fen and I couldn't find a single person to ask for directions.'

Then she began to bring a picnic basket and it seemed that in some way she was trying to re-create the times when I had been working for her father and she and the others would swoop down on me at lunch-time and bear me off for picnics.

'The Nine Bridges!' she said. 'We came here once – Tom and Ralph went swimming – and you and Martin caught those little fish – do you remember?'

I remembered: and if I could not share her enthusiasm it was because I did not want to remember. There was something, too, a little strained and forced about Blanche's gaiety on these expeditions. She would bring the gramophone and jig about on her own to the music almost like some parody of the flapper of a few years ago; or she would challenge me to running races across water-meadows, where the new green was like the nap of baize. Not once did she mention Victor and only gradually did I come to realise that this revealed more of what she was thinking than if she had talked of nothing else.

Then she wanted me to go to dances with her. I put her off a couple of times before giving in and going with her to a rackety sort of roadhouse, off the main road down the valley, where a band played watered-down jazz in an upstairs room whilst young men made cautious bets over billiards in the room below. I did not fancy going again and I said so.

'Oh! all right then,' Blanche said quite lightly.

Then when we were driving back into Billingham an unlit bicycle swerved in front of us and we nearly hit it. It made me think of Tom and the way he had died and I began to be uneasy about leaving Blanche alone in this mood. And then as we pulled up in my street Blanche said, 'We needn't go there again, you know. We could find somewhere else.'

For a moment I did not speak and Blanche, with a sudden naked appeal in her voice, said, 'Jenny, don't back out on me. I need you.'

'What about Martin and Ursula?' I said.

'Oh well – it's no use asking them,' she said, 'they're an old married couple now,' and all at once I felt I understood as I had not before. In her hungry pursuit of diversion Blanche was seeking to deny the very fact of her marriage. I had been unnerved by the sensation of being pressed back into the past but that was the very process she wished for.

And so I agreed to accompany her again and we went to a very formal and correct hotel dance where a young man with a pencil moustache attempted to monopolise us and came out with such a string of malapropisms that neither of us could keep a straight face. 'My feelings are ambidextrous about that one,' he said. 'But I hate it when people won't diverge any sort of opinion on anything, don't you? No enthusiasm. Legarthic sort of people.'

There was something even more frenzied and hectic about Blanche's gaiety that night and it was only later, as we sat out in a quiet annexe room, that I learned why.

'Victor came up,' she said. 'To sort things out and get things straight – that's another of his phrases. Poor man, he thought it would only take a few apologies – a few cries of "I need you" and so on – and I'd be back with him like a shot. I told him it's no good. We're better apart. He knows now. I'm not going back to him and that's that.'

'What will you do?'

'Stay at St Germain House. Victor won't discuss formal separation yet – he still thinks he can get me back. Mother's being motherly, bless her, and Martin's happy to have me around. Of course there's Ursula – but I shall have to put up with that.'

'What about Ursula?'

'We don't really get on. Oh, she's a nice enough person. We'd get on perfectly if she wasn't married to Martin. But she nags at him so. Not exactly nags – she just always expects too much of him.' All the instinctive Crawthorne solidarity was in her words. 'She makes him feel like a failure. I think she loves him but she doesn't understand him. I almost think she wants him to be like Victor – very businesslike and practical. Martin should have married someone who understood him, don't you think?'

'Let's try one of those ices,' I said.

In the late surge of spring I went often with Blanche out to the country, gorging my senses on greening corn and hawthorns splashed with milky blossom, and hunting the copses, on upland to the west, for bluebells and lily of the valley. But I avoided going to St Germain House, making excuses if she asked me to drop in and say hello to the others. It was when we were returning from one of these drives one Saturday in May that Blanche stopped to get petrol at a small garage at Newburn, on the main road on the northern edge of the town.

Newburn had already been incorporated into the municipal borough of Billingham, but in those days it was still very much a village: there were several one-storey thatched cottages dating back two hundred years and the surrounding pasture, on the edge of fen, was farmed by Billingham's main dairy. The only signs of things to come were the motor traffic on the road and the garage itself.

There was a single petrol pump in the front yard. The house was a slate-roofed brick box: in the typical fen way, there were more outhouses than house proper. As we drew up at the pump I could see, at the back, something like a long cow-shed open at one end filled with old scrap cars and beyond that more sheds amongst a few scrubby, sterile apple-trees. Hens ran about the oil-spattered forecourt like panicked Keystone Cops as Blanche sounded the horn. Something about the rusting jumble in conjunction with the hens struck me as familiar and so in a curious way I was not surprised at all when Robert Snowden came hurrying round from the back yard, wiping his oily hands on a rag.

He said good morning and went to the petrol pump and only then did he see me.

'Hello,' I said. 'It's been a long time.'

'I didn't know you were back,' Robert said. He stood there grasping the handle of the pump and staring at me.

'I haven't been back long,' I said. 'How are you?'

'I'm very well,' he said, 'thank you,' and he seemed so startled that he did not ask me how I was.

'You work here?' I asked, stupidly I suppose; but Robert smiled and with a sort of mixed awkwardness and pride said, 'Yes – well, I live here. It's my place.'

'Oh! I didn't know.'

He stood there at the pump, not moving, for some moments longer, and then I said, 'Blanche, you remember Robert, don't you? Robert Snowden,' and I saw that she had not recognised him at first.

'Of course, hello – you used to keep the farm – and Tom always said you should go into cars.'

'That's right,' Robert said, and the sight of Blanche seemed to wake him and he began to fill the tank.

I had heard, from my parents, that the Snowdens had left the old farm and moved east across the fen to where Mrs Snowden had family. I said: 'Do you live here all alone?'

'Just me and the hens,' he said. 'I've only been here three months. That's why it's still a bit of a mess.'

That seemed to me quite an understatement. Blanche paid Robert and he went into the front room of the house, which had been knocked into an office, to get change. One of the hens ran in after him. Through the dirty window, hung about with bright sheet-metal advertisements for tyres and oil and a rusty tin Michelin road-map, I saw him groping for a cash-box amongst piles of papers and Blanche said, 'Dear God, imagine living here all on your own. He must have a heart like a lion.'

'Yes,' I said; but in fact the prospect did not appal me as it did Blanche. There was something rather compelling in the idea of taking on such an isolated barnyard of a place and something very typical of Robert about it too.

Robert came back with Blanche's change, and as I saw him fruitlessly wiping and rewiping his oiled hands before passing it to her I remembered the way he had seemed to be dazzled and immobilised when confronted with Blanche's beauty. Blanche started the engine and I said, 'I suppose you're in a good position here for passing traffic.'

'I reckon it's just about the best position in Billingham,' Robert said. 'I was lucky to get it,' and again a modest pride seemed to shine out from his face, lighting up the dark fixed eyes above their smudges of perspiration. And as we said goodbye and drove away I thought that there, at least, was a person who knew just what he wanted.

That evening I told my mother about meeting Robert at the garage at Newburn.

'I hope he looks after himself,' she said. 'I'll bet he doesn't eat properly. All on his own like that. You can never trust a man to eat properly in that situation.' The thought of incomplete domesticity was disturbing to her and soon she was hunting about in the pantry for what we could spare and then rolling out pastry on the kitchen table. 'I dread to think what his kitchen must be like,' she said. 'I'll bet his mother would have a fit.' And so the next morning, in spite of my grandmother, who like a pocket Cassandra was declaring that people these days were always expecting something for nothing and the world had gone mad, I bicycled over to Newburn with a basket of pies and sausage rolls and a great wedge of my mother's highly sustaining Dundee cake.

It was a beautiful clear May morning, the air fretted with the sound of Billingham's many church bells. Where the main road ran through the village there were horse-chestnuts, richly in blossom, and I could smell the ripeness too of a long grass-field up behind the garage. There was no answer to my knock and I went round to the back yard. A big tom-cat watched me from the peak of a rusting crag of scrap as I peered into the sheds and then I saw a pair of legs sticking out from under a car. I was rather afraid of making Robert jump and knock his head on the underside of the chassis: I stopped at a distance and then stooped down, calling his name.

I saw the muscles of his thighs tauten as he pulled himself lithely out from under the car. Above the waist he was wearing only a singlet and I remembered, in a flash of sharp unpleasantness, that last time at the farm, the shouting at John and the blood dripping on the floor. Then all at once that was dispelled as Robert smiled and stood up.

'Hullo again,' he said, and looked at his grimed hands. 'Sorry – I don't get to shake hands with anybody nowadays.'

'I knocked at the house,' I said. 'My mother's been doing some baking and she sends her best and wondered if you'd like these – she knows how busy you must be.'

I think I phrased it in this way because of an image I had of Robert as a somewhat prickly and touchy person and through some hazy idea of his taking against 'charity'. But as he looked into the basket he gave a low whistle of appreciation.

'Real food,' he said. 'I've forgotten what that smells like. Do thank her for me, won't you? I've been meaning to go over and say hello some day but I just don't seem to get time.'

'Be careful of the apple turnovers,' I said. 'I made those.'

'Apple turnovers too. I shall eat myself silly.'

'You're working on a Sunday?' I said.

'Oh, just tinkering. I'll probably have a sit-down

this afternoon. Look, are you in a hurry? I mean, would you like to have a look round the place?'

'I'd love to,' I said.

'Of course there isn't much to see,' he said, but again his dark face seemed to flush upwards with pride. 'It'll be better when I get things sorted out. Just let me go and get a shirt on . . .'

The long open outhouse had once been, as I had thought, a cowshed; and one of the other sheds had been a stable. Part of the yard was still cobbled. Crazy sheets of corrugated-iron and lengths of gas-tarred timber alternated with patches of mossy lime-stone wall, and altogether there was a peculiar min-gling of farmyard and automobile, meeting not unpleasantly in a single odour made up of petrol and straw, of axle-grease and old dung.

'The place was empty for a long time,' Robert said. 'The chap who started it up as a garage developed TB and had to go into the sanatorium at Cawley. It's leased from the old lady who lives in that place up there – ' he pointed up the grass-field to a redbrick farmhouse in the distance – 'and she let me have it on easier terms, what with it being half derelict, and the slump as well. She's a nice old stick. I'd been looking for something like it since we sold up the farm. We had to: I know Dad would have hated it, but it was hopeless. Mum's living with her sister over Wisbech way – her sister does market-gardening. The two of 'em are making a good thing of it now. Mum always said it takes a woman to drive a hard bargain and folk say the pair of 'em together are unstoppable. I'd like to see a buyer cheat *them*.'

'What about John?'

'He went and got work in London. It suits him

better. I get a postcard from him now and then. We get on all right once we're away from each other,' he added with a certain grimness.

'And Margaret miles away,' I said. 'Things always seemed so secure at the farm – I'd never have believed it could all break up like this.'

'Oh well, you can't stick at the same thing for ever.' With a certain shortness that I recognised now as shyness he said, 'How'd you get on in London then?'

'All right,' I said. 'But I realised it just wasn't for me, in the end.'

Robert was silent a moment.

'I always thought that,' he said.

Behind the last shed was the hen-coop and beyond that a stretch of garden, bordered by the sparse apple-trees and fenced off at the end by a hawthorn hedge marking the boundary of the field.

'I'm going to dig this over when I get time,' Robert said. 'Grow cabbages and lettuces – perhaps a few spuds.'

'Thought you'd finished with farming,' I said; but I smiled, not wanting him to think I was mocking him.

'I have,' he said, smiling too. 'I've found what I want to do.'

He took me into the house, talking of how he hoped to make a living. 'There's the petrol – I could do with another pump really. You get no end of cars coming through: folk in the village complain about the traffic. Second-hand dealing – there's plenty of space for that. Course, I've got to get my name known as a mechanic. I did two years at night school getting qualified, but you've got to get people to come to you and then recommend you to other people. And then some time I'd like to do hire cars as well – but that will have to wait.'

Inside the house smelt musty and Robert put up absent patting fingers to the wallpaper where little spiral peelings curled down from patches of dampness. 'I keep meaning to strip all this. Perhaps just do it over with whitewash – like we had it at home. When I get time . . .'

In the dingy passage I stopped as I saw the old barometer that Robert had once bought hanging on the wall. 'Oh! I remember that,' I said.

'Chap offered me twelve pounds for that. But I wouldn't take it.'

Behind the front office there was a tiny sitting-room and then a kitchen-scullery and wash-house. The sitting-room contained a slate fireplace, two ancient armchairs, a framed picture of Queen Victoria's Diamond Jubilee, and an aspidistra like a monstrous spider. The centre of the kitchen-scullery was a deal table covered with dog-eared motoring periodicals: in the sink there was a toppling landslide of unwashed crockery. The wash-house had a copper and a great cast-iron mangle like a medieval rack. Upstairs only Robert's bedroom was furnished, and there was no light. 'I've made do with candles upstairs so far,' he said as we negotiated the narrow staircase down again. 'But the days are getting long now – it'll be light till ten soon so that won't matter.' Everywhere there were little pieces of the innards of cars, as if the yard outside, like a creeping jungle, were slowly infiltrating the house.

'Sorry about the mess. I keep meaning to have a good clear-out,' Robert said, and for the third or fourth time he added: 'When I get time.'

He was insistent that I should have some tea,

though it was no easy matter to find clean cups or, indeed, the teapot. We drank the tea at last sitting at the deal table, while one of the hens pecked around the threshold of the back door, watching us.

'That's Henrietta,' Robert said. 'She's a real old matriarch. The old girl up at the house gave her to me.'

'What about that cat in the yard – is that yours?'

'Oh! he adopted me, really. He comes in when it suits him. I haven't got a name for him – he doesn't look as if he wants one.'

He lifted the teapot and saw that it had leaked, leaving a stained ring on the table. 'I must give this a scrub some time,' he said. Then for the first time a shade of doubt crossed his face and he said, 'I suppose it all looks a bit of a shambles, doesn't it?'

'You'll soon get it sorted out,' I said. It was a shambles, but there was something hopeful about it. I thought of my digs in London and how I had prettified them and how, after all, it had meant nothing. I saw a sort of integrity in Robert's solitary exertions here, forging his own life, that I admired at the same time as it sharpened my own dissatisfaction.

The office, which he showed me last, was slightly more tidy. 'People see this,' he said. 'You've got to make a good impression.' There were pigeon-holes behind the desk and some sort of effort at order but still the paperwork was in confusion. Bulldog clips chomped at unsorted wedges of bills and invoices and cheques.

'Mum always did the books at the farm,' Robert said, dubiously handling his account-books. 'I've been taking one of these correspondence courses.

I'm getting on gradually.'

I said, 'I could do that for you. I've done book-keeping. I could sort out your accounts for you.'

'Oh no! I couldn't put you to that trouble. It looks like a big job.'

I felt the continued presence of a layer of mistrust between us as Robert shook his head and put the books back and said, 'No, no, I can manage.'

'Really,' I said, 'I'd like to. I have plenty of free time. I could just set the books straight while you're so busy. I'd be glad to do that.'

'Well . . . If you really wouldn't mind.'

I could see that he had embraced his industrious solitude and that just for a moment he had feared losing even a little of it. Then he looked at his books again and laughed. 'I must admit I've been having a bit of a struggle with these,' he said. 'Thank you.'

So the following week, whenever my father did not need me in the shop, I cycled out to the garage and began to put Robert's accounts in order. I told him I did not want to get in his way and I worked at the desk in the office, by the dim light of the smeared window, beneath an old calendar with art-deco advertisements of speeding sports cars. Inevitably in combing through the haphazard files I had to go sometimes to Robert to ask him about things and I began to take him cups of tea at the same time and soon I did not worry about being in the way. I found that he liked to have someone there. We would stand and drink our tea amongst the apple trees and Robert would talk of his plans for the garden. We would put milk down for the cat and I would go in search of the small, warm white eggs laid by the hens while Robert perched on the bonnet of one of his scrap cars, his hand inky-black against the white mug of tea. We talked about Margaret and Bill and about places we remembered around the farm and presently, for the first time, we began to be friends.

When I had the accounts up to date I tidied the office, though I was careful to ask Robert first; and then, without having to ask, I began to turn up at any time to help with the house. I brought odds and ends of food from my mother and sometimes, when I asked Robert what he had had to eat lately and he answered vaguely that he had had something last night, I would cook a meal for him on the old range.

'I don't think my mother would approve of this,' he said, as he ate eggs and bacon and mushrooms that I had picked behind the house early that morning. 'She'd say trust a man to find someone to wait on him.'

'Oh! you needn't think I shall make a habit of this,' I said, with mock severity; and again for the first time, we laughed together.

It was in the everyday experience of working side by side that the old coolness there had been between us disappeared. In all our past association we had somehow always begun to grate against each other, progressively, in frozen misunderstandings. Now I felt that I began to understand Robert. The intense solitariness that had baffled me before I now saw to be germane to him; the difficult unyielding manner to be natural to someone who spent much time in a world of his own. With the house, the books, the cars, the hens, and the garden, and all the absorbing business of the life Robert was building for himself, there was no need for us to refer to the past. The simple matters of work were enough and this in turn relaxed me, so that I felt the slow disentangling of the perplexed coils of feeling that had made me so restless and without contentment.

The June weather was warm and bright and I remember how we had the doors of the house always open when I made a start on cleaning the inside. I put on a spare overall of Robert's and scraped off the peeling wallpaper and washed down the walls and then took up the sitting-room carpet and beat it on the line outside. The carpet was filthy and great clouds of dust went up until it looked as if we were having a bonfire. I was completely coated with it. When Robert saw me he gave a shout of laughter.

'You look like a Kentucky Minstrel,' he said; and he brought a car wing-mirror to show me my blackened face, with white eyes and teeth.

'I've never been so dirty,' I said, and I laughed too. 'And I don't care.'

When the walls were clean I began to paint them with whitewash that Robert fetched from town in an ancient, battered and clapped-out Sunbeam, like a decayed aristocrat, that he ran about in. I kidded him about that Sunbeam.

'Garage-owner,' I said, 'expert mechanic – and look what he drives.'

'Oh! You know what they say – the cobbler's children always go without shoes,' he said.

But I was careful not to kid him too much in case the hard suspicious look should close over his eyes as it used to: I remembered the times when I had preened myself on what I saw as my elevation to the rarefied world of the Crawthornes, how vain I had been and how this had brought out all the chafing hostility between us.

When the walls were painted the sitting-room looked bigger. I washed the oil-stained antimacassars from the armchairs and cleaned the sooty fireplace and took down the picture of Queen Victoria's Diamond Jubilee, which Robert said made him feel miserable.

'My grandfather used to have a picture of Mr Gladstone in his front parlour,' I said. 'I always used to think he was watching me.'

'Probably was,' Robert said. 'Old Glad-Eye they used to call him.'

In the attic I found a framed mirror, slightly foxed with damp, and I polished it up and hung it where the picture had been.

'Now you can see yourself for a change,' I said, and Robert looked at himself in the mirror with a genuine surprise, scraping his hand across his strong black stubble. 'I shall have to smarten myself up some time,' he said. 'I can't remember when I last had a tie on.'

But it was part of the pleasure of those days that neither of us felt the need, as it were, to have a tie on. I liked the informality of going there at any old time, sometimes in the early evening when through the open doors came the summer sweetness of the hayfield, ready for cutting, and of honeysuckle that grew in loose unchecked fans by the water-butt. Often Robert would still be in the workshop: I would hear the clank of his wrench and call out hello and go and feed the hens, seeing them come like hurrying fat ladies as the corn rattled into the enamel bowl. I learnt too how to work the petrol-pump, and sometimes when Robert had to go out for a while I would mind the place for him, sitting on a bench outside the front door and listening for the unmistakable exhaust-coughs of his clapped-out Sunbeam.

One Sunday my father came over to look round the garage. 'Jenny did this,' Robert said, as he showed him over the house, 'oh – Jenny did that too,' and soon a sort of awkwardness and formality came over him and he said: 'I keep forgetting to thank her for it all.' And I was glad when at last my father left because somehow I did not want to be thanked: Robert had never thanked me before and it seemed cold and inappropriate to what I had begun to see as a rough partnership, without fixed roles.

Throughout this time I still saw Blanche quite often. She continued to drive about the country as if in some frantic quest for the happy days before her marriage and, when I was not at the garage, to descend on me and carry me off with her. Then one day I was in the office going over the week's bills when I saw Blanche's sleek white car draw up outside.

'Your father said you were here,' she said when I went out to her. 'My goodness, you look well.'

'I feel well,' I said, and I told her how I had been helping Robert get settled in.

'That reminds me,' she said, 'I think I might have found a customer for your friend. Is he here?'

Robert came round from the yard just then, and Blanche said, 'Mr Snowden, hello – I was just telling Jenny I think I've got you a customer. A friend happened to mention to me the other day that he couldn't get a decent car mechanic in Billingham – he said he'd been to Watson's and they were swindlers. So I told him about you. I fibbed and said you'd fixed my car in no time for a very reasonable price – and then of course he asked me what had been wrong with the car, which served me right.'

She laughed. 'I think I mumbled something about gaskets.'

Robert, after a moment, laughed too. 'Well, thank you very much,' he said. Just for that moment he had looked transfixed and baffled and I recalled my own bafflement, when I had first met the Crawthornes, at the way they enfolded you with sudden intimacy, including you.

'It's a pity you haven't got a sign,' Blanche said. 'Then it would catch people's eye as they drive past.'

'I keep meaning to get a sign,' Robert said. 'That's another thing I must remember.'

We showed Blanche around the garage. She stepped nimbly between pools of oil, an incongruous figure amongst all that rust and scrap and the great clutching weeds where the tom-cat hid. She was fascinated and she wanted to see all of it.

'Tom would have loved this,' she said once. 'He would have been in his element.'

She saw over the house too, and was far more interested, I noticed, than she had been in the grandly echoing rooms of her own house in Bayswater.

'It must be very satisfying,' she said. 'Doing everything yourself. That's rich coming from me – I've never done anything. Well, you've both made me feel more thoroughly useless than ever.' She pulled on her gloves. 'There's one thing I can do to help though – I can drum up some more custom for you. I see no end of people who drive and I'll tell them all. I'll be a sort of human circular.'

'Thank you very much,' Robert said. Again a sort of self-imposed stiffness immobilised him. 'I'll have to see about that sign.'

It was not until later that Robert referred to Blanche. We had begun to paint the kitchen ceiling and he was on the stepladder while I was washing brushes in the sink.

'That was – very nice of your friend earlier,' he said slowly. 'You know – recommending me to someone.'

'Yes,' I said. Privately I had my doubts whether anything would come of that: I did not doubt Blanche's sincerity but I knew too well how good the Crawthornes were at saying what pleased.

'Didn't you say she was married?' Robert said after a pause.

'Yes.' I told him, briefly, about the circumstances of Blanche's return to St Germain House: there was no point in making a secret of it. I was brief because I did not want to think about all that. It had no place here: it was a twist of complication where everything was pleasantly uncomplicated and straightforward and easy. It raised the ghost of all the hostility and resentment there had been between Robert and myself, when I had been so proudly, blindly absorbed by the Crawthornes that I could hardly see him or anything else. I was sure that he was thinking of these things, and sure enough he said, after another pause: 'You used to be very thick with them at one time.'

I finished washing the brushes. Henrietta was dithering on the threshold of the back door and I went to shoo her away and then stood there a moment breathing in the soft summer air. The hay had just been cut and warm waves of its scent beat on the breeze and with the same gentle beating came the call of a ring-dove from the trees below the garden.

'I just happened to meet up with Blanche again,' I said. 'I don't have much to do with them any more.'

'No?' Robert put down his brush and stared at the ceiling for a long time. 'She makes me feel like a bit of a clod. Sort of clumsy. You know?'

I nodded. In fact Robert, for a big-boned and rangy man, was not at all clumsy. But I knew what he meant: the feeling, when you were next to Blanche, that you were altogether too bulky and earth-bound.

'Still,' he said, 'it was nice of her to mention me.'

Again I did not think anything would come of that but I was proved wrong the very next day when a man brought in a Wolseley to be serviced, telling Robert that Mrs Blanche Prentice had recommended him. The man stood talking to Robert for some time on the forecourt. 'Good luck to you,' he said. 'We need a decent garage at this end of town.'

The Wolseley was a handsome affair that seemed to lift its big patrician nose at the disembowelled bangers in the yard.

'That's a car,' Robert said. 'That's something like.'

'You'll have one like that some day,' I said.

'Oh, steady on!' he said. He laughed. 'I've got to keep my feet on the ground, you know.'

He took the Wolseley for a test drive round the village and he invited me to ride in the back. 'Go on,' he said. 'You can pretend I'm your chauffeur.' He put on an old peaked army cap that he had found in the attic and a stiff collar and a pair of heavy leather driving gloves and I sat in the back waving grandly to some of the village children playing by the pond.

'Where to now, m'lady?'

'Oh! home now, Snowden. I'm having the bishop for tea.'

'Makes a change from crumpets.'

Amongst all this pleasant nonsense I was struck, probably because of seeing Robert in unfamiliar clothes, by a memory of meeting him at the Agricultural Show when he had been a steward. I thought of him as he was then and I said, looking at the short soft hairs at the nape of his neck: 'I never thought I'd ever be ordering you around.'

'Why not?'

'Oh . . . I used to be a bit intimidated by you, I suppose.'

'Me?' He flung his head round in surprise, his eyes meeting mine, so that for a moment he was driving blind, and then turned back to the road. 'Not half as frightened as I was of you.'

We did not say anything more about that; but somehow it seemed we did not need to and I felt, half with pleasure and half with a refiring of my old defensive unease, that some fundamental point had been cleared up between us.

Soon after Robert had done the job on the Wolseley, Blanche began to call at the garage often: it seemed to become a focus for her restlessness, appropriately enough as she spent so much time in the white car with the coffee-coloured plush that gave it the look of some luxurious piece of confectionery. All the minutiae of making a living were new to her and she had something of the delighted curiosity of a child with a toy shopkeeping set.

'You need to keep all the receipts for your expenses,' I explained to her in the office, 'for when you make up your tax returns.'

'I always wondered what people did with receipts,' she said. She had a way, very droll and engaging, of coming out with the most innocent questions in a tone of perfect gravity.

'What do the laundry say when they have to deal with these?' she said, indicating Robert's oil-stained overalls; and I had to explain to her that Robert did his own washing in the copper.

It was not long before another acquaintance of Blanche's brought his car in for service. Robert was very grateful to her for helping him get custom and it was his gratitude that began to break down his shyness of her. He still seemed to find something perennially startling about her: her beauty, so diametrically opposed in its bright delicacy to his own sinewy darkness, seemed to afflict him with a sense of unreality, his eyes glazing as if they had looked upon the mermaid or the unicorn. But the vital warmth that sang out of her, so appealing and direct, inevitably put him at his ease too. And it was because of this gratitude that he accepted when Blanche invited the two of us to St Germain House one evening.

'Martin and Ursula are having people round for drinks,' she said, 'so I thought why not ask my special friends too? You need a break after all the work you've put in – both of you. We'll open up the terrace. It's been re-paved at last – Ursula's idea.'

'I didn't know what to say at first,' Robert said to me later. 'It doesn't sound like my sort of thing. But she's been so kind, it would have looked bad to refuse. I shall have to put a tie on at last. It won't be any more formal than that, will it?'

'Oh no!' I said. 'They're not like that.'

'Drinks on a terrace, eh?' he said with amiable wonder. 'It's like something on the films.'

As Robert said, it would have looked bad to refuse; but I was not easy about it. The mention of the terrace raised memories that I wanted to shun.

With Robert and the garage I had found a sort of equilibrium: our work together through those summer days seemed to soothe the chafing and gnawing that had made me tiresome to myself. Now Blanche disrupted that equilibrium. It was not possible to feel resentful of her, but I did feel myself tightening again, withdrawing behind a defensive screen, as Robert and I drove to St Germain House in the clattering Sunbeam.

'I don't know,' Robert said as we passed between the gateposts. 'I'm afraid I'm going to feel terribly out of place.'

'You'll be all right,' I said, with a casualness I did not feel.

'Oh! it's all right for you,' he said. 'You've done all this before,' and in those words there chimed a strained and unhappy note between us that had not been there for a long time.

But it was typical of the Crawthornes that there was no question of anyone being made to feel out of place. There were perhaps a dozen people there besides ourselves; but from Mrs Crawthorne and Blanche and Martin and from Ursula too there came that familiar, bemusing impression that you were the one person above all they wanted to see. For some time Mrs Crawthorne took possession of Robert and I heard her, like a bony inquisitor, pumping him about the garage just as she used to pump me. It was as if, with the ebbing of the flesh from her body, that pulsing curiosity came more nakedly to the surface.

It was quite early on in the evening when I noticed that Ursula, very elegant in a black chiffon and lace evening dress, seemed to take two drinks to everybody else's one. It did not seem to affect her – except that her voice, always clear and superbly confident, became louder until it could be heard all over the room.

Someone spoke of the re-paving of the terrace and Ursula, sitting on the sofa beside Blanche, said: 'Of course that's only a start. All the grounds at the back of the house need clearing. From behind the tennis-court to the park gate it's just a wilderness.'

'But there are some wonderful old trees there,' Blanche said. 'It would be a shame to get rid of them.'

'Oh! I don't mean chop everything down. Just thin it where it's overgrown. I say we ought to make a start now, while the weather's good, but I can't get Martin to agree.'

'It's the question of money,' Martin said. 'The roof and the terrace have already set us back this year.'

'Oh, there's money, of course there's money. Victor's doing wonders with it – telephone Victor and see. Well, what's wrong?' she said, aware of patches of silence around her. 'Surely we can still mention Victor's name, can't we? Blanche is still married to him. You don't expect me to pretend he doesn't exist, do you, Blanche?'

'That would be silly,' Blanche said, with the tensest of smiles.

'We don't have to worry about money with Victor in charge,' Ursula said. 'Look how he made his own fortune – and what is he, just past thirty?'

'The slump's made things more difficult for everyone,' Martin said.

'It's people like Victor we need to get us out of the slump. You either give in to the slump or fight it.' Ursula's voice rose above all the others. 'I'd rather be a fighter.'

A curious thought occurred to me, hearing Ursula

talk of Victor, hearing Blanche defend the old shabby jungle of the grounds. It was that a stranger, knowing nothing of these people, might well assume that Victor and Ursula were a couple and likewise Martin and Blanche. At that moment all the correspondences and empathies seemed to point in that direction. And in the same moment I was struck by the way Martin was looking at his wife. If the look was certainly not fond then neither was it irritated or impatient. It was, in the most alarming way, neutral. It was as if they were nothing more than fellow guests: you could almost imagine him, later, remarking on this very pretty, rather insistent woman he met at a party.

I was disturbed by these thoughts. I had several drinks but without effect: a sort of cold wakefulness suspended me. Soon afterwards people began to drift out to the lamplit terrace and there I found myself in a group with Martin and Ursula and Blanche and Robert, who was nursing a weak whisky. Blanche was full of talk about the garage.

'Jenny's been helping with the renovation – you ought to see it. They've done such an amazing job on the house. I'll tell you what, though – I was doing my publicity bit the other day and someone said they'd never noticed the garage was there. It's because from the outside there's nothing really to show, except the petrol pump.'

'It'll be better when I get a sign,' Robert said.

'Yes, that will help. But have you thought of doing anything with the frontage? I mean the forecourt's just a patch of earth at the moment.'

'It does want smartening up,' Robert said. 'In time—'

'I've just thought of something,' she said. 'Martin,

have we still got those old stone tubs? The ones that were on the terrace.'

'They're down by the gardener's shed, I think,' Martin said.

'You don't need them, do you, Martin? I was just thinking how nice they'd look on the garage forecourt. You could line them along the drive – perhaps plant them with miniature shrubs – it would attract attention and signal people to turn off. Martin, can we have them?'

'You're welcome.'

'Oh no, really,' Robert said, 'I couldn't – it's very kind but I couldn't—'

'Of course you can,' Blanche said. 'The place is crammed with that sort of thing. I'll show you them now – come on. While it's still light enough.'

Without a word Robert followed her: surrendering as I had done to that blithe spontaneity which seemed to make the most trivial things delightfully worth doing. Immediately they had gone Ursula said to me: 'Jenny, come on now, tell me – don't you think all that wants clearing?' She waved a hand in the direction of the spinneys, a bronzy mass in the late summer evening light.

'Well, no,' I said, as temperately as I could, 'I rather like it as it is.'

'Oh! you're just like Martin,' she said. She shook her head at both of us. Though she was so emphatically feminine she could look, at such moments, very like a pouting boy. 'You're a romantic like him. He prefers a poetic mess. Don't marry a romantic man, Jenny. They can be more stubborn than any.' She dipped her red lips into her glass, found it empty. 'Take it from me, romance isn't everything,' she said, and went to get another drink.

317

'Will you have it cleared?' I said.

'Oh, I should think so, sooner or later,' Martin said. His voice too sounded strangely neutral. 'We've done a lot of alterations inside as well. Most of the upstairs rooms – the old playroom. Blanche wasn't too pleased about that. All those old toys gone – you remember how sentimental she was about them.'

'Yes.' I remembered the playroom. As I thought of it all my unease about Blanche and her visits to the garage crystallised. I saw that, for all the genuine kindness of her interest, it was nothing more than a toy to her. And in that same cold clarity of vision I saw something common to the Crawthornes: their love of toys. Very grown-up toys, and in poor Tom's case – the fast cars – fatal; but the impulse to pick them up and play with them was fundamentally childlike.

'I suppose it must all seem very changed from when you were here, Jenny,' Martin said.

The air across the terrace was haunted with the perfume of roses. On the lawn below, as the sun set, long shadows stretched themselves and colour leaked out of the grass.

'No,' I said. 'Not really.' Essentially St Germain House had not changed at all. It was as if it resisted change and I wondered if that was what made Ursula fling herself against it, digging things up and throwing things out: I wondered if that was what made her stalk about like a lithe, sceptical boy, loudly impatient of romance. The terrace might have been re-paved, but it was still the same terrace on which I had danced alone with Martin. The past was so strong that I felt I only had to close my eyes for a moment and the transformation would be complete:

Mr Crawthorne and Tom would be there and Ursula and Victor would never have been heard of. But I did not want to close my eyes: I wanted to keep them wide open.

'What are you doing these days?' Martin said, leaning on the balustrade.

'Helping out at the shop. Helping out at Robert's garage.'

'You don't regret leaving London?'

'No,' I said. 'Why?'

He looked at me for some moments, thoughtful. 'Someone once said that every decision you make is wrong. Which I suppose means every decision you make is also right.' I saw that Martin too had had quite a few drinks, though he was not as well fuelled as Ursula. 'Do you remember when you were a child and you had to choose between some sweets or something like that – and you'd be told to hurry up and make up your mind? Make up your mind – they always made it sound a quick, trivial sort of thing – like pulling your socks up. And yet there's *Hamlet*, the world's greatest tragedy, and it's about a man who can't make up his mind. I read somewhere that if you present two identical bowls of food to a certain animal – I forget which, a mule or something – it can't decide which to eat and it'll starve if you don't take one away. I can't believe it's precisely true. But it seems to have more truth in it than just "make up your mind".' His voice dropped suddenly. 'You always used to deflate me with a joke when I talked like this.'

'I think that's Ursula's job,' I said. 'Not mine.'

He seemed not to mind the sharpness of this. 'I don't think you've changed after all,' he said. 'When I first saw you again – when you came back with

Blanche – I thought you'd changed. But I don't think you have.'

'Did I hear my name?' Ursula was back. Her glass was already nearly empty again. Her eyes flicked with bright and aggressive alertness from me to Martin and back, her face tilted to the lamplight like a hard and shapely jewel. 'What have you two romantics been cooking up, then? How to save the gardens from wicked Ursula who's got no soul? You shouldn't listen to him, Jenny, even if you are a romantic. I had to force him to have the roof fixed. How can you be nostalgic about slates? Do you have this disease of nostalgia, Jenny?'

'I'm only twenty-one,' I said. I did not much like being so breezily labelled as a romantic.

'Oh, don't let that stop you! Martin can be nostalgic about last week, can't you, darling?'

She ruffled his hair. It did not appear to be a gesture of fondness.

'Why,' Martin said, 'what happened last week?'

Ursula took no notice of this. With the same jewel-like edge she smiled at me and said: 'Do you know in that jungle over there there's even a statue? The whole place is so overgrown that nobody knew it was there. I found it a month or so ago. And Martin actually insists that it stays where it is. Some hideous old thing covered in mould.'

I was aware of Martin looking at me. The shared secret was a burden I did not want: it was too intimate and disturbing like the memory of the terrace; and it was because of this that I said, 'I know. I've seen it.'

'*You've* seen it?' Ursula said. 'When?'

'When I worked here,' I said.

'Well! They certainly gave you the run of the

place, didn't they?' She kept drinking while she spoke, repeatedly, not looking at her glass but maintaining a sort of roving stare at Martin and me. 'Of course it's different for me. I only married into the family, after all. Perhaps I'd get on better if I came here as a secretary. Perhaps the Crawthornes would actually let me in then.'

'You are a Crawthorne,' Martin said. 'You took the name.'

'God! It takes more than that,' Ursula said. 'It takes more than a certificate to make you a Crawthorne.'

The most terrible and in a sense most shocking thing about all this was Martin's continued air of neutrality. Nothing about it seemed to surprise him. He and Ursula were not happy together: clearly they were blazingly unhappy and I think that Ursula was, in her way, trying to challenge that fact, desperately hurling herself against it. But for Martin it seemed to be a settled thing. The apparent look of disinterest in his eyes was that of a player who sees that the game is lost.

I was relieved when Blanche and Robert reappeared. Blanche was saying something about the garage forecourt and Robert was listening attentively and nodding. I could tell that he was relaxed at last because he had his hands in his pockets: he had not quite known what to do with his hands all evening.

'Robert's going to bring a trailer for the tubs tomorrow,' Blanche said. 'I must ask Mother if we've got any shrubs we could give him as well.'

'I thought it was a garage,' Ursula said. 'Not a tea-garden.'

But Blanche did not rise to this. The idea of the

garage had taken hold of her completely and it was as if she could not see anything else. Her enthusiasm infected Robert too and before we left he spoke of the sign. 'I must see about that sign,' he said. 'I must get that sign done.'

As he drove me back home he mentioned the sign again.

'What do you think? Just "Snowden"? Or should I have initials?'

'Oh, initials, I think,' I said. 'It's a pity your name's not George. Then you could have "Geo. Snowden". Or "Chas." for Charles. But then people would think you're a butcher. Have you noticed how butchers are always Geo. or Chas.?'

I spoke lightly to cover the perplexities I was feeling. They stemmed from what had happened on the terrace and also, more directly, from the matter of the sign and the stone tubs. With Robert still just scraping by the sign seemed to me a trivial matter and it was unlike his practicality to be so concerned about it.

'It's a sight to see, that house,' he said. 'Those great high ceilings . . . I expected it to be stuffy but they're very friendly, really, aren't they?'

'Yes.'

'Blanche's husband – did you ever meet him?'

'Yes,' I said. 'I met him.'

'What's he like?'

I remembered Victor Prentice, the boyish good looks and the eyes that were always wandering as he spoke to you, restlessly alert for something new.

'I can't say I liked him very much,' I said.

'Hm.' Robert nodded, as if I had confirmed something he was thinking. 'You know – I think Blanche is rather a sad woman really. I know she's got that light sort of way. But I think there's something sad about her. Don't you?'

'Perhaps.' I felt that I had perceived something about the Crawthornes that night, a thread that ran through all of them, but it was something more elusive than sadness. If I was being objective about them I might have used the word flawed. But it was with a deepening of my perplexities that I realised I was not objective now about anything.

About a week later I went to the garage one morning to find not only the sign-writer there but a builder's van too. The rough earth of the forecourt had been dug up and two men were mixing concrete.

'You need a concrete forecourt,' Robert said. 'You get cars pulling in all day on that muck – think of it when the weather turns wet.'

'How much are they charging?' I said.

'Oh! he's quite reasonable, this bloke. Dad had him do some work at the farm once. He's always reasonable.'

Blanche arrived not long afterwards. She stood with me and watched the concrete being poured.

'It will look so much better, won't it?' she said. 'Especially when the tubs are set out. It'll catch people's eye.'

She stayed most of that day, watching the builders and the sign-writer; and I thought again how much she was like a child absorbed with a new toy. After she had gone I sat in the office for a while going over the accounts. The sign-writer had left his bill and I reckoned that when the builder's bill was added to it Robert would not break even this month.

Robert came into the office.

'The sign looks a treat,' he said. 'Don't you think?

I'm pleased with the sign.'

I watched him wander about the office, long-legged and fretfully energetic, and then go and stand at the open door and look out at the drying concrete.

'I've been thinking about Blanche,' he said. 'She asked us to that party and I feel like I ought to return her hospitality – you know. It seems like we ought to do something. Sort of say thank you. But I don't know quite how to do it. It's not exactly the place for cocktails.'

'You could ask her to tea,' I said.

'D'you think she'd come?'

'I'm sure.'

'That's an idea. The three of us could have a real old Sunday tea – like the ones at the farm – d'you remember?'

'I remember.'

He smiled. 'We'll ask her then.' He looked out again at the forecourt. 'It did look a mess – she's right. It wanted doing.'

I closed the account-book. It was an indication of a new and troubling development in my life here that I did not speak to Robert about the accounts. If I had been just a book-keeper or even just a friend I would have said to him straight out that the improvements were costing money he really could not afford. But it was no longer as simple as that. I watched Robert's taut figure silhouetted at the doorway and I felt, with relief but also with bewilderment and dismay, the slow unravelling of feeling that had been so long coiled and suppressed within me. It was no longer as simple as that and I could not say anything.

Three

The old lady who lived at the farmhouse up above
the hayfield behind Robert's garage was a widow
who had lost both her sons in the war. She lived
alone except for a girl who came in to clean and a
parrot in a big square cage. She came tottering down
to the garage once or twice to see the improvements,
wearing a long hobble skirt and patent leather shoes.
'I don't often venture,' she said to me. 'I don't often
stir. But I like to be neighbourly.' She made a little
tour leaning on Robert's arm.

'I took to him straight away,' she said of Robert.
'He reminds me of my eldest. Except he was fair,
and blue-eyed, and he wasn't so tall.

'And he wore glasses,' she added.

I was amused, but it was after this that I learned
about the two sons in the war. 'The house is like a
shrine,' Robert said. 'Pictures of them and her husband everywhere. She's got no family at all.' So to
be neighbourly in return I took up to the house that
night some scones that I had been making in the
range. It was a very warm evening and in the old
lady's parlour it was like a greenhouse amongst the
heavy framed photographs and the moulting parrot's
feathers. But the old lady was garrulous with com-
panionable pleasure and when at last I got up to go,

aware of a patch of sweat like a damp hand in the hollow of my back, she went to a drawer. 'Let me give you this, my dear,' she said. 'Take and read. Take and read.'

She pressed into my hand a religious tract, printed on the garish smudgy pulp-paper that has always characterised such things, inquiring whether I was Ready to Stand before My Maker. I took it back to show Robert, who smiled wryly and opened a cupboard to show me a whole sheaf of them. 'I don't like to throw them away,' he said.

The next day, however, a very different gift was sent down from the farmhouse. I came to the garage in the early evening to find Robert examining two bottles of elderflower wine, sent with the old lady's compliments.

'I don't know,' Robert said, holding a bottle up to the light. 'It's very nice of her . . . but a friend of Mum's used to make this stuff and we always ended up tipping it down the drain.'

It had been a day of thick close heat. All that afternoon thunderstorms had lurked about a daffodil-coloured sky without ever breaking and on the horizon there were still metallic little palpitations of summer lightning. The brick kitchen was stifling after the cooking of a panful of Henrietta's dainty eggs and we stood outside, lifting our faces for air and looking at the parched cracked earth of the garden.

'No,' Robert said, glancing up at a sky mottled and sulky with clotted heat. 'It's not going to break tonight. I reckon I'll get the hosepipe out and give this garden a water.'

'Shall I make some tea?' I said.

'No. Tell you what. Let's taste that wine and see

what it's like. Then at least we won't have to fib to the old stick if she asks us whether we've tried it.'

Robert had no glasses: we tasted the wine in tea-cups. It was a surprise. It had a pale and delicate flavour that was also, in the muggy heat, remarkably refreshing.

'Well,' Robert said, smacking his lips. 'I've heard her boast about her home-made wines but I always took it with a pinch of salt. Shall we have another?'

We had another, and then another, toasting the old stick. 'Cheers,' we said. 'Good health to her.'

Then Robert went to water the garden and I went to give the hens a little feed and shut them up in the pen. I stood for a while by the pen, listening to their soft evening croonings. I could feel all the heat of the day quivering in the air, compressed under the lemon-coloured sky, and my body too seemed flushed and swollen with the heat beneath my thin summer dress.

Thirsty, I fetched another cup of the pale fragrant wine and took a cup out to Robert. He drank it thirstily too. I picked up the still running hose where he had laid it on the ground and played it over the hard earth. The wine seemed to set up a dancing in my head, light and rarefied, that was very like the distant tremor of the heat over the stubble of the hayfield; and when I saw Robert had his back to me I could not resist it. I pointed the hose at him, catching him square in the seat of the pants. He leapt up in the air so exactly in the way that people did in the slapstick films that I doubled up with laughter. I could not even run as he came after me, but he slipped on the wet ground anyway and fell down.

'You shouldn't drink if you can't hold it,' I said.

'You little beggar!' He scrambled up from his hands and knees. 'You cheeky beggar! You wait till I catch you!'

Robert chased me across the garden. From a low branch of one of the apple trees the tom-cat watched us with feline reservations as we laughed and shrieked about. Then Robert succeeded in grabbing my arm and before I could wriggle away he had poked the nozzle of the hosepipe down the back of my dress. The shock of the cold water was so great that for a moment I believe I just stood there rigid with an expression of utter surprise on my face, and this made Robert laugh so much that he sat down on the ground again, weakly, and could not move.

At last I gave him my hand to help him up and as I did so I noticed something. It was raining.

'And there was you saying it wasn't going to break tonight!' I said.

'Oh! well, you shouldn't listen to that – I'm a motor mechanic – what do they know about the weather? Red sky at night – motor mechanic's delight . . .'

From the back doorway we watched the rain drumming down, in steaming torrents, glistening here and there in moments of sheet lightning. The cat shot in after us like a furred missile. For some moments we listened to the rain, smelling its freshness, and then I became aware of another sound. It was the dripping of my soaking wet dress on to the brick floor.

'Oh dear,' Robert said, looking at the drips. 'I did that, didn't I?'

'Yes,' I said, and I laughed again because, with the subtle wine-elated dancing still going on in my head, it did not seem to matter. 'I could put the frock in front of the stove. It would soon dry. Have you got anything I could put on?'

'Overalls?' he said, and that set us laughing again as we thought of when the dust had turned me into a Kentucky Minstrel. 'No,' he said. 'I know – I've got a dressing gown. It's hanging on the side of my wardrobe.'

So I went to Robert's bedroom and slipped out of the frock and put on his dressing-gown. Robert took the frock downstairs and I lingered a moment at the landing window, breathing in a wonderful gust of rain-cool air that bellied out the shabby net curtains. Then something caught my eye in the corner of the hayfield visible from the window.

'Robert!' I called.

'What is it?' He came up the stairs.

'Look there – see? A fox.'

The fox was trotting up the hayfield away from us. It looked like a ripple of flame against the stubble. 'See better from the next window,' Robert said, and we ran into the spare room and from there watched the fox, long-bodied and purposeful in the rainy twilight, cross the length of the field, stopping now and then to look jauntily over his shoulder.

'Look at him,' Robert said. 'Just as if he didn't give a damn for anybody.'

We sat crouched on a packing case beneath the window, watching, until the fox disappeared into the hedgerow like a flame blown out. The room was filled with a hot silence, underlined by a hiss of rain, and with a thick peppery smell of dust. For a peculiar moment, as I looked at Robert in profile beside me, I thought again of when I had seen him at the Agricultural Show in the steward's jacket and breeches and he had reminded me of some illustration, some picture I could not place.

'I've never seen a fox round this way,' Robert said. 'I shall have to make sure that hen-house is secure.' As he turned his head he glanced at my left arm, with the floppy sleeve of the dressing-gown rolled up to the elbow. He put his fingers to a red mark on the skin above the wrist.

'Did I do that?'

'Oh! I hadn't noticed it.'

'I must have done that. When I grabbed you. Sorry.'

His fingers did not move and I said: 'Well, I got you first. I started it. With the hose,' and then I touched his shirt. 'Look – your shirt's still damp.'

The top buttons of the shirt were undone and I found my hand had slipped inside. His chest beneath my hand was warm and hard as a sweating apple. The delicate fires of the wine seemed to dance again in my head and all at once I could not look at Robert. His hand stroked gently up my left arm and I felt it tremble as it grazed the tip of my breast. Without volition I inclined towards him, my other hand on his thigh, my eyes as if magnetised on a soft hollow at the base of his throat. The sound of a car door slamming seemed scarcely to penetrate the thick dusty silence and it was only as the voice called at the front door that we sprang apart, frozen and startled.

'Anyone home? It's only me.'

'My God, that's Blanche,' Robert said.

We ran down. Fortunately the stairs descended to the back of the house, so I was able to be in the kitchen, turning my frock in front of the stove, when Robert brought Blanche through. She was shaking the rain from a scarf that she had put round her head and there were beads of rain too on her face.

'Hullo, Jenny – Oh! dear – did you get caught in it?'

'Yes,' I managed to say. 'Soaked.'

'I came out with the hood down – Martin swore the rain wasn't going to break tonight. Why do we always believe another person when they say something about the weather?'

A prolonged torment of nervous embarrassment went through Robert and me as Blanche sat down, talking of the heat and the rain, and stroking the humped back of the cat who screwed up his eyes as if he wasn't sure whether he liked it or hated it. I fumbled about at the sink rinsing cups and plates and Robert stood stiffly in the middle of the kitchen, his arms at his sides, exactly as if someone had told him to stand there and not move. At last Blanche said: 'Well! you two are quiet tonight,' and this remark seemed to wake Robert at last, so that he said something in apology and asked if she would like a cup of tea.

'No, I can't stop,' Blanche said. 'I just came over to ask you about something. You know you said you were thinking of moving into hire-cars at some time – well, some friends of Mother's have got an old limousine they want to sell. A Chrysler, I think Mother said. They want something a bit more practical. But I thought it sounded ideal for a hire-car – you know, special occasions and so on. And I wondered if you'd be interested.'

'Well . . .' Robert licked his lips and hesitated. 'I dare say it would be expensive—'

'I think it wants some work doing to it. And I could get it cheaper for you – I know them quite well. What do you think? Shall I at least find out about it? They're away today but I could telephone them tomorrow and get some more details. Shall I do that?'

Blanche's face seemed to glow more brightly through the beaded raindrops. I watched Robert.

'Yes,' he said, 'please. If you wouldn't mind. If you could find out a bit more about it—'

'I'll write it all down – I'll get it all mixed up otherwise.' She got up. 'I can bring you all the details on Sunday – I'm looking forward to that.'

'Sunday?' Robert said. 'Oh! yes, of course – the tea.'

The terrible tension of embarrassment persisted after Blanche had left. Curiously it seemed not to unite us but to separate us, in a sort of reversal of complicity. I put on my dress, still not quite dry, and after a few forcedly casual spurts of conversation about the rain and the tea on Sunday I got ready to go.

The elation of the wine had left me and a reaction seemed to set in that brought back, tighter than ever, all the mistrustful defensiveness that had been so slowly broken down since my return from London. What had happened in the dusty spare room had alarmed me: I shrank from thinking of it. The springing up of this barrier of resistance made the next few days, at the garage, awkward and unrestful. Robert, caught up in shyness of his own, seemed not to know how to meet me and for a time it was as if we had not changed at all since the old jarring misunderstandings of two years ago.

What sharpened this edge between us was Blanche. Another of her eager suggestions for improvements to the garage was to have the front of the house painted. 'And an awning – she thinks an

awning above the door,' Robert said. I felt, with
impotent annoyance, that he was missing the point.
All that could come later, it seemed to me: the main
thing now, with all his capital spent, was to make a
living. I watched with mounting irritation as he stood
out again on the newly concreted forecourt, frowning up at the house, measuring with his eyes. But I
was afraid too that my irritation at these things had
deeper and more troubling roots. I was afraid that
it was not just misjudgement but blindness that was
making Robert like this and that it was Blanche who
was the cause of the blindness. I remembered the
way Blanche's brilliance used to strike him physically, leaving him dazzled and motionless. Now he
was caught in the full blast of all the charm and
vitality and enthusiasm that was so curiously compelling and intoxicating in the Crawthornes. My father's
favourite euphemism for intoxication was 'under the
influence' and it seemed to me uncannily appropriate as I watched Robert spending more and more
of his time following up Blanche's suggestions,
speaking her name with a repetition of which he
seemed to be unconscious.

'Blanche reckons that would be best,' he said.
'That's Blanche's idea. That's what they've got at
Watson's, so Blanche says.' But still I only watched
and could not say anything of this.

On Sunday, when Blanche was to come to tea, I
bicycled out in the morning to a place I knew by the
river, out to the west where the valley opens up into
a broad bowl of meadows and cornfields. There was
a shallow place behind a disused lock where some
children were swimming and I lay in the grass for
some time watching them. The thundery weather
had passed and it was a morning of pure July heat

and bleached tufts of cloud in a blue sky. There were butterflies flickering in sparks of colour above the flags by the bank and across the valley I could see a line of haycocks that seemed to wobble fatly in the haze of distance. As I lay there a succession of sharp, angular thoughts – of Robert and the garage and Blanche and even of Jocelyn in London – turned and revolved in my mind and then at last seemed to settle. The sun on my face relaxed me and for perhaps an hour I lay there, not moving, and not thinking of anything at all.

Then suddenly I got to my feet. I knew that more than anything else in the world I wanted to see Robert again. It was a plain and uncomplicated piece of knowledge; nothing else seemed to matter. I got my bicycle and cycled back into town.

I went to the garage early in the afternoon, with a basket of food for the tea. I found Robert washing watercress in the sink.

'Picked this from the stream this morning,' he said. 'Smell.'

The cress was wonderfully fresh. 'I've got a cos lettuce,' I said. 'And some radishes and celery from Dad. And a currant loaf from Mum.'

'I've got some ham,' he said, 'I hope there's enough. What do you think? Did I get enough?'

We laid the table and washed the salad things and as we fussed together around the kitchen I felt the clear mood that had begun by the river that morning refine itself into happiness. I was relaxed again, working side by side with Robert; and when we stood back to look at the table, covered with a clean lace cloth and crowded with food, pleasant against the freshly whitewashed walls, Robert said with satisfaction: 'Never know this place, would you?'

'It looks lovely.'

'I reckon I'd still be living in all that mess if you hadn't come along, you know,' he said.

'Oh, well – I'm sure you wouldn't,' I said confusedly.

I went outside to gather a few heads of rambler rose from the back wall for the table. A late skylark was somewhere up above the field, making a sweet disturbance in the warm, still air. When I came back into the house Robert had put on a tie and jacket. He looked at himself in the mirror we had hung, pushing back his thick, black, uncombable hair.

'Finishing touch,' I said, and threaded one small rose-head into his buttonhole.

'I feel like I'm going to church,' he said.

'You look very nice.'

'So do you.'

An acute wish went through me that we were having tea alone; and Robert said, looking at the table: 'You know, I've half a mind to start.' But just then there was the sound of a car at the front of the house, and we went out to meet Blanche.

'This is a professional call as well, you know,' she said. 'I'm having trouble with the car. It took ages to start this morning. And every time I slow at a junction the engine sort of dies and I have to start it again. I don't feel quite safe in it.'

Robert listened to the engine running for a few moments. 'Better leave it with me,' he said. 'I can look at it in the morning.'

Blanche was wearing that day a soft white dress of crepe de Chine with a yoked collar. The white, as always, set off her pure buttery blondeness, and as the westering sun struck low through the kitchen window it caught and magnified the faint golden down on her bare arms. Over tea she spoke of the Chrysler limousine, passing Robert a piece of paper on which she had written the details.

'It's quite a plush sort of thing,' she said. 'It would be ideal for hiring out for weddings. I've spoken to the people and they'll knock something off the price for you. They live just outside Norwich – the address is on the back there. What do you think? If you want to go over and see it I can telephone them.'

The talk of the limousine went on for some time, Blanche's eyes seeming to shine more brilliantly blue and excited as the sun declined and the room, with its one small window, filled with shadow; and Robert's eyes in turn seemed to become more dark, fixed and lost, never leaving her brightly animated face as he nodded and replied and was carried along by her.

'It's black,' she said, 'which is probably not the best colour. You could respray it – perhaps blue. Blue would look good. It would be something with a touch of luxury about it for people to hire – something special. Then you could have it photographed for advertising. A photograph against an impressive background – somewhere in the cathedral precinct perhaps. No – you could have it done at St Germain House – we could find a bit of the house that isn't falling down.'

Typically, Blanche did not eat much of the substantial spread, taking bird-like bites here and there of ham and cress. All the time Robert, who still had a farmer's appetite, worked his way steadily through the food, but it was as if he were hardly aware of eating at all; once or twice I saw him look down at his plate with a sort of bemused surprise. It was as if, as the room darkened, he became aware of

nothing but the enchanting oval face across the table
and the musical voice spinning out plans that opened
out into further plans like a series of secret gardens.

'That's another thing – I went to Watson's scout-
ing out the opposition, and when I came away they
gave me a card – a bit of a shabby one. It would
pay you to have some really nice cards printed.
Father used to have calling-cards printed – he was
very old-fashioned like that – and he used to have
them done at a funny little place over at Huntingdon. I'm going there next week – I'll get a quotation
for some cards for you.'

As this went on I was seized by a growing feeling
of unreality, heightened by the premature dimness
of the room while ripe sunlight still lingered outside.
With rising unease I saw that the garage, which
was Robert's living and which he had worked at so
tirelessly, was turning into a fantasy. For Blanche it
was something around which to weave her skittish
imagination, just like the doll's house in the playroom that she had always wanted to climb into. It
was a fantasy that could be endlessly embroidered
and Robert was caught up in it too.

At last I got up, abruptly, said, 'Everyone had
enough?' and began to clear the table; and as I took
Robert's plate he looked startled again as if he did
not quite know where he was.

While I made tea Blanche stretched out her legs
with her characteristic cat-like uncoiling and looked
around her. 'You've done wonders with this house,'
she said. 'I'll never forget when I first saw it and I
thought it was hopeless. Now it's really homely –
you feel you could live here. There's a nice feeling
when you come in.'

'Well, it wants plenty more doing to it,' Robert

said. 'It's not half finished yet.'

After tea we went out into the garden. The cat, cocky with an audience, swaggered about the trees chasing the bees that still droned sleepily about in the evening warmth. Blanche's eye fell on the old converted cowshed and on the patched roof.

'Doesn't the rain come in?' she said.

'A bit,' Robert said. 'I was patching it up the other day. Of course eventually it'd be best to have a proper workshop . . .'

'What sort of thing? What will it be?'

'Well – brick-built, with double doors at either end ideally . . .'

By now I had had enough of this. I went inside and when Blanche came to say goodbye – Robert was taking her home in the Sunbeam – I was finishing the washing up. I said goodbye, I suppose, rather shortly. A furious pressure to say something about what was happening to Robert was building inside me like steam in a kettle. I listened to the cracked exhaust of the Sunbeam banging away into the distance and then went into the office and got out the account-books.

The books were lying open on the table when, after about half-an-hour, Robert came back.

'Oh! you've washed up,' he said vaguely, coming into the kitchen. 'I was going to do that.'

I stood by the table, where the open books were. Looking back I can see there must have been something stagey about this; but melodrama only strikes us as ridiculous when our feelings are not engaged and at the time I was deadly serious.

'I'm going over to Norwich tomorrow to have a look at that Chrysler,' Robert said, wandering over to the back door. 'I stopped in at St Germain House for a minute and Blanche telephoned the people to make an appointment for me . . . Are you busy tomorrow? I mean, do you think you could open the garage up – just for a while?'

'I'll open it up all day,' I said. 'You can't afford to close it at all the way you're going.'

'Eh?' Robert said. He turned from the door to look at me, and I saw from his eyes that he was hardly there at all. He was rather like a man who is drunk; but I knew it was not alcohol that had gone to his head.

'You still haven't paid the builder's bill,' I said. 'Look – look here at the books.' He looked, but he did not seem to see them. 'How on earth can you afford to buy a limousine?'

'Oh! Blanche is going to get it cheaper for me. Blanche knows the people – she's arranged it—'

'So you've decided already. You've decided you're going to buy it even though you haven't seen it.'

He seemed, at last, to see how angry I was.

'I didn't say that. I just said I'm going to have a look at it. There's no obligation, Blanche says—'

'You're going to buy it because of Blanche. Because it's Blanche's idea.'

He was frowning. 'What's all this about? Yes, it's Blanche's idea. She has some very good ideas. You can't get hire-cars like that in Billingham—'

'But you haven't got the money. Where's the money coming from?'

'I went to the bank on Friday to see about a loan—'

'Oh, *God*.'

I sat down. Absurdly, some vestige of my parents' pacific gentility moved in me, aghast at the idea of having a scene.

'I want to get on,' Robert said. 'There's nothing

wrong with thinking big, is there?'

'No,' I said quietly. 'But it's not you thinking, it's Blanche.'

He stood darkly frowning down at me, his square shoulders stubborn. 'What's that supposed to mean?'

'I mean you do everything she says. I mean you're spending money you haven't got because of her.'

'Blanche has helped me a lot. She's got me custom. She's taken a lot of interest in the garage and I don't see what there is against that.'

'It's just a toy to her,' I said. 'It's just a toy and she can always put it down again and that's just what you can't do.' Suddenly I was saying something I had not meant to say. 'They're all like that – the Crawthornes. They're very charming and very lovable and they just see life as a lot of toys for them to play with.'

'Of course you would know all about that,' Robert said.

I looked up. It was as if some fine-drawn surface between us had snapped.

'Yes, I do know them,' I said. 'I'm not saying Blanche means any harm. I just don't want to see you get involved – get all caught up with her.' He was glaring at me: his eyes were like stones and I said, weakly, disconcerted: 'I'm just thinking of your welfare.'

'It doesn't sound like that to me. I'll tell you what it sounds like to me. It sounds like you don't want me to get on.'

'I do—'

'You don't want to see me get on and all because of the Crawthornes.' There was a sort of clenched and dogged ferocity about Robert that reminded me of that day at the farm with John: I knew that the scene was here and that I had been mad to think I could avoid one. 'By God, you've changed your tune. It was different when you were so thick with that family, wasn't it? Don't you remember? You could hardly bring yourself to speak to me then.'

I knew then that all the old animosities between us had come home. I glimpsed, too, for the first time, the true depth of the hurts that had been created two years ago, the wounds that at the time I had been too blindly proud to see; and the revelation of this, on top of my changed feelings for Robert, kept me frozen and silent as he raged at me.

'It was different then. The Crawthornes were the bee's knees then. I didn't get a look in. But now you're not flavour of the month with them any more. That's what this is all about, isn't it? It's you we're talking about, not me, not Blanche. You're peeved because you wanted to get in with that family – you practically crawled to them – but they dropped you and you can't forget it.'

I would be lying if I said this did not hurt me. It hurt perhaps more than anything that had ever been said to me and it hurt all the more because of the truth in it and because it came from Robert whom I had begun to love. But at first the hurt did not really sink in: it was like one of those blows that cause a great cold numbness before the bruise appears. For the moment all I could think was that nothing I had said had made any impression on him. He had not really heard it. That was the terrible thing: it had been useless my speaking out at all.

'And so you've taken against Blanche. Well, leave Blanche out of it. She's taken a very kind interest in this place and I don't see why I should turn that down.'

'Blanche is a married woman,' I said. I was hitting back, of course: it is a reflex as uncontrollable as a physical one.

'What's that got to do with anything?' Robert said; but his anger seemed to lose a little of its towering calm. 'I know that. And I think she's a sad woman – she's not been treated well and I'm sorry for her.'

There did not seem to be anything for me to say after that. I got up to go.

Outside, while I got out my bicycle, Robert stood with his hands jammed in his pockets in a sort of fuming irresolution. It was the sort of exquisitely balmy and scented evening that in its sheer serenity seems to mock at human emotions. As I got on my bicycle Robert raked his hand through his hair and said: 'I don't know what we're quarrelling about Blanche for.'

'No,' I said. 'I'm sorry,' and rode off.

When I arrived at the garage next morning Robert was in his shirt sleeves and stockinged feet, polishing his shoes.

'What are you doing here?' he said.

'You're going to Norwich today, aren't you?' I said. 'To see that limousine?'

'Yes, I am.'

'Well, I said I'd mind the garage.'

He put the shoes down on the kitchen floor. 'You don't have to,' he said.

'I said I'd mind the garage and I will,' I said. 'Unless you don't want me to?'

The bruise had come up now and I was smarting

dangerously: Robert must have seen that, for he said quietly, 'No, not at all. I'll leave you the spare keys.'

The account-books were still out: he must have been looking at them. I took them back into the office. When I went outside again I found Robert looking at Blanche's white car where she had left it in the yard.

'I'd forgotten about this,' he said. 'I'll have a look at it tonight if I get time. I should be back this afternoon. If I'm not, well – you know how to lock up and everything.'

I nodded, and went to get a broom to sweep out the office. I did not like the part I was playing; it was stupid. But it was the only way I knew to stop myself screaming at him. I was counting up the petty cash when the Sunbeam bucketed away.

The morning passed quickly. A few cars stopped for petrol and a man came to look over the scrap cars in the yard for spare parts. At midday an old village denizen called Albert whom I had got to know came by and stood out on the forecourt chewing tobacco and talking of the hot weather. Albert could construct a whole conversation on the weather and indeed I had never known him talk of anything else. I remember as I stood there how the heat of the concrete struck up through my shoes and how, even as I smiled and chatted, a great wave of burning resentment went through me every few minutes at the memory of what Robert had said last night.

I was just getting ready to close for lunch when a car drew up. Looking through the office window I saw a man in a light jacket and flannels get out and stand looking up at the house. Then he lifted his hand to push back his gold-brown hair from his forehead and I recognised Martin.

'Hullo, there,' he said as I went out to him. 'I've just come to have a peep at this place that Blanche is always talking about.'

'This is the place,' I said.

He looked at the stone tubs arranged along the drive. 'Thought I recognised her handiwork.'

'Oh yes,' I said, waving a hand around. 'They're all Blanche's ideas.'

I noticed Martin's car. It was a yellow Talbot sports tourer, very glamorous, except for the large dent in the right fender.

'Extravagant thing, isn't it?' Martin said. 'It was Ursula's choice. She drives it mostly.'

'Robert could knock that dent out for you.'

'Could he? Trouble is there'd soon be another one. Ursula drives like—' For a moment I thought he was going to say *like Tom*, and our eyes met in understanding. 'Like the wind. So how's business? Does he make a living out of it? I suppose the slump's made it more difficult.'

'Oh, he doesn't let a little thing like the slump stop him,' I said. My bitterness was so close to the surface that Martin could not help but notice it and just then I didn't care.

I showed him around the yard. He seemed not to take much notice.

'Actually, Jenny, it was you I wanted to speak to,' he said. He hesitated. 'Are you going anywhere for your lunch?'

I said I had a packed lunch and I was going to take it down to the stream. 'If you'd like to come I'll toss you a sandwich or two,' I said, 'if you're good.'

I do not know what he made of this brittle flippancy: I do not know why I adopted it, except that there was something brutal about it that suited my mood. He only smiled a little and said, 'Just your company will do for me.'

The stream was actually an old drainage cut, emerging through a culvert by the pub, that ran out of the village between banks tangled with hawthorn and briar. As we walked down the rough path by the stream Martin talked casually of the garage and the good position it was in but I was not really listening. My mind was flaring again with the pain of what Robert had said to me and with the fact that he had gone to buy that limousine. I thought of all the work he had put into the garage, of our contented days there with the cleaning and painting, the old cow-shed and the scrap cars and the hens and the tom-cat: and the simple fact of his going to Norwich after the limousine appeared to me in the shape of a monstrous betrayal.

I sat down and began to eat my sandwiches, whilst Martin stood looking at the stream. At such times there is something offensively trivial and ludicrous about food and it was inevitable, the way I crammed them in, that I would choke. Martin knelt down beside me, patting my back, and then without fuss poured some tea from my thermos flask and handed it to me. 'Here,' he said. 'Drink that.'

There was something childishly comforting about these little ministrations. I thanked him and he smiled and stood up again, jingling the change in his pockets and looking down into the green stream.

'I wanted to apologise for the other week,' he said. 'The way Ursula behaved. I got the impression you really didn't want to be at that party anyway and it was tough on you having to put up with that.

It was my fault: I'd rather been infuriating her that day and she lost patience.'

'What about?'

'Oh! the business of clearing the grounds – all that. You know how these little things blow up. I read in a newspaper once where a woman bumped her husband off and when they asked why she said it was because his dentures didn't fit and it got on her nerves. There is a weird sort of logic in it, isn't there?'

'What are you going to do about the grounds?'

'Oh, we've reached a compromise.' He gave a smile that was half a wince. 'I gave in.'

'Well,' I said, 'I really didn't notice anything that night anyway.'

Martin shook his head. 'It's all right. You needn't pretend. You couldn't help but see how Ursula was. You saw it. It wasn't anything personal to you – she's like that all the time now.'

'Martin,' I said, 'you shouldn't talk to me about Ursula like this. It's not my business.' How like Blanche he was, I thought: in just the same way she had thrust at me her confidences about Victor; it was as if for the Crawthornes the only safe ground was intimacy. And the echo of Blanche was even stronger as he said, 'But it's precisely you who I can talk to about it. It wouldn't be right with anyone else, but you – you understand. You always understood us.'

I wasn't sure about that. After what Robert had said I wasn't sure about anything. I thought I had become finally neutral about the Crawthornes; but part of my anger with Robert came from fear that what he had said might be true – that it was jealous pique, not concern for his welfare, that had made me warn him against getting involved with them.

'In fact I wanted to ask your advice,' Martin said.

'Me?'

'You. Don't sound so surprised. It's natural to ask advice of someone you admire, isn't it?'

I stared at him. 'I don't think that's very funny.'

'It's not meant to be. I'm simply saying I admire what you did – the way you went to London and just changed everything in your life. I've been thinking a lot about that. The way you made that decision and acted on it. That's what I want to ask you, Jenny. How does one do that? Take hold of one's life and change it?'

'It wasn't that difficult for me. I didn't have any permanent ties.'

He looked away. 'As I have Ursula.'

'If it's about Ursula,' I said, 'then I've told you – it's not my business.'

'Look, I'm not blaming Ursula. It's me – it's me I've got to change. She's the way she is because of me. Life's not how she hoped it would be and she's disappointed. And I just know I've got to do something – the way you did. Make the change. It's in my hands.'

'What's brought all this on?' I said.

He sat down next to me, and looked straightly at me. 'Meeting you again. Of course.' He plucked a blade of grass and chewed it. 'You've been very generous. Not many people can resist the urge to say *I told you so*.'

'Why should I say that?'

'Because you had me sized up from the beginning. You always said that I should stick to the music – that politics wasn't for me. You saw through me. Look, I'm not just chewing over old regrets. Oh yes,

I'd do it all differently if I had the time over again. But it's *now* I'm thinking about. You made the break – changed yourself. Ursula's not happy with me. How do I make myself the person she wants me to be?' And again uncannily echoing Blanche he said: 'In a way I think she wants me to be like Victor. She was very keen on him taking control of Father's money and I know she wants me to be more involved in that. Even go into partnership with him.'

'Do you want that?'

'Well . . . it would please Ursula.'

'You'd still be the same person though. You can't just change like that. Do you think when I went away to London it was because I'd decided to change? It was because I had to. There wasn't any choice in it.' All at once as I looked at Martin I did not know what I felt for him: it was as if there was a great vacuum where my feelings should have been. 'I had to get away, because of you. You know that.'

He was very still: a bee came blunderingly and settled on his sleeve for a moment and he did not brush it away.

He said softly: 'I know. And I'd give anything to take that back.'

The bee flew away.

'You never did slap my face for it, did you?' Martin said.

'No.'

'You should have done.' Suddenly he was smiling, teasingly, his face quite close to mine. 'It's not too late. Give it a slap now. Go on.'

I laughed, confusedly. 'No.'

'Go on. A free slap.' His face twinkled with the old grave mischief, darkening rather than brightening the blue eyes. 'Go on. An unrepeatable offer. Pick a cheek.'

'I can't slap in cold blood.'

'How about if I give you a reason, then?' he said, and leaned over and lightly kissed me.

'Martin, don't,' I said. The vacuum loomed and yawned dangerously.

'I'm sorry.' He sat back. 'Think of it as the first kiss of summer.'

For some moments I could not speak: and Martin let the silence lie there. At last I gathered up my basket. 'I ought to be getting back to the garage.'

He put out a hand to help me to my feet. 'So you think there's no hope of changing me, eh?'

'I can't give you any answers, Martin,' I said. 'Really.'

'I know . . . I know. It's just so good to talk to you again – it always *feels* like you've given me an answer. I know when I first saw you again – when Blanche brought you back – you didn't want anything to do with me. I realise that. I'm just saying that – well, I'd still like to see you.'

' "We can still be friends" – is that it?'

'Oh dear!' He laughed. 'Do people really say that?'

We walked back to the garage. As Martin got into the dented car he said: 'He was a farmer, wasn't he? Robert?'

'His family were.'

'He doesn't miss that, then?'

'Oh no. This is what he wants.'

'Good.' Martin started the Talbot's engine: the roar it gave was slick and powerful. 'There's nothing worse than knowing you made the wrong choice.'

Robert was not yet back when it was time to close the garage. I fed and watered the hens and, mindful of the fox, checked the pen was secure and then

checked the padlocks on the shed doors. I had just
locked up the house and was getting out my bicycle
when I heard footsteps. But it was not Robert: it
was only Albert making his ambling return through
the village. I got on my bicycle and sped away to
escape another dose of folk meteorology.

Back home I minded the shop after tea and then,
after listening to the wireless a while with my family,
slipped off to bed, pausing only to be informed by
my grandmother that in the old days people had
conversations instead of creeping off to their rooms
and it only went to show. But once in my room I
could not face the thought of bed. It was a warm
night and for some time I sat at the open window,
listening to the shunting of goods trains that in fine
weather seemed to carry all over Billingham, and
torn by tortuous cross-currents of feeling. I still
seemed to feel the imprint of Martin's lips, like
a brand. Then I seemed to surface out of all this
turbulence holding the single thought that I should
go back to the garage and see if Robert were back
yet.

It was late; but the compulsion of this strange idea
carried me downstairs and out to the shed to get my
bicycle. I was only stopped by the sight of my father
standing in the garden looking at the stars.

'Hello, love,' he said. 'Couldn't you sleep?'

'No,' I said. 'It's warm, isn't it?'

'It is. I fancied a breath of air myself.'

Flatly, I saw the impossibility of explaining to my
father that I was going to pelt out to Newburn, at
this time of night, for no real reason at all. I stood
with him a while, looking at the stars and listening
to the grinding and clanking, uncannily magnified,
of the goods trains.

'Always makes me want to go on a train when I hear that,' my father said. 'I haven't been on a train for ages. I always wanted to be an engine-driver when I was a lad. Funny thing is, there's Ted Carr who's been a driver for years, and when I was at school with him he was dead set against going on the railway. I suppose you never do know what you really want.'

I went back to my bedroom and at last lay down. I punched my pillow long into the night and I seemed to have been asleep only a few minutes when my mother came to wake me.

'There's someone to see you,' she said. 'Mrs Prentice.'

It was only a quarter to seven. 'What on earth can she want at this time?' I said.

Blanche was waiting for me in the garden. I was struck, coldly, by a memory of Ralph doing the same thing when he brought me the news about Tom.

'Jenny, I'm so sorry to disturb you this early,' she said. 'Do apologise to your mother for me. I thought I should come and tell you before I go.'

'Go where?' I was groggy.

'London. Home. Victor needs me.' And so she began to tell me, in the bright morning garden, that Victor's company had gone bust.

'If only I'd listened . . . That time he came up to Billingham to ask me to come back, he mentioned that there was some investigation into his accounts, some irregularity. And he kept saying in his letters that there was some trouble – but I just threw them away. I thought it was a ploy to get me back. But it's true. They're going to appoint a receiver.'

The enormous solemnity of this announcement

was so incongruous coming from Blanche that I scarcely believed I was awake.

'I've had no sleep. He's been on the telephone to me half the night. He's sick with worry – and I had to keep talking to him because he sounded so desperate I was afraid he'd do something silly.'

'Oh, Blanche. I'm sorry.'

'I can't believe it's Victor's fault. He brought in this junior partner a while ago and I never quite trusted him. I'll bet that's what's at the bottom of it. I know there are businesses going to the wall all the time these days, but I can't believe Victor's to blame . . . So you see. It makes our differences all rather meaningless, doesn't it? I've got to be with him. I've got to go back.'

Again it was a little bizarre to hear this tone of tragic loyalty in Blanche's small light voice, as she stood there slender and elegant as a fashion-plate, tapping her gloves against one poised leg.

'You're going now?' I said.

'Train at seven-fifteen. You do see, don't you? I have to be with him. I have to show him he's not alone.'

'Yes,' I said. 'Your car—'

'I can't wait for that. Oh! yes – you'll say goodbye to Robert for me, won't you? Jenny, I've a cab waiting, I must go. I'm sorry I can't stay any longer. I'll write just as soon as – well, as soon as we know where we are.'

She kissed me. Her skin was cool and fresh. I said: 'I hope you'll be all right.'

'I'll be all right. It certainly puts things in perspective, doesn't it?'

She gave a rueful little smile. As I went out with her to the waiting cab it was borne in on me, through the haze of sleep and surprise, how well Blanche looked. She had never looked more alive. There was a washed brightness about her eyes that was probably from tears and fatigue but also appeared like excitement. As the cab drove away I remembered her saying how she longed for a real drama in her life and I realised that now, at last, she had got what she wanted.

She had left me the task of saying goodbye to Robert for her. Last night I had been full of urgency to get to the garage and see him; now I put it off throughout the morning. It was the thought of giving him that short casual message that dismayed me. I had been more right than I knew when I had spoken of her picking up Robert and the garage as a toy that could easily be tossed aside again. But I did not know how to tell him without seeming to crow: after that terrible row two days ago, I saw no way to tell him that Blanche had simply forgotten him without appearing to draw some malicious satisfaction from it. And I could not feel any satisfaction: the thought of Robert's reaction gave me a peculiar queasy dread.

I went to the garage at last just before noon. It was a day of scorching glare, heat bouncing off roads and paths in harsh oven-waves; and when Robert came out of the workshop at my call he screwed up his eyes against the light as if in sudden pain.

'Hullo,' he said. 'Everything all right yesterday?'

'Yes,' I said.

'Sorry I was a bit late back. I stopped off at Fakenham, had a look round a scrap-dealer's there.' He drew a sunburnt forearm across his forehead. 'Hot today.'

'Shall I make some tea?'

'Please.'

I went into the house and put the kettle on the hob. The dark kitchen was startlingly cool after the torrid heat outside; the tom-cat had found that out and was lying on the brick floor in an abandoned attitude. I was so preoccupied with Blanche's bombshell that I had not even thought to ask Robert about the limousine.

Robert came into the kitchen. His shirt clung to him.

'They always find the coolest place in summer and the warmest place in winter,' he said, looking down at the tom-cat. 'Shall I rub his tummy?'

'No. Your hand would look funny without fingers.'

Just then I burnt my own fingers on the handle of the old tin kettle. I ran them under the tap. Robert came over and took my hand. 'Let me see,' he said.

'It's nothing,' I said. Somehow I could not bear him being kind to me with what I had to tell him: and in this confusion I blurted it out.

'Robert, Blanche asked me to say goodbye – she's gone back to London. She came to see me early this morning.'

I told him about Victor. He continued to hold my hand, palm upwards, as I told him; and an expression of purest puzzlement grew on his face.

'I don't believe you,' he said. He let go of my hand.

'That's what happened,' I said. 'She—'

'No.' He shook his head, emphatically, over and over again. 'No, no, that can't be right. She wouldn't just go like that. Not like that – I don't believe it.' With a dogged sort of reasonableness he went on: 'There's her car. Her car's still here – I was just working on it this morning. And those cards – she was going to see about those cards for me.'

'It was urgent. She had to go—'

'But she *hates* him. She told me that she . . . It was all finished – you said so yourself! She wouldn't go back to him whatever happened.'

'She has.'

Again he shook his head. 'There's her car. Her car's still here.' He kept returning, with a terrible flat logicality, to the car. 'She wouldn't just go like that. That's not like her.'

I wanted to say that it was exactly like her; that it was more like her, as it were, than anything she had ever done. But I knew now that Robert would not listen.

'What did she say?' he demanded. 'She must have said something else. What else did she say?' Beneath his peremptory manner I could see there was unease too and even pain: at the idea that Blanche had, after all, simply turned her face from him without a thought.

'She was in a hurry,' I said feebly. 'She just said to say goodbye.'

Robert stared through me. His lips moved as if he were inwardly struggling to the solution of some infuriating but basically solvable problem.

'I don't understand. Her husband made her miserable. You know that. Anyone could tell. Why should she go back to him? It seemed like she was just starting to be happy again – she loved this place – she put a lot into the garage. She had all these plans for it. I just don't understand.'

Suddenly he picked up the kettle I had put on for tea and took it into the wash-house and began stripping off his shirt.

'What are you doing?' I said.

'I've got to get ready.' He began to lather his face.

'What for?'

'I've got to take Blanche's car to her. She'll be lost without that. I'll drive it down to London. And then I can find out what's really happened. She can't have gone back to him – not properly. She just wouldn't.'

'You're going now?'

'Yes, of course.' He looked at me, chin lifted as he shaved with hasty strokes. 'I've got to see her. She surely can't have been quite in her right mind. She'll want her car. She needs her independence – from him. You know the address, don't you?'

I stared at him. 'I can't remember it.'

He shrugged. 'If you won't tell me, I'll go over to St Germain House and ask there.'

I was damned if I'd tell him. 'What about the garage?'

'I can't think about that now.'

He rinsed his face, and as it came up from the water smooth and fresh and, to me now, tormentingly handsome, it seemed to have all the set stubbornness of obsession. Bitterness rose in me, acid-like. 'You needn't think I'm going to mind the place for you again,' I said.

'I thought Blanche was your friend,' Robert said. 'Anybody would think you're enjoying this from the way you're going on.'

I could not speak. I watched him take a clean shirt from the clothes-horse. I think I was very close to slapping his face at that moment: except that it would have made no difference.

'You're really going, aren't you?' I said.

He did not need to answer. I stared at him a moment longer and then turned and walked out.

Somehow – I don't know how, as between fury and tears I was cycling virtually blind – I got home. My grandmother was sitting in the garden wearing a sun-hat, more gnome-like than ever, as I slammed my bicycle in the shed.

'Why do young people these days have to rush about everywhere?' she asked me. 'We were taught to sit still when I was a girl. I never even had a bicycle –'

'Oh, shut up!' I cried and, to my astonishment, for the first time in my life, she did.

All that afternoon I worked in the shop. Women then often stayed in the shop, talking, for half an hour or so, holding their purses in folded hands, until they sighed and said they must be getting on, as if you had kept them: but nobody talked to me that afternoon. I think my baleful glare must have frightened them.

After tea a thin ghost of a cool breeze blew up at last, and I said I was going for a walk. I wandered aimlessly into town – but I knew quite well where I was going in the end. I had not quite given Robert up: a little whisper of hope suggested that he might have thought better of it. He might not have gone to St Germain House to find out Blanche's address after all; and the whisper told me to go over there and find out.

In the market square I saw Mr Silvani with his ice-cream cart. Later many Italian families came to Billingham to work in the brick-pits but I think the Silvanis, who lived at the other end of our street, were the first. I stopped to speak to him, and it was because of this that I noticed the sports Talbot with the dent in it, parked among the cars in the middle of the market square.

I walked on, crossing the railway bridge, towards St Germain House. If it was Martin who was out in the car, then that was all to the good: Martin was part of it all, and I would feel easier just asking Mrs Crawthorne. But when the maid answered the front door it was Martin's voice I heard immediately, behind her.

'Who is it, Lily? Who is it? Is it her?'

Martin came thundering down the stairs and then stopped.

'Oh! Jenny. I thought . . . Hello.'

He looked terrible: both drained and a little wild. He stood there gazing at me and uncomfortably I said: 'I'm sorry to disturb you. I just called to ask if Robert had been here today.'

'Robert? Oh! yes. He was here this lunch-time. Wanted Blanche's address – he'd still got her car in dock or something. You heard about Victor, of course.'

A great wave of blackness left me so seared and empty that for a moment I could not answer.

'Yes,' I said. 'I heard.'

Martin glanced over his shoulder and then took my arm. 'I have to talk to you. Mother's here – come out to the garden.'

I let him guide me. We went through the old study – I hardly recognised it, for all Mr Crawthorne's shambles of books and Eastern artefacts were swept away – and out by the french doors into the garden.

'I have to talk to you,' Martin said again. He steered me down the lawn to the shade of the trees, where I had first met the children – long ago in what

seemed another life. 'I have to talk to someone
who's sane. It's been like a madhouse here. I
thought – when I heard the door I thought it might
be Ursula. She went off in the car – she shouldn't
have been driving. She's been on a blinder all day
– you can guess why.'

I felt numb and stupid and merely looked at him,
not understanding.

'Victor. He was handling all our money. I put
most of it into some construction project of his.
Cast-iron investment, he said. So you see – it's not
just Victor's losses.'

He looked back at the house, its rows of windows
glowing squares in the late sun.

'So Ursula went through the roof. She was already
unhappy about things, and now the prospect of
being on our uppers . . . There was a terrible row.
She said that she'd thrown her life away, marrying
me. Well – we both said some pretty awful things.
I don't know what time she started on the drink,
but she kept at it all afternoon. And then she stormed out. She wouldn't say where she was going—'

'I saw the car,' I said. 'It's all right. I saw it parked
in the market square, on the way here.'

'You're sure? She didn't go far then.' He grimaced. 'I've an idea where she ended up. The Jubilee
Hotel, or the Great Northern. She goes there to
tank up. I'd better go down there and find her. She
was in no state to drink any more. Jenny – do you
have to go? Will you come with me?' All at once
he seemed to emerge from his distraction: his voice
softened in that intimate way that made you feel
you were the only person in the world for him just
then. 'Please. I need you.'

For a moment I thought of the garage – closed

and empty. Again I felt seared, choking on ashes of futility.

'All right, Martin,' I said.

The sun was sinking as we walked into town but there was still a dusty, embalmed heat about the streets. Martin carried his jacket over his shoulder.

'I'll have to go down to London and see Victor as soon as possible,' he said. 'I would have gone with Blanche this morning but she insisted it was something she had to do on her own. Funny how it took something like that to bring those two together again. I always doubted whether they were suited – but now I think deep down they are.'

'Yes,' I said. 'They are.' I remembered the way Victor's eyes, while he talked to me at that party in London, had darted restlessly about, looking always for something new: I had not known then just how alike he and Blanche were.

We came to the market square at sunset. A last pure lance of golden light struck the upper stone of the old merchants' houses as their feet were swallowed up in shadow. There were still cars parked in the square; but the dented Talbot was not amongst them.

'It was here,' I said. 'Just here. She must have gone.'

The light melted, dream-like, on the old roofs.

'Hell,' Martin said. 'I suppose she might have moved it . . . Let's just look in the hotels. Make sure.'

There was no one in the lounge of the Jubilee. We went over to the Great Northern, and Martin asked if his wife had been in: obviously they knew her. No, the waiter said, he had not seen her.

'She's probably gone home,' I said. 'She's probably gone home to sleep it off.'

'I suppose so.' There was a certain flatness, of fears that had begun to dissolve. 'Well, I could manage a drink myself, could you?'

The dusty, thickly draped lounge was cool. In a savage sort of disenchantment I accepted, and like Martin had a whisky, strong, that burned through me. Briefly all my angry resentment at Robert glowered and re-lighted and then died again, spent and bleak.

'What did your mother say to all this?' I said, breaking the silence.

'She's taking it on the chin, of course. As long as Blanche and Victor are together, she says. And she seems to think Ursula's father will bail us out. I don't think she quite sees what's happened to Ursula and me. Or she won't see it. She won't admit that Ursula and I have come to the end of the road.'

His eyes met mine. I said: 'Isn't that what Blanche thought about her marriage?'

'It's a bit different with us. Poor Jenny, you always get dragged in, don't you? Thank God you came along to the house today – I think I'd have gone off my head without you. Let me get you another drink. No, it's pretty well finished – because there's got to be love, hasn't there? And that's gone, for me. I know I can tell you this. There just comes a day when you look at a person and there are all sorts of feelings there but love isn't one of them . . . You must have guessed.'

'Not really,' I said. 'I've guessed wrong about you before.'

'Did you? You probably didn't. You probably knew me better than I knew myself.' He laid his hand on mine, very gently. 'I met you here once, didn't I? Off the London train. I was in a mixed-up mood – over Ursula. Irony of ironies. And you somehow made me feel better . . . It's a pity I'm too vain to wear spectacles, isn't it?'

'What?'

'Short-sighted. I can never see what's right under my nose. I didn't then. It would have been better if I had.'

'How do you know that?' I wanted to remove my hand from beneath his; but somehow, while he was speaking, I could not: somehow that music kept me still, listening.

'Because seeing you again has made me realise what I missed. And now my marriage is in a mess, my whole life's pretty well in a mess if you like – and yet being with you it doesn't seem to matter.'

His fingers stroked mine. The lounge had filled up considerably and he leaned close to me, his low voice somehow shutting out the noise of other voices, putting me in possession of a secret like a gift.

'That's how I know what I missed, Jenny,' he said. 'That's what makes me wonder if it's not too late.'

A sudden explosion of laughter from a fat man at the bar made us both jump. Martin glanced round and then smiled at me. 'So much for my best lines,' he said.

I smiled too. It was impossible not to when Martin smiled at you in that way. And yet that was just the trouble. I remembered Ralph once saying that Martin's charm was so habitual he could not help using it. He wanted things to be all right: he wanted me to make things better. Suddenly I had such a vivid and overpowering sense of his irresponsibility

that for a moment I was actually frightened of him:
it was as if the room was full of gas and he had
smilingly, teasingly, struck a match.

I pulled my hand away. 'I can't help you, Martin,'
I said.

'Oh, Jenny, you can,' he said. 'If you only knew—'

The fat man at the bar gave another loud burst
of laughter, slapping his companion's shoulder; and
as I looked up at him I saw a woman standing in
the doorway to the lobby, staring at me. I saw the
bobbed hair and the high-cheeked oval face but still
it was a second or two before I realised who it was.

It was Ursula. When I looked again she was
gone.

'What's wrong?' Martin said.

'Ursula – there. She just went out again.'

Martin flung his head round and made a move to
get up. Then he sighed and sat down again.

'Oh! what's the point,' he said. 'There's nothing
to do or say anyway. Let her go—'

'You came looking for her,' I reminded him. 'You
ought to see if she's all right.'

'Do you want me to?'

'It doesn't matter what I want,' I said carefully.

Martin finished his drink. 'All right then.'

We went out to the car park. A humid darkness
had fallen, barely stirred by breeze. The car was not
there.

'I'm getting tired of this,' Martin said.

'So am I,' I said. 'Go home, Martin. Go and see
her there. Sort things out.'

'All right. I'm in your hands.'

We crossed the Station Road back into town and
walked in silence down the Causeway. There was a
smoky murmur from the open doors of pubs. At the

corner of the Causeway, where I would turn off to go home, I stopped and said goodbye.

'It's all right,' Martin said. 'I'll walk you home.'

'No,' I said.

'It's no trouble. I'd like to walk with you—'

'No, Martin,' I said.

I would walk no further with Martin. Somewhere – I could not have said at what precise moment – I had made a very clear decision. I was going to keep faith with Robert; and whether in fact Robert wanted me or not did not affect that decision at all. I was finished with the Crawthornes. I had been in love with Martin – or rather, I had been in love with the intoxicating family of which he was the concentrated essence. But now we had come, in the truest sense, to a parting of the ways.

'Jenny,' Martin said softly, holding out his hand. 'I do need you.'

'Even if that were true, it wouldn't make any difference,' I said.

His hand dropped; then he lifted it again in a little wave. 'I'm sorry,' he said. He turned and began to cross the street; and in the same moment I heard the great roar, rising to a screech, of an accelerating engine and in the sudden glare of headlights I saw the dented wing of the car that was being driven straight at him.

'Martin, look out!' I screamed.

I do not know whether he heard me or not. He whirled round as the car bore down on him: I saw his eyes luminous as a rabbit's in the headlights. It all seemed to happen in slow motion. The car missed him by inches as he flung himself on to the kerb, his jacket whipping and flapping in the slipstream. Ursula's mouth was open as she gripped the wheel:

I don't know if she was shouting or screaming because I could hear nothing above the howl of that powerful engine as the car hurtled past. At that speed there was no chance of stopping at the corner. The Talbot slewed across the junction and with a hideous noise smashed full into the side of a car inching out from the left turning, driving it with the force of a train right across to the other side, in a ghastly waltz of headlights.

The sudden silence that followed was uncanny, broken only by the continued reedy wail of a motor-horn and then by footsteps as people began to come running. There was a glow and a flare in the summer darkness as an engine caught fire. I bent down to Martin, sprawled on the pavement, but he was not hurt. He just looked as if he did not want to get up again.

Four

I do not know what time I got home that night. I know it was late. I had been long giving statements as a witness to the police: and then there had been a period of violent shivering, in a sort of delayed shock, and endless cups of sweetened tea, so that the short summer night was well advanced by the time I climbed into bed. Even then my mind was a whirling carousel of distorted images. Ursula had been taken to the hospital. Someone – it was not Martin, but a passer-by – had pulled her clear of the wreckage before the fire had taken hold. She had been conscious. The man driving the other car had not been so lucky. He had died before they could get him to hospital.

Yet though I had had only a few hours of troubled sleep I was up early in the morning. Some almost animal instinct directed me. Straight after breakfast I cycled out to Robert's garage.

Robert was not there. I did not think for more than a moment about where he might be. Whether he was still in London, what had happened with Blanche – I paid little attention to these questions. They had nothing to do with the decision I had made last night. In the brilliance of the July morning, undeadened as yet by heat, that decision was even clearer and more unequivocal. It was Robert that I wanted: it had taken a slow painful process to make me realise that, and Martin too had had his part in it. The agony of that first rejection by Martin had left me with a fear of love that had to be broken through. To be whole again I had to acknowledge my love for Robert instead of mistrusting it; and so whatever he felt for me in return – if anything – I must accept too. There was no other way.

I still had the spare keys, so I opened up the garage for business. I put down corn for the hens, and made a note that the corn-tub was nearly empty. I went across the road to the cottage with a rudimentary shop in the front room to buy a pint of milk. I swept out and tidied the office and washed up the plates in the kitchen. I did all these things in a mechanical and also curiously ceremonial way. It was almost as if I were performing an incantation, a rite to bring Robert back. And in the same way when a man brought in a car and asked to see the mechanic I said he would be back later.

'So I can bring it in this afternoon, then?' the man said. 'Definite?'

'Yes,' I said. 'He'll be here.' It was an invocation.

Between serving at the petrol-pump I went into the yard to see if there was anything I could do. The tom-cat reclined on the roof of a scrap car, airily surveying his domain of rusting chassis and tyres and weeds and miniature lakes of oil with surfaces of broken rainbow. Then I saw Robert's shabby old Sunbeam, parked by the cow-shed, and noticed how dirty it was. So I got a bucket and sponge and chamois leather and washed the car and then with brush and dustpan cleaned out the interior. There was an old leathery smell about the cracked and wrinkled upholstery and the faint staleness too of rich cigars, smoked by the first owner as he drove in a vanished world before the slump. Then, with the day so fine and dry, I decided I would wax the car too. For nearly an hour I worked on it, bringing a lustre at last to the battered paintwork and the chrome, whilst the tom-cat stalked around me, occasionally sniffing at the rags and the chamois with fascinated grins of disgust.

Just as I finished a van pulled up for petrol; and when I came back to the yard my eye was struck by the transformation I had wrought. In the summer noonday Robert's car shone as if it had the sun inside it. I felt enormously satisfied.

I closed up for lunch. In the kitchen there was the remains of a pie that I had baked the other day but I only picked at it. The unnatural and rather fevered energy that had driven me all morning was suddenly gone and I felt exhausted. I sat for a while in the sitting-room. The armchair was the one Robert always sat in. It was moulded with his shape and I remembered the way he would sit there after a day's work, his long legs stretched out, talking of things done and things left to do. In relaxation his voice would get lower, rumbling from his chest in contentment, as he scraped his hand back and forth across the black stubble that he could never quite shave as close as he wanted it.

I made the memory go away and took down a book from the shelf above. There were not many books; mainly a set of encyclopaedias of the sort that the newspapers offered in the circulation war of those days. It was the first volume and it opened at *Apollo*. There was an engraving of Apollo as the charioteer of the sun: and then with a jolt I saw another picture, the original of the reproduction statue in the trees behind St Germain House. I clapped the book shut. I made as if to get up: there was plenty to do, the front windows to be cleaned, a pile of advertising circulars to be sorted. But the tension of lack of sleep and the furious work of the morning had caught up with me: my legs felt weak and there was a woozy sort of singing in my head. The thought of lying down, just for a few minutes, was wonderfully attractive.

I went up to Robert's bedroom and took off my shoes and lay down on his bed. The window above it was ajar and through it came stealing the scent of the tea-roses that grew in drooping clumps on the outer wall: they needed tying back and I made a mental note that there was another job I could do. I promised myself that I would rest for a short while, and seeing a tin alarm-clock on the night-table I reached out and took it down to set it to ring in half an hour. I could not see how to set it and I must have been still wearily fumbling with it when I fell asleep.

It was the footsteps on the uncarpeted stairs that woke me: the sound intertwined with the trailing ends of a dream I had been having and then Robert's voice called: 'Hello?' and I snapped awake. I sat up on the bed as he came in.

Often people will say, jokingly, 'You look how I feel': and that was very much how I felt as Robert stood in the bedroom doorway. There was a sleepless strain in his eyes, narrowed and puckered as if the light was too strong for him. His thick hair was uncombed and he badly needed a shave.

'Sorry,' I said. 'What's the time? I must have dropped off – hope you don't mind, I—'

'No, no.' He leaned heavily against the door-jamb. 'Time? Oh, I don't know. Must be . . . I don't know.'

I was still sitting up on the bed. All at once my heart was thundering. I said: 'Did you see Blanche?'

'Yes. I gave her back her car . . .' Robert frowned, seemed to struggle to focus his thoughts. 'You opened the garage up for me?'

'Yes,' I said. 'Oh! there's a man bringing his car in for service this afternoon. About half-past three.'

'Half-past three. Right . . . Thank you. For opening up and everything.'

He rubbed one hand up and down his arm, his eyes hooded, so that I could not see them.

'There's some milk,' I said, 'if you want some tea—'

He shook his head. 'I'll – I'll get something in a minute.'

'You look tired,' I said.

'I didn't get much sleep. Spent the night in this – well, called itself a hotel, just a boarding-house really. Near King's Cross.'

Why? was the question that naturally offered itself, but I could not ask it. I could not say any more: I could only wait. I was aware again of the scent of the tea-roses below the window, pastel and faded just like the pattern of rose on the bedroom wallpaper.

Robert came in slowly and sat in the white-painted wicker chair. One of his ties was on the back and he ran it through and through his hands, his elbows on his knees, as he spoke.

'It was late before I got to see Blanche. I kept calling at the house but there was no one there. I didn't know what to do. I just sat in her car outside the house all evening. It's such a posh street, isn't it . . . I think people looked at me a bit suspiciously, the way I was sitting there. I think I dozed off for a while. Then I woke up and there was a taxi drawing up outside. Blanche got out, and her husband . . . They looked as if they'd been out on the town. They were in evening dress, and they were sort of laughing. They started going up the steps – you know, Blanche hadn't even noticed that it was her car parked outside.' He glanced at me, his dark face drawn and painfully honest. 'Anyway, I went after them, and said – and said I'd brought the car. They couldn't quite believe it, really, and then they sort of laughed again. I suppose it was funny, really. Me bringing it all that way. Her husband said something about how that was one asset they'd got left. They just looked – sort of happy. They said thank you. I mean Blanche was kind, and said I shouldn't have, and how would I get home, and she must pay for the petrol and everything . . . and I said that I was coming down to London anyway. I don't know why I said that. She didn't ask what for. They just sort of thanked me again and went in – they just sort of . . .'

His voice ran down. He sat in stunned fashion, the tired shadows under his eyes making him look physically bruised. Picturing the scene, I thought of the word that he could not bring himself to say. They had dismissed him.

'So then I didn't know what to do. I wandered about for a while, I suppose . . . It was late. So I ended up at this place, and got a room – dingy sort of place. I didn't really get any sleep – I just kept thinking, what on earth am I doing here? I felt a fool.' He put his chin in his hands. Saying those words seemed to leave him more stunned and sapped than ever. 'I felt a fool.'

Suddenly, with a peculiar inconsequence that was perhaps a result of my not being long awake, I thought again of Robert in his steward's outfit at the Agricultural Show and remembered at last what picture it was that he had reminded me of: it was an illustration of Heathcliff in some children's edition of *Wuthering Heights*. And even as I grasped this I saw that it was mistaken after all. He did not look like an illustration in a book. He just looked like himself, and though it had taken a long time for me to see it, that was all I wanted.

'I don't know what I was expecting when I went there,' he said. 'It's just that she always seemed so interested, sort of made you feel special. It got so as I just didn't think – I didn't know what I was doing – I know that sounds stupid—'

'No,' I said.

'God, that boarding-house was an awful place. There was this wardrobe like a coffin and this folding-bed and I just lay there and kept thinking, how on earth had I got there. I just didn't know what to do. I couldn't face coming back . . . When you said – when you told me not to get mixed up with them – I just thought it was sour grapes. I said some awful things to you, didn't I?'

'Yes,' I said. 'But it doesn't matter.'

'It does, though, doesn't it?' His bruised, trance-like eyes met mine with decision. 'All that work. All the money I've poured down the drain.'

'You can survive that.'

'It isn't just that, though,' he said. Suddenly he examined his hands with intense concentration. 'I know you're angry with me. I don't know – how much.'

Was I angry with him? I had been, a little while

ago, extremely angry with him: it was not much of an exaggeration to say I could have killed him. And in a way all the reasons for anger were still there. But I thought of how, when he had first walked in, I had had a sense of looking at myself; and I saw now that the resemblances went deeper. Yes, the anger was there, but my understanding seemed to make a leap over it. Robert had lost his head under the spell of the Crawthornes – and of all people in the world I was the one who could understand that, and forgive. I remembered a time when I too had been enchanted by them, blindly swept into their orbit, so that nothing else seemed quite real any more. I thought of Martin last night, the alluring accents of his voice, begging me to help him, to make things all right: and how near I had come to yielding again to that destructive magnetism. How could I blame the man sitting in the wicker chair across the room, when it was myself I was seeing?

'I'm not angry,' I said.

He looked grim and unconvinced. 'Those things I said. I don't know what I can do – what I can say . . .'

'Come here,' I said.

In understanding him, I understood myself. The last of my defences seemed to crumble and fall as I held out my hand to him. I had mistaken the dourness of the loveless years, cautiously shunning pain, for growing up: I had mistaken for maturity what was actually a shrinking from its consequences. I remembered Jocelyn saying, 'You're all take and no give': I had misjudged even him. Because love hurt I had been afraid of it and had forgotten that it could be wonderful too.

'I've made such a bloody fool of myself,' Robert said. 'You've seen it.'

'We're even, then,' I said. 'Aren't we? Come here.'

He came slowly over to the bed, as if not knowing what to expect, but with a sort of trustfulness. He sat down beside me, looking into my eyes, wondering.

'It's all right,' I said. 'You see?' and I kissed his face. 'I've been waiting for you to come back. I didn't know, but I waited . . . It's all right now.'

He lifted his hands, slowly, as if they were suddenly too heavy for him, and placed them on my shoulders: and after a moment he kissed me.

No, you could not trust the Crawthornes; and I did not know and still do not know whether to blame them for that. Whatever flaw it was that ran through them, it tended to destruction – of themselves and of others; yet they seemed not to know it. I found, and have always found, a final judgement on the Crawthornes as elusive to the grasp as everything else about them; but when Robert leaned over and kissed me, the need for judgements was gone.

'You're tired,' I said. 'We needn't open the garage yet. Lie down here a while.'

I lay back, and he lay down beside me, beneath the open window. I put my arms around his neck and as he kissed me again I knew that I was no longer tired; and as I looked up into his eyes I saw that neither was he.

He lifted his head.

'Jenny,' he said. 'Whatever have you done to my car?'

I laughed with my mouth against his face, holding him. From the window I caught the scent again of the roses, carried on the warm breeze of July: and in that tender air I felt, even at summer's height, the promise of a new season.

A selection of bestsellers from Headline

FICTION

STUDPOKER	John Francome	£4.99
DANGEROUS LADY	Martina Cole	£4.99
TIME OFF FROM GOOD BEHAVIOUR	Susan Sussman	£4.99 □
THE KEY TO MIDNIGHT	Dean Koontz	£4.99 □
LEGAL TENDER	Richard Smitten	£5.99 □
BLESSINGS AND SORROWS	Christine Thomas	£4.99 □
VAGABONDS	Josephine Cox	£4.99 □
DAUGHTER OF TINTAGEL	Fay Sampson	£5.99 □
HAPPY ENDINGS	Sally Quinn	£5.99 □
BLOOD GAMES	Richard Laymon	£4.99 □
EXCEPTIONAL CLEARANCE	William J Caunitz	£4.99 □
QUILLER BAMBOO	Adam Hall	£4.99 □

NON-FICTION

RICHARD BRANSON: The Inside Story	Mick Brown	£6.99 □
PLAYFAIR FOOTBALL ANNUAL 1992-93	Jack Rollin	£3.99 □
DEBRETT'S ETIQUETTE & MODERN MANNERS	Elsie Burch Donald	£7.99 □
PLAYFIELD NON-LEAGUE FOOTBALL ANNUAL 1992-93	Bruce Smith	£3.99 □

SCIENCE FICTION AND FANTASY

THE CINEVERSE CYCLE OMNIBUS	Craig Shaw Gardner	£5.99 □
BURYING THE SHADOW	Storm Constantine	£4.99 □
THE LOST PRINCE	Bridget Wood	£5.99 □
KING OF THE DEAD	R A MacAvoy	£4.50 □
THE ULTIMATE WEREWOLF	Byron Preiss	£4.99 □

All Headline books are available at your local bookshop or newsagent, or can be ordered direct from the publisher. Just tick the titles you want and fill in the form below. Prices and availability subject to change without notice.

Headline Book Publishing PLC, Cash Sales Department, PO Box 11, Falmouth, Cornwall, TR10 9EN, England.

Please enclose a cheque or postal order to the value of the cover price and allow the following for postage and packing:
UK & BFPO: £1.00 for the first book, 50p for the second book and 30p for each additional book ordered up to a maximum charge of £3.00.
OVERSEAS & EIRE: £2.00 for the first book, £1.00 for the second book and 50p for each additional book.

Name ....

Address ....

....